MW00583454

CHEMICAL
CAPTURE

CHEMICAL CAPTURE

DEBBIE BALDWIN

Tampa, Florida

CHEMICAL CAPTURE
Published by **Gatekeeper Press**
7853 Gunn Hwy., Suite 209
Tampa, FL 33626
www.GatekeeperPress.com

The editorial work for this book is entirely the product of the author. Gatekeeper Press did not participate in and is not responsible for any aspect of that element.

Library of Congress Control Number:
ISBN (hardcover): 9781662938177
ISBN (paperback): 9781662938184
eISBN: 9781662938191

*Dedicated to all the readers
who understand books provide perspective,
knowledge, and insight.*

"You have to keep this con even after you take his money.
He can't know you took him."

–Henry Gondorff
The Sting

CAST OF CHARACTERS

Nathan Bishop
Nickname: North
Height: 6'2"
Hair color: Chestnut
Eye color: Green

Head of Bishop Security. Former Naval Intelligence Officer. Consumed by the childhood abduction of his neighbor, Emily Webster, Nathan dedicated his life to helping those in need. Read their story in Book 1, *False Front*.

Miller Buchanan
Nickname: Tox
Height: 6'5"
Hair color: Dark brown (buzzed very short)
Eye color: Brown

Nathan's number two at Bishop Security and former Navy SEAL. After Emily's friend, reporter Calliope Garland got in over her head with an investigation, the six-foot, five-inch warrior came to her aid. Read their story in Book 2, *Illicit Intent*.

Andrew Dunlap
Nickname: Chat
Height: 6'0"
Hair color: Black, shaved bald
Eye color: Dark brown

One of the original SEAL Team members at Bishop Security. Nicknamed facetiously for his taciturn nature, the quiet African American possesses an almost uncanny sixth sense.

Jonah Lockhart
Nickname: Steady
Height: 6'1"
Hair color: Sandy blond
Eye color: Sage green

His SEAL brothers call him Steady because of his calm nature. It's not until Twitch's college friend, the pink-haired Very, moves in next door that Steady finds himself decidedly unsteady.

Leo Jameson
Nickname: Ren/ Renaissance Man
Height 5'11"
Hair color: Dark brown
Eye color: Hazel

The Teamguys call him the Renaissance Man because Ren has an encyclopedic knowledge of topics ranging from Astrophysics to Zoology. For years, Ren has been captivated by Sofria Kirk, a brilliant CIA analyst, but he keeps her at a distance, fearing she is too young.

Camilo Canto
Nickname JJ
Height: 6'0"
Hair color: Dark brown
Eye color: Gold

Former SEAL and current Bishop Security operator, Cam worked undercover for the CIA. Last year, an old enemy abducted Cam and brought him to Mallorca, where he took on a drug cartel and joined beautiful archaeologist Evangeline Cole on a treasure hunt. Read their story in Book 3, *Buried Beneath.*

Hercules Reynolds
Nickname: Shorty
Height 6'0"
Hair color: Light brown
Eye color: Blue-gray

Marine sniper Herc joined Bishop Security after getting mixed up in an illegal arms deal. He is related to Nathan Bishop by marriage—his grandmother, Maggie, is married to Nathan's uncle Charlie Bishop.

Finn McIntyre
Height: 6'2"
Hair: Sandy brown
Eyes: Cobalt blue

After being captured on a SEAL mission, Finn was tortured for three days, leaving the right side of his face terribly scarred. Bitter and isolated, Finn left the Navy and joined the CIA. After burning his bridges with The Agency and alienating his friends, Finn takes off to try and get his life back.

Charlotte Devlin
Nickname: Twitch
Height 5'4"
Hair color: Copper red
Eye color: Sky blue

The Bishop Security cyber guru is a tech genius. Nobody knows exactly what happened between Twitch and Finn McIntyre, but it has left both their hearts damaged.

Emily Webster Bishop
Height: 5'6"
Hair color: Honey Blonde
Eye color: Violet

After being abducted as a child, Emily lived under the false identity of Emma Porter but never forgot the kind boy who had lived next door, Nathan Bishop. She rediscovered Nathan as an adult while Nathan helped protect her from a continuing threat. Read their story in book 1, *False Front*.

Calliope Garland Buchanan
Height 5'8"
Hair color: Black
Eye color: Ice blue

Now a Bishop Security operative, Calliope Garland worked as a reporter for The Harlem Sentry. While investigating a sketchy hedge fund manager, Calliope found herself in possession of valuable financial data and a priceless, stolen work of art. Tox protected Calliope from the threat. Read their story in Book 2, *Illicit Intent*.

Verity Valentine
Nickname: Very
Height: 5'6"
Hair color: Fuschia
Eye color: Marble gray

Very is Twitch's best friend from college. She recently moved next door to Steady and works as a chemist at a private lab. When she learns of Steady's calm reputation, she can't resist riling him.

Sofria Kirk
Height 5'5"
Hair Color: Mahogany brown
Eye color: Dark brown

CIA analyst Sofria Kirk has helped the team out on numerous occasions. The exotic beauty has a rare gift for detecting patterns, and the CIA has put her skills to use. While she is highly effective behind a desk, Sofria dreams of going into the field.

Evangeline Cole
Nickname: Evan
Height 5'6"
Hair color: Caramel brown
Eye color: Caramel brown

Evan is an archaeologist who met Cam Canto while on a dig in the caves of Mallorca. She immediately fell for the gorgeous former SEAL. Evan now lives in Beaufort and is continuing her studies. Read their story in book 3, *Buried Beneath*.

CHEMICAL CAPTURE

Maggie Bishop
Height 5'5"
Hair color: Steel gray
Eye color: Gray-blue

Wife of Nathan's uncle, Charlie Bishop, Maggie is the self-appointed mother hen to the group. She has lived in Beaufort her whole life and raised Herc, her grandson, and Bishop Security sniper.

Charlie Bishop
Nickname: Cerberus
Height: 5'10"
Hair color: Gray
Eye color: Green

Nathan's uncle is a Former Secretary of Defense and a successful businessman. After retiring to the Barrier Islands, Charlie continues to consult on National Security, but his main focus is rehoming and working with retired military dogs.

PART ONE

Setting the Trap

CHAPTER ONE

Beaufort, South Carolina
July 18

Very Valentine switched on her high beams and scanned the dark roadside for the address. Rain spattered the windshield enough to obscure her vision but so sparingly that one swipe of the wipers blurred the view more. The tourist season in the South Carolina Barrier Islands was long over, and a stifling summer heat blanketed the charming coastal region. As she drove farther and farther away from the quaint inns and luxury beach homes, her anxiety mounted.

Noting the ache in her hands, she eased her grip on the steering wheel. This degree of planning and detail allowed reason to keep pace with impulsiveness, which was unnerving. Very was a lioness. She never hesitated to get involved to right a wrong or defend a friend, and she never backed down from a fight. Rarely considering factors like risk and consequence, Very simply acted. But now that her most important battle was about to begin, an unfamiliar fear crept from her toes to her bright pink ponytail.

Up ahead, Very spotted the entrance to the Ocean's Edge Resort, the irony immediately apparent. The peeling turquoise paint and the half-working

"Vacancies" light did not bode well for the accommodations. Three wooden planks comprised the sign at the entrance. The bottom one had fallen off, so the "Resort" part was tipped up against the support pole. She pulled into the packed-sand lot and parked.

A drizzle cut through the mist, providing little relief from the oppressive heat. With a Charleston Riverdogs cap covering her hair, Very hurried to the row of rooms covered by the exterior second-floor balcony. She marked the room numbers as she passed each graffitied, dilapidated door. A TV was blaring in room 13; a couple was arguing in 16. When she spotted 18, Very looked to her left, then right. She checked the deserted parking lot behind her. After reassuring herself that her visions of lurking spies and assassins were simply that, *visions*, she knocked on the door.

The latch didn't secure in the jamb, and the door opened with the force of Very's gentle taps. She stepped into the room, pushing the door closed behind her. Water was running in the bathroom.

"Hello?"

He entered the bedroom, toweling off his hands, and met her gaze.

The force of Very's embrace as she threw herself into his arms knocked a laugh out of him. "Easy there."

"I'm just happy to see you," she said

"You see me all the time." He held her at arm's length and used the hand towel to dry the rain on her face.

"You know what I mean."

The man gestured to the small, round table, and Very took a wobbly seat. He joined her.

The moment had come—a revenge plot twenty years in the making.

He referred to Very as "Marie Curie." She called him "Charles Darwin." from this point on, most electronic communication would halt—only planned, coded texts or, in an emergency, calls from the stash of burner phones.

"Phase one will commence this week," he said.

Very nodded.

"After you download the research, we should know right away if the mark has taken the bait."

"Lab security will alert Krill," Very said.

"The important thing to remember is that things will happen that we don't anticipate. Don't let that throw you. Don't volunteer information; be prepared to think on your feet."

"Okay." Very blew out a breath. "I can do that."

"Yes," he chuckled. "You can."

Charles Darwin continued reviewing the plan.

Very listened intently. "I think we're ready."

He withdrew a slender flask from his jacket pocket and took a fortifying swig. "Let's go over it again."

She protested, "I've got it."

Charles Darwin patted her hand with a patient smile. "A plan like this is like painting a house. The most important part is the preparation."

He reviewed their assignments one final time. Then, Darwin leaned forward, lacing his fingers. "There are two things I know."

Very waited for Darwin to impart his wisdom. She had known him for most of her life, and he never wasted words.

"First, there are no coincidences. If something is unexpected, a person showing up at the same places, or a surprise visitor, just know it's intentional, and alter your behavior accordingly."

"What's the second thing?" she asked.

Darwin grinned. "Human nature will always reveal itself. People can't deny who they truly are. And who is Armand Krill, truly?" he asked.

Very answered the question. "A man with no limit to his greed."

Darwin toasted her with his flask. "Then let's hit him where he lives."

They left the motel separately, Very departing first. She hurried across the desolate parking lot, feeling only marginally safer knowing Darwin was watching through the slats in the window blinds. The rain had kicked up, and Very pulled the hood of her sweatshirt over her cap as she fumbled in the pouch for the key fob. Once she was safely behind the wheel of her Volvo, Very tossed the ball cap into the backseat, gripped the immobile steering wheel, and gave it a shake. The time had arrived. All the planning and preparation were about to come to fruition. Very was a chemist, a researcher; nothing gave her more satisfaction than using her mind to solve a problem. She was an alchemist turning theory into reality.

She and Darwin had set up the dominoes with precise detail.

Very was about to tip the first tile.

CHAPTER TWO

Armand Krill's Manhattan home was an expansive but inconspicuous sandstone manse tucked on a side street off Fifth Avenue in the shadow of the Metropolitan Museum of Art. Built in 1901 by Armand's great-grandfather, the home was one of the few Gilded Age mansions still standing in Manhattan. The eighteen thousand-square-foot residence stood four stories tall and occupied nearly a third of the block. Two stone lions guarded the front door at the top of five semi-circular stairs. Much like its owner, the house was austere and uninviting.

In his seventy-three years, the CEO of Parasol Pharmaceuticals had been rich, and he had been poor. He preferred the former. So much so that Armand Krill had done everything in his power over the course of his career to ensure a reversal of fortune never again struck the Krill name.

Armand Krill sat at the head of the dining table, which required three chandeliers to illuminate, and inspected his place setting. Noting a water spot on the dessert spoon, he signaled the maid to replace it by pinching the utensil between a boney thumb and finger and dropping it onto the Aubusson rug. It gave Armand a modicum of pleasure to see the girl's hand tremble as she replaced the spoon with a freshly polished one. Three generations of Krills looked down on him from the oil portraits fencing the room. He lifted the tumbler etched with the Krill family crest and toasted his ancestors. His frivolous father's financial missteps had been righted. All was well.

It was an extravagant residence for a man who had spent most of his life alone, but Krill, or his staff, used almost every room—with the exception of the six perfectly decorated guest bedrooms on the fourth floor that had never been occupied. Krill neither wanted nor expected guests, but the rooms were there just the same, a bitter reminder that for Krill to achieve his goal and restore the flow of generational wealth, he needed generations.

It was the reason he tolerated his two incompetent sons. The older boy was a high school history teacher in Vermont, the other an artist in Seattle. Whenever Krill thought or spoke about his younger son's "occupation," the word dripped with disdain as if he were saying, *bookie or hitman.* Truth be told, Krill would have preferred either of those to his son's chosen profession. Neither boy would contribute to the Krill coffers, but at least they had both given him grandchildren. Not the grandchild he wanted, but Armand supposed that was the plight of Rockefellers and Vanderbilts; you couldn't choose the spawn for whom you were providing.

Krill had a cordial relationship with his relatives. He saw them once a year during the holidays. He could have done without the visit, but his sons no doubt needed to ensure they were still in the will, so he suffered through an awkward meal and the perfunctory exchange of gifts. Last year, his younger son, *the artist,* had given Krill a small zen rock garden. With uncharacteristic sensitivity, Krill had waited until the family had departed to toss it in the trash unopened.

Krill concluded that it made no difference if, generations from now, his progeny were tech titans or accountants or bums. He would ensure that the name Krill held the same reverence and power as Getty and Ford, regardless of the capabilities of his heirs.

Krill's motive wasn't about leaving his idiot children with a trust fund. He had lived through the destruction of a fortune, and he was going to ensure it never happened again. It didn't matter that his sons had turned their backs on the family business. And his daughter, well, she had shown the wrong kind of interest and paid the price.

This was about more than money. It was about legacy.

After eating his lunch and without acknowledgment to the staff, Krill set his napkin beside his plate, climbed the palatial central staircase, and returned to his office.

He sat behind the antique desk in the same study where his grandfather had entertained Franklin Roosevelt. The original name of the company founded by his great-grandfather was Krill's Medicines and Tonics. During World War II, they provided most of the first aid provisions for the soldiers. In the nineteen fifties, his grandfather changed the name to Parasol Pharmaceuticals when he began branching into prescription medications.

The Parasol Corporate Headquarters was housed in a midtown highrise, but Krill rarely went there. He preferred this office, the desk where his grandfather had worked. The old man's pipe tobacco had infused the cherry wood of the paneling and bookshelves. Krill thought he could smell the fruited smoke, even now. His grandfather had made his first million in this room. It would be the room where Krill made his first billion.

Today Krill was on the verge of a windfall that made his grandfather's government contracts look like loose change. Parasol's breakthrough arthritis medication, Mobilify, had just received final FDA approval. After the requisite press conference, the drug would hit the market. The sales of Mobilify (along with Parasol's other medication that treated Mobilify's main side effect) would make Armand Krill a billionaire in under a year.

He had tap danced around FDA regulations and negotiated insurance contracts to charge the maximum price for Mobilify. He had spent a small fortune developing it, after all. He would recoup his investment and then some in only months. Mobilify was a license to print money.

Krill was reading over the legal paperwork and memos from his executives and the government regulators when a tap on the door had him looking up. His secretary Jessica, a capable woman in her mid-forties, stood at the threshold, a thick white envelope in her slender fingers.

"Excuse me, Mr. Krill. You wanted to be informed when this arrived. It's the letter you've been expecting."

Krill nearly shot out of his seat, but at the last moment, he forced himself to remain calm. He summoned Jessica with his fingertips. "Yes, yes. Bring it to me."

His assistant passed him the letter and left.

Krill ran a gentle hand over the rich paper, turned it over, and touched the wax seal–two interlocking Cs over a horse's head–the unmistakable symbol of the Cavalry Club. He had been waiting for this to arrive for weeks. What perfect timing. With due reverence, he broke the seal and withdrew the engraved card.

Leaning back in the leather desk chair, Krill tapped the thick card on the wide armrest. He was close, so close. Soon his chair would be a throne.

Soon he would be king.

CHAPTER THREE

The Sand Bar was packed to the gills. Winter residents of the Barrier Islands had headed to cooler climes, but vacationers and locals were out en masse. Jonah "Steady" Lockhart was dressed in his standard bar attire–a Hawaiian shirt and shorts. Tonight he had the added accessory of a blue sling. It was minor as gunshot wounds went, but it still hurt like hell. He had sustained the injury on a recent Bishop Security op, shoving his friend Camilo "Cam" Canto out of the way when a mercenary got the drop on them. Cam's fiancée, Evan, had expressed her gratitude by dropping off meals daily despite Steady's insistence that Cam would have, and had, done the same–any one of them would have. They were former SEALs, brothers; their bond ran deeper than friendship.

Steady sat at the bar with Andrew "Chat" Dunlap, both men nursing an IPA from a local brewery. With his muscled physique, ebony skin, and bald head, Chat was an intimidating presence. He was also a man of few words and a calming force in Steady's life. They balanced one another. While Steady was talkative and devil-may-care, Chat was serious and observant. The man had a mischievous side and could throw shade with the best of them, but that was an aspect of Chat only those in his inner circle ever got to see.

Steady knew if he glanced to his right, his friend would be assessing him with eyes that saw too much. Steady couldn't tear his gaze away from the dance floor where Very Valentine was laughing with her friends–her presence was like a homing beacon.

Since moving to the area last year, Very had not only reconnected with her college best friend, Bishop's cybersecurity expert, Twitch, but had become close with the entire group. She was currently two-stepping badly with Miller "Tox" Buchanan's wife, Calliope. The girls were bumping into other couples and trodding on toes, and nobody seemed to mind.

Most of the women were dressed for a night out in short dresses and slinky sandals, but barefoot in cut-offs and a cropped yellow T-shirt, Very Valentine was the sexiest girl in the room. Hell, she was the sexiest girl in the state. Unfortunately, Steady wasn't the only one who thought so. He took a violent swig of his beer as he watched yet another drunken reveler sidle up next to her.

Verity Valentine had been called Very since she was a child and couldn't pronounce her name. And while it seemed logical that a small child might shorten or misspeak their name due to a speech impediment or developmental delay, Steady thought that on some cosmic level, she had declared the more accurate moniker. Everything about Verity Valentine was *very*.

Very had captured his undivided attention from the first time he laid eyes on her. She was renting the beach house next door to his, and he had accidentally spied her through his telescope while stargazing one night. *Yes, accidentally*, he insisted. With her neon underwear and hot pink hair, it was no wonder she had stolen his attention. Very Valentine half-dressed, dancing around to the Ramones eclipsed any constellation in the sky.

She had a brilliant mind, a smart mouth, and an effusive personality, all crammed into a package that heated his blood. They fought like cats and dogs most of the time, a first for him. While Steady enjoyed pushing people's buttons, it was a revelation to discover he had a few buttons of his own.

There was something else too. Beneath Very's brash exterior, something simmered, a hidden pain. It was easy to miss, but Steady paid attention, particularly to Very. On rare occasions, he would see it—a flash of anguish in her eyes, gone as quickly as it had appeared. She was well-practiced at keeping it hidden.

Steady had long ago mastered the art of concealing old wounds. He recognized a kindred spirit.

Jonah Lockhart wasn't the fastest swimmer or the best target shooter or most adept at hand-to-hand combat; what he was, was calm. He never panicked, never lost his cool, and his unwavering composure had saved the lives of his brothers on more than one occasion.

Steady had earned his nickname on his SEAL squad. The men were pinned down in a firefight, and Steady had been trapped under a crashed supply truck. With the adrenaline and strength of ten men, his teammate Miller "Tox" Buchanan had lifted the truck and pulled him out. With a fractured leg, Steady had hobbled to an abandoned Huey on the outskirts of the insurgent compound, done a patchwork repair on the helicopter, and flown his team to safety. After the helo had sputtered and slammed to the ground a safe distance away, Tox had wrapped him in a bear hug and lifted Steady in the air with an appreciative (and painful) shake. *Nothing gets to this guy. Outmanned ten to one, and he's replacing a fuel line like it's a Sunday afternoon in the motor pool. Steady as a rock.*

Steady could remain even-keeled in an ambush; pinned down by the enemy, his pulse never went above 80. Yet somehow, this five-foot, six-inch firecracker made his skin feel too tight on his body. All that equilibrium went out the window when Very Valentine entered a room.

The song changed to a classic Lil John song, and the dancers obeyed the lyrics: Bending over to the front and touching their toes. Steady had a buffet of asses to peruse, but he couldn't avert his gaze from the two perfect half-moons peeking out from the hem of Very's shorts.

"You know, you could just ask her to dance," Chat said with a smile in his voice.

Still facing the dance floor, Steady perched his good elbow on the bar behind him. "Let me ask you, my clairvoyant friend. What do you make of her?"

"She's a mystery."

Steady agreed, but he wanted to know why Chat thought so. He dangled his beer by the neck of the bottle. "Very? Come on, man. She's an open book."

A new song came on, and Chat turned to watch Very dance. Her bright pink ponytail bobbed as she jumped.

"Sometimes people open their cover, so you don't read the pages," Chat said.

Steady thought about Chat's assessment. With her hot pink hair and exuberance, Very turned heads, but there was so much more to her if anyone bothered to look. And Steady bothered–far too often for his own good. Her body was fit yet somehow soft. Steady watched her dance, the way the curves of her body moved beneath her clothes. Very grabbed her friend Calliope's arm as she stumbled, revealing the aspect of Very Valentine that captivated him the most; she always seemed to be taking care of everyone around her. He sometimes wondered who was taking care of her.

Chat interrupted his reverie. "If you asked every guy in this bar to describe Very, I bet they'd all say the same thing."

"Pink hair," Steady agreed.

"It's funny," Chat said contemplatively, then pointed to the dance floor with his beer bottle. "With the hair and her energy, she's the most noticeable girl in the place. But she could probably rob a bank, and no one would be able to describe her beyond that."

Steady could. Very had hazel eyes with tiny sparks of gold. They turned a dark green when she was mad or turned on; brown when she was happy. Her smile was almost too big for her face, and the way Very's lush lips parted slightly when she was thinking gave him too many dangerous thoughts. He had to admit, however, that beneath the surface, Very Valentine was a tough nut to crack.

He tilted his head to the side, a tawny curl falling across his forehead. "Twitch is her oldest friend, and she told me she doesn't know much about Very's past–never even met her parents."

"Nothing particularly strange about that," Chat said.

"I guess not."

"She drives a Volvo," Chat commented absently.

"Yeah, so?"

Chat waggled his empty bottle, and the busty bartender delivered two fresh beers. "These are on me. You guys make the view from behind the bar so much better." Then she pointed at Chat. "We on for tomorrow?"

"Six a.m. I'll meet you there," Chat said.

"You better get your beauty sleep, or you'll get your ass kicked."

Chat pasted on his panty-dropper smile and said, "Same goes."

When she sauntered away, Steady asked, "Six a.m.?"

"She's a Black Belt in taekwondo."

Steady sat up straighter. "Impressive. I bet she's got some moves."

Ignoring the innuendo, Chat said, "I'm going to talk to Nathan about having her come in and teach a class at the office. Our hand-to-hand could use some sharpening." Nathan Bishop was their brother-in-arms who now ran the security company where they both worked.

Steady traded out his beer and returned to the topic that took up most of the real estate in his brain. "What about her car?"

"Hmm?"

"You said she drives a Volvo."

Chat checked the score of the ballgame on the muted TV as he spoke. "She seems like the type to drive a little VW convertible or a Mini like Twitch's, no? But she drives a Volvo SUV. Someone influenced her car choice. Probably a parent who cares about her safety. More importantly, she listened."

Steady waited for Chat's additional insights, but his friend rotated his stool and looked across the room. Very was skipping her way through the crowd to the back hall that led to the restrooms. It was then Steady noticed the guy who had been dancing in her orbit trailing behind. It shouldn't have been an alarming scenario; patrons were coming and going from the back of the building. In addition to the restrooms, the hall led to a pool room and an exit. Gripping his beer bottle a little too forcefully, Steady turned back to the bar.

Still dancing, Very stood outside the bathroom in a short line. She was smiling at the girl in front of her when a hand circled her wrist and pulled her down the hall into the empty pool room. She rested against the edge of the table as her uninteresting dance partner invaded her space.

"Want to keep dancing?" he asked, his beer breath wrinkling her nose.

"Of course. I'll be out there as soon as I use the little girls 'room," she said.

"How 'bout right here?" He leaned forward, aiming his lips at her neck.

Very leaned back and placed a hand on his chest. "Easy, tiger. Let's head back."

He pressed his body to hers, undeterred. "You are so fucking hot."

Very was well-versed in fending off aggressive men. She shifted her stance and prepared to knee him in the balls when the weight on her body lifted. The guy flew past her shoulder, landing on the pool table, his face banging against the felt.

He howled, "What the fuck?"

Steady Lockhart stood in front of her, six feet of coiled rage. One arm was in a sling–he had thrown the guy halfway across a pool table one-handed. She was struck dumb by the sight. Steady always wore a cockeyed grin with a cozy, Southern aphorism on the other side of those enticing lips. Very had been a little too fascinated with his mouth, lips that were soft and naturally stained red and set into a face that had alarm bells clanging in her head the second she first laid eyes on him.

At this moment, however, she saw none of the blithe, easygoing man who had been nursing a beer at the bar. Standing before her was a warrior, furious and lethal, and she had never been more turned on. Her body softened with an ache to be near him. Fighting the urge to lose herself in his strength, she reinforced her walls.

Her dance partner flipped onto his ass and put a hand to his bloody face. "I think you broke my nose."

Very turned back to Steady and said with as much anger as she could muster. "What the hell do you think you're doing?"

Steady stood stock still and, turning his gaze away from the guy on the pool table, said, "Trying really hard not to kill him."

It wasn't a figure of speech.

The guy scrambled off the table and fled.

Very stared at her unwelcome savior and couldn't fight the rush of pleasure she felt at seeing the pulse drumming in his neck and his one hand fisted at his side. While upset with his intrusion, she loved that she seemed to be the only person capable of getting a rise out of the even-tempered operative.

She licked her lips. "I don't need you rushing in to save me, Steady. I had the situation under control."

"What am I supposed to do, Very?" He threw out his good hand. "Stand here and watch some asshole maul you? I can't do that."

"Try."

"No."

"I'm perfectly capable of defending myself. Do you think this is the first drunken idiot who tried to cop a feel?" It was the wrong thing to say.

Steady's gaze lasered into her, his voice just south of shouting. "I'm not going to apologize, Very. That guy had it coming. I know you can fend for yourself. But you shouldn't have to."

He looked so frazzled and angry. And while Very always enjoyed riling the unflappable Jonah Lockhart, at this moment, she felt the need to soothe him. "I appreciate your thoughtless and misguided effort."

Steady laughed. "Christ, maybe we need a code word."

"A what?"

"You know. A code word, like rutabaga or some shit. A word for when you need me to step in and rescue you."

"Rutabaga? What the hell is that?"

"It's a vegetable."

"I don't need a freaking code word, Steady, because I don't need to be rescued. Ever. Just mind your own business."

He stepped forward to within reach and looked down at her. "I'm not gonna do that, Very."

She fisted his T-shirt and pulled him closer. "You are impossible."

When his lips touched hers, Very's knees buckled. She pushed to her toes and wrapped her arms around his neck. Steady backed her against the pool table and took charge of the kiss. His unencumbered hand started on the side of her neck, then traced the curve of her body down to her ass. Very let herself get lost in the commanding pressure of his lips, the perfect finesse of his tongue, the warmth of his body. For the first time in a long time, she let go.

That kiss.

It started like a flash of lightning. Then came the thunder. A deep, rolling echo through her body. Thrilling and frightening.

A squeal of laughter from a group of women in the hall had them jumping apart.

Steady jammed his hand into his pocket and jerked his chin over his shoulder. "I'm just gonna–"

Very spoke over him awkwardly, pointing straight and to the left to indicate the restroom. "Yeah, I need to stop in–"

"Sure." Steady stood for a moment, then beat a hasty retreat back to the bar.

She waited a full minute to ensure the coast was clear, then, after texting the girls in their group chat that she was calling it a night, slipped out the back entrance.

Steady made a beeline for the front door, pausing only long enough to throw some cash on the bar next to Chat.

"Everything okay?" Chat asked.

"Yeah, man. I gotta get going. Early start tomorrow."

The second bartender was tossing a bloody cloth into the trash. "Steady, you're paying to refelt that table!"

Steady waved him off and returned his attention to Chat.

"What's going on tomorrow?" Chat continued, a hint of playfulness in his voice.

"Nothing, just, I want to get a jump on the day."

Chat nodded. "Got it."

"See ya."

"Hey, Steady?" Chat stopped his forward momentum once again.

"Yeah?" Steady sighed.

Chat shoved a cocktail napkin against his friend's chest, and Steady trapped it with his hand. Chat tapped his own lips. "The shimmer is nice, but the pink isn't your color."

Steady eyes widened, and he quickly swiped the paper over his mouth, only to find no trace of lipstick. He should have known. Very didn't wear pink shimmer lip gloss. Chat was openly grinning, his white teeth striking against his dark skin.

"Asshole." Steady crumpled the napkin, tossed it at his buddy, and left. Chat's laughter followed him out the door.

Steady jogged over to his jeep and climbed in the doorless driver's side. Turning the ignition, he glanced up to see a bright pink head of hair darting through the parked cars. Her Volvo bleeped, and the lights flashed as she unlocked it remotely. *What the hell?* Was she sneaking out on him? Of all the ridiculous, immature, chicken-shit moves. Did she honestly think she needed to escape? That he would turn into some swooning, obsessed puppy? Gravel kicked up as Very pulled out of the parking lot.

Without wasting a second on self-reflection, Steady gave chase.

When they came to the long stretch of empty road that led to their neighboring beach houses, Steady drove into the opposing lane and pulled up next to Very. Her eyes doubled in size, and she hurried to lower her window. "Steady, what are you doing? Get out of that lane!"

Ripping off the sling to steer, he pointed at his driveway, and Very turned in without argument. Steady hopped out of the Jeep and stalked to her car just as she flew out, already yelling.

"Are you out of your mind? What the hell do you think you're doing?"

Steady didn't break stride as he came nose-to-nose with her, cupped her face in both hands, and kissed her again. She didn't pull him closer, nor did she back away. She stood still as a statue and reciprocated. After a long moment, Steady tore his lips from hers.

"I can't fucking take it anymore, Very. It's been months, *months*. The bickering, the goading, the teasing, all in the name of stifling this unending, raw ache."

She stood two feet away, frozen as he continued. "You lit the fuse last December, and the fire's about to hit the dynamite. So either explode with me or run."

She catapulted into his arms. Steady gripped her thighs as she locked her ankles around his waist, her flip-flops hitting the ground behind him. Very sank both hands into his mop of hair and kissed him like there was no tomorrow. Unwilling to break their connection, Steady staggered up the exterior stairs with Very in his arms and his lips locked with hers.

She pulled back and looked at his arm. "You're bleeding," she panted.

The stitches in his bicep from the bullet graze had popped at some point. He hadn't noticed. "It's nothing."

"We should rebandage it," she said, then bit his chin.

"If you can wrap gauze with my head between your legs, go for it."

She kissed him again, reignited as Steady pushed open the unlocked door and barreled into the house. Shifting his grip on her ass to one-handed, Steady began attacking their clothes. He bumped the entry hall table with his knee, righted himself, then donkey-kicked the front door closed with a slam.

Very was awash in sensation. Every touch, every movement felt so right. It was as if Steady had a thousand keys to a thousand locks on her body and was slowly releasing each one. He dropped her onto the couch and came over her, his lips exploring her neck, then wandering down to her clavicle. Very needed his mouth everywhere. She peeled the T-shirt over her head and tossed it. Steady unclasped her bra and pulled the lemon-yellow straps down her arms. She expected him to dive back in, but when Very looked up, Steady was staring at her with so much hunger in his sage-green eyes, she nearly combusted.

"So fucking beautiful," he said.

She arched her back, encouraging him. Steady took the hint and returned his mouth to her body. She felt her cutoffs slide down her legs. Every touch of his hand, every brush of his lips sent her deeper into this ocean of desire. His hand traveled slowly, purposefully, to the place she needed him most. He sank a thick finger inside her, then a second. When his thumb hit its target, Very thought she might simultaneously melt and explode.

She moaned, and Steady redoubled his effort. He gripped her leg behind her knee, urging her open, and she earnestly complied.

There was no stress, no worry, no fear; everything was color and bursts of light. Very locked eyes with Steady. It made no sense. This was a man she resented, a man she disliked. She had spent months cultivating her irritation with his balanced, untroubled attitude. At this moment, on the brink of a momentous release, Very couldn't find it within herself to care. Steady was so giving, so powerful, and for one brief wink of time, she wanted to surrender.

But she couldn't. Against her will, Very's rational mind caught up with her pleasure center, and she forced herself to face reality. This was the most critical time in her life; her singular focus was imperative. She needed to stop this brewing fascination dead in its tracks.

And Very knew exactly how to do it.

Steady had to be dreaming. Touching Very was like taking flight, and he never wanted to return to earth. The scent of her hair, the lust in her eyes, the feel of her skin, it was all perfection. Every little sound that escaped her lips drove Steady on; he wanted to lose himself in her body and never return. The way she responded to his touch drove him mad. He was going to spend all night making her feel good, and Steady whispered the same into her ear as he nipped her lobe.

When Very rested her hand over his erection, he nearly blasted off. He needed to be inside her, to join their bodies, but each step on this path felt so pure, Steady found himself in no rush to reach the end of the journey.

Very was close. He felt her body gearing up for the climax–the first of many if Steady had his way. He was so lost in her hazel eyes, he didn't understand what was happening when he felt her small hand circle his wrist.

"Wait. Stop," she said.

Steady withdrew his hand immediately, concern coloring his words. "What's wrong?" He corked his frustration and sat back on his haunches.

Very moved them, so they were sitting side by side and took his hand. "I just think we should slow down. Talk."

Running a hand over his face, he blew out a breath. "Yeah, sure. What's on your mind?"

"Well, it's finally happened with us. This is going to be so great." Very scooted closer.

"Yeah," he replied. "Wait. What's going to be so great?"

"Us. Dating. Being a couple."

Steady couldn't process her words. His dick was fighting to escape its confines, and the willing woman beside him was saying things that didn't compute. "What?" was all he could muster.

"It's crazy to think of you as my boyfriend, finally, after all this time."

"Yes." He blinked. "Crazy."

"God, Steady, I want to wake up with you every morning."

Wait. What?

"Oops," she giggled. "Did I say that out loud?"

"Um," he huffed a laugh, "yeah."

"Oh, my God." Very rested her head on his shoulder. "Let's get a dog!"

"Huh?" What the fuck was she doing?

Very turned to the side, hooked her arms around her legs, and rested her chin on her knees. "Yes! It's perfect—a little dog, like a Yorkie or a dachshund. We'll name him Buddy. He can live here, and we'll share him."

"Huh?" All he could do was stare at this new, slightly psychotic version of the woman he had pursued relentlessly for months.

"I figure I'll be here all the time anyway. Just picture it: you, me, and little Buddy taking walks on the beach. Oh, I'm really into baking right now, so maybe you could walk him while I try out a new recipe. I'd love to be able to make a nice meal for your parents when they come to visit." Very fell back on the couch and propped her bare feet on his lap. "I'm learning how to make apple fritters."

What the hell is happening?

Steady shot up like an admiral had just entered the room, causing Very's feet to flop back onto the cushion. Steady wouldn't have guessed it in a million years, but there she was, lying there with hearts in her eyes. *Holy shit, she's a clinger.* And then–

She giggled.

In all the time he had known and fought with and flirted with this woman, he had never once heard her giggle. Laugh? Sure. Guffaw? Once or twice. Chuckle? Definitely. But giggle? It was *bizarre*.

She ran her eyes over his body, noting the erection that still tented his shorts. "Feeling frisky, Baby?"

The answer was yes. Despite the crazy coming out of Very's mouth, her pink hair splayed on the throw pillow, and that warm, inviting body posed on the couch was almost enough to summon Steady back to the asylum. Almost.

"You know what? You're right. We should take it slow. Why don't we call it a night, and we can, you know, take it one step at a time. I'm going to jump in the shower." He exhaled into his hand. "Beer breath." He tripped on the leg of the coffee table and stumbled toward the stairs.

Still topless, Very followed him across the room and wrapped her arms around his waist. "Shoot, you're right, but I want to join you," she cooed.

Steady pushed her to arm's length. "That's okay."

She snatched her bra off the floor and spun it around. "Text me later, okay?"

"Just try and stop me." He forced a toothy grin.

"Kay." She pouted, "Bye."

"Bye-bye."

When the front door closed, Steady ran to the window, ensuring her car had left. He shifted into the kitchen and watched as the Volvo traveled the short distance to her driveway. When Very reached her front door, she turned and spotted him. Fighting the urge to hit the floor, Steady stayed where he was until Very disappeared into her house. His phone buzzed on the area rug where he had dropped it. Snatching it up, he read the notification.

Very: Making sure I got home safe. So sweet.

The words were followed by a string of emojis Steady couldn't bother to decode. Frustrated and confused, he made his way up the stairs, still not comprehending what the hell had just happened.

CHAPTER FOUR

South Island, South Carolina
July 20

Steady blinked one eye open, squinting against the sunlight. Every muscle in his body ached. He slept like he had spent the night perched on the edge of a cliff. As the night passed, Steady half-dreamed, half-wondered how his evening had gone so horribly wrong. He was finally, *finally*, seducing Very Valentine. And then, halfway into what was proving to be the most mind-blowing physical encounter he had ever experienced, she went bonkers.

Very was so magical, so unattainable, it had never occurred to him that she might be trying to rope him into a relationship. The painful conclusion was as clear as the ceiling fan spinning above the bed. Angry and disappointed, Steady kicked off the sheet and plodded naked to the shower.

Steady fell back against the locked bathroom door with a groan. In the mirror, he caught sight of his reinjured arm. He grabbed the first aid kit from the cabinet and set it on the sink. In the shower, his thoughts continued to race. He spent five minutes cleaning his body and twenty minutes standing under the hot spray, trying to make sense of the situation. He always knew Very was crazy, but crazy in a *let's fuck on your porch swing, then skinny dip in the ocean* kind of way. Not in a let me cook dinner for your parents after a one-night stand kind of way.

After rebandaging his arm and wrapping a towel low on his hips, Steady trudged across the bedroom and grabbed sweatpants and a T-shirt from the dresser. Movement outside caught his eye, and Steady glanced across the way to see Very hurrying out her front door. She had a messenger bag slung over one shoulder and was holding a travel mug. She looked like she did most mornings when he spotted her rushing off to work—business as usual.

Steady shook off the strange feeling simmering in his gut and got dressed. When his head pushed through the neck hole of the T-shirt, he looked out the window again as Very hopped into her SUV and sped off without a backward glance. Something gnawed at him, but Steady brushed it away and reminded himself there was now yet another woman in Beaufort he would have to dodge.

CHAPTER FIVE

Parasol Labs
Ridgeland, South Carolina
July 20

Very stood at the plexiglass hood at her lab station, her hands through the arm holes and secured in the gloves, and prepared the slides. She was analyzing the makeup of the natural antihistamine in stinging nettles and comparing it to a synthetic version; it was the basis of the new allergy drug Parasol was developing. After affixing the sample to the slide with paraffin, she moved to the microscope. She studied the sample, then exited the workroom to record her findings at her desk.

Rohit, her coworker, greeted her with a head bob, the music in his earbuds producing a rhythmic thump. Very took her seat at the desk beside him and woke her computer. Rohit plucked out an Airpod and turned to face her. "I drove to Charleston last night to hear Shipwreck'd. Freaking awesome."

Rohit was a music aficionado–everything from Beethoven to Beyonce, didgeridoo to DJs. If it produced a sound, Rohit was interested. Very's musical tastes were broad but not nearly as diverse. She always enjoyed hearing about her friend's adventures road-tripping up and down the eastern seaboard to catch a show. When he loved a performance, he would talk like a WWF announcer in the ring introducing the fighters. He did it then.

"They blew the roof off the building, building, building," he echoed for effect.

Very laughed. "Glad it was worth the trip."

"Shipwreck'd in the house." He drummed on his desk.

"Woot, woot." Very pumped her hands over her head, flat palms to the ceiling.

The other researcher in their pod was Jeffrey. He was neither irritated by Very's chitchat nor a participant. He worked. Occasionally, if Rohit and Very got carried away, Jeffrey would look up with a blank expression. Very had come to know it as his *please shut up* face.

As if she had conjured it, Jeffrey lifted his head.

Rohit cleared his throat and stood. "If you need me, I'll be downstairs. I need to destroy some old samples and clean out that fridge."

Very said, "I'll go with you. I have some housekeeping to do too."

She picked up a stray ballpoint pen and returned it to the coffee mug she had repurposed as a pencil holder. As she withdrew her hand, her finger skated over the blade of an X-Acto knife sticking out of the cup.

"Dammit." Very sucked her finger into her mouth, soothing the wound. After pulling a tissue from the box, she pressed down on the tiny cut.

Rohit stood over her shoulder. "What the hell, Verity? Why is there an X-Acto knife in there? That's just asking for trouble."

Very tossed the tissue while Rohit peeled a bandaid. "It had a little cover. It must have come off."

"Ya think?" Rohit chided as he secured the plaster. "Keep that thing in your desk. It's dangerous."

"Ah." Very found the small safety cardboard, slipped it over the blade, and then deposited the X-Acto knife into a drawer. "There."

"You, of all people." Rohit chuckled as they walked to the stairs. "We must keep sharps away from you at all times."

"It's nothing," Very replied, wiggling the injured digit at her friend. "Come on. I need to make sure you don't destroy my viable samples."

Rohit returned to his story of the previous night's concert, and together they made their way down to the secure storage area.

Very double-checked her sample tray in the freezer and confirmed one test tube surreptitiously marked with a small, red dot was where it should be. After offering to pick up lunch, she retrieved her things and left the lab.

The ParaPharm cafeteria was bustling with researchers and office workers. After placing her and Rohit's lunch order, she stepped into an open seating alcove and sent a text.

Marie Curie: *Sunny skies in Ridgeland today*

Charles Darwin: *Noted*

Dropping the disposable phone back in her purse–she would get rid of it later–she grabbed the food and returned to work.

CHAPTER SIX

Very pulled into her driveway and stopped the car with a jerk. It was only six–she usually stayed later, but she needed to get out of that lab.

The day had moved at a snail's pace. Very devoted most of her time to transcribing research and organizing projects. Really, she had spent the hours waiting for the Sword of Damocles hanging over her head to fall and split her in two. Whenever Dr. Kemp, the lab's Primary Investigator, opened his office door or Malcomb Everett, the chief administrator, answered his phone, she froze.

Usually a master at managing her anxiety, Very couldn't get her churning stomach to calm. So much was at stake. She had only needed to accomplish two small tasks today. The first was to make sure the sample of the early version of Mobilify was hidden in her sample tray. The second thing–she glanced down at her bandaged index finger with a smile.

She hadn't even accessed the research that would trigger the chain of events. But what if it didn't work? What if they just fired her? What if they didn't notice at all? What if, what if, what if?

Then, like a compass needle seeking true north, Very turned her head to the house next door and allowed her mind to rest on Steady. He was so grounded, so sedate, that the mere thought of his jade-green eyes and golden-brown hair settled her. It was strange, this duality. On any given day, Jonah Lockhart was making her blood boil. Nevertheless, there was just something about him, something buried beneath the surface, that soothed her tattered nerves.

Still sitting in the driver's seat, she leaned down and peered through the palm trees. His jeep was gone. The house seemed empty. Good, she thought. "That's good," she said aloud, convincing herself.

Very had employed what had proved to be an effective tactic for getting rid of unwanted men. She simply removed the thrill of the chase by being overly interested, *too* overly interested. A wave of disappointment crashed over her. Despite the risk and the terrible timing, she wished they'd taken things further. She'd known him for the better part of a year, and they'd been flirting for most of it, but last night would be an isolated incident. Very would have liked to have the true memory of being with Steady rather than just the fantasy that played on a loop in her head.

She imagined the vee at his hips,

the flexing muscles of his back,

the flop of hair on his forehead as he moved above her.

The one real image that planted itself deep in her mind with intractable roots was the look on Steady's face when he touched her. And that face. That beautiful, heart-stopping face. Very wanted to see that expression every day for the rest of her life.

No. Very screeched her brain to a halt.

As much as she wanted to recline the driver's seat and nod off to Steady's commanding, vulnerable presence, Very forced her legs to move. Grabbing her things, she pushed open the car door and dragged her exhausted body into the house.

She couldn't risk it.

And by "it," she meant the plan.

Not her heart.

CHAPTER SEVEN

South Island, South Carolina
July 22

Steady awoke alone in his bed, the dream of Very Valentine half-naked and splayed under his body, still clinging to his consciousness. Regardless of how that night ended, their time together had spiraled into an ongoing sexual fantasy that had him throbbing with unprecedented force. Torn between lingering in the dream state and satisfying his need, he reluctantly peeled himself off the mattress and lumbered to the shower. Under the hot spray of the water, Steady gripped his erection, imagining his gorgeous neighbor on her knees, taking his length between her perfect lips. He exploded on a shout, holding a hand out to brace himself against the force of the sensation. Continuing with his shower, he washed away the mirage and focused on how Very had shattered the euphoria with her crazy. For one brief, shining moment, he thought *maybe*. But no, Very Valentine was needy and manipulative. *Just like all women.* With that frigid reminder, he toweled off and got dressed.

Steady was doctoring his coffee when his dad's familiar shave-and-a-haircut knock had him hurrying to the door.

"It's your house, Dad. You don't need to knock." Steady pulled open the door and hugged his father.

Louis Lockhart was sixty-three with a full head of graying sandy hair and a warm smile. Wearing khakis and an oxford with the cuffs rolled to his forearms, he was as dressed down as Steady had ever known him to be.

Louis stepped into the house. "I won't be writing a parenting book any time soon, but I know enough not to enter one of my kids 'rooms without knocking first."

Steady smiled. It was his dad's signature line. Whenever Steady fought with his brothers or got in trouble, Louis Lockhart would sit him down in one of the oversized patio chairs. His dad would make some off-hand comment about the yard or the weather. Then, he'd say *I won't be writing a parenting book anytime soon, but I gave you a curfew for a reason.* The truth was, with the six of them and their teenage drama, Louis Lockhart probably could write a parenting book.

Children rarely see or admit family resemblance, but not even Steady could deny he was his father two-point-oh. From features to mannerisms, he was his father's son.

His dad sank his hands into his trouser pockets and slowly perused the space. "Jonah, this is impressive. Last time I was in this room, I was standing in two inches of sand staring through a hole in the wall at half a deck."

Steady had moved into the beach house after yet another tropical storm had all but destroyed it. Rather than let his dad sell it, Steady saw the win-win of moving in and rehabbing the place. It was only a twenty-minute drive to the Bishop Security office, so he could enjoy free housing while he helped out his family.

"Wait'll you see the new deck. Finn crashed through the rotted floorboards last winter, so we ripped the whole thing off and rebuilt it."

"And Finn? He's doing better?" his father asked.

Finn McIntire had been captured and tortured on a SEAL op. They had rescued him, but the experience had scarred him physically and emotionally.

"So much better, Dad. He ran off to a small town in West Virginia last winter and got his head straight. He and Twitch are together and having a baby."

"Glad to hear it. I worry about you boys. Sherman was right; *War is hell.*"

Steady knew his dad questioned his career—knew he worried. It was a blessing and a curse. His father had a bad heart. The last thing he wanted to do was add stress to his father's life. His dad had told him repeatedly that it would cause him more heartache if Steady didn't follow his path. So he did. The entire time he served, Steady made sure to check in and assure his father that all was well. Even when it wasn't.

"Want to see the new deck?"

"Lead the way, son."

"Coffee?"

"Please. Your mother has me off caffeine, but I sneak in a little high-test here and there."

Steady popped a decaf pod into the Keurig and retrieved a mug. With a quick peek under his T-shirt, he confirmed that the bandage on his arm was secure and undetectable. Fortunately, the sling was in his bedroom upstairs. His father had undergone bypass surgery two years ago, and Steady was going to do his part to keep him around as long as possible. When the coffee had brewed, he passed the mug to his dad, grabbed his own, and pulled open the sliding glass doors.

The deck was his pride and joy. Between his teammate and best friend, Cam's expertise from growing up in Miami and their sniper, Herc's construction skills, the Bishop Security men had built one hell of a sexy deck. The top level held a dining area and covered outdoor kitchen. Three steps descended to a lower section with cushioned wicker seating and a hammock. From there, another set of wide stairs led down to the beach.

His dad was a man of few words. A simple *well done* was high praise, and his disciplinary talks were usually one sentence: *if you could go back and relive it, what would you do differently?* So when his father glanced around and said, "I think I could live the rest of my life on this deck," Steady grew two inches.

"It's pretty sweet," Steady agreed. "You gonna tell me what's up? Because I know you didn't fly down here at seven in the morning to tour the remodel."

Steady pulled out one of the sturdy black dining chairs and set his coffee on the table. His dad did the same.

"Got a call from an old college buddy. Head of Emergency Medicine at a hospital out west."

"Aw, shit. I was on painkillers. I forgot he asked me about you."

"Imagine my surprise when he told me he patched up my son's gunshot wound."

"It's nothing–barely a scratch."

"Just wanted to see with my own eyes that you were in one piece. You haven't been injured in a long while."

Steady unconsciously rubbed his leg. "Yeah. It's fine, Dad."

"Good to know."

"What else is going on?" Steady was desperate for a change of subject, mainly for his father's sake.

"The merger with Haven Hotels was finalized last week. The company's new name is Lockhart-Haven Group, and we now own forty-two properties."

"That's really somethin', Dad."

"Your mother and I agreed I would retire six months after the merger."

"I think that's great. You don't need all that stress."

His dad took a sip, then set the mug down. "And you're doing your part passing off this shit decaf as real coffee."

Steady grinned. "I still can't get away with anything."

"Deception isn't your strong suit. That's something to be proud of."

Steady frowned. Why did the word deception send his mind to Very?

Louis pinned his son with a look and said, "Well, something's on your mind."

Steady knew exactly what was occupying his thoughts, or rather *who*, but he sure as hell wasn't going to admit it. "Any plans for retirement? Bingo night? A cruise?"

Louis chuckled. "I'm not going to be sitting on the porch playing checkers. Your mother's bucket list is longer than a Russian novel."

Steady laughed too. "I'm sure mom has plenty to keep you busy. I'm happy for you, Dad."

"Let's wander down to that inviting couch and enjoy the view."

Steady grinned. The best thing about his dad was his ability just to be. They had spent hours together in quiet, mutual moments, stargazing or fishing or walking in the woods. Steady had learned to be comfortable in his own skin by osmosis.

Together they sat and watched the waves retreat from the shore. When Very jogged by in the morning mist, Steady couldn't take his eyes off that hypnotic pink ponytail and those damned little shorts she always wore. She didn't look his way, didn't act like she even knew him. That was a relief. Or was it? Something was gnawing at his gut, but Steady couldn't put his finger on exactly what. Louis Lockhart said nothing, but Steady felt the couch cushion shake with his dad's silent chuckle.

CHAPTER EIGHT

Parasol Labs
Ridgeland, South Carolina
July 22

The Parasol Labs 'campus was dark and quiet when Very returned to work at ten p.m. The security guard, used to seeing her at odd hours, lifted the gate and ushered her through. After parking in her usual spot, she waved to the man patrolling the grounds, swiped her access card, and entered the building.

The lab was a concrete and glass monument to modernism. The three-story atrium was bright and welcoming—potted palms bracketed the circular reception desk, and the cream leather furniture invited visitors to relax and admire the art or glance out at the lush landscape. Parasol's PR department often gave tours of the facility, and the building reflected the company image.

Very moved through the space, summoned the elevator, and ascended to the second floor. The doors parted to a dark silence. She remained in the soft light of the elevator car and stared into oblivion with familiar trepidation. It was always irrationally unnerving before she stepped into the hall and activated the motion-sensitive lights. Very imagined the floor disappearing beneath her in that first step and falling into an abyss. But sure enough, as she forced her feet forward, the area around the elevator banks lit up, revealing the usual, unremarkable hall. Every few feet she walked, another section came to life. Each advancement was like a bad dream, staring into a haunting void, imagining a waiting killer, then waking up and seeing a simple, benign space. Despite her level-headedness, Very couldn't help but imagine a demon lurking in the black, nor could she stifle the small sigh of relief as each section of the hall illuminated. Why she felt this apprehension, she couldn't fathom. In her experience, monsters didn't hide in the shadows; they stood in the spotlight.

Her lab was the last on the long, sterile corridor that branched off at even intervals into a dizzying labyrinth. When Very started working here, she had been relieved her workspace was off the main hall; she had visions of wandering the white maze in a Kafka-esque ordeal.

When she touched her thumb to the pad, and the light on the wall flashed green, Very pushed open the heavy door and entered. The main room was an open office space where each scientist had a desk. Security cameras dotted the corners of the ceiling, unobtrusive but for a small red light. The lab where Very and her colleagues did their benchwork was beyond a glass wall at the back.

After logging on to her computer, Very brought up the secure archive and entered the password. Incorrectly.

The notification flashed: Login Failed.

She tried again.

Login Failed.

With a frustrated breath, mindful of the security cameras, Very reached into her tote and retrieved her planner. Flipping to the back, she checked the password. She quickly typed in the correct sequence and accessed the research archive.

Without further delay, Very slipped the flash drive into the machine and downloaded the information she needed. Then, she withdrew the device and slipped it into her pocket. That completed, she stayed at her desk, as instructed, and read over the team's research update.

After twenty minutes and no alarm bells or security presence, Very gathered her things and left. The lights had timed out, and the hallway was dark. She had walked about halfway, the lights again coming on section-by-section, when the soft ping of the elevator sounded from the shadows.

Very froze, a mouse in a maze. Her instinct was to run and hide; she had been doing it for years, and the strategy had never failed her. But something told her to stay put. Darwin's words rang in her ears: *never show your hand.*

Jimmy, one of the night guards, stepped off the elevator. Backlit by the dim light of the car, he walked to the nearest corner. Suddenly, the entire hall was flooded with blinding light. He approached her at an even pace, checking locked doors as he went.

Very walked forward. Ten yards away, she smiled and waved. "Hey, Jimmy."

He didn't respond, simply continued walking straight toward her. When he was two feet in front of her, blocking her way, he paused, his face blank. Very masked her fear with what she hoped was a mildly confused expression. She forced her feet to remain planted, standing her ground.

After a seeming eternity, Jimmy said, "There is a switch on the wall at both ends." He pointed to one end of the hall, then the other. "To light the whole corridor. Chase away the ghosts."

Very followed his extended hand to what was indeed a light switch she had never noticed. "Wow. How did I not know that? Thanks."

"Your brain is thinkin 'bigger thoughts." He had a gentle southern accent, a soft lilt to his voice that reminded her of a certain charming SEAL.

"Well, that's a convenient excuse anyway." She gave a self-deprecating laugh. "Have a good night."

Jimmy lifted his hand in a half-wave, tucked both thumbs into his utility belt, and continued on in the opposite direction.

Very forced herself to walk at a reasonable pace as she made her way out of the building. In the safety of her car, with the doors locked and the interior lights off, she screamed into the crook of her elbow. After reassuring herself that all was well, she retrieved the burner phone from her messenger bag.

Fat raindrops slapped the windshield as she texted.

Marie Curie: *Clear skies in Ridgeland.*

Charles Darwin: *Glad to hear it.*

Marie Curie: *Have a good night.*

Doing her best not to burn rubber in the parking lot, Very drove out of the ParaPharm Labs lot and headed home, going straight into the oncoming storm.

PART TWO

The Hook

CHAPTER NINE

Armand Krill posed before the standing mirror in his bedroom and double-checked his appearance. His blue blazer was nondescript but expertly tailored, and his gray slacks had a perfect crease leading down to his leather oxfords. His thinning hair was combed straight back, highlighting a jowled, hawkish face.

He had received word of the approval of his membership by messenger two days prior. After paying the initiation fee and filling out the required paperwork, Krill was free to use the Cavalry Club at will. He would certainly avail himself of the services of the chefs, barbers, tailor, shoeshine man, librarian, bartenders, and masseuses—perhaps not the personal trainers or the squash pros.

Located just four blocks from his home, the Cavalry Club was a haven for well-heeled scions of the Manhattan elite. Krill had spent his life earning back his family fortune, and now he would reap the benefits of having an old-money name with the new money to back it up. For most of his life, places like the Cavalry Club had been inaccessible, despite the fact that his grandfather and great-grandfather had been members. Armand Krill's father had been a dallying playboy, happy to indulge his every whim without concern for his family. He'd lost millions on idiotic investments–fly-by-night ideas of his drunken friends–and spent money like there was no tomorrow. But there was a tomorrow, and when it came, the Krills were nearly broke. Krill had worked tirelessly–and unhindered by integrity–to refill the family coffers.

Finally, he had the means to congregate with his ilk. And congregate, he would. Krill planned to have breakfast every morning at the club.

He gave the sport coat a final pass with a lint brush and fastened a platinum clip on his paisley necktie—ties were required in all parts of the club except the fitness areas. The buzzing cell phone on his bedside table pulled Krill from his perusal. After checking the screen, he answered immediately.

"Yes?"

"Mr. Krill, this is Micah at the Highridge lab."

"What is it?" Krill asked, gathering his wallet and a monogrammed handkerchief.

"I don't think it's anything concerning, but you asked to be informed personally of any irregularity. I know security is heightened with the new drug coming out."

Parasol's new arthritis drug, Mobilify, would change lives, primarily his.

"Last night, a chemist at the lab accessed the secure research archive. Two failed login attempts triggered a warning. Probably nothing, but it is unusual for a scientist to be accessing the archive."

"What did he access?"

"She," the guard corrected. "Verity Valentine downloaded the double-blind studies for an early version of Mobilify."

Krill bristled. "Send me the information she accessed."

"Yes, sir."

"I want her monitored."

There was a pause on the line. Then Micah said, "Lab activity or comprehensive?"

"Comprehensive."

"Understood."

Krill ended the call, a strange worry boring into his brain. A scientist researching in an archive wasn't out of the ordinary, but Krill's paranoia had served him well over the years. He needed to make sure this female scientist was clean. Nothing was going to interfere with the release of Mobilify. Nothing.

After he slipped his wallet into his breast pocket and rechecked his appearance in the standing mirror, Krill dropped the phone into his briefcase. Electronics were frowned upon in most parts of the Cavalry Club, and Krill needed to make a good impression. He was incapable of being obsequious, his arrogance forbade him from pandering, but Armand Krill, more than most, knew the value of worthy alliances. It was the only thing lacking in his return to prominence. With an army of Cavalry Club members behind him, Krill would be unstoppable.

CHAPTER TEN

Beaufort, South Carolina
July 29

Steady's favorite hole-in-the-wall burger joint was packed. He scanned their round table in the back corner of the room, feeling like the odd man out. Finn McIntyre, his brother from the SEALs, had been through hell and was now getting his well-deserved reward. He had returned to Beaufort with the love of his life, Bishop's cybersecurity chief, Charlotte "Twitch" Devlin, and they were expecting a baby in September. Cam Canto had been on a different SEAL squad, but he and Steady had grown close, working side-by-side at Bishop Security for over a year. Cam, too, had fallen. With his Latin looks and unusual golden eyes, Cam never lacked female attention, but once he set his sights on Evan Cole, the beautiful archaeologist he had met on an op in Mallorca, his playboy days were over.

Miller "Tox" Buchanan was the old married man of the group. The gorgeous and enigmatic Calliope had felled the 6'5" warrior. Tox had run to protect her after she stumbled upon financial information that some exceedingly dangerous people wanted at all costs. Now they were married, and they, too, were expecting. Their missing teammate, Leo "Ren" Jameson, was taking a long-overdue vacation helping his new girlfriend, Sofia Kirk, move for a new CIA embassy assignment in Amman, Jordan. His buddies were dropping like flies. Before long, he might be the only single guy on the team.

Fine by me.

The disastrous end to his encounter with Very reaffirmed his commitment to bachelorhood. It had been a week since their night together, and Steady had successfully managed to dodge an awkward run-in. It had been surprisingly easy, in fact.

His thoughts drifted to their brief encounter–the way she had clung to him like a lifeline, the exhilaration of touching her, the intimacy. It was so much more than just a wild, passionate hookup. And that's what made her crazy behavior all the more frustrating.

The new waitress, hired for the season, leaned over his shoulder and placed a fresh beer in front of him.

"Is your girlfriend late?" she ran her hand down his shoulder and squeezed his injured arm. Steady hid a wince.

He had left the sling at home tonight; he wasn't sure why. It was a good conversation starter, an easy way for interested women to approach. For some reason, tonight, he just wasn't in the mood.

Steady leaned back to get a look at the waitress. She had "college student" written all over her, from the bouncing blonde curls to her cherry red lip gloss to the perky tits striking distance from his face. All she was missing was a sorority T-shirt and AirPods.

"Hmm?" Steady asked.

"Well, you're the only solo one at the table, and you keep checking the door. So, I figured you must be waiting for your date."

Had he been checking the door? Yes, he was avoiding Very and an awkward encounter like the plague. Or he wanted a repeat performance. No. It was the first thing. He was sure. If she walked in, he planned on slipping out the back before she could get to their table. Cowardly? Yes. Easy? Also yes.

The pretty waitress leaned closer. "If you get ditched, I'll cheer you up with a game of pool." She gathered some empty plates from the table and sauntered away.

"A game of pool?" Tox taunted.

Steady deadpanned, "I'm not lookin 'to adopt. If she's twenty, I'll pick up the tab."

"What is it about women and pool?" Cam asked. "Why is it so hot?"

"It's chalking the tip and that little blow. The first time I saw Calliope do it, I almost bought a pool table." Tox kissed his wife's neck.

Calliope shifted back and speared Tox with her ice-blue gaze. "He's just flattering me into agreeing to get a pool table."

Tox pulled her back to his side. "I may have an ulterior motive, but it's still true. You chalking a pool cue is sexy as fuck."

"No, *hermano*. It's bending over for the shot. Evocative." Cam squeezed Evan's hand.

Steady rested his forearms on the table and cradled his beer. "There's sort of a nasty innocence to it, you know?"

The women burst out laughing.

"What?" Steady asked.

Evan leaned into Cam. "There's nothing innocent about it, Steady. Most women know exactly what they're doing when they play pool with a guy." She picked up her knife with an exaggerated pout and mimicked blowing on a cue, eliciting a growl from her fiancé.

Twitch grabbed a breadstick from the basket. "One time in college, Very hustled an entire fraternity. Granted, she's an amazing pool player, but she also wore this little sundress that crept up *almost* high enough to show the goods. Paid for our spring break trip to Destin." Twitch punctuated the story with a bite. Finn placed a protective arm around her shoulders and cradled her belly with his other hand.

The mention of the clinger had Steady's eyes darting to the door.

"She's not coming," Twitch said.

Faking ignorance, Steady replied, "Hmm? Who?"

"You know who. Very. She's working on some project and has been practically living at her lab."

Steady sat back with a huff.

"Is that relief or frustration? I can't get a read," Tox said.

The waitress returned, shouldering a large tray, and proceeded to distribute the food.

Evan grabbed the ketchup. "We heard you guys made out. What's the big deal?" She smacked the bottom of the bottle.

"She told you? Great. So I guess it was a big deal if she's gossiping to her girlfriends." Steady wondered how much Very had shared with her girlfriends about that night. He absolutely, unequivocally did not want people to find out. But. A teeny tiny part of him wanted to know if Very had the same mind-bending experience. Even now, the mere memory launched a flash flood of sensation.

"She isn't gossiping, Steady," Calliope brought him back to the conversation. "I saw you. That night at the bar, I went to find Very in the bathroom when the guy she was dancing with came running out of the game room with a bloody nose." She forked a bite of salad. "I went to check it out."

Steady downed his beer. "It was nothing."

"That was not nothing. *That* was like coming too close to the sun. I was fully prepared to watch you two do it."

When all eyes found her, Calliope defended, "What? They both seem like exhibitionists."

There was muttered agreement around the table. Even Steady pursed his lips and tipped his head in a *you've-got-a-point* expression.

"Fine, it was a hot kiss." Steady modified the story to make his point without revealing the extent of his encounter with Very. "But afterward, she acted all…" He took a long pull of his beer. "Let's just say there are anacondas with looser grips."

"Yeah, that's perplexing." Tox held the half-pound burger in one hand and took a bite.

Calliope elbowed her husband as she snatched a fry from his plate.

"I guess you never really know a person." Evan pinched her lips together.

Finn, who, up to this point, had been content to eat his meal and hold Twitch's hand, blurted. "I can't do it." He ran a palm down his scarred face.

"Finn," Twitch scolded.

"I'm sorry. I can't." He tucked an auburn strand behind Twitch's ear, then turned to Steady. "Dude, you are getting played like Pong."

"Damn, and it was just getting fun." Cam slapped a hand on the table in mock annoyance.

"What the fuck is going on?" Steady demanded.

Twitch rested a hand over Steady's as if she were about to deliver bad news. "It all started our third year of college. Very and I lived with three other women in this little house we rented back behind the fraternities in Charlottesville. One night, three things happened."

"The perfect storm," Tox added.

Twitch extended a finger as she continued. "First, one of the girls had been completely ghosted by this lacrosse player she was crazy about, so she started sneaking around, following him." She added a finger. "Two, our other roommate told her boyfriend of six months that she loved him, and he hadn't said it back, so she threw all his stuff out her window. The third thing that happened was crazy."

"Seems like we already crossed the county line on that one," Steady grumbled.

Ignoring him, Twitch said, "Very had hooked up with this guy in her chem lab, and he was obsessed with her. I mean, one make-out session over a Bunsen burner, and the guy was in love. He showed up at our door, sent flowers, and texted constantly."

"Stalker," Calliope shuddered.

"Totally," Twitch confirmed. "That night, he drove his car onto our tiny front lawn, stood on the hood, and started yelling for Very. I asked her if she wanted me to call the police. That's when it happened."

"What?" Steady urged. "What happened?"

"The perfect storm," Twitch repeated Tox's words. "Very walked outside and ran up to the guy. I came out with her but stayed by the front door. She said this was the grand gesture she had been waiting for, that they should get married and have babies and rent a little house together while they finished their degrees. I mean, the performance was Oscar-worthy. After thirty minutes of pure insanity—she was naming their pets and asking if she could call his mother, 'mom'—the guy left, and we never saw him again."

"The stalker became the stalkee." Evan toasted the air with her wine glass.

"Okay, yeah, so she got rid of a barnacle. I'm not seeing the connection." Steady polished off his beer.

Finn rubbed Twitch's back and, leaning forward to look around her, gave Steady a meaningful stare.

Twitch continued, "Steady, whenever Very doesn't want to, um, pursue a relationship—which is every time—she pulls this overly-clingy act. We call it the commphobe. It's short for commitment-phobe. She sends the guy running, so she doesn't have to deal with the awkward 'it's not you, it's me 'stuff."

Steady snagged a chicken wing and gestured with it as he spoke. "Twitch, get to the point of this story."

"I thought I did."

Six pairs of eyes all looked at him with a mix of amusement and sympathy.

"Wait. Are you saying she commphobed *me*?"

"Well, it's a noun, not a verb, but yes. That is what I'm saying." Twitch made a yikes face and leaned back against Finn.

"That's ridiculous," Steady insisted, but his mind was racing.

Twitch pointed at him with the nub of the breadstick. "Did she name your imaginary pet?"

Steady mumbled, "Something about a Yorkie named Buddy."

Twitch popped the last bite into her mouth.

The chicken wing hit the plate, and Steady shoved his chair back a foot. "You're saying that pink-haired, lunatic minx played me?"

Cam turned to Tox. "Now he's getting it. Do you think he's getting it?"

"Not sure yet. It seems like it's starting to sink in, though. I imagine getting fooled on top of getting dumped may take a minute to process." Tox pointed the tips of his index fingers together and rolled his hands.

Twitch patted Steady's forearm and threw him a bone. "The point is, you don't have to constantly worry about running into her. She's perfectly sane. Well, she's not perfectly sane, but she's not completely nuts."

That evil, conniving, psychotic, fantastic, sexy, devil-woman. Steady had so many thoughts and feelings running through his brain he could barely sort them. He should have been relieved, but he wasn't. Very Valentine had thrown down, whether she knew it or not. Steady may have been an easygoing guy, but he never walked away from a challenge.

Slowly, deliberately, Steady wiped his hands and face with the red-checked napkin and tossed it on the table with a flourish. When he looked up at his friends, his grin was broad and evil.

"Oh shit," Tox shook his head. "I know that look."

"Yes, you do, my brother," Steady replied. "And why don't you share with the class what this look says." He pointed to his own face.

Tox mumbled under his breath.

"Once more, for the cheap seats," Steady urged.

"It's on," Tox repeated.

Steady shoved his chair back and stood. "Oh, you got that right. It. Is. On."

Tox groaned. Cam laughed. "That's a dangerous game, son."

Twitch once again provided the voice of reason. "Steady, relax. I'm sure it was an epic kiss. Very just, she's not looking for anything right now. She's crazy busy at work and settling into her new life here. It's not—"

"Oh, hell, no. I swear to God, Twitch, if you pull that *it's-not-you-it's-me* shit, I will throttle you."

Finn, who, a year ago, would have flipped the table at a remark like that, tossed a french fry at his friend's head with a laugh.

Steady repeated, "Don't you dare *it's-not-you-it's-me* me."

"Who's Mimi?" Tox asked, then returned to his meal.

Twitch gave Calliope an exasperated sigh. "Why do I bother?"

"Well, guess what?" Steady leaned forward, palms flat on the table. "She may think it's not me, it's her, but it's fucking me, not her, and I'm going to deliver that message in person, so we're all clear on the 'who it is 'part of the relationship or lack thereof. Me, not her. You got me?" Without waiting for a reply, Steady stormed out.

Cam broke the silence. "English is my second language, so…"

Tox clapped him on the back. "Don't worry, bro. That wasn't English."

CHAPTER ELEVEN

South Island, South Carolina
July 29

The dilapidated Jeep bounced along the beach road, and Steady stuck out his arm like a soccer mom to prevent the bag of groceries from spilling forward into the footwell. After charging out of the bar, he made a quick detour to the Piggly Wiggly for supplies, then drove as fast as the engine would allow, straight toward Very's house. The Jeep squeaked and rattled in protest. He needed a new car but couldn't seem to part with the old girl. His parents had given him the Jeep when he went to college, and it held priceless memories— road trips, spring breaks, and more than a few intimate encounters.

Steady couldn't fight the grin that spread across his face. So Very Valentine thought she could outwit him with her little reverse psychology act. *It's not you; it's me, my ass.* He passed his driveway and headed to Very's next door.

As he approached the driveway, Steady's headlights caught on a black SUV sitting on the sandy shoulder, half-hidden by bushes. After parking in the driveway, he walked out to the main road and looked again at the abandoned vehicle. He moved closer, checking for signs of car trouble–a flat tire or smoking engine. Seeing nothing, he continued, passing the tailgate and approaching the driver's-side door.

No one was inside. A Coke can sat in the drink holder, and a fast food bag was in the footwell. In the back seat, there were swim trunks and a soccer ball. Nothing remotely suspicious. It wasn't the first time Steady had seen a car parked out here and busted kids sneaking onto the beach for a little late-night fun. Out of habit, he memorized the license plate. Steady would chase them off later. Right now, he had bigger fish to fry.

He grabbed the flowers and groceries from the Jeep and turned toward the front door. He had a woman in his sights, and he was going hunting.

Very couldn't imagine who would be knocking on her door at this hour. Her actions at the lab earlier had her jumpy and mildly irrational. With a deep breath, she reminded herself of Darwin's sage advice: *don't make assumptions; respond to facts, not emotions.* With forced calm, she walked to the door, flipped the deadbolt, and pulled it open a crack. Rather than the ninja assassin she was half-expecting, she was met with six feet of handsome she had been avoiding.

There on her doorstep, with a cockeyed grin and a bag of goodies, was Jonah "Steady" Lockhart.

She took an unconscious step back, and despite her whispered, "what the fuck?" she couldn't help the bolt of excitement–and relief–that shot through her.

"Why is your door locked?" Steady asked.

She never locked the door. Half the time, it was standing open, with just the screen door closed. Very ignored the question. She couldn't explain her apprehension anyway.

"Steady?"

He didn't wait for an invitation. With a canvas bag in each hand and the grocery store bouquet tucked under his arm, he led with his lips. He kissed her with more intensity than she would have thought possible through the crack of a door with his hands full. Her bare toes curled on the welcome mat.

What the hell was he doing here?

"Hey there, Cupcake. Surprise," he said through the gap.

Very staggered back a step. Unfortunately, the action pulled the door fully open, and Steady strode in. He was too attractive for his own good. Very knew the type. He was the messy-haired, wrinkle-shirted frat boy who looked as sweet as honey but, in reality, was the worst kind of heartbreaker—the kind that made you believe he was anything but.

She voiced her thought. "What are you doing here?"

"Just being neighborly," he winked.

Fuck that boyish Southern charm. His accent wasn't thick; it simply colored his words, adding a lyrical quality to his voice. What the hell was he doing? She was sure her clingy girlfriend act had sent him running for the hills. Maybe she needed to double down.

"Steady, I'm so happy. I've always dreamed of having a boyfriend who dropped by with surprises. I'm so bummed I have to work tonight."

"You gotta eat, Very. You relax while I whip up dinner. Pretend I'm not here."

Like that was even a remote possibility. She couldn't look at his ridiculous Hawaiian shirts without imagining the stacked abs beneath. Steady smelled like the beach and looked like a sunset. Ever since *that night*, when she thought about him, her body responded. Jonah Lockhart was a complication she could not afford.

"How 'bout a rain check, lover? I'll come over next week and cook for you. I promise it'll be worth the wait."

Steady took both of her hands in his. There was mischief in his sage-green eyes. "I thought we should talk about our relationship. You know, really peel the onion on our feelings."

Very could see in an instant her tactic had been discovered. She pulled away, put the coffee table between them, and gave it one last try. "I waited all day for you to text, baby."

"Cut the shit, Very."

Frustrated and anxious, Very dropped the act like a barbell hitting the floor. "It was one night, Steady. The world didn't stop turning. Angels didn't descend from the sky." The lie burned her tongue, but she continued. "Chalk it up as another one of your infamous hookups. That's all."

He strode to within a foot of her but kept his hands in his pockets. She could see his length through his pants. Why on earth was her tirade turning him on?

"It was more than just a hookup, and you know it," he said.

"You're delusional. You just don't like that I'm not following you around like a puppy because your magic moves cast some sex spell."

He didn't respond, and that spoke volumes.

Very pointed at him. "That's it, isn't it? You can't accept that I'm not interested in you."

"I can accept it just fine. What I can't do is *believe* it." He ran a thumb down her cheek, and Very momentarily basked in the gentle touch before grabbing his wrist and shoving him away.

"What the fuck?" Steady stepped back.

"Give me a break. You're the king of the hit-and-run. I was making it easy on you, Steady."

"Maybe I don't want easy with you."

"Oh, please, your pride is wounded. You're happy to do the pump-and-dump as long as you're the one who gets to do the dumping."

"That's not what this is about," he grumbled.

"Isn't it? Admit it. You're here because your ego is bruised. You like to be the one to pull the ripcord."

"Jesus, you make me sound like an asshole."

"If the shoe fits." She turned and walked back to the kitchen.

Steady followed. "You don't know the first thing about me."

"I know you'll have to move soon because you've slept with every woman in Beaufort."

"I don't lie, Very. I don't make promises."

"It doesn't fucking matter what you say, Steady. It matters what you do. You can tell the waitress or the beach bunny that it's just a little fun and that it's a one-and-done situation, and she's still going to imagine she's the one that will tame you."

"That's not my fault. I'm untameable." He shot her that winning smile.

She stepped into his space and spoke with her breath on his lips. "Yeah, well, so am I. Now pound sand."

"Seriously? You're kicking me out?"

"Yes! God, for a smart guy, you're a big fucking dope."

He threw his hands out to the side. "Fine. You're not interested. Whatever. Good. Glad we're on the same page."

Both in denial, she thought, then banished the idea. Steady didn't wait for a snarky comeback; he simply spun on his heel and marched out the door with a slam. A second later, the door flew open, and he strode back into her personal space. Without thought or decision, Very wrapped her arms around his neck and pulled him down. The kiss was an avalanche of lust and frustration and attraction and confusion. Their minds were fighting their bodies, and, at the moment, the bodies were winning.

This time it was Steady who pulled away, leaving Very on the edge of a cliff. "Like I said, Darlin', glad we're on the same page."

With that soft, parting promise, he turned and strolled out. Very released a snarl of frustration, slammed the door, and stood alone in the ensuing silence, aroused and conflicted.

Steady trotted down Very's front steps and hopped in the Jeep with a grin. He'd just had a throwdown, a full-on shouting match, when the closest Steady came to confrontation was sending back cold french fries. Very had insulted him, scolded him, faked being interested in him. So, why was he in the best mood with a hard-on threatening to break his fly?

He knew exactly why. She was faking her faking. She could pretend all she wanted, she could snarl, she could lie; that kiss told him everything he needed to know.

As he turned the Jeep around in the driveway, the headlights swept across the trees and shrubs on the far side of the property. Something caught his eye, movement in the bushes closest to the house. He remembered the car parked on the side of the road, and the hair on his forearms prickled. Knowing the Jeep's lights would hide his actions, Steady slipped out of the car and raced in the shadow of the house to the spot where he had seen the disruption. As he crept into the brush, a figure abandoned any attempt to remain hidden and bolted out of the darkness. Steady clocked the man as he gave chase–he was wearing jeans and a T-shirt and held a pair of binoculars in one hand. As Steady skirted a tree, his shoulder bumped the trunk, sending a bolt of pain through his healing bullet wound.

The man broke out of the trees, rounded the SUV, and peeled away before he closed the car door. Steady stood in the dark road and held his freshly bleeding arm, confirming he remembered the plate number of the rapidly fleeing vehicle.

He trudged back to the Jeep, perplexed and concerned. He made the conscious choice not to mention the intruder to Very, telling himself that he didn't want to upset her rather than admit his ego wouldn't allow him to return to her door. More than that, something else lurked in the shadows of his mind.

She had locked her front door. She seemed on edge when he first arrived. Was Very in trouble? Was she afraid?

Steady wanted to resort to his tried and true method of letting things play out; he wanted to believe the guy in the bushes was just a benign trespasser checking out the private beach. But he couldn't. So, after returning the jeep to his house, Steady walked back through the trees and up Very's driveway to the road. It had been a long time since he had been on night watch, but the routine fell easily upon him. He walked the perimeter of the property and contemplated Very's security. The residents of this island took their safety for granted; houses rarely had alarms, and most of the time, doors were unlocked if not open. Steady retraced his steps. Everything was quiet except for his racing thoughts. There was one precaution Steady had been considering for a while, so he pulled out his phone and texted Charlie Bishop, his boss Nathan's uncle. Charlie would be able to help. Returning the phone to his pocket, Steady continued his patrol.

It was still dark when Very woke from a fitful sleep riddled with dreams of a cocky, charming pilot. She quickly showered and brushed her teeth. As she walked back across the bedroom, something out the window caught her eye. Ignoring the ball of dread in her belly, she crept to the side of the curtains and peeked out. There, standing at the entrance to her driveway, Steady stood like a sentinel. What was he doing? Had he been out there all night?

Her fear faded to something warm and comforting, then quickly morphed into anger. Jonah Lockhart was going to ruin everything with his misplaced concern. She went to her closet, pulled a burner phone from a shoebox hidden on a high shelf, and texted Charles Darwin.

Marie Curie: *There may be a complication with my neighbor.*

Darwin: *How so?*

Marie Curie: *He's persistent. Shows up without notice. Asks questions.*

Very wandered down to the kitchen and pulled a box of cereal from the cupboard.

Darwin: *Is the meeting still proceeding as planned?*

Marie Curie: *Yes, delivering the package next week.*

Very gathered her thoughts and sent a follow-up text.

Marie Curie: *He just… makes me nervous.*

Darwin: *There are always going to be complications. You need to manage the situation.*

Marie Curie: *Understood.*

Very powered off the disposable phone and deposited it in the kitchen drawer. With her elbows on the island and her hands cradling her chin, she pondered Darwin's words. *Manage the situation.* How on earth was she going to manage the unmanageable Jonah Lockhart?

CHAPTER TWELVE

New York City
July 30

Armand Krill sat in his library and skimmed the paper copy of the *New York Times Book Review*. He had no interest in popular fiction or prose of any sort, but he liked to be abreast of cultural news. One never knew when a passing knowledge of a best-seller would be an entré into a coveted conversation.

His vision blurred as he jumped from one synopsis of wretched drivel to the next. At his limit and preoccupied, Krill snatched his phone from the end table and called Micah, the head of Security at the Ridgeland lab.

"This is Micah."

"It's Mr. Krill. I'd like an update."

"As you know, the scientist in Dr. Kemp's lab removed a flash drive containing Mobilify research."

Krill bit back a remark. It would take more time to explain to the idiot that he knew the situation.

When Krill said nothing, the man continued, "I have been surveilling Ms. Valentine at work and her home on South Island."

"Have you discovered anything?"

"Sir, I believe Ms. Valentine may have hired a bodyguard."

Krill nearly dropped the phone. "Elaborate."

"Well, I was in the bushes observing Ms. Valentine's activity when a huge, muscular individual spotted me and chased me. I outran him and left the scene."

"Stand down for the moment. I'll let you know if further action is required."

"Yes, S–"

Krill ended the call, cutting off the guard's affirmation. It was apparent Micah was coloring his version of events. Nevertheless, one thing seemed clear: the in-house security staff was out of their depth.

It was time for more fitting measures.

Krill tended to overreact. A former VP at Parasol had once told him he swatted flies with a sledgehammer. (Krill had demonstrated the accuracy of the criticism when he had subsequently terminated the man.) Yes, Krill was inclined to go with the nuclear option. Some may consider it overreacting; Krill called it decisive.

He entered another number as he moved through the house and down the central staircase.

His man's voice was soft and controlled when he answered. "Mr. Krill."

Krill's heartbeat calmed. Alonso Mitchell was his best-kept secret, a thief in the night who could unearth the most arcane information and solve the stickiest of problems. He operated without conscience and without remorse.

"Mitchell, I have something I need you to look into."

Mitchell's response was succinct. "Of course."

"A scientist in Ridgeland accessed the secure archive and downloaded research on an early version of Mobilify. It may be nothing, but I'm not taking any chances where Mobilify is concerned."

"Understandable."

"I'll forward you the information," Krill said.

"I'll get back to you."

Mitchell waited for Krill to end the call. Alonso Mitchell knew his place.

CHAPTER THIRTEEN

South Island, South Carolina
August 1

Steady gathered the items from the house and walked out the sliding glass doors, down the deck stairs, and across the beach. He spread the quilt out on the sand and set down the cooler. He glanced over at Very's house. The lights were out—nobody home. Ever since he had run the intruder off, Steady had been paying close attention to the happenings next door. Not that he needed an excuse.

Three days had passed, and Steady had spent each one preoccupied with Very. Every time he swam or sat on his deck looking out, he thought of her. The ocean reminded him. The crashing waves echoed her passionate kiss; the roiling water, his tangled emotions; the curl of a whitecap, the curve of her hip; and the undertow was Very's unrelenting hold on him, pulling Steady into welcome oblivion.

He thought back all those months ago when he first saw Very Valentine. He had brought his telescope out to the beach, but something far brighter than a star had captured his attention–Very in the house next door, dancing like no one was watching and writing chemical formulas on a whiteboard. He hadn't met her, hadn't heard her voice. He didn't know the first thing about her. But something changed inside him as he spied Very through the telescope–a fundamental shift as if the cells in his body had dissolved and reformed.

He didn't like it.

Steady was a master at keeping the fairer sex at a distance. Once, on leave, he ran into a woman he had hooked up with the previous year. She told him she'd never felt better about herself than when she got the blow-off from him. He was that charming.

His encounter with Very was a one-off, but come on. Jonah Lockhart had once fucked a girl on a rappelling line. He'd gone down on a performer backstage at Coachella. He'd engaged in activities with women that were illegal in several states. Why was one interrupted night with Very Valentine knocking him on his ass?

It was nothing.

Maybe if he kept repeating that, the words would be true.

Who was he kidding? Steady had never experienced anything like it. That night was staggering.

Then there was the aftermath. Steady was the king of the charismatic rejection, of sending women away with a smile and no expectations, but Very? She had beaten him to the punch, more eager to chalk the encounter up to an isolated moment of weakness than he had been. And if he was being honest, he hadn't been eager at all.

The rush of feelings Steady experienced whenever Very was around sent his normally calm pulse racing. He wanted to fight with her. He wanted to talk to her, and he wanted to sleep with her. Again and again. Badly. If one fumbling encounter could elicit that kind of response, he couldn't even fathom what sex with her would be like. He ached to learn all her idiosyncrasies–the places on her body that drove her wild, her preferences, her kinks. *Dammit*, he was doomed to spend the rest of his life walking around with a hard-on.

What was it about this woman that put Steady in a tailspin? Yes, she was beautiful, but Steady had known plenty of stunning females. Something about Very whispered to his psyche. Whenever she was near, he felt her hand reach out, silently asking him to take it, but when he looked down at his own open palm, there was nothing there. He would sometimes find himself grasping the empty air, checking for some trace of her presence. The sensation left him feeling somehow incomplete.

Very Valentine was a mystery. Chat was right. She hid behind a facade of openness, like a locked diary concealed in the hollowed-out pages of a book; the volume was in plain sight, but the secrets inside were inaccessible. It didn't really matter; there wasn't much that could bridle the lust that pounded through his veins.

He didn't know how and didn't understand why, but from the moment he had first laid eyes on Very, no other woman had so much as turned his head. It was more than her bright pink hair and her neon lingerie; Very's vibrancy came from within, and all other women paled in comparison.

The realization had produced nothing but aggravation and turmoil, in response to which Steady had redoubled his efforts to elicit the same reaction from her. He bickered, needled, teased, and cajoled. Had he been a third-grader, Steady would have stuck his thumbs in his ears and blown a raspberry. It was all too much. It was all too *Very*.

Steady had a habit of coming to the beach at night to clear his head. Sometimes he would swim. Occasionally he would use the telescope. Sometimes he would just sit and listen to the waves and shore birds. He had been meditating in some form since he became a SEAL, and this quiet stretch of beach was the perfect place to reboot—the perfect place to purge his mind of a particular pink-haired obsession.

He was just losing himself in the hypnotic rhythm of the surf when he felt someone approach. He turned his attention from the white caps to the woman walking barefoot toward him. In the twilight, he mapped her face. Very was beautiful in any circumstance. She never ceased to take his breath away. But this night, she seemed troubled and tired.

Without a word, she sat next to him, crossed her long legs at the ankle, and leaned back on her hands. Steady watched as she stared at the darkening sky and breathed in the ocean air.

He seemed to know instinctively that this was not the time for their typical sniping and banter, so he joined her perusal of the heavens. For two hours, they sat and took in the night without a word spoken. Then, Very leaned over, kissed him on the cheek, and left.

Steady watched her until she disappeared into the house next door—nothing in the sky as mesmerizing as the view of Very Valentine walking away. Again.

Very entered the beach house, a marching band of sensations parading through her. The primary one being guilt. She had to figure out a way to handle Steady; his interference could topple the entire house of cards. But she couldn't think of how to leash him. Avoiding him had backfired, so tonight, she had done the opposite and approached him. The second she sat by his side, she was struck dumb, overwhelmed by the unexpected feeling of contentment that blanketed her. Very felt the outline of his body next to hers—knew the way her chest fit into the gentle curve under his thick arm, how the round of her hips melded with his narrow waist. It was like they were two pieces in a five thousand-piece puzzle just sitting there on the table next to each other, waiting for the puzzler to notice the match and click them into place.

She had never met anyone like Jonah Lockhart. She'd met plenty of guys who were just like the mask he wore, the persona he showed the world. She had hated that flippant shrug-and-a-wink guy, and yet she had been drawn to him even then. She was now beginning to see that the real Jonah Lockhart was someone else entirely. They hadn't said a word on that beach, but she felt his depth and caught a glimpse of the man he didn't show to the world. And she was absolutely sure of one thing; she wanted more than a glimpse. Very craved a full view of this complicated man. He may pretend like nothing got to him, but Very had the distinct sense that Steady felt things deeply.

The rest of her emotions trailed along behind—excitement, arousal, trepidation. She stood at the sliding glass doors and stared out at the now-empty beach, trying to reconcile the strangest feeling of all. One she hadn't felt in so long, she was nearly incapable of labeling it. And yet, as she stood there watching black waves edged with white foam, Very knew precisely what it was.

She wasn't alone.

Steady stepped out of the bathroom in a cloud of steam and toweled off. Through the entire shower, a thorough brushing of his teeth, and even flossing, he tried to come to terms with what had just happened.

Never in his life had he experienced such a synergy. It was as if some force in the universe had surrounded them for that brief moment, allowing them to understand the other without words or actions. There had been no joke on his lips, no practiced come-ons. He and Very had simply existed. The silence had allowed him to remove his armor, and thoughts formed and flowed without restriction. What's more, he felt Very doing the same. He couldn't read her mind, but he sat in quiet acceptance while she reciprocated.

Two lost souls, adrift, had lashed themselves together and found the shore.

Steady tripped over the leg of the dresser and stubbed his toe. "Ouch, shit." He hopped to the bed and muttered, "I have a bullet wound that doesn't smart this bad." As he leaned down to inspect the injury, his head bumped the telescope, knocking the tube, rotating it away from the sky and right toward Very's bedroom window.

Inches from the eyepiece, he continued toward the lens. The next thing he knew, he was watching Very Valentine getting ready for bed.

She had taken a shower, then changed into sleep clothes: an oversized hoodie and pajama shorts. It was the sexiest outfit Steady had ever seen. For a second, his mind drifted. What would it be like to have Very in his bedroom, performing this effortlessly seductive routine every night?

Very stood in an open space facing him and did some sort of Tai Chi routine. She moved with fluidity and grace, getting lost in the exercise. It was this activity that had Steady questioning his actions. Her ritual was private, meditative, and the angel on his shoulder forced him to acknowledge he was crossing a line. But then that pesky devil weighed in. There was something so salacious, so forbidden about his spying; he couldn't stop.

Fantasies ran amuck in his head. His brain ping-ponged between voy-euristic images–Very in his bed: on all fours, straddling him, beneath him. His body responded, and Steady ripped his head away from the telescope. What the fuck was he doing?

He moved the telescope to the corner of the room, slammed off the lights, and threw himself into bed. "You are definitely going to hell."

He punched his pillow and rolled to the other side. Across the way, he spotted Very. She was standing at her window looking right at him. With slow, deliberate movements, she peeled off the hoodie and dropped it to the floor. Then, wearing only a white camisole and a smirk, she closed the blinds.

Goddamn, she was spectacular. Steady remained on his side, looking in her direction. They were separated by fifty yards of beach, two walls, and a dozen trees and bushes. Yet, as Steady closed his eyes, he felt Very's presence as if she were curled up in bed beside him.

CHAPTER FOURTEEN

New York City
August 2

A rmand Krill sat in a burgundy velvet armchair in one of the Cavalry Club's many opulent lounges. He had requested a room for a private meeting, and the manager had directed Krill to this elegantly appointed space known as The Presidential Parlor. As he took in the room, he saw why. The walls were lined with oil portraits of all the Cavalry Club's past presidents, starting with the first man in 1885. Krill stood and scanned the walls like a museum visitor, noting the familiar names of titans and moguls. These were the men with whom Krill was now associated. They would become his bridge group and complete his golf foursome. He would do whatever was necessary to ingratiate himself with the members. They were the epoxy that would cement his fortune.

On its face, Cavalry was a social club, a venue for parties, a location for a weekly squash match. Beneath the surface, the machinations of high society were in full swing. Sons were given jobs in exchange for asset reallocation. Daughters were betrothed part and parcel with corporate mergers.

Since being granted membership, Krill had made good use of the club. He arrived early each day like clockwork, took breakfast in the morning room, read the news, and casually introduced himself to members. On this day, however, he had requested a private lounge.

Armand Krill was displeased, and one or both of these men were responsible. Malcomb Everett, the administrator at the lab in question, was already seated as a uniformed attendant showed Carson Kemp, the Ridgeland Lab's Principle Investigator, to the remaining chair. As usual, Everett was impeccably dressed and obsequious. Kemp was disheveled in a tweed jacket and mismatched tie. He was a pleasant man whose face showed all of his sixty-three years.

Everett and Kemp were both relatively good employees. Everett had joined the team six months ago after leaving a go-nowhere administrative position at a prestigious New York hospital. The concern with Everett was that he changed jobs frequently. On the positive side, Everett was ambitious, a quality Krill respected.

Carson Kemp had been a lead researcher at several Parasol labs during his twenty-eight years with the company. In that time, Krill had been pleased with Kemp's willingness to maximize Parasol's profits. Krill preferred employees with moral agility.

Armand made a point of checking the time on the A. Lange and Sohne watch that circled his slender wrist. Dr. Kemp took a seat. "Apologies for the slight delay, Armand. I was unaware that a tie was required. I had to wait while the attendant fetched me one." Kemp tugged at the knot like the thing was choking him.

"Promptness is a choice, Kemp." Without waiting for additional simpering, Armand Krill addressed the matter at hand, directing his comments to Malcomb Everett. "When I hire an employee, I entrust my staff to ensure that employee is above reproach."

Everett was quick to recover from the scolding. "I can assure you, sir, every staff member is vetted according to protocol."

Krill sipped his coffee and returned the delicate cup to the saucer. "Be that as it may, it appears we have some suspicious activity at Ridgeland."

Malcomb Everett asked, "How so?"

"As you know, nothing leaves the lab without authorization. If a worker wants to take home a bag of chips from the vending machine, it must be cleared by either you or another senior staff member." Krill looked pointedly at Dr. Kemp.

Kemp said, "That is the protocol, Armand. I can assure you, it is being followed."

Armand nodded to a deferential assistant who stood unnoticed in the corner, and the man stepped forward. He held up the tablet in his arms and started the security video. In the footage, a white-jacketed researcher with pink hair was working on a desktop computer. The woman glanced around, then plugged a flash drive into the machine and entered a command. A moment later, she removed the device and slipped it into the pocket of her lab coat.

When the clip ended, the assistant retreated, and Armand waited.

Dr. Kemp spoke up. "That's Ms. Valentine. She's a dedicated researcher and a trusted member of my staff. I assure you, if she's breaking lab protocol, it is only to work on her project at home."

Krill drummed the arm of his chair. "Possibly. However, I've been fooled by more innocent-looking creatures than this woman. The incident, and all of our security protocols, will be investigated.."

"Understood." Malcomb accepted the coffee from the waiter, but Krill stopped him before he could lift the cup to his lips.

"That is all."

Krill picked up the paper copy of the Wall Street Journal and turned his attention to the front page. A moment later, he was alone in the expansive room, and the club attendant had opened the double doors that led to the main hall. Krill glanced up to see a man being escorted down the elegant hall by a suited staff member. Two men who were obviously security and a beautiful, efficient-looking blonde trailed behind. Krill couldn't explain his fascination other than the man had an air about him; he was regal. He half expected the club manager to genuflect. Krill knew it was unseemly, but he couldn't stop himself from leaning over the chair's cushioned arm to follow the entourage's path.

The man lifted his hand—a slight tip of the wrist—and the assistant quickened her gait. She stumbled on the carpet, upending the satchel she carried. No one moved to help or even broke stride. She quickly gathered the scattered items and caught up with her employer, who had moved beyond Krill's line of sight.

What did catch his eye was the amber pill bottle still rolling across the carpet. Krill's curiosity and self-interest propelled him from his chair, and he walked into the grand hall and picked up the prescription.

Out of habit, his eyes went first to the medication, a standard blood pressure treatment—not the one Parasol produced. He read the patient name on the label:

Johan DeVold.

Of course.

At the cursory glance, what Krill had thought was the arm of a pair of glasses must have been the elastic of the eye patch DeVold was known to wear. It was rumored Johan DeVold had been blinded in one eye by an East African warlord in an altercation over a disputed diamond mine. Krill could feel his heart race, and he unconsciously repositioned the pill bottle in his palm with due reverence.

The DeVold family was the epitome of generational wealth. Johan was the son, grandson, great-grandson, and great-great-grandson of one of the richest families in the world. DeVolds controlled most of the diamonds that were mined in Africa. There were buildings at both Krill's boarding school and college named for the family. Krill envisioned his younger self, on full financial aid, walking to his campus job in Harvard Square and stopping to stand before a dedication plaque lauding the largesse of the DeVold family.

Without hesitation, Krill hurried after the group. When he reached the end of the grand hall, DeVold and the bodyguards were gone, but the female assistant was standing in the hallway, speaking with the manager.

Krill cleared his throat, and the twosome looked up. His first impulse was to apologize for interrupting, but he quickly reminded himself that he was the member, and these two people were his subordinates. He held the prescription bottle between his thumb and forefinger. "I believe you dropped this."

The assistant's blue eyes widened in near-horror, and she stepped forward and took the bottle from Krill's outstretched hand. With a curt "thank you," she returned the medication to her bag and resumed her conversation with the staff member.

Refusing to feel awkward or dismissed, Krill said, "You're welcome," and returned to the lounge where one waiter was setting a fresh cup of coffee beside his seat, and another stood with a cloche-covered plate. The white-jacketed man set the plate down and removed the cover revealing Krill's usual breakfast of cut cantaloupe and the club's signature popover with a small dish of homemade seedless raspberry jam and a flower of perfectly softened butter.

Krill ignored the food and summoned his assistant. After bringing up the lab security footage, Krill once again observed the pink-haired woman as she transferred the data. Despite Kemp's insistence that this Miss Valentine was above reproach, he saw a glimmer of deception beneath her professional facade.

Spotting the manager who had escorted Johan DeVold, Krill waved him over.

"Yes, Mr. Krill."

Unwilling to reveal he had read the prescription bottle, Krill said, "The man you were just with. I think I went to school with his father."

"Heinrich DeVold is an Oxford man, sir. I believe you attended Harvard."

Ignoring the manager's tone, Krill continued probing. He needed information. "That's right. I met him at an event. Will his son be in town long? I'd like to send my regards to his parents."

"Mijnheer Johan DeVold will attend a private meeting tomorrow and is scheduled to speak at the U.N. later in the week. I am unaware of his travel plans."

Krill wanted to pry every nugget of information from this man, but despite the manager's role to provide any and all needs to the members, Krill knew the man's foremost directive was to guard their privacy. The manager looked uncomfortable, as though he had already said too much.

"Is there anything else, sir?"

"Nothing, thank you." Krill dismissed him.

The manager stepped closer and spoke softly despite the fact they were the only people in the room. "Oh, and Mr. Krill? Electronics of all kinds are strictly forbidden in the main lounges. If you need to use your phone or computer, I can escort you to the business center."

Mortified and miffed, Krill tucked the phone and tablet into his briefcase, secured the clasps, and returned to reading the paper, opening the pages with a sharp snap. When he looked up, the staff member was gone.

Despite the chastisement, Krill felt a surge of excitement. Johan DeVold was precisely the sort of man Krill had hoped to encounter when he joined the Cavalry Club. After gathering his things, he stepped through the sweeping archway of the main lounge and into the equally impressive hall. Rather than turning left and making his way to the grand split staircase that descended to the lobby, Krill turned right and followed the path DeVold had taken. When the hall ended at a full-length portrait of Benjamin Franklin by Charles Wilson Peale, Krill surveyed his options.

He knew the hall to the left led to the elevator bank, private dining rooms, and staff offices. To his right, the carpeted hall was wide and short and stopped at a set of closed double doors flanked by two complete suits of armor as if medieval knights were guarding the room. He had never really noticed that the corridor went in both directions.

"*Izvinite menya.*" A man brushed by, excusing himself in Russian. The man walked the short distance and disappeared into the room without a backward glance. Krill had an image of attempting to follow and the two suits of armor crossing their swords to block his path.

Krill balled his fists, pretending to admire the painting before him, and listened, wondering if Johan DeVold was in that room with the Russian, perhaps negotiating a secret deal or hosting a luncheon. After long minutes of silence, Krill left the club.

Outside in the August heat, the tree-lined street was quiet, and Krill began his usual walk of four blocks to his Upper East Side home. At the end of the Cavalry Club building was a gated alley Krill assumed was used for deliveries and staff entry. For the first time since he had joined, the gate was open, and a smoke-gray Rolls Royce Wraith sat idling, facing out, just shy of the sidewalk.

"Armand?"

Krill turned to spot an old schoolmate, Jerome Washburn, walking toward him.

"Jerome, hello." Krill had never liked the incipient brat, but he was rich and well-connected by birthright.

"I haven't seen you since our fiftieth reunion, old boy."

"We'll be seeing more of each other. I've just been admitted to the Cavalry Club."

"Wonderful news. I hadn't heard. That's odd. They usually send an email announcing new members. I must have missed it." Washburn glanced at the building. "Or they've got their hands full with this messy business." He leaned closer. "Rumor has it, it's vermin."

Krill had no idea what Washburn was talking about, but, rather than admit he wasn't abreast of club gossip, he simply nodded along with a mimicking chuckle.

"Well, I'm headed out to the country. August in the City is too much for me. See you around the clubhouse, Krill."

Krill was about to resume walking when the side service door to the Cavalry Club opened. Simultaneously, the chauffeur emerged from the car and opened the back passenger door while two bodyguards appeared from the building and flanked Johan DeVold as he walked unhurriedly and ducked inside the Rolls. With a black Suburban following, the car pulled past where Krill stood and drove away. Krill felt like a serf watching the king pass by in a royal carriage.

Armand Krill stewed the entire walk home. He had paid a small fortune to join that club, but clearly, he did not have access to *all* the privileges afforded to members. Stuffing his old resentments back into their metaphorical box, he focused on the quandary. Every problem was solvable; however, the method of solution varied. The first step toward gaining a solid foothold at the Cavalry Club would be a simple introduction. Krill would have to wait for a chance to present himself to DeVold without looking like a squealing teen in the presence of a pop star.

For now, all he could do was watch and wait for an opportunity. He certainly had more pressing matters to occupy his time.

CHAPTER FIFTEEN

Beaufort, South Carolina
August 2

Steady reclined on the couch in Tox and Calliope's living room. Coco, their eighty-pound Rottweiler, had wedged herself between his body and the back of the sofa, forcing Steady's arm into the perfect position to scratch her. Tox trotted down the stairs with a duffle bag in each hand and Calliope's purse around his neck. His wife was four months pregnant, and Tox wasn't letting her lift a finger.

Calliope leaned over the second-floor banister with a smirk and called down to Tox, "Can I walk down the stairs by myself? Is that okay?"

Without missing a beat, the big guy bounded back up, swooped Calliope into his arms, and descended, holding her like a bride.

Steady ate a grape from the bunch resting on his chest and fed one to the dog, who promptly spit it into the cushions. "You gotta toughen that baby up. He's never going to make it through Hell Week if you're carrying him around everywhere."

Tox threw a flat glance at his friend. "He's doing just fine. Plenty of time for training."

Calliope elbowed her husband. "*She's* doing just fine. I do yoga every morning with her."

Tox looked surprised. "You do?"

"Yep. I asked Doctor Mills, and she thought it was a great idea. So zip it, and let's go. Steady, the fridge is yours. Twitch and Finn are coming by for Coco after work."

"Their house is a fucking kennel," Steady joked.

Finn had returned to Beaufort after spending four months in the remote West Virginia town of Purgatory, confronting some old demons and taking time to heal his battered soul. When he came back, Finn wasn't alone. He and Twitch now had an eight-year-old foster child, Auggie, they were in the process of adopting and, to Steady's point, two lackadaisical bulldogs.

Calliope looked around, going through her mental checklist for when she and Tox were both out of town. "The dogs all get along. Twitch said most of the time, they just lie around."

"Where did you say you were headed?" Steady asked.

Tox grabbed both bags and headed out to his Defender. "New York. Calliope's parents are off on another adventure and wanted to see with their own eyes what I've done to their daughter." He waggled his brows. "Little Miller Buchanan junior is going to meet grandma and grandpa."

Steady smiled. Tox had always wanted a family of his own. His happiness was written all over his face.

"Miles is in the City, probably whitewashing a congressman's affair with a high-end hooker or confiscating cell phone video of some billionaire's shady dealings. So we're meeting him for dinner."

Tox's twin brother, Miles, was a fixer. He and Tox had been reunited after twenty years, each thinking the other twin was dead. Miles had been hired to retrieve a valuable piece of art that had ended up in Calliope's possession. Amid murder and danger, Tox had not only found the love of his life, but he had also discovered his long-lost brother.

Steady scratched Coco behind the ears. "That's cool."

"You never know what Miles has gotten himself mixed up in," Calliope said.

Steady tossed a grape in the air and caught it in his mouth. "Well, if you're letting your pregnant wife go, it can't be too dangerous."

Tox pointed at his friend in agreement as Calliope repeated, "*Letting?*"

Steady looked at Tox wide-eyed while his friend darted back out the door. He rolled off the couch and hopped to his feet. "I'm gonna grab your milk and leftovers. Have a good trip."

He skirted Calliope, who was still giving him side-eye, and hid behind the open door of the fridge.

"Just for that, I'm *letting* Twitch and Finn have the rest of Maggie's lemon pound cake." Calliope stalked outside after Tox.

Steady popped up, his arms full of perishables, and set them on the kitchen island next to the dessert in question. He loaded everything, including the cake, into the picnic basket Calliope had left out for him. Then he looked over at Coco, who was watching him from the couch with a bland yet somehow accusatory look.

"You keep your mouth shut," Steady threatened the dog.

Coco buried her head under a throw pillow as Steady gathered up his haul and left.

CHAPTER SIXTEEN

Parasol Labs
Ridgeland, South Carolina
August 2

Alonso Mitchell pulled into Parasol Labs, parked his sedan in a handi-capped spot, and got out of the car. It was well after 8 p.m., but the summer sun was still out. None of the guards questioned him; none even looked him in the eye. They knew who he was. With quiet efficiency, Mitchell strode across the lobby to the elevator bank and swiped his all-access card. On the second floor, his footsteps echoed in the silence as he walked to the end of the hall.

The lab where Verity Valentine worked was unoccupied. Mitchell casually strolled around the room with his phone opened to the security application. He watched himself on the screen and confirmed the camera coverage was thorough, noting blind spots. The head of the lab, Primary Investigator Carson Kemp's office was dark—he tried the handle—and locked. The video coming from Kemp's office was unsatisfactory. Mitchell reprogrammed the camera. No one was above suspicion.

After clearing the room and making the necessary surveillance adjustments, Mitchell crossed to his destination: Verity Valentine's desk. Mitchell was more than observant. He was a deducer. Ms. Valentine's desk told him plenty. The lack of family photos, the single unsent beach postcard, and the snow globe all told a story of a woman with no ties, a woman with secrets. Mitchell attached one button camera on the lamp at the back of the desk and another on the rear wall aimed at her computer. After fine-tuning the coverage, he stepped back. Armand Krill now had a bird's eye view of everything Verity Valentine was doing.

He picked up the snow globe and shook it, sending glitter swirling around the winter scene of a mother and daughter building a snowman. He replaced the object with a careless thunk, and a tiny piece of paper fluttered. No, not a piece of paper, the back of a bandaid.

Mitchell scanned the desk. There, on the page of an open notebook, was a lone drop of blood. After fishing a plastic bag from his jacket pocket, he ripped the page from the spiral. The little pink-haired researcher had left him a gift. He secured the item, tucked the bag back in his pocket, and walked out.

Funny thing about people who think they're one step ahead; they always end up staring at someone's back.

CHAPTER SEVENTEEN

Bishop Security Headquarters
Somewhere outside Beaufort, South Carolina
August 3

Steady stood in the open doorway of Nathan Bishop's office. The head of Bishop Security waved him in, then held up a finger as he finished a phone call. Steady had been with Nathan since he left the SEALs, and Nathan resigned his commission with Naval Intelligence. In the following years, Nathan had evolved from an isolated, mission-focused man who played the part of a socialite playboy a little too well to a happy, contented husband and father. He had always been the picture of professionalism in impeccably tailored suits and with an air of competence. His emotional transformation, however, had been dramatic. Case in point, the pair of toddlers who sat on the floor in the corner alternating between stacking plastic donuts on a stick and throwing them at each other.

Steady glanced down at his own ensemble: cargo shorts, battered Nikes, and a short-sleeved tropical shirt—this one a turquoise explosion of pineapples. He had found a box of the ridiculous things when he moved into his parents' beach house last year and started wearing them mostly to annoy Cam. Steady was pretty sure the shirts had belonged to his grandfather. He also suspected his mother, in her subtle but unyielding way, had stolen them from dear old dad and hidden them in the attic storage space.

Despite his scruffy nonchalance, looking at Nathan had him vowing to up his game in the wardrobe department. Nathan's subsequent sarcasm cemented his thought.

"Important meeting later?"

"Very funny. You know I was going to offer to take the Tasmanian Twins to the park." Steady shot his thumb over his shoulder at the boys. "But if you want, I can go home and change."

Nathan grinned, something else that had been a rarity before he found his wife, Emily. "The magic words. Take these two on a field trip, and you can show up to work in a clown costume."

Charlie, the more rambunctious twin, spotted Steady and abandoned his project and his brother to hurry over. Jack, the quieter twin, took the opportunity to correctly stack the plastic donuts by size without his brother's interference.

Steady picked up Charlie by his armpits and threw him to the ceiling, eliciting a squeal. "Hey buddy, you like to fly? I'm gonna take you flying one of these days." He tossed the toddler again.

"Rosemary?" Nathan spoke into the intercom on his phone.

"Yes, sir," Rosemary replied.

"Can you take the boys upstairs and see if there's any fruit or snacks in the kitchen?"

Nathan's assistant, a capable-looking woman in her mid-fifties, appeared in the doorway. "Maybe we'll see if we can get Sesame Street to stream on that big TV."

Nathan mouthed thank you as Steady set Charlie on the floor, and Rosemary took each boy by the hand and led them out.

"Why are the twins at the office? Breaking them into black ops a little early, aren't you?"

Nathan released an exaggerated sigh. "Emily's taking Charlotte for her nine-month check-up. Maggie wasn't available, and, as you know, we're firm on the no nanny stance."

Emily Bishop had been abducted as a child, and the family nanny had been instrumental in executing the crime. She was a badass mamma bear but struggled with reconciling her past trauma.

"It's no chore to take them to the park. I'm also thinking about starting a new construction project. How would you feel about a treehouse for the boys?" Steady asked.

Nathan seemed lost in a happy memory. "Emily got stuck in my old treehouse when she was a child. We were neighbors in Connecticut. I had to rescue her."

"First of many rescues," Steady quipped.

"She rescues me every day, so it's only fair I do my part."

Steady laughed. "Well, happy to take the mini monsters to the park."

Nathan sat back and crossed one leg over the other. "What's on your mind?"

Steady ran a hand through his hair and shifted uncomfortably. "It's Very."

He half expected Nathan to laugh or roll his eyes, but his boss remained quiet, waiting for him to continue.

"A couple of nights ago, I was over at her place, and she was acting a little squirrelly."

"How so?"

"Well, the door was locked for one thing, which was weird. But that's not the big thing."

"What is the big thing, Steady?" Nathan pressed.

"As I was leaving, I caught some guy in the bushes with a pair of binoculars. When I chased him, he ran to his car and sped off."

Nathan picked up a pen and drummed it on his desk. "That is concerning. You think it's a stalker?"

"I don't think so." Relieved he wasn't crazy, Steady continued. "I noticed the car when I pulled in. Got the plate."

"And I assume you used company resources to locate the owner."

Steady didn't bother making excuses. He knew Nathan understood. "Twitch ran it. The car belongs to the Head of Security at Very's lab."

"Parasol Pharmaceuticals," Nathan said.

"Yeah."

"I read something about them recently." Nathan turned to his computer and entered the company name into the search bar. "Ah, yes, Parasol is releasing a new drug in the coming weeks. Wall Street is bullish on its success; the company's stock price has shot up."

"Why would they be spying on Very?"

Nathan countered, "It could still be a stalking situation. Plenty of obsessions develop in the workplace."

And with your neighbors. Steady didn't voice his thought. "Could be," Steady acknowledged. "But I don't think that's what it was."

"What did Very say?"

"I didn't tell her. At the time, I just figured it was some kid sneaking onto the beach or some guy camping. But it's gnawing at me."

"There's a remedy for that."

Steady sighed. "Yeah, I'll talk to her."

Nathan said, "I will say that the company owner, Armand Krill is a real son of a bitch. He has been accused multiple times of overcharging for basic life-saving drugs and was manufacturing addictive opioids decades before the Oxy crisis."

"So maybe this Krill joker thinks Very is doing something sketchy, but he's sketchy, so maybe her sketchy isn't sketchy at all."

"Once again, your eloquent logic is flawless," Nathan deadpanned.

Steady continued, "There's no way she's doing anything illegal. Her moral compass points due north."

"You're suggesting perhaps Very is a whistleblower," Nathan said.

"Well, that hadn't occurred to me, but now that you mention it, I think it's possible."

Nathan sat back in his chair and looked up at the ceiling. Steady had come to think of it as his boss's thinking pose. After a long moment, Nathan tilted forward, resting his forearms on the desk.

"We have no dog in this race. Parasol is not a client, and neither is Very."

"I just want to make sure she's okay," Steady said.

"All right, then. Steady, as of now, you're on a mandatory two-week medical leave."

"Oh, come on." Steady protested and gestured to his arm. "It's practically all healed up."

Nathan ignored the protest. "What you choose to do in that time off is up to you. Come into the office if you need to catch up on paperwork. Or," He paused for effect. "Stay home and rest up. Enjoy the scenery. If you happen to notice any unusual goings on *as a concerned neighbor*, let me know."

Steady nearly had a Pavlovian arousal response. His boss was all but telling him to watch Very.

He jumped to his feet. "Copy that."

"Steady, you obviously have some…" Nathan paused, searching for the word. Steady knew the feeling. "Relationship with Very."

Before Steady could protest, Nathan held up both hands. "I simply mean you know her personally."

Steady couldn't argue with that. He did know her, and worse, he wanted to learn more.

"Yeah?"

Nathan straightened a stack of files with a thump on his desktop and said, "Just make sure the person stalking Very Valentine isn't you."

Steady opened his mouth, then closed it. He didn't know what he was going to say. Rather than tossing out an impertinent reply, Steady acknowledged the order with a sharp nod and left his boss's office. He took the stairs two at a time to the third-floor lounge area. When it came to Very, Nathan's words of caution may have been too late.

Standing at the entry of the open space, Steady watched the scene before him. Bishop Security's third floor held a bright chef's kitchen with an expansive granite island and an inviting seating area punctuated by a flatscreen. Evan Cole, Cam's fiancée, kissed him goodbye as he headed off for an assignment. It was nothing dramatic, just a shared, intimate moment. Finn was at the counter doctoring Twitch's tea in a mug that read "Currently Debugging." Twitch was standing next to him, buttering a piece of toast. Finn slid the cup in front of her and kissed her temple. Nathan's son Jack sat quietly on the couch watching John Legend play piano with Elmo. Rosemary had caught little Charlie in a rare moment of calm and was brushing his mop of blond curls.

What was this life his friends had discovered? This calm understanding that they had found their soulmate? This blend of wild passion and quiet surety? Steady squelched the ache in his gut and strolled into the room with a joke on his lips. He was good at shoving that feeling of longing away; he had been doing it most of his life.

As he moved to the kitchen and grabbed a Coke from the fridge, his mind strayed to his new *assignment*. Well, nothing new about it if he was being honest. He had been watching Very Valentine with exaggerated interest for almost a year. Now, however, he had a legitimate reason to peel back the layers of this complicated, intriguing woman. Running a finger across a vein in the granite, he cautioned himself to remain professional, to retain the casual air that at once made him approachable and kept him distant.

He didn't know how long he stood there contemplating his predicament, but the next time he looked up, Rosemary was standing across from him, holding a little hand in each of hers.

"Ready, Mr. Lockhart? They can't sit still another minute."

"Oh really? And it's Steady, by the way. Mr. Lockhart is my dad."

Rosemary rephrased, "Ready, Steady?" Then laughed at the rhyme.

"They can't sit still, eh? Can't sit still?" Steady dropped to a catcher's stance, grabbed Charlie and Jack around the waist, and hauled them up like luggage. He spoke over the squeals. "All right then, I'm off to the park. If you see the twins, tell them that's where I'm headed." He rotated from side-to-side sending the boys spinning. "Where did those little crib lizards go?"

Rosemary waved them off as Steady strolled to the elevator with a little boy under each arm. He reran his conversation with Nathan and contemplated his strategy to help Very. Funny, as willing as she was to step in on behalf of others, Very Valentine bristled at the idea of someone stepping in to help her. Well, what she didn't know wouldn't hurt her. The first thing he needed to do was a little recon at Parasol Pharmaceuticals. Sounded easy enough.

CHAPTER EIGHTEEN

New York City
August 4

Armand Krill sat behind his antique mahogany desk and acknowledged the man who appeared in the doorway without being announced. Alonso Mitchell stepped into the room and stood between the two forest green leather guest chairs. Wearing a nylon windbreaker and khaki trousers, he looked more like a tourist than a private detective, but Krill guessed that was the point. Mitchell had coarse dark hair that was tinged with gray and dead eyes. He was sure Mitchell had been a good man once—before three tours of duty had turned him to stone. Krill smirked. People like Mitchell weren't born disconnected; some emotional transfusion had replaced blood with ice water. Or perhaps he had always been ruthless. It made no difference to Krill.

An accordion folder was tucked securely under Mitchell's left arm. And, if Krill wasn't mistaken, the man had a look of satisfaction on his usually stoic face.

Alonso Mitchell had worked for Krill for nearly thirty years. To this day, Krill didn't know how Mitchell managed to gather the information he did, but his services were invaluable, and Krill compensated him accordingly. Utterly forgettable in appearance and manner, Mitchell possessed skills ranging from hacking to safe cracking to breaking and entering. Alonso Mitchell could find a skeleton in the closet of The Pope.

In all his years of service, Mitchell had only failed Krill once. Twenty years ago, Krill had ordered Mitchell to watch his wayward daughter, yet she had eluded him. It took Krill's men over a year to locate and deal with Patricia Krill. Her daughter, Amelia, Krill's granddaughter, had vanished. Decades of stellar service hadn't faded the blotch on his record.

"You have something for me?" Krill asked.

"I completed the background checks and psychological profiles of the employees at the High Ridge lab. Those files have been delivered to your midtown office at Parasol Headquarters."

Krill knew Mitchell's version of background checks was far different than the cursory investigations conducted by HR. His eyes wandered to the file under Mitchell's arm.

Without preamble, Mitchell set the folder on the desk, unwound the string closure, and opened it. "There is an issue with one researcher." He withdrew a thick envelope and placed it on the desk. "This is what the standard company background check discovered." He retrieved a second, thinner envelope and put it on top of the first. "This is what I found."

Armand opened the smaller envelope, unclipped the passport-sized photo from the upper corner, and read the contents.

Mitchell spoke, "I never stopped looking for her, sir."

Armand tossed his half glasses on the desk and rubbed a hand down his face. "And yet she's been under your nose?"

Mitchell didn't reply.

"You think this young woman is Amelia?"

"I don't think it. I know it. She cut her hand at the lab last week. I was able to retrieve a blood sample. I had your lab do a DNA analysis before I came to you with the information. Verity Valentine is Amelia Krill."

Krill picked up the small photograph. "She's working for Parasol. Why?"

"I can think of two reasons," Mitchell said.

Krill waited for Mitchell's astute analysis. He always thought Alonso Mitchell would have been an excellent Chief Operations Officer. Krill had never met anyone so adept at assessing a situation. Of course, Krill would never hire Mitchell to be COO—he was too good at this work. What's more, Mitchell would never accept the pay cut.

"I think it's safe to assume her appearance at ParaPharm is not coincidental. Either she's returned and taken a job through normal channels to prove herself. After a certain amount of time, she could come to you and show that she's earned her place beside the throne."

Armand glanced at the photo, covering the pink head of hair with his index finger as he imagined that scenario playing out. "Or?"

"Or Ms. Valentine has embraced her deceased mother's theories and has taken a job at Parasol to search for damning evidence."

"Which theory seems more plausible?" Krill asked.

"Time will tell." Mitchell took a small envelope from his pocket and passed it across the desk. "I've added additional surveillance to Ms. Valentine's work areas. No one knows about it but the two of us. I emailed you a secure link to access the cameras from your phone and computer. I'll be checking the feed daily, but if you'd like to review video footage or watch it in real-time, just open the file and enter that username and password." He pointed with his chin at the slip of paper Krill had withdrawn. "Nothing Verity Valentine does at ParaPharm labs will be unmonitored."

"What about her home?"

Mitchell shrugged. "Be easy enough to do. She's staying at Dr. Kemp's beach house on South Island, so we have access to the keys and the alarm codes. I scoped it out. She's gone all day at the lab and goes out a lot at night. Most of the homes are vacant—the snowbirds have flown north for the summer. The house next door is occupied, and she seems friendly with the neighbor.

I showed his picture to your Parasol guard, and he confirmed that's who ran him off."

"Does he need to be handled?"

"The neighbor? No. Micah, your guard? Maybe. He was more than a little humiliated that some rich beach bum got the drop on him."

Krill recalled the Parasol guard's ham-handed efforts to surveil Ms. Valentine's residence. He had definitely made the right decision bringing in Mitchell. "When this business is settled, I will reevaluate lab security. If you're confident the neighbor poses no threat, we'll move on."

Mitchell reassured him, "Probably best if the neighbor thinks it was a random occurrence. I'm heading back to Beaufort tonight. I'll stay apprised of the situation."

"Mobilify is scheduled to be released. Nothing can interfere with that drug hitting the market."

"Understood." After working for Krill for this long, Mitchell knew when the meeting had ended without having to be told. He said, "I'll wait to hear from you," and left the room as unobtrusively as he had entered.

Krill inserted the device into his computer and entered the username and password Mitchell had provided. He toggled between surveillance cameras, watching the activity in the lab. Everything appeared normal. Krill brought up the archived research on Mobilify that Verity Valentine had copied. It shouldn't have been concerning. Drugs went through dozens of variations before they were perfected, and researchers often referred to earlier experiments.

Nevertheless, something pecked at his brain. Mobilify was going to market. Verity Valentine was working on a different project. Why was she poking around in old research that didn't relate to her current assignment?

Returning to the security feed, Krill watched the pink-haired woman. She was diligent and focused—utterly unsuspicious. He examined her profile, the turn of her nose, the slope of her jaw. The familiarity was undeniable. Krill touched her face on the screen.

Verity Valentine was Amelia Krill. His granddaughter.

CHAPTER NINETEEN

South Island, South Carolina
August 4

Very secured her hair in a ponytail as she walked through the sand. Steady was already relaxing on the blanket. He didn't turn her way, but Very knew he sensed her presence. She took her seat beside him on the empty beach. The air was heavy, thick with heat and expectation. Out at sea, a storm brewed.

They had continued this shared meditation for the past several nights. Tonight, Very broke the silence. "I'm an only child," she said. Then she asked, "Do you have brothers and sisters?"

"I'm the oldest of six, five boys and one girl. Technically, they are my half-siblings. My sister is the baby. Shep, the oldest, is my stepbrother."

Very rested her cheek on her knees as she listened.

"June, my birth mother, left Dad and me when I was a baby." Steady looked out at the water and spoke casually as if he were talking about the weather. "My dad met her at a party. She was runner-up for Miss North Carolina. Dad went ass over teakettle. They bought a little house in Charlotte, had a baby, me. Life was good."

"But not good enough," Very surmised.

"Her talent in pageants was country singing. Dad said June always felt she was destined to be a big star. He's quick to point out his own failures to take some of the heat off her. He was busy starting his business, gone all the time. He knew she was unhappy but ignored it; hoped the problem would go away."

"It didn't go away," Very said.

"No, she did. Ran off to Nashville with some promoter who promised to make her the next Naomi Judd."

"Did she succeed?"

"Nah. She cleaned out their savings account when she left. Got swindled by the promoter. She moved out to Hollywood to try and get discovered. Same old story."

"Do you ever see her?"

"She'd show up on our doorstep from time to time asking for money. One time—I was maybe seven—June visited. She said to me, 'Jonah, give your mother a hug.' I ran over to my stepmom and hugged her. She stopped coming by after that. She worked as a spokesmodel early on. Got some gigs at boat shows and conventions, stuff like that. She married the owner of a car dealership when I was ten or eleven. I think she's happy."

Very nodded against her knee. She was discovering a quality about Steady. He always seemed to be more concerned with the well-being of others than himself. Here he was telling her about a woman who abandoned him for her own selfish pursuits, and he was glad she was happy. Very had stood in the ruins of the destruction caused by one man's greed. She wasn't nearly so magnanimous.

"Wife number two was Marissa."

His face darkened, and Very lifted her head. Steady, the insouciant, moment-to-moment guy she had come to know, looked... *pained*.

He seemed to hesitate, then returned his gaze to the dark ocean. "Dad married her quickly. I was three. I think he thought I needed a mother more than he needed a wife, you know?"

"Sure," Very agreed.

"She came from the right family and looked the part. I think Dad was happy he found someone."

She glanced down and noted Steady was gripping the quilt.

"What happened?"

"She really took to the role of society wife. She was on charity boards, volunteered at The Mint Museum, attended luncheons and bridge clubs. She ticked all the boxes."

He blew out a big breath. Without conscious thought, Very rested her hand over his fist.

"She didn't hire a nanny or a babysitter or anything. When she would go out, she would leave me alone."

"Oh, my God."

"It's gonna sound worse than it is," he said. Lightning flickered in the sky.

"What?"

He tilted his head up to the stars. Very noticed he did that when something troubled him–like the sky was his solace. "Before she married Dad, she used to have this big dog. A Great Dane, I think. Marissa got rid of the dog, but she kept the kennel in the garage."

"Oh, Steady, no."

"I mean, when you think about it, it's not the worst thing. It was probably about the size of a playpen."

Very bit her tongue. What kind of person could put a toddler in a cage?

"I don't remember it. But I hated our garage. Dad said if he was holding me and he even walked near it, I would start crying and cling to him like I was falling off a cliff."

He released the quilt and turned his hand, interlacing their fingers. It wasn't a romantic gesture. Very saw it for what it was, a lifeline.

"It went on for about a year, I guess. She'd go to her garden parties or tennis lessons, and I'd spend hours in that kennel."

Cage, she thought. He was spending hours in a cage.

"She'd put a bowl of dry cereal in with me." He shook his head with a huffed laugh, no doubt thinking the same thing she was: *like a dog*.

"It took Dad a while to catch on. Longer than it should have. I was underweight and had diaper rash even though I could use the toilet."

Very's eyes stung, and she gave his hand a reassuring squeeze. "I want to kill her."

"Yeah? Well, so did the universe."

Without breaking their connection, Very turned fully to face him. "What happened?"

"She had a little too much wine at lunch one day. Ran a red light and crashed into a fuel truck."

Very turned back to the water and scooted so their bodies were touching.

"Nobody could find me. Dad thought I was in the car."

"Oh, my God. He must have been frantic."

"He realized it that day. He came home trying to figure out where I was and found me in the garage. Saw what she'd been doing."

"She's lucky she's dead. I want to kill her myself," Very repeated.

Steady smiled then and tipped his big body into hers. "It was a long time ago. I don't even really remember it."

Very surreptitiously swiped at the dampness on her cheek.

"Dad took a leave of absence, and for a year, it was just the two of us. After that, he worked from home. Those are really my first memories–Dad teaching me how to ride a bike and taking me fishing."

He chuckled, and it warmed her heart. He had gotten through the tough part, and now he was enjoying the story.

"When he went back to work, he took me with him. I didn't go to preschool or kindergarten. I raced around our hotels and sat on the cleaning trolleys while the housekeepers pushed me around. It was awesome. One time,

I manned the guest book at a wedding reception. I was six. I wore a little tux and had all the guests sign. The bride danced with me. It was a great childhood."

Minus the witch who locked you in a dog kennel. Very shook off the thought. Steady focused on the positive. She admired that about him. He was a glass-half-full kind of person. She was not.

"That's your dad's business?"

Steady nodded. "Lockhart Hotels. He has twenty or so properties now, and he's in the middle of a big merger, but at the time, we had five."

"That's cool."

"Dad met Lara when she came in to interview for a job."

"Lara?"

"My stepmom. He finally got it right. Lara applied for an accountant job. She walked in, and Dad was trying to work while I was throwing little shampoo bottles I'd stolen from the housekeeping cart and having a tantrum."

"That doesn't sound like you," Very said.

"I know, right? Dad wasn't big on discipline."

Because he felt guilty. She met his gentle gaze and knew he was thinking the same thing.

"Anyway, Lara walked right over, hauled me off the floor, and sat me next to her on the couch. She had a son my age, so she knew just what to do. Dad hadn't known I needed a nap, so she laid me down and covered me up, and I fell asleep. The touch of a good woman calmed me right down."

"Now *that* sounds like you."

"Dad married Lara when I was seven. She's my mom. She's the only mother I've ever known. So to answer your question in the longest possible way, I have one stepbrother, three half-brothers, and a half-sister, but none of us think of it like that."

"I'm sorry that happened, Steady."

"I've got a terrific mom and dad. I'm lucky," he said.

"I'm glad."

For a while, they sat, enjoying the silence and watching the distant storm.

"My mom died when I was six." Very never talked about her family, but something about this moment, *this man,* created a safe space where she could share herself.

"I'm sorry," he said.

"I don't remember much about her. That's the hard part, trying to hold on to her image and feeling it fade."

"Any fond memories?"

Very felt the corners of her lips creep up. "Sometimes a random thing will trigger a memory–the inside of a seashell, the sound of crunching through dry leaves. The smell of a Christmas tree makes me think of her. "

"What happened after she passed away?"

Very wanted to tell Steady everything. God, she had been standing in quicksand for so long, and here he was, gentle and confident, offering a hand. She started to speak when Steady shot to his feet and took off running across the beach.

Steady raced along the sand. The flash of light he saw behind the dunes was brief but unmistakable.

Someone was out there, watching them.

Thunder rumbled in the distance as he mounted the first low hill, then skated down the far side. The action was hell on his bad leg. No one was there. He stood in the knee-high beach grass and listened. To his left, a twig snapped. Steady took off again, running toward their houses. He emerged from the trees just as red taillights disappeared around a bend in the road.

"Shit. Fuck." He kicked the gravel and hiked back to Very. He sat beside her, unsure how to ask what he wanted to know.

"Steady? What's going on?"

"I need to talk to you."

"Okay."

She pulled away, ostensibly to face him, but Steady knew Very was creating distance.

"A couple of nights ago, I chased off a guy in the bushes outside your house."

Scattered raindrops began to fall. "Oh."

"I didn't mention it because I didn't think it was a big deal. Just now, somebody was hiding in the dunes. I didn't see him, but a car was driving away when I got to the road."

Very was staring down at the quilt. Steady placed two fingers under her chin and lifted her head. He felt her sigh.

"Steady, you know people sneak onto this beach all the time. There are probably people out there right now." The rain picked up, and she held out her hand to catch the drops. "Well, maybe not now."

He tilted his head to the side. "I don't think that's what's goin 'on here."

Steady noticed Very's defenses go up. "What do you think's going on?"

"Not sure. Anything weird happening at work? Anybody payin 'a little too much attention to you?"

She lifted her face to the sky, eyes closed. The rain on her cheeks looked like tears. Steady waited. This was the moment. She would either tell him the truth or remain closed off to him.

"I don't know. Maybe."

"Care to elaborate?"

"There's a security guard who keeps asking me out, Micah. I'm sure he's harmless."

"Okay." He tried to suppress his doubt.

"So, yeah, thanks for keeping an eye out. I really appreciate it."

She was lying. Steady didn't know what else he could do. He couldn't make Very let him in. After a heavy silence, he replied, "Sure. No problem." He climbed to his feet, and she joined him. A gust of wind brought the downpour.

"I'll help you get the stuff into the house," she said.

"That's okay. I got it." He made quick work of gathering the blanket and cooler.

"Steady." Very stopped him with a hand on his waist.

A flash of lightning lit Very's face, and Steady caught a glimpse of that anguish she tried to hide. He wanted to help her. He would help her. He just wished she would trust him. It wasn't something he could force. Steady knew that much. So, as the rain came down, he leaned forward and kissed her wet cheek.

"Have a good night."

"You too." Very licked the raindrops from her lips and gave him a thankful smile. Then she turned and ran through the torrent to her house.

Barely cognizant of the weather, Steady walked inside and stood dripping on the kitchen floor. Something burned in his chest. Yes, he wanted to make sure Very was safe, but he also wanted to know what she was hiding.

Very entered her house and locked the door behind her. After checking the other doors and windows, she walked to the kitchen and dried her face with a dish towel. Who had been watching them on the beach? Maybe it was Darwin checking on her. Maybe Krill had spies. All this speculation would drive her mad.

And then there was Steady. She couldn't believe she had almost told him her most guarded secrets. God, what was she doing? Darwin wanted her to keep Steady on a leash. Instead, she seemed to be forging this intimate bond with him. How was this even happening? Steady was a hotshot who treated women as temporary—understandable considering his childhood. Very had her own scars. As a result, she sought out people who were loyal and reliable. As much as she had wanted to open up and tell Steady everything, she couldn't cross that line. She needed to keep an eye on him because he was keeping an eye on her. She couldn't allow Steady to meddle. Any interference, even well-intentioned, could shatter the plan.

She needed to continue this charade with him, forging this bond of friendship and teasing him with the possibility of something more. That was the way to manage him. And if she was up half the night agitated by arousal more intense than she had ever known, well, that was the price she would have to pay.

CHAPTER TWENTY

V ery knocked on the front door of Twitch's bungalow and came in, balancing a cardboard coffee tray and a bag of treats.

"Twitch?" she called.

"In the kitchen," came the reply.

Very followed her best friend's voice and found Twitch sitting at the kitchen table with her feet propped up. As always, her laptop was open in front of her.

"How are you feeling, sweetie?"

"Swollen." Twitch moaned.

"Little Devlin-McIntyre will be here before you know it," Very soothed.

"That's more terrifying than my fat ankles." Twitch laughed.

"Where's Dickhead and the crew?" Very asked.

Twitch replied casually, "He took Auggie to see the Revolutionary War cannon."

Very had started referring to Finn as Dickhead years ago after he had broken Twitch's heart in the worst possible way. Very had intended it as a show of solidarity, but now that Twitch and Finn were all loved up, the nickname had morphed into a strange term of endearment. Twitch didn't bat an eye at the moniker. Even Finn now joked about it and occasionally used the nickname in a less-than-wholesome way.

Very took a seat at the table and pulled the herbal tea from the tray. Twitch was drinking the foul concoction in place of her usual coffee. Holding the cup far from her nose, Very passed it over. "Bleh. How do you drink that?"

"It's good," Twitch defended, but Very saw her make a face as she smelled it.

Outside, a car alarm blared, and Very jumped in her seat. The siren stopped.

"You okay?" Twitch asked.

"Of course. I'm fine."

Twitch snagged the bag of pastries and withdrew a cherry danish. "What's going on?"

Very had so much going on and so many secrets, she could barely keep her lies straight. "Not much." There was one truth she could tell, however. "Steady is driving me crazy."

Twitch's blue eyes sparkled as she leaned closer. "Do tell."

Very popped the lid off her caramel latte and blew on the surface. "Don't get all gooey-Twitch on me."

"Oh, please." Her friend snorted. "I haven't been gooey-Twitch since college."

"Admit it. You're gooey again. Pregnancy has re-gooed you."

Twitch fed a bit of pastry to the droopy bulldog who had suddenly appeared and rested his head in her lap. "Don't beg, Bruce." She scolded in a soft voice as she fed him.

Very rolled her eyes. "You're really driving the lesson home, you big dope."

Twitch's eyes lit with affection.

Very smiled at her soft-hearted sidekick. She had moved to Beaufort with vengeance on her mind, but the best part of being here had been reconnecting with her best friend. Looking at her now, Very realized how much she had missed Twitch. She was kind and brilliant and insightful–Very was lucky.

With that sentiment foremost in her thoughts, she said, "He's not what I thought he'd be like."

Twitch dipped her finger in the cherry center of the danish and licked. "He puts up a good front–like someone else I know–but deep down, he's an angel."

"Well, *angel* might be a stretch."

Twitch ignored her. "You know, on the SEALs, he rescued the guys. Saved their lives. All of them–Finn, Tox, Ren, and Chat."

"He never said anything," Very replied softly.

"He wouldn't. None of them ever brag about their own actions. Tox told me the story a few years ago. They were ambushed by insurgents. Steady had been pinned under a truck, but they got him out. He ran half a mile on a broken leg, stole a helicopter from the terrorist camp, and flew the guys out."

Very pushed back the swell of emotion that threatened to choke her and took a slow sip of coffee. "Wow. That's unbelievable."

"Steady almost died from the leg injury. They didn't realize it at the time, but the bone nicked his femoral artery. He barely made it to the hospital. You can tell sometimes he limps."

Very had noticed. She'd even wondered about it, but she hadn't asked. And knowing Steady, he would have shrugged it off with a joke. She could practically hear his voice: *just an old war wound, Darlin'. Nothin 'a good rubdown can't fix.*

Twitch went on, "He had a bunch of surgeries, and now he has a metal rod in his leg. He earned a Silver Star for that rescue. You'd never know it, Ver, but Steady is the biggest hero in the group."

Very sagged back in her chair. Would she ever stop discovering wonderful things about this man she had so misjudged? The answer that whispered through her mind surprised her. She hoped not.

CHAPTER TWENTY-ONE

Parasol Labs
Ridgeland, South Carolina
August 5

Parasol Labs had begun giving scheduled monthly tours of the new facility to journalists and industry professionals as a PR move. They had expanded the service to include members of the public after a social media rumor that the lab was housing puppies for experimentation and testing went viral. Tour attendance had dropped off since the lab was up and running, and the locals had assured themselves that no adorable beagles were being caged and tortured. Today five people were waiting for the guide to begin. Steady took in the small group. As they waited, he introduced himself and discovered the twenty-something girl was a chemistry student at a local college. An older man with thick glasses and a spiral notepad was an aspiring novelist researching his thriller. The black woman in her mid-thirties was a journalist writing a puff piece on the boon the lab had created in the local economy. The last member of their group was a portly woman in a kaftan who was still not convinced about the dogs. She informed Steady she had a hamburger in her purse, hoping any imprisoned pups would catch the scent and begin barking.

Steady sat on the cream leather couch and drummed his fingers on his thighs. He glanced at the clock: ten past nine. The tour was starting late.

"This is unusual," the would-be animal savior said. "I've taken this tour every month, and it always starts right on time."

Steady reassured her that the cause for the delay was most likely benign and not, as the lady theorized, a mad dash to secure and hide dogs.

At quarter past, a man walked through the front door. The guy had a military bearing, and Steady made sure the button camera affixed to his Hawaiian shirt captured his stone-cold face. Steady clocked him as he moved to the periphery of the seating area and then gave a subtle nod to the receptionist sitting behind the semi-circular desk. A moment later, a smartly dressed woman with a bright smile and a tablet in her hands crossed to the group.

"Good morning, everyone. Welcome to Parasol Labs, where we are redefining pharmaceutical development with humane and sustainable research. My name is Annette. I'll give you each a visitor pass. Please keep them around your necks at all times." She checked her tablet as she distributed the lanyards. "Mr. Dorfman, Miss Cramer. Oh, hello, Mrs. Mancini; nice to see you again. Mr. Lockhart, Ms. Petrey, and..." She glanced at the lurking man who stepped forward and took the badge before she could say his name–if she ever intended to.

The tour began, and Annette, their guide, led them through a pristine cafeteria, where she informed them that was where the tour would wrap up if they wanted to indulge in a freshly baked pastry or enjoy a fair trade cup of coffee before they left. Continuing, they walked by a glass-walled conference room where a suited man delivered a Powerpoint presentation to a group of fascinated executives sitting around a table. The whole thing looked staged.

Steady hoped he wouldn't run into Very, although he was prepared for the possibility. She would be pissed. Steady rubbed at his scruffy beard, fighting a grin. Why did the idea of Very Valentine all fired up get him so hot under the collar? As they continued down the hall, he felt a chill creep up his spine, and he turned to see the latecomer keeping pace behind him.

"Ah, here are Dr. Kemp and Mr. Everett." Annette pulled his attention to the front. "Good morning, gentleman. This is the monthly tour group."

Steady knew Very worked for Dr. Kemp. He'd met Kemp a handful of times–he owned the beach house next door that Very was renting. After spotting Steady in the small group, Kemp acknowledged him with a smile. The other guy, Everett, looked a little too slick for his own good. He wore an expensive watch and cheap shoes, a designer tie, and a rack suit. He cared about appearances.

Dr. Kemp pretended to tip an imaginary hat. "Well, hello, everyone. I hope you're enjoying your behind-the-scenes peek at Parasol." Steady couldn't help but notice Everett rolling his eyes. He captured images of both men, then turned back to his lurker.

"We didn't meet. I'm Jonah." Steady extended his hand.

The man kept his hands in his pockets. "I know who you are. I'd like a word."

Annette waved the group forward. "Now, if you follow me, we'll let these gentlemen get back to their important work, and we can look at one of Parasol's state-of-the-art laboratories."

The man gripped Steady's bicep right over his healing wound, and Steady had the feeling it was intentional. With his free hand, he opened an unmarked door and entered a small room filled with monitors. A security guard sat behind the desk, trying to mask his unease by adjusting the equipment.

"I need the room."

The guard, whose nametag read "Micah." scurried away. He was definitely the guy Steady had chased off the other night. Steady had bigger problems than this pipsqueak at the moment.

Still holding his injured arm, the man pushed Steady into a folding chair and then took the seat Micah had vacated behind the desk.

"What are you doing here, Lieutenant?"

Steady's eyes widened at the title, but he remained calm. "Just checking things out."

The man's face spread into a vicious smile. "So, that's how you're going to play this?"

"Well, if I'm being honest, I did hear some rumors about animal testing. I'm a big dog lover."

With both forearms on the desk and his hairy fingers laced, the man replied, "You have no idea what you're doing, Lieutenant Lockhart. No idea the problems you're creating. Problems for Parasol. Problems for Parasol *employees.*"

Steady straightened. "Is that a threat?"

"It's a warning. You're shining a spotlight on things best kept in the shadows. Forget about Parasol Pharmaceuticals."

"Yeah, I don't see that happening."

"When I was in the military, a guy in my platoon threw a grenade to clear an insurgent safe house. The house was empty, but the blast shook the foundation of a neighboring building, and falling stones hit our informant and killed him. If I were you, I'd think about that before I pulled the pin."

Steady had a clear image of flying over the desk and breaking this guy's neck. One clean snap. Then he would smooth out his shirt and walk out of the building like it was a Sunday afternoon stroll in the park. The man must have seen the menace in Steady's unwavering stare. He broke off first, saying, "You can see yourself out."

S teady was sitting on the wicker couch with a fishing hat pulled over his eyes when the stomp of trainers on the deck steps had him lazily looking up.

"What the hell were you doing at Parasol Labs today?"

Steady sipped his beer. "Shh, Look." He pointed to a large trunk of beached driftwood. "A momma sea otter and her baby."

Very spun to the water, and despite her palpable rage, when she spotted the frolicking animals, she couldn't seem to stop the "Awww" from escaping her lips. She watched the adorable exploits, then turned back to Steady, marginally soothed.

"Steady, why did you tour my lab?"

He shrugged. "I was curious."

"Curious?"

"Interested."

"Well, stop," she said. "Steady, it's a tense time at work right now. You're going to get me fired."

"Why would taking the company tour get you fired?"

"I don't know, but everyone is on pins and needles with this new drug coming out. Stop poking around in my business."

Steady slid the fishing hat off his head and sat up. "Very, I was just making sure you were okay. I don't like people coming to your home in the middle of the night."

She rounded the glass coffee table and sat beside him. "I appreciate your concern. I do." Very placed her open palm on his cheek. "Just please express it in another way."

When she leaned in, Steady met her halfway. Their previous kisses had been like storms: heated and passionate. This kiss was like the tide rolling in. It started slow, almost hesitantly. It took Steady a beat to realize he was actually kissing her. Gradually, he explored her mouth, his hands roaming her back, pulling her to him.

_____ arated, Steady mapped her face. Very looked dazed and ____ _red her throat. "Well, that's a better way to express an interest." ___ t fall in love with me, Darlin'." He winked.

No worries there, hotshot. I don't believe in it," she replied.

"What? Love?"

"I mean, I believe in love in a general sense—attachment, affection. I love Twitch. I love my family. I love my friends. But romantic love? It's all hormones and compatibility."

Steady turned to face her fully. "Darlin', we are surrounded by some of the most amazing love stories out there. Emily and Nathan? Tox and Calliope? Cam and Evan? Twitch and Finn? Even with all that evidence to the contrary, you think romantic love doesn't exist?"

Very sighed. "I don't know what's true for them. I only know what's true for me. I'll never be that dependent on another person."

Steady watched the otters swim off. "A Valentine who doesn't believe in love."

She shot back, "And a Lockhart whose heart is locked."

"Amen."

She stood and headed for the stairs. "Okay, then. Glad we're on the same page."

When her feet hit the sand, Steady called, "Hey, Darlin'?"

"Yeah?"

"How'd you know I took the tour?"

She paused before answering, "Dr. Kemp told me."

CHAPTER TWENTY-TWO

New York City
August 6

As soon as the hour permitted, Armand Krill entered the Cavalry Club, bypassed the uniformed attendant without acknowledgment, and took his usual table in the morning parlor. He sat placidly while the waiter whipped open the linen napkin with a flourish and laid it across his lap. Another young man set the *Wall Street Journal* and the *New York Times* beside the place setting, then poured the coffee.

Glancing around the room over the rim of his cup, Krill instantly spotted Johan DeVold, with his black eye patch and perfectly tailored suit, shaking hands with a man in a thoub. When the two men parted, DeVold took a seat at a corner table where his assistant sat at the ready. DeVold was so accustomed to the ministrations of staff that his own actions were uninterrupted by the buzzing around him. It was only when the final servant had stepped away that Armand Krill saw his opportunity.

Krill knew everything about every medication Parasol Pharmaceuticals produced and a considerable amount about the drugs of his competitors. He knew their chemical makeup, side effects, and, most importantly, at this moment, their negative interactions.

Krill was no altruist. He didn't donate to charity and never spared a thought for those less fortunate. He had his own problems. If Armand Krill was performing a good deed, *he* was the ultimate beneficiary. Without a hint of selflessness, Krill stood to intervene.

Krill approached DeVold's table and was met with a wary gaze from the assistant and a welcoming smile from DeVold. Johan set his spoon to the side and looked up.

Krill said, "Forgive this intrusion, but yesterday, your assistant dropped a bottle of your medication."

DeVold turned an impassive face to the young woman who didn't meet his gaze.

"I have a bit more knowledge than most. I'm in pharmaceuticals."

Krill noticed DeVold clenched his jaw, clearly upset at this invasion of privacy. Krill rushed to the point. Extending his hand to DeVold's breakfast, he said, "You cannot eat grapefruit with that medication. It interferes with its effectiveness, sometimes completely."

Concern overtook DeVold's discomfort, and he murmured to his assistant, "Call Dr. Cho." Without missing a beat, the woman stood and left the room.

DeVold flattened his hands on the tablecloth and muttered, "To think I was trying to start a heart-healthy diet."

Krill almost didn't hear the remark as the glint from DeVold's drumming fingers caught his eye. His stomach plummeted as he fought to tear his gaze from the signet ring on DeVold's left hand. The symbol–the letter V, surrounded by a laurel wreath and bisected by a sword–had been seared into his childhood memory. Krill staggered back a step, then regained his balance, his eyes never leaving the ring.

The assistant returned, took her seat, and spoke into DeVold's ear. He summoned the waiter with a slight lift of his hand. After correcting his order, he stood.

"I am in your debt," DeVold said.

Krill introduced himself. "Armand—"

"Krill, yes." DeVold interrupted. "Parasol Pharmaceuticals. Diamonds are a dangerous business, Armand. I rarely enter a room without knowing who's in it."

Krill shook DeVold's hand with barely leashed enthusiasm. "I'm happy to help."

DeVold replied dismissively, "Mr. Krill, I have to leave. I'm speaking at the U.N. Louisa will give you my information. If there's anything I can do for you, please don't hesitate to ask."

The assistant stepped forward, and Krill was again struck by her vivid blue eyes. She handed him a card and, with cool reserve, said, "This is Mr. DeVold's personal cell. We ask that you simply keep the card. It is imperative that you do not save the information on any electronic device. Understood?"

She waited for Krill to consent before releasing the card. Then without comment, she followed her boss through the phalanx of guards to the car.

The Rolls Royce had already disappeared from view when Krill returned to the sidewalk. He slipped the card into his billfold and replaced it in his breast pocket.

He knew what he would ask of Johan DeVold.

As a young boy, before their family's reversal of fortune, Armand had sat with his grandfather in the study of the same home he now occupied. The senior Krill told young Armand about the Vitruvian Society: where they met, what they did, the secrecy. Krill had been wide-eyed with interest.

The Vitruvian Society was a mythic cadre of the world's most powerful men who controlled everything from governments to the economy. And members had only one identifying symbol: a gold signet ring. His grandfather had worn one.

Years later, the family coffers nearly drained, Armand Krill had walked by the Cavalry Club wondering if the suited men coming and going had any idea of the arcane group that assembled there. He would shove the apron for his after-school busboy job further down in his bag, bitter and humiliated—furious with his father for squandering his inheritance.

Young Krill would stare at the club monogram etched on the glass doors and vow to rebuild his family's wealth and ensure it was never again depleted.

With a spring in his step, Krill headed home. This new drug was going to make him a billionaire. Now he just needed to establish the infrastructure to ensure the Krill name was forever linked with money and power.

He patted his chest where the business card was safely stowed. Johan DeVold had just handed him the means to achieve his goal.

CHAPTER TWENTY-THREE

New York City
August 6

Tox and Calliope sat at a cozy corner table at the West Village restaurant. They had spent four days with Calliope's parents, and Tox needed a vacation from the vacation. After shopping in every baby boutique from SoHo to the Upper East Side, he and Calliope now had enough baby shit to start a preschool. Fortunately, the Acostas were meeting friends in the Bahamas and needed to set sail. Tox and Calliope had spent the day at a South Hampton marina on her parents 'yacht. Clemente Acosta, Calliope's stepfather, was a former Portuguese Prime Minister, and her mother was a renowned poet. They lived outside of Faro and, now that Clemente was retired, spent their time traveling the world. Tox was unused to the lifestyle Calliope's parents enjoyed, but being aboard a ship, any ship, felt like home to the former SEAL. Following a lavish lunch and relaxing afternoon pampering his pregnant wife, they had waved to Clemente and Elara from the dock as the ship headed off to Exuma. After four days of being on his best behavior, Tox was ready for a drink.

Calliope yawned. "Boy, a day in a lounger in the sun really takes it out of you."

Tox put a big hand over her slight baby bump. "The bear cub is sapping your strength."

She whispered into the crook of his neck, 'Not all my strength."

Tox growled, "Let's go back to the hotel. Miles will understand."

Calliope reluctantly pushed him away and tipped her head toward the front of the room where Tox's twin brother stood scanning the tables. "You can explain it to him yourself."

Tox lifted his hand with a smile. "Damn."

Miles spotted his hard-to-miss brother and crossed to the table. The men hugged, an embrace filled with affection. Tox had spent twenty years without his twin; he never took a moment they spent together for granted.

"The Waverly Inn. Good choice. Try the Amish chicken," Miles said as he took the third chair.

Calliope made a face, and Tox rubbed his wife's back. "Please, no mention of poultry, Mi. It makes Cal sick."

"A thousand pardons, Sis. They have a great New York strip with these amazing mashed potatoes."

Calliope set the menu aside. "Done."

They ordered their meals, and Miles said, "So, a day on a yacht with the in-laws? That couldn't have been too painful."

"My dad had the chef prepare Tox his own seafood tower. The three of us shared the other one." Calliope shook her head.

Miles waited while the server poured the wine and then lifted his glass. "He knows my brother well."

"Come on. It's tiny tiers of shrimp and crab. It's barely enough food for one person," Tox defended.

"There were four lobster tails on it," Calliope countered.

Tox just shrugged.

Miles laughed. "Next time you're in town, we'll go to Peter Luger's for the thirty-eight-ounce porterhouse."

Tox perked up. "Calliope's mother wants her to see some fancy Manhattan specialist. At the time, I thought it was a dumb idea, but now that a Porterhouse is involved..."

Calliope laced her fingers with his. "The appointment's in two weeks. Totally unnecessary, but it's their first grandchild."

Miles's expression was kind, even though Tox knew he couldn't relate. "I'll make a reservation."

Pulling a piece of bread from the small loaf, Tox searched Miles's gaze. "So, is New York home now? You're talking like you live here."

"I seem to have developed a soft spot for Manhattan." Miles was no doubt referring to the fact that this was where they had reunited after all those years. "And it's a hell of a lot closer to Beaufort than Paris. Especially with my little niece on the way."

"Nephew," Tox corrected.

Miles looked at Calliope for a long moment. "I don't know, Miller," Miles called Tox by his given name. "I think there are going to be some pink bows in your future."

Tox waved him off. "How are you keeping busy?"

Miles shook out his napkin and placed it across his lap. "This and that."

"Come on, Miles. How many politicians are there who need your help? They can't all be sending dick pics and taking bribes," Tox said.

"You'd be surprised." Miles moved his wine glass to make room for the salad. "But." He paused while the waiter brandished the pepper mill. "This time, I'm helping out an old friend."

"How? 'Tox asked.

Miles tapped his fingertips together, and Tox felt a surge of nostalgia. It was a gesture his twin had used when they were young boys, before they had been separated. Much like then, Tox had the same mix of excitement and trepidation. Those drumming fingers meant Miles was scheming.

After a pause, Miles said, "About six months ago, I got a call from a guy I worked with back when I was starting out. He needed my help." He leaned forward in his chair. "Running a con."

"Please tell me you're not doing anything that could land you in jail."

"Everything I do could land me in jail, dear brother. At least this time, I'm sticking it to the rich and powerful instead of helping them avoid accountability."

"Who's the mark?"

Miles wiped the corners of his mouth. The napkin came away, revealing an evil grin. "Just another corporate CEO who thinks he's untouchable."

Calliope smiled. "It feels good to be working for the good guys, doesn't it?"

Miles mirrored her expression, then his face fell. He polished off his wine and refilled the glass. "Most of the time."

Calliope paused with a grape tomato speared on her fork. "Do I want to know?"

Miles picked up his butter knife, then set it back down. "It's not the job." He sighed. "Do you remember Clara?"

"The art student? From Columbia University?" Calliope asked.

The team met the Art History Ph.D. when Calliope had discovered a lost Degas.

"Among other things, yes," Miles said.

"Interesting," Tox goaded.

Miles shot his brother a look. "It's the opposite of interesting. She has a boyfriend. Her father is protective. So, he asked me to get the lay of the land."

Tox stole one of the olives Calliope had pushed to the side of her plate. "And?"

Miles stabbed at his salad with more force than necessary. "I asked Clara to help me with this little project so I could keep an eye on her."

"And maybe keep her away from this boyfriend?" Calliope asked.

"I haven't even seen the chump, but I figure if Clara's with me, she's not with him." Miles smirked.

"Interesting," Tox repeated, drawing out the word.

"The only thing interesting about it is that I now owe Clara a favor. A big one. I swear I spend my life doing favors and cashing them in."

"And Clara? A squeaky-clean, Ivy League art student is helping?"

The server arrived, and Miles said, "Trust me. Clara Gautreau is many things, but squeaky-clean isn't one of them."

CHAPTER TWENTY-FOUR

South Island, South Carolina
August 6

Steady set the telescope up on the beach and positioned the folding sports chairs. His bare feet sank into the sand as he stared at the dark ocean. The air smelled of salt and sea life, and the waves lapped a gentle rhythm on the shore.

He spread out the quilt and sat with his hands locked around his knees. He stayed in that position only a moment before falling to his back to stare at the sky. It was a perfect, cloudless night, and Steady mapped the constellations.

He had loved the sky for as long as he could remember. From pointing out cloud shapes with his mom to trying to touch the blue by jumping from the roof of his family home (and breaking his leg), the expanse had always fascinated him. On his fifth birthday, his grandfather had taken Steady up in an old crop duster he had lovingly restored in the spare barn on his North Carolina farm.

The instant the wheels left the makeshift runway, Steady was a goner. He never wanted to touch the ground again. Steady had the extremely rare distinction of being both a SEAL and a Naval Aviator. He had been flying planes since he was a teenager. In the Navy, he had started in Pensacola, flown combat missions, and trained as a drone pilot before switching to the SEALs. If it went up in the air, Steady could fly it. Whether in the cockpit of an F-35 fighter jet or puttering through the sky in his Cessna, when he was flying, he was free.

"Looks like star gazing is on the agenda."

Staying flat on his back, Steady turned his head and spied a pair of slim legs. He hadn't been sure Very would show tonight after their heated run-in on his deck, but here she was, looking like heaven.

"Hey, Darlin'," Steady drawled.

"No bad guys to chase?" Very sank down next to him and pulled a raspberry-flavored water from the cooler.

"Even Superman takes off his cape every once in a while."

They were a different couple on these nights. Sure, they'd trade jabs and joke around, but there was a synergy. The sexual attraction that simmered between them was back-burnered, and something else took its place—a shared desire to connect. They were two people who used wit and deflection to hide their vulnerabilities from the world. Somehow, here on this quiet beach, they had created a safe place to bare their souls.

Steady smiled as Very took her usual place on her back beside him. "What are we looking at tonight?"

Steady locked his hands behind his head. "See that cluster of stars shaped like a double-u? That's Cassiopeia. Neptune stuck her up there for braggin' about her looks."

"Seems excessive," Very commented.

"Well, the gods weren't exactly 'let the punishment fit the crime' kind of beings," Steady chuckled. "Hell, Neptune tied Cassiopeia's daughter to a rock to be eaten by a sea monster, and she didn't do anything wrong."

"Sometimes parents really screw you over."

Steady looked at Very, but she was still gazing at the sky. "Sometimes," he agreed. "In this particular case, the daughter, Andromeda, was rescued by

Perseus, and they married. So maybe Cassiopeia didn't screw her over as much as change her fate."

"That's a nice way to look at it," she said.

"When I was a kid, my dad and I would come out here to look at the stars. That's why I brought the telescope tonight. Want to take a look?"

"Yes. That sounds really cool." Very pointed to the sky. "What's that big group of stars?"

Steady pulled Very to her feet and led her to one of the chairs. Standing behind her, he guided her head to the telescope. "See it?"

She adjusted the tube slightly. "Yes."

"That's Scorpius. He hunts Orion. You can't see Orion because he hides from Scorpius in the summer and only appears in the sky in the winter."

"I thought Orion was the hunter," she said, still looking through the scope.

"Correct, but the gods sent Scorpius to hunt him. You can pick your myth as to why but they all seem to revolve around the idea that Orion got too big for his britches."

Very looked up at him. "So Scorpius hunts the hunter," she said.

"Exactly." In the moonlight, Steady could just make out the Mona Lisa smile playing on her lips.

"I like that."

Steady heard something in her voice–the way she said those three simple words–there was a depth to it, a satisfaction.

They sat side-by-side, sharing the telescope and staring at the spangled sky. The tips of their elbows touched. It was the only point of contact. Steady had the oddest sensation. It was an *awareness*, as if a spider were spinning an invisible web between them, using each of their bodies as an anchor and connecting them with silken threads.

"I want to show you something." Steady shifted the tube, checked the sighting, then offered the view to Very. "See that bright star in the middle?'

"Yes."

"That's a double."

"What do you mean?" she asked. Very lifted her head and looked his way.

"A binary star. It's actually two stars that are connected. They're somehow bound together and share the same orbit."

"Why?"

"Not sure." Steady tipped his head up to the sky. "There's a lot going on out there that we don't understand."

"I like to think there's a reason for things, an order to the universe," Very said.

"You gotta learn to embrace the unpredictability of it all. That's the key."

"Oh, *that's* the key? Thank you. I've been pondering the meaning of life for years. Who knew it was so simple?"

"Yep. Just go with the flow," Steady quipped.

"I don't think I can. Sometimes there are things that need to be set right."

"Very, I'm a SEAL. I understand a fight for the right reasons."

"I know." She sighed. "You know I had a rough start in life, and that feeling of–I don't know–injustice? Betrayal? It's always there."

"Sorry to hear that."

"Maybe it's stupid. My biological family was pretty fucked up. I got lucky."

"You know what they say: most family trees bear nuts."

"Who says that?" She brought her arm down and elbowed him in the ribs.

"People. People say it." he defended.

"You big dope." She softened her declaration by scooting closer and resting her head on his shoulder. Then she pointed to the sky. "Show me something else."

Steady shifted and brought his arm around Very's shoulders in a motion that shouldn't have been familiar. It was as if she had always been meant to be there, like he had saved this spot in the nook of his shoulder just for her.

With his free hand, he pointed to the horizon. "I'll show you Cygnus, the swan. Then you gotta teach me something cool about chemistry."

Very followed the line of his arm and said, "Deal."

After the celestial show, Very stood and brushed the sand from her legs. "Thank you for showing me. That was cool."

"Where's my chemistry lesson?"

"I do have some cool tricks up my sleeve, but I'll show you another night. I'm exhausted."

Steady stood and gave Very a mock bow, then began gathering his things. She helped him fold the quilt and dump the melting icy water from the cooler. Steady zipped the telescope into its case, and Very sidled up to bestow her nightly kiss on his cheek. At that moment, Steady remembered he wanted to tell Very about an upcoming lunar eclipse and turned his head.

Very's lips touched the corner of his mouth, and in an instant, he felt that same invisible web adhering them. Tentatively, Steady moved his head to align their mouths. They stood there, frozen in the moonlight, Steady waiting for some indication from Very. Then the tip of her tongue skimmed their lips, and Steady exploded like a bullet from a gun.

With one hand cupping her neck and the other pulling her body against him, Steady kissed Very with the pent-up desire he had been bottling since that one incredible night. And, as he knew she would, Very returned the kiss with equal fervor. They were both strong-willed, sexual people, but the kiss was not a battle; no, it was a dance.

Instinctively they melded, her body sinking into his. Their lips and tongues moved in sync as if they had kissed for hours and hours in another life. Steady thought he could stand there kissing her all night, drowning in the sensation of her body against his, of her hands in his hair, of her heel curling around his calf. He was so lost in the moment his lips chased hers when she pulled away.

Very wobbled on her feet and took a moment to compose herself as she stared at her tangled fingers. She blew out a deep breath, then lifted her gaze. "Well, goodnight."

"G'night, Very."

Halfway back to her house, she turned back. "I'm glad you brought the telescope tonight. It makes things interesting. Lots to look at."

And with that provocative farewell, Very slipped inside. Steady grabbed the telescope, left the rest of the items where they were, and raced back to the house. Looked like he was going to get that chemistry lesson after all.

Steady fell twice running up the stairs to his bedroom. He had the telescope set up and the chair in place in record time. He aimed the tube toward Very's bedroom window and adjusted the focus. She came into the room without the slightest change in behavior. The thought crossed his mind that maybe what she had said on the beach hadn't been an invitation. He banished the idea; of course, it was. Very knew the most erotic thing about this was that it was forbidden. She wasn't going to put on a show. But man, was she putting on a show.

Very went about her bedtime routine in her usual unhurried fashion. She peeled off her clothes on the way to the bathroom, then emerged minutes later in a towel. Steady only caught bits and pieces of her various stages of undress–only when she was positioned in front of one of the two windows that faced his house. Very passed by one window in a towel. By the time she arrived at the next, she was in a robe. She fluffed her pillows, scrolled through messages on her phone, and picked up her laundry off the floor. It was a mundane evening ritual and the most erotic thing Steady had ever seen. Very disappeared from view again, then materialized in front of the window, wearing a T-shirt and sleep shorts. She looked across the beach toward his bedroom. Steady kept his eye to the scope. With a soft smile in his direction, she closed the blinds.

Steady looked up then and, with a mirroring smile, said, "Sweet dreams, Darlin'."

CHAPTER TWENTY-FIVE

South Island, South Carolina
August 7

Steady entered the house with a thick folder tucked under his arm. Chat gave him shit about the paper copies of the information, but Steady preferred to hold the pages in his hands. His computer skills were proficient, but there was something about the physical copies of photos and documents. It's just how he was–old school.

In the small den at the front of the house, Steady sat at the scarred wooden table where his grandfather used to tie fishing flies. Hard copies of the photos he had taken on his tour of Parasol Labs were spread out before him. Using Chat's computer genius and some next-gen facial recognition software, they were able to identify everyone he had encountered. He set aside the pictures of his fellow tour attendees in a neat stack, then started a second pile with the Parasol employees.

He looked through the information paper clipped to each photo, finding little of note. Malcomb Everett, the lab administrator, looked ambitious and shady. Steady knew Very's boss, Carson Kemp, from when he occupied the beach house next door. Kemp had worked for Parasol for thirty years and had what appeared to be an illustrious and well-compensated career.

Nothing else jumped out. Steady stopped when he came to the last photo in the stack. The anonymous goon from his tour of the lab. Alonso Mitchell.

"Gotcha," Steady muttered.

Chat was able to match Mitchell's face to his military record. It was scant. Mitchell had served in the Army for six years after enlisting at eighteen. After three tours and an honorable discharge, Alonso Mitchell took a job working security at Parasol Pharmaceuticals Manhattan office. After that, nothing. Steady turned the paperwork over to check the back of the page, but there was no additional information.

Steady had a bad feeling. Very was wading in dangerous waters. He ran a hand down his face and tossed the stack of photos onto the table.

Standing in the kitchen and contemplating dinner, he glanced out the window at Very's dark house. Twitch had mentioned the girls were meeting at their local watering hole for a night out. After a brief internal debate, Steady decided he needed a drink.

CHAPTER TWENTY-SIX

Beaufort, South Carolina
August 7

"She knows I watch her." Steady swiveled his barstool toward the table of women and gave his back to his friend.

Across the room, the object of his attention, Very Valentine, sat at a round table with her friends. She gestured with a brightly-colored cocktail and pointed at Twitch, who was shaking her head in protest. Next to her, Nathan's wife, Emily, covered her face with her hands, her shoulders shaking with laughter. Evan Cole, the fiancée of the man currently sitting to Steady's right, was just returning from the restroom to take her seat to Very's left.

Cam spun his mug on the weathered bar and nodded. "Sure, sure, then that makes it okay. I'm sure the cops will see your side of it."

Steady spun back around. "No, dude, I mean, *she knows.*"

Cam slipped a hand through the handle of his beer mug and lifted the glass to his lips. "I'm gonna need a little more, hermano."

Steady hooked his foot on the rung of Cam's barstool and leaned closer. "Remember that night last winter? You stopped by?"

At Cam's blank expression, Steady continued, "Very had just moved in next door. I had the telescope set up on the beach." He rolled his hands in a *remember now?* Gesture.

Cam cocked his head in confusion.

"Dude, I spied on her, jumping around in her underwear."

Cam grinned. "Yeah, I knew what you were talking about. I just wanted to hear you admit it."

Steady drove his fist into Cam's bicep, causing beer to slosh onto the bar.

Cam grabbed a cocktail napkin from the stack and sopped up the spill. "Go on."

A waitress walked by with a tray full of drinks and ran her free hand across Steady's back. "Hey, handsome. I get off early tonight."

Steady took her hand and kissed the back. "Sweetheart, there's nothing I'd rather do, but my parents are coming in for a visit, and I'm gonna be tied up for the next few days. And not in a good way." He winked.

"Damn." She squeezed his shoulder. "Another time?"

"You bet."

The waitress hurried off, and Cam said, "Are your parents really coming to visit?"

"Nah." Steady tossed a peanut into his mouth. When he returned his gaze to his friend, Cam was scowling.

"What?"

"I will pay the tab if you can tell me her name."

Steady scrunched his face. "It starts with a K." He snapped his fingers once, twice. "Kayla. No, Kaylee."

The bearded bartender placed a fresh beer in front of him. "Kaitlyn, dipshit."

"Kaitlyn! Yes, that's it. Cam's buying."

Cam waved him off. "Get back to the creepy peeping."

"Right." Steady looked over his shoulder at the table of women and caught Very staring right back at him. She lifted her brows in challenge before being pulled back into her conversation. "So after that night last winter—well, it was a day or so later when she called me a pervert—I put the telescope away. I set it in the corner of my bedroom."

"Uh-huh," Cam said, a hint of suspicion in his voice.

"Last week, I got out of the shower, and I was walking across the bedroom, and I stubbed my toe on the leg of the bed. Hurt like a motherfucker. Anyway, I was hopping around, and I knocked the telescope. Look, I know it sounds sketchy as hell, but I swear to you, this is how it went down. The thing was pointed right at Very's bedroom, and my head was directly over the eyehole." Steady tossed up his hands and stage whispered, "What was I supposed to do? It was like the universe was telling me to take a peek."

Cam tilted his head back and forth, his eyes on the ceiling.

"What?" Steady asked.

"Just trying to decide if a judge would see it that way," Cam replied.

"Hold on. Let me finish." Steady took a long draw on his beer. "I'll skip past the telescope adjustments and focus."

"By all means." Cam pulled the bowl of peanuts in front of him. "Wouldn't want to shatter the romance."

"The sarcasm is neither amusing nor appreciated."

With a hand on each of their shoulders, the Bishop Security sniper, Hercules Reynolds, stuck his head between the two men. "Sarcasm about what?"

Cam moved over a stool to let Herc sit between them. Hercules Reynolds was their sniper. He was also the youngest guy on the team, and it showed. Whatever his behavior after hours, Herc was reliable and professional—the guy could shoot a baseball in a blizzard from a thousand yards. Herc had saved the lives of both men flanking him.

Cam shelled a peanut and tossed it in his mouth. "Steady's stalking Very."

"She's spoken for? Damn. She's hot." Herc pointed to Cam's beer and nodded to the bartender.

"She not fucking spoken for. And I'm not stalking her. And don't you even think about it. If you'd let me tell the story," Steady defended.

"Who's stopping you?" Herc accepted the drink and took a healthy swig from the bottle, the sincerity of his question belying Steady's exasperation.

Cam caught Herc up. "He's got a telescope in his bedroom, and he's explaining how he *accidentally* started spying on Very."

"Yes, exactly." Steady held out a hand toward his friend. "Thank you. Accidentally and consensually, I might add."

Both men gave Steady their attention as he turned his back to the table of women and told the story. "So I looked through the eyepiece. I mean, I was bent over the thing. It's right there."

Cam explained to Herc, "He stubbed his toe."

"And there's Very." Steady mouthed, "In the bedroom."

"And suddenly, your toe wasn't the only thing throbbing." Herc held up his hand for a high five and was met with two blank faces.

Steady continued, "Anyway, it wasn't like a scene in a porno or anything. She was just getting ready for bed, but I couldn't look away. After a couple minutes, she looks up, and you know what she does? She walks over to the window and stands there for a second. Then she peels off the hoodie, smiles, and reaches up and closes the blinds."

After a pregnant pause, Herc said, "Whoa."

"I know. So, a few nights after that, I take another peek, and Very takes it up a notch. She's just out of the shower and wrapped in a towel. She walks out of my line of sight, and I see the towel fly across the room. Then she walks back into view in a robe and closes the blinds. Again."

"Show's over," Herc accurately surmised.

"I want to float a theory." Steady and Herc turned their attention to Cam, who continued, "Is it possible that Very doesn't know you're watching? That perhaps, she's just going through her nightly bedtime routine and then closing her blinds, so the sun doesn't wake her in the morning? Is it possible you've concocted the mutuality of this exchange, and you're just spying on an innocent woman?"

Steady paused with the beer mug at his lips, considering. "I guess it's possible."

"Steady," Cam admonished.

"But highly unlikely." Steady drained his mug. "No. She knows. She's not Evan."

"What's that supposed to mean?" Cam asked.

Steady navigated the minefield deftly. "I just mean, Very's impulsive, maybe a little reckless. Possibly an exhibitionist." Steady wanted to use more favorable terms like uninhibited and erotically charged, but he didn't want to risk unintentionally insulting Cam's beautiful but bookish fiancée.

"And Evan's not?"

Steady shifted on the bar stool. "No, dude, I'm sure she's those things. In a good way. I mean—"

"Relax, hermano. I'm messing with you."

"Fuck" Steady tipped his head toward the ceiling. "Well, cut it out. This woman is making me crazy enough as it is."

"I've never seen you like this," Cam said.

"Like what?"

"Un-Steady." Cam grinned, and Steady flipped him off before waving down the bartender.

CHAPTER TWENTY-SEVEN

South Island, South Carolina
August 8

The drive from Steady's house to the Bishop Security office was twenty minutes, and this morning, every one of them was filled with thoughts of Very. She was the polar opposite of every woman he had ever encountered. He thought of the countless dates and barroom conversations where he would nod along as a girl talked about why social media was her calling or how the homeless man outside her building was an inconvenience.

Very's career was noble. She was dedicating herself to creating medicines to heal people. What's more, she was a good person. Steady saw it in the way she supported her friends and in the way she acted. One time, on a run on the beach, she came across a loggerhead sea turtle nest. She had alerted a local conservation group and spent the morning working with a bunch of nature nerds roping off the area and making signs.

Steady could tick off Very's positive attributes all day. Hell, he hadn't even gotten to her looks. She was beautiful and curvy in all the right places. More than that, she glowed. There was a light inside of Very, and, like a ship lost at sea, he steered toward it. He wasn't sure if Very was a lighthouse guiding him safely into the harbor or a Siren luring him to his destruction, but he was powerless to make the distinction.

Steady's jeep drifted onto the shoulder, kicking up gravel. The driver behind him laid on the horn. He righted the car and, with a wave to the guy in his rearview mirror, continued on.

Where was he? Of course, he was thinking about that pink-haired demon. The thing about Very that captured him most of all? She had this embedded sense of purpose. Like she was on a mission, working toward a goal. It was woven into her DNA. Steady had felt that way once: intentional. On the SEALs, he had that drive, that zeal. Now? Now he had a job. It was a good job. He liked what he did, loved his coworkers, made a good living. But was something missing?

One of the many reasons Steady loved to fly was how calming and freeing it was. Whenever his brain turned into a lottery ball air popper, he would take to the sky. There, he could contemplate the vast expanse before him and close the door on unsettling thoughts. Surrounded by an endless sky, personal problems felt insignificant. Whenever Steady's thoughts turned inward, he did his damnedest to shut them down. Best not to tug at those threads.

Steady nearly bypassed his exit and, amid a chorus of honking horns, swerved the jeep across a lane to get off the highway. With a shake of his head, he turned on the ancient radio and caught the end of a Coldplay song while he took in the South Carolina landscape.

When he came to the unmarked timber gate that resembled the entrance to a genteel horse farm, Steady pulled into the Bishop Security campus. The drive was a ribbon of asphalt through bucolic fields dotted with horses. When he reached the converted schoolhouse, Steady pulled into his spot in the back lot and hopped out.

Nathan's Uncle, Charlie Bishop, was talking to the handler who took care of the dogs that patrolled the property. The dogs were retired combat veterans, and Charlie Bishop had been instrumental in finding them proper homes. Steady grinned. Who would have thought that a former Secretary of Defense, a man who couldn't spend all his money if he lived to be a hundred, would find his calling rehoming military dogs? Charlie dipped his toe in espionage from time to time, helping out the Bishop team, but really his days were spent with his four-legged friends. On top of that, when Charlie moved to the little Barrier Island fishing village over a decade ago, the confirmed bachelor met the love of his life, Maggie, and married for the first time at the age of sixty-three.

Steady genuinely liked Charlie Bishop, he was gruff and cantankerous, but the guy had a heart of gold. So when Charlie had called and asked Steady to come to the kennel, he didn't waste a second. Steady broke into a jog, hoping he knew the reason Charlie had wanted him to come by.

"Just the man I wanted to see." Charlie removed the stub of an unlit cigar from between his lips and dropped it into the side pocket of his battered jacket.

"What's up?" Steady asked.

"I got your text."

Steady had messaged Charlie after he found the bozo hiding in Very's bushes. A dog would provide some added security. On top of that, he had wanted a dog since he moved into the beach house. Charlie whisted to the handler, who came over with a small yellow lab on a leash.

If Steady had trouble sorting his complicated feelings for Very, he felt no such confusion here. It was love at first sight. He dropped to his knees and scratched the dog behind the ears, unashamed by his baby talk. "Who's a good girl? Who's a good girl?"

"I've got the perfect canine for you, Jonah. This is Tilly."

Steady looked up with a smile. "She's the one."

"She's a therapy dog and a bomb sniffer. She's three years old."

Steady commented, "That's young."

"That's what I wanted to talk to you about. She was injured in a training accident. She can't serve."

Steady ran his hand over the dog's body, from soft ears to wagging tail. "She looks healthy to me."

"Perfectly healthy," Charlie confirmed.

"So what's the issue?" Steady asked.

"She's deaf."

Steady took the dog's face in his hands and looked into her big brown eyes. Tilly jutted her muzzle forward and licked him on the chin. Above him, Charlie chuckled.

Steady stood and dusted off his pants. "How do I take care of her?"

Charlie scooped up the leash and put it in Steady's hands. Then he passed him a small book. "You'll need to add some words to your ASL vocabulary."

The team used basic American Sign Language to communicate silently during ops.

"Copy that." Steady shook the leash, and Tilly came to his side. "You ready, Tilly girl?"

"Deaf, Jonah," Charlie scolded.

"Right." Steady thumbed through the book of hand signals.

Charlie pulled a yellow bandana from his back pocket. "Use this to get her attention."

"Thanks, Charlie. I love her already."

Charlie stuck the short cigar back in his mouth. "I knew you would, kid."

With a shake of the bandana, Steady and his new best friend jogged off toward the office. Tilly had a new human.

CHAPTER TWENTY-EIGHT

South Island, South Carolina
August 9

Steady stood at the kitchen counter, finishing the sandwich he had made himself for dinner and studying the handbook of commands for Tilly. She was already family. The yellow lab sat obediently beside him. He hadn't realized how most ways to communicate with a dog were non-verbal. Tilly conversed in her own way too. When Steady was in his head or feeling low–two aspects of his personality he rarely showed the world–Tilly would press her soft body against him, her warmth comforting.

He ran through some basics with Tilly, finally remembering to stop speaking the words aloud. Steady threw her rubber toy, and she waited for his order to fetch it. Each time, Steady rewarded her with a small treat and a scratch.

The strangest thing Tilly did involved Very. Whenever Steady saw his beautiful neighbor jog by on the beach or spotted her out on her deck, Tilly would push the top of her head against his leg. Sometimes, Steady would just think about her, and there was Tilly. There was no force behind it, just a reassuring pressure. A nudge? Steady didn't know what the dog was trying to tell him, but he found the gesture endearing.

He glanced out the side window of the kitchen and spotted the woman in question. Very was at her sink, loading the dishwasher. Steady felt the flat of Tilly's head against his calf and smiled.

Very was dancing to a song in her head, or maybe she was wearing earbuds. Steady couldn't see from this distance. He confirmed it was the latter when Very stopped swaying, dried her hands, and grabbed the phone from the counter. She listened and paced. When the call ended, Very buzzed around the room, gathering her things. With her bag over her shoulder and her key fob in her hand, she stopped. Very turned, looked out the window, and met his gaze for one brief moment before hurrying out the door.

In the months that he had known her, Steady had been on the receiving end of a lot of looks from Very—angry, teasing, sarcastic, joyful, sultry, and even embarrassed. But, in that split-second look, he saw an unreadable something he had never seen in Very Valentine's eyes before.

In another instant, she was climbing behind the wheel of her SUV. He could hear her tires spinning against the gravel in the darkness, and then she was gone.

Steady didn't think, didn't debate, didn't analyze. He signaled to Tilly, who scampered to the door, scooped up his keys, and, in under a minute, he was following her from a discreet distance.

Steady pulled into the expansive parking lot of the Roadtrip Diner. It was late, but the well-traveled highway ensured customers at all hours. He took a parking spot in the second row facing the glass windows that lined the side of the restaurant. He immediately spotted Very's pink hair as she walked through the dining room and greeted a man in a booth. Tilly pressed her head against Steady's bicep, and he gave her a pat as he observed. The man she was meeting stood and kissed her cheek. The guy was built like a string bean, but Steady felt an unwelcome swirl of jealousy in his gut. A waitress refilled the string bean's coffee and set a mug before Very. They spoke calmly, Very nodding along. The man cleared a space and put a laptop on the table. After typing for a moment, he spun the screen to Very. She looked at it, then opened her bag and passed the man a flash drive which he inserted into the machine. He smiled and then mimicked wiping sweat from his brow.

Steady's eyes swept the diner. A child was having a tantrum at one table. At another, some truckers were eating. Then, his gaze landed on a man at the counter. He wore a feed cap pulled low and was looking at some sort of brochure. Steady saw a rack of them by the front door. Just as Steady was about to move on, the man looked up and stared directly at Very and her companion. It was the man who had threatened him at Parasol during his tour of the lab– Alonso Mitchell. Even from the parking lot, Steady sensed his menace.

The string bean stood and gathered his things. Very gave the guy a little wave, and he headed out the door. A moment later, Mitchell stood and followed. Steady drummed his thumbs on the steering wheel while he waited for Very. The entire way home, he wondered what Very was mixed up in and why.

When Steady pulled his Jeep into the driveway, he stopped short. Then he eased the car beside the Volvo and parked. Pushing the front door of the house closed behind him, Steady glanced across the room to see the half-open sliding glass door leading out to the deck. As he crossed the room and peered out, Tilly wandered over to her dog bed, unconcerned. Very sat on the lacquered wicker couch, her arms locked around her knees. She looked lost.

"Very?" he said as he came around and sat beside her. "You okay?"

"You followed me,"

Steady sighed. "Yes. I was worried about you."

He braced himself for a dressing down. Very was private and fiercely independent. Steady knew she would be pissed, and he didn't care. Nothing could have prepared him for what she did.

Very released her legs from her grasp and crawled into his lap. Straddling him with her arms around his shoulders, Very buried her face in his neck and whispered, "Thank you."

Steady released a relieved chuckle. "Not the reaction I was expecting, Darlin'."

"I know." Very pulled back and rested her forehead against his. "Don't do it again, but tonight, I felt you watching me." She met his gaze. "It was nice."

When her eyes wandered down to his lips, Steady got the hint. He leaned forward and kissed her, slow and deep. Very pushed back and stood, and Steady waited for her to say goodnight. She didn't speak, though. Instead, she grabbed the hem of her T-shirt and pulled it off. Then she unclasped her bra and tossed it on the couch beside him. Steady sat frozen, afraid to move, afraid to shatter this dream. Very tucked her thumbs into the waistband of her flowy miniskirt and slid it down her legs. She stood before him in a white thong. Nothing could improve the vision–until she turned and walked down the deck stairs and out to the beach.

This was his fantasy. This was the woman he knew. This was the woman he wanted more than air, more than sky. When Very reached the water's edge and turned, Steady stood. He grabbed the back of his T-shirt with his good arm and pulled it over his head. Then he kicked off his trainers, pulled the blanket from the back of the couch, and stalked after his prey.

Very watched Steady prowl toward her like a lazy tiger roaming the Savannah. He unfurled the blanket she hadn't noticed. Then, he sank to his knees before her. With his hands on her hips, Steady slipped his fingers under the elastic of her thong, dragged it down, and pulled one lean leg over his shoulder. On his knees with her body open before him, he explored her with one long, slow lick.

He murmured, "You taste like heaven."

Steady worshiped her. He was rough and reverent, with his tongue and teeth, and Very felt herself falling. He rested a big palm on her lower back, then slid it down into that forbidden crease. With the mere threat of his finger pressed against the taboo bud, he pushed her body closer. It was too much and not enough. Very didn't know whether to arch back into the hand behind her or grind forward into his unrelenting mouth. She was drowning. She was flying. And then she exploded in a shattering orgasm.

Steady lowered her onto the blanket, and Very gave in to the relief of surrender. He kissed her and ran his nose down hers. "Feeling better, Darlin'?"

"Not yet." She rolled on top of him and kissed her way down his broad chest.

Steady gripped her sides and pulled her back. "This is just for you tonight."

"Then let me enjoy myself," she said.

Very's lips retraced the path until she settled between his legs. She opened his fly. Steady lifted his hips to help her efforts, then propped himself on his elbows.

She wasn't intimidated by much, but Steady's erection, thick and long before her, gave her pause. Determined and thrilled, she took him in her mouth.

The tide was coming in. Steady could feel the foamy waves lapping at his feet. The sea could swallow him whole at that moment, and he wouldn't have noticed or cared as long as Very kept doing what she was doing. The fall of her pink ponytail had slipped over her shoulder and brushed his hip. Her short nails were digging into his thighs. And her mouth, God, her mouth. He had pictured this in his mind over and over. His imagination didn't compare to the real thing.

Steady was lost. Each surge of the ocean echoed the press of Very's body. The water's retreat seemed to pull every worry, every suspicion, along with it, into the dark depths. Nothing remained on the beach but peace and pleasure. The stars in the sky remained when he closed his eyes, exploding into bursts of light. As much as he wanted to wait, to drag out this feeling for hours, he couldn't. He tried to warn Very with a groan and a squeeze of her shoulder, but his signal only fueled her. She gripped him tighter, sucked harder, and he erupted.

He wanted to toss Very onto her back and lose himself inside her, but not tonight. She had been off, vulnerable, and Steady wanted sex with Very to be a culmination of all the lust and fire they had been stoking for all these months.

With a satisfied grin, she crawled up his body, tracing his abs with her fingers, and settled under his arm. His girl was back.

Waves lapped the shore, reaching their legs, then retreating.

"We're getting soaked," she said with a laugh.

"I think the ocean could carry us off to parts unknown, and I wouldn't mind a bit."

Very snuggled closer. After a moment of quiet, she pinched his side. "So, are we getting a dog?"

Steady squirmed from the tickle, then laughed. "Well, about that–"

"Relax, you big dope. No crazy tonight."

"A little crazy," he countered.

"Yeah, the good kind."

"Can you come inside?" He wanted to introduce her to Tilly.

"I better get back."

Steady sat up, pulling her with him. Very stepped into her panties, then covered her chest with her hands as she hurried to the deck for her clothes. She pulled the T-shirt over her bare breasts and held onto her bra. He was getting hard again just watching her.

When she returned to where he lay, Very dropped to her hands and knees and kissed him. "Good night, Steady."

"G'night, Darlin'."

As she walked away across the sand, Steady called, "Hey, Very?"

She turned back to face him. "Yes?"

"If you need me, you know where to find me."

She nodded her understanding and continued home, leaving Steady naked on the beach, wishing for things he wasn't sure he could ever have.

Every second Steady spent with Very felt like a crushing weight being lifted from his shoulders. The ocean rushed up and retreated, and he reluctantly stood and gathered up the blanket. He saw Very's footsteps in the sand and fought the nearly irresistible pull to follow.

If someone had asked him a year ago, Steady could have confidently affirmed he didn't understand love. Yes, his friends had fallen hard, but he couldn't relate. It was as if he had never tasted chocolate, and his buddies were trying to describe it. Steady could appreciate their enjoyment, but he couldn't comprehend the flavor. And then, one day, a snarky, pink-haired girl sat next to him in the sand in complete silence. She was the chocolate bar–with a few nuts added. Every quiet moment that passed, Steady felt his heart reaching out to her. He wanted to know her pain. He wanted to feel her body beneath him. He wanted to kiss her on a dance floor.

Steady was a man who spent his life dodging women and avoiding commitment, but he suddenly found himself in foreign waters. He wasn't sure what he was feeling, but he could practically taste the chocolate on his tongue.

CHAPTER TWENTY-NINE

Bishop Security Headquarters
Somewhere outside Beaufort, South Carolina
August 10

Steady found Nathan in his office. His boss nodded to the small conference table by the windows, poured himself coffee, and joined him.

"Well, it must be important if you put off your weekly Saturday trip to the airfield."

Steady flew every weekend when he wasn't on an op. "Yeah, I'll head over there in a bit, but I needed to talk to you."

Nathan sipped his drink, waiting for Steady to continue.

"Last night, I followed Very to a diner outside of town. She gave some guy a flash drive. I clocked another guy there too. The same guy who threatened me during the lab tour–some Parasol hired gun named Alonso Mitchell. He left right after Very and her friend, and it looked like he followed the friend."

"I see."

"Boss, I don't know what the hell is going on with Very, but somethin' ain't right."

"I agree," Nathan said.

" I know you think I'm fishing in a dry pond, but I'm telling you, Very is mixed up in something."

"You're right."

"All I ask...wait. What?"

"Steady, I agree with you. Very is up to something."

"What makes you say that?" Steady asked.

Nathan's answer surprised him. "Twitch. She mentioned that Very hadn't been herself lately, and, against my better judgment, I had her look into it."

"What did she discover?"

"According to some internal memos Twitch accessed, they caught Very downloading data from a restricted archive about the new drug Parasol is releasing. It could be nothing, but on its face, it's questionable."

"That could be what she handed off last night."

Nathan continued, "Keep an eye on her, Steady. Full surveillance. Krill and his team are watching Very. The man you saw at the diner is proof. Parasol is releasing Mobilify soon, and they want to ensure nothing interferes with that. I have no doubt Armand Krill will do whatever it takes to get that drug to market. Let's make sure Very is safe."

"Understood."

Nathan walked over to his desk and picked up a file. "Chat mentioned he gathered data from photos you took on a lab tour. Here is some additional information on the key players at the lab." He passed it to Steady.

"Anything interesting?" Steady asked.

"Some. Malcomb Everett, the lab administrator, is in debt. He likes to gamble and has expensive taste. He's maxed out several credit cards."

Steady flipped through the pages of the paper file, following along.

"The Principle Investigator–that's the lead scientist–Carson Kemp has worked for Parasol since the nineties. His movement within the company is interesting. It looks like his transfers among labs coincide with the release of new drugs."

"And then there's Very Valentine." Steady's voice held a note of disbelief. A chill crept down his spine as he recalled the man in the dunes. He slapped the file closed and stood. "I'm on it."

"Steady." Nathan's voice stopped him at the door.

"Yeah?"

"This is an observe-and-report situation. Do not involve yourself with whatever is going on at that lab. Even if something looks suspicious, unless Very is in immediate danger, stand down."

"Copy that." With that halfhearted confirmation, Steady headed to the airfield. A little time in his Cessna would clear his head.

CHAPTER THIRTY

New York City
August 10

A lonso Mitchell stood at attention in the doorway to Krill's office and waited. Mitchell had known Armand Krill for nearly thirty years and was practiced in when to move and speak. When Krill looked up, Mitchell stepped fully into the room.

"Verity Valentine, your granddaughter Amelia Krill, is a model employee. She arrives early and leaves late. She is well-liked by the entire staff and regularly updates her superiors on her research."

"But," Krill prompted.

"But, she's raising some red flags with me," Mitchell said.

"How so?"

"For one thing, as you know, she has permission to work remotely. She was granted that because she started working before the lab was fully operational, and her supervisor Dr. Kemp, simply allowed her to keep virtual access to the lab because she works odd hours and quite obsessively. Strange decision on Kemp's part, but not unreasonable."

Krill nodded in a get-on-with-it fashion.

"While she can't link to the lab intranet from her external laptop, she can remove data on a flash drive without being questioned."

Krill laced his fingers and drummed the pads of his thumbs. "Have Kemp revoke her access. Nothing leaves that lab without my express consent."

Mitchell continued, "Two nights ago, I followed her to a coffee shop outside Beaufort, South Carolina."

"What was she doing there?"

"Meeting a friend."

"Go on," Krill said.

"The friend was a classmate in her Master's program. He is also the head of research at ProbeX Labs. Verity gave him a flash drive. I suspect it's the information on Mobilify she downloaded from the lab archive."

Krill summoned his assistant.

"Yes, Mr. Krill?"

"Bring me a complete workup on ProbeX Labs."

"Certainly."

When the assistant closed the door behind her, Mitchell said, "I'll continue to monitor her activity."

"That won't be necessary. I have something else I want you to look into."

With almost ceremonial purpose, Krill opened the desk's center drawer, withdrew a letter-sized envelope, and held it out. Mitchell flipped up the unsealed flap and skimmed the pages. "The Vitruvian Society?"

"That's everything I know about it."

Mitchell returned Krill's notes to the envelope and slid it into his pocket. "You've mentioned this group over the years."

"Yes, my great-grandfather was a founding member. He brought my grandfather into the fold in the nineteen forties."

"Right around the time his business took off."

"That's no coincidence. Vitruvian paved the way." Krill tapped his lips, a faraway look in his eyes. "I thought the group had disbanded, but it seems I may have been mistaken."

Mitchell cast a skeptical glance. "You think this syndicate still exists?"

"With good reason. Look into it. Information will be difficult, if not impossible, to find. My expectations are low."

"Well then, I look forward to exceeding them."

When Krill remained silent, Mitchell asked, "Any instructions regarding Ms. Valentine and ProbeX Labs?"

"I'll handle that."

Krill dismissed him by rotating his desk chair back to his monitor and returning to work. Confident Krill comprehended the gravity of the situation, Mitchell turned and left.

CHAPTER THIRTY-ONE

South Island, South Carolina
August 10

Very wandered out of the house and down the driveway to the large oak by the road where she usually began her stretches before her morning run. Tied to the fence post next to the tree was a leash. At the end of it was a dog sitting obediently and watching her approach. A big blonde tail thwapped the ground, and Very didn't hesitate to rub the fur behind the animal's ears.

"Hey, buddy. What are you doing out here?"

Very's hands scratched around the collar, and she felt a rolled piece of paper tucked into the tags. She pulled it out and read the note.

Dear Ms. Valentine (May I call you Very?),

I am a yellow lab named Matilda. (You may call me Tilly.) Steady Lockhart is my human.

I am deaf.

Below the sentence was the dog's name spelled out with little hands.

Charlie Bishop brought me to Beaufort when I could no longer serve my country. Steady thought you would take me along on your runs because I am only three, and I need a lot of exercise. My commands are simple and easy to learn. Steady left a book for you.

Very looked around and spotted the pocket-sized book leaning up against the tree trunk.

Steady said you don't believe in love, but I'd wager you already love me. I'm pretty fucking lovable.

Very shook her head at the sky. "You big dope."

She continued reading. *Please don't call Mr. Lockhart a big dope. He knows what he's doing. Now let's get going.*

P.S. Steady left a bag of my favorite kibble on your deck with a new bowl and a Tempur Pedic dog bed. In case we want to have girly sleepovers.

P.P.S. He also left a chew toy that makes an annoying squeak.

P.P.P.S. What are we waiting for?

Very dropped down beside Tilly and hugged her. "Hey, sweet girl."

When the dog didn't respond, she picked up the book, found what she was looking for, and signed, *"Good girl."* Then, she held the leash up in the universal signal for walk.

Tilly stood with her entire backside wagging. Very took another few minutes to study the basic commands, then jogged off down the road with Tilly at her side.

It was a mild day with a nice breeze coming off the ocean, but even after staying in the shade for most of the run, Very was a sweaty mess, and Tilly was panting. She climbed Steady's exterior steps and knocked on the front door. When no one answered, she entered the house.

Steady's home was suitably nautical, decorated in navy blue and white. There was a ship in a bottle on the mantle, and the newly redone kitchen was surprisingly clean. To her right, there was a cozy office. She released Tilly from her leash, and the dog bounded over to her water dish, but Very stayed where she was and stared into that small room.

Her feet propelled her toward something she was sure she didn't want to see. On a wooden table opposite the desk was a series of grainy photos and printed information. There were candids of her coworkers, Micah, the Head of

Security, and even Dr. Kemp. He had photos of random employees and tour attendees, even one of Annette, the bubble-headed PR woman. She pushed around the papers on the table. Steady had made notes on each person, their background, their job, their home address.

Spinning around, Very sprinted to the stairs. She wasn't angry. She was terrified.

Steady stood shirtless in front of the bathroom mirror and lathered his face. He had been so eager to speak to Nathan, he had forgotten to shave. He lifted the razor to his cheek when the bedroom door flew open and banged against the wall.

"Steady, what the fuck?"

He grabbed the towel hanging around his neck and wiped the shaving cream from his face. "Darlin'..."

"Don't *Darlin'* me! You have got to stop poking around at Parasol. You're going to ruin everything!"

"What do you mean?"

"I mean, there are things going on, things about to happen, and your interference is going screw everything up."

Her words lost steam as she scanned his naked body. Those hazel eyes turned forest green, betraying her interest. Steady invaded her space. "Tell me what's going on, Very."

She looked torn but replied, "I can't."

He cupped her cheek. "You can trust me, you know."

"I know." She rested her forehead on her bare chest. "I know," she repeated. "It's not my decision to make."

So she was working with someone on whatever scheme she had devised. It didn't really matter. He would do anything to ease the fear coursing through her. Steady pulled her close and wrapped Very in his arms. "Okay, Darlin'." He tipped her head up and kissed her forehead, then her cheek. Steady spoke into her ear. "I'll back off. But I'm here if you need me."

Very whispered, "I do need you."

Steady fell to his knees and pulled her running shorts and cotton panties down her legs. His hands traveled up her tan thighs. On a deep inhale, he placed a provocative kiss at her bare apex.

He growled, "I like you dirty, but you need to relax." Steady stood and led her into the bathroom. After starting the shower, he peeled the sports bra off and freed her perfect breasts. He cupped and kissed them, then pulled her under the spray. Steady took his time washing the sweat and sand from her body. By the time he finished shampooing her hair and sponging her back, he was on fire. He turned Very to face him and nearly staggered. Droplets of water clung to her lashes, and her hazel eyes were hungry. He had waited to do what he wanted long enough.

After wrapping Very in a towel, he lifted her into his arms and carried her to the bed. Removing a condom from the nightstand, he came down over her. She urged him forward with her heels at the small of his back. Steady cradled her jaw with one hand and guided himself to her waiting body. "Keep those walls down, Darlin', and hang on."

With a soft kiss and a reassuring grip on her body, Steady pushed forward with a powerful thrust. She buried her face in the bend of his neck and encouraged him with her hands on his back. He buried himself inside her, and Very muffled her moan in his bare chest. He waited, processing this feeling. Then she looked up at him. And the world stopped turning.

Her face was a glorious mix of surprise and happiness and awe–not of him, of them. He knew it because he was sure his expression reflected the same thing back to her.

She tilted her hips and said, "Give it to me, Lockhart."

"That's my girl."

Steady surged forward again and again, swallowing her gasps with his lips over hers. With deliberate, powerful strokes, he moved inside her, his hips pistoning in a rhythm that had her body tightening around him. He was awash in sensation. Very's eyes were a firework display of green and gold, her hands squeezing his back and her soft sounds, a measure of what drove her wild. Steady was lost. And he was found.

"You with me, Darlin'?"

"I'm with you."

Stars exploded behind his eyes, and Steady's body shook like he was standing on a fault line. He muttered, "Fuck, fuck, fuck," before collapsing onto her soft body.

Very watched as Steady disposed of the condom, settled into the bed, and tucked her under his arm. She had come to think of that soft nook beneath his muscled bicep as her spot.

In her first year of college, Very had a Chemistry professor who began the class by telling the students that when two substances come together and produce a reaction, they are forever altered. Their goal as chemists would be to understand how that happens and why. She couldn't explain what had just occurred between them, but Very knew it changed everything.

She lifted her head from his chest to find Steady staring as he smoothed back her hair with his big palm.

"You okay?"

"Okay?" she breathed. "Definitely not. I'm not sure there's a word to describe what I am."

Her body shook gently from his chuckle.

Very cupped his beautiful face in her hands. He looked young and vulnerable. He looked hopeful. She smiled. "I know you're a one-and-done kind of guy, but please tell me we can do that again." It wasn't lost on Very that this was the type of comment she might make if she were trying to scare him off, but this time she meant it.

Steady kissed her, and a bolt of arousal warmed her blood.

"I think I could do that every day for the rest of my life," he said.

The declaration startled them both. "I think you're sex drunk."

He didn't take the out. "Maybe."

A sunbeam warmed the sheet, and Very looked up. "That's some skylight." Half the ceiling was transparent.

"Added it when I had the roof replaced. The front of the house has an attic, but I get to see the stars. Oh, and check this out." He fiddled with something on the wall, and the skylight glass darkened.

"You and the sky," she said.

"What do you mean?"

"I just notice whenever you're quiet or thinking, you look up at the sky."

"I guess that makes sense. All I ever really wanted to do was fly."

"Really?" She couldn't hide her disbelief. Very hated airplanes.

He continued, undeterred, "I keep a little Cessna at the airfield. I was there this morning–every Saturday like clockwork. Best part of my week is being up in the clouds.

"If you say so."

"What? You don't like to fly?"

"I've only been on a plane once. Coming home from college for Christmas one year. It was a puddle jumper from Charlottesville to New York in a storm. I nearly crawled into the lap of the guy sitting next to me."

"I doubt he minded," Steady commented.

"He minded. I screamed like I was on fire. Never again."

"We'll get you back up there, Darlin'. I promise you'll love it."

Very hid her smile. She couldn't explain it, but she absolutely loved it when he called her Darlin'. Maybe it was that he only did it when they were flirting, or maybe she liked how it hinted at his Southern roots. Or perhaps it was that she had never heard Steady call anyone else by that particular nickname. Maybe he had. Maybe he did it all the time, but Very chose to believe that this particular endearment was for her alone.

Very kissed his neck. "We'll see."

"It's the safest way to travel, you know." The backs of his fingers skimmed over her breast, then moved lower at a maddeningly slow pace.

She spread her legs, encouraging him. "I know, but it doesn't make me feel any better."

Steady rolled to the side, putting her body under him. "Darlin', there are other ways to fly."

And with that, he set to work making her soar.

Very opened her eyes. It had to be past two. They had spent half the day in bed. Steady was snoring softly, wrapped around her like a blanket. Even in his sleep, he was protecting her. That was Steady–always more concerned about other people than himself. She turned to her back to watch him sleep in the midday light, the ache between her legs reminding her of how thoroughly Steady had loved her. She knew long before she ever kissed him that he would be wicked in bed: giving, attentive, *endowed*.

It had been an overload of feeling–Steady above her, below her, inside her. In the safety of Steady's arms, Very could no longer deny the truth surrounding her.

She was falling in love with him.

Something clicked in her mind. Steady was nosing around in her business because he cared, because he wanted to keep her safe. Very needed to face facts; she had gone over Niagara Falls in a barrel and was trying to fight the current. It was time to adopt Steady's mantra and go with the flow. She trusted Steady. The only way to proceed was to get him on board. It was time to tell him the truth.

Very would have to speak to Darwin and explain the situation. For the longest time, it had just been the two of them, planning and waiting. Very was sure of one thing, however. If she confessed her scheme to Steady, he would move heaven and earth to help.

Tomorrow she would text Darwin, and then she would tell Steady everything.

CHAPTER THIRTY-TWO

New York City
August 11

Armand Krill's greenhouse was a small, pristine structure at the back of the home just off the solarium. Every day, without fail, Armand visited this sanctuary to check on his vast array of orchids. Monitoring the soil moisture and trimming browning leaves was a meditation for Krill. He took great pride in the exotic blooms.

Krill didn't bother to look up when his houseman announced the arrival of Carson Kemp, the Primary Investigator at the Ridgeland lab. Kemp entered the room, tripping on the threshold and nearly barrelling into Krill.

"Your flowers are beautiful," Kemp said.

"Orchids," Krill corrected.

"Yes, of course. Orchids. I send one to my mother every year on her birthday. She's in assisted living. Flowers, er orchids," he amended, "really brighten up the place."

Krill's tolerance for chitchat was less than zero. When Kemp touched the petals of a delicate dendrobium, Krill nearly stabbed his hand with the clippers.

After setting the tool on the work table and removing his gardening gloves, Krill got to the matter at hand. "There is an issue with one of your scientists."

Kemp's bushy eyebrows shot up. "Verity? Still?"

Krill confirmed, "Verity. Still."

"How would you like it handled?" Kemp asked.

"As you know, I like to keep my employees 'best interests at heart."

"Of course," Kemp agreed. If there was a hint of skepticism in his voice, Krill ignored it.

"My concern is that the stress of the job is getting to her."

Kemp started to argue. "I don't think her work is particularly stressful–"

Krill cut him off with a lifted hand. "A routine mental health check is in order."

"I can have her check in with wellness this week," Kemp said.

"First thing Monday, Kemp. Issues such as these need to be addressed immediately."

"Of course."

Krill grabbed the misting bottle from the window sill and spritzed the blossoms. Kemp correctly interpreted the action as a dismissal and turned to go.

Krill halted him. "Oh, and Kemp?"

"Yes, sir."

"Please make sure any old samples of Mobilify have been destroyed."

"All research samples are disposed of after testing."

Krill's thumb froze on the plunger mid-spray, and he slowly turned to Kemp, his expression blank.

Kemp immediately rephrased, "I will double-check, sir. Triple-check." He backed out of the room, turned, and hurried off.

Irritated, Krill returned to gardening.

He tended the flowers with less care than usual, casting a glance back at the doorway where Kemp had fled. He understood the man's apprehension; Kemp had been around a long time and, no doubt, saw the handwriting on the wall. Krill was going to send Verity to the Hale Center.

Krill reasoned that he could have reassured Kemp he had no intention of harming Verity Valentine, that he simply needed to ensure the meddling woman didn't interfere with the launch of Mobilify. Seventy-two hours under lock and key in the psychiatric facility would ensure Verity, or rather Amelia, did nothing to cast doubt on the validity of Mobilify. His granddaughter was a devious little thing. Krill nearly smiled. He was more devious.

None of that was information that the old scientist needed to know. Kemp was a cog in the wheel, paid to do a job. That was all.

Krill inspected a bloom as he recalled little Amelia Krill. She had been a precocious child, always asking questions. The young woman had been poisoned with idealism and storybook ethics. Despite this adversarial start to their reunion, Krill was convinced he could sway Verity Valentine's resolve.

One way or another.

PART THREE

Roping the Mark

CHAPTER THIRTY-THREE

New York City
August 12

The midtown offices of Parasol Pharmaceuticals were discreetly housed on the upper ten floors of a nondescript skyscraper bordering Rockefeller Center. The fortieth-floor lobby was an expanse of white marble. A semicircular reception desk sat in the center under the gleaming silver ParaPharm logo: two back-to-back Ps under a stylized umbrella. The company slogan: *Curing and Caring,* was written below in bold lettering.

Today Krill was holding a small press conference for industry media and select guests. The upcoming release of Mobilify was being announced to an audience comprised of medical professionals, including Carson Kemp from the Ridgeland lab, journalists, and local politicians. Krill would not be doing the talking. They had a dashing marketing executive with a toothpaste smile for this precise purpose. As the CEO, he would simply stand on the stage and nod approvingly at the announcement. The PR witch had requested that he smile—the nerve.

The press conference, however, was not foremost in his thoughts today. He had another reason for coming into the office, which required an in-person meeting with members of his executive board, several of whom he would never dream of inviting into his home.

Krill seldom came into the office, the rarity of his presence apparent in the surprised and fawning faces of the executives and their minions as he marched down the hall. Armand Krill paid no mind to the immaculate space, nor did he acknowledge the attractive and perfectly groomed receptionist who sat eager for affirmation or instruction. He strode across the lobby and through the double doors a second assistant held open.

Only one man ventured out to address him, Arthur Drabek, his CFO. Well aware of Krill's aversion to chitchat, Drabek skipped the small talk and fell into step beside Krill.

"Armand, the prospectus has been drafted, and all the materials are on the conference table in your office."

"Good. Where are Stanley and Wainwright?" Walter Stanley, the in-house head of Mergers and Acquisitions, was the third attendee, and Wainwright, the Director of Compliance, was the fourth man.

"Waiting in your outer office," Drabek replied, keeping pace.

Krill was in an exceptionally good mood. Mobilify was set to launch. The drug Parasol manufactured that would treat Mobilify's common side effect was readily available, and he was about to quash the small uprising within his ranks.

He didn't speak the language of compliments, but nonetheless, Krill found himself uttering a single word of encouragement, as much for himself as his underlings.

"Excellent."

A lackey pulled open the massive doors to his outer office with a flourish, and Krill swam in the image of the young man tossing rose petals on the carpet as he strode past. He was the king in this domain, and today he was expanding his empire.

CHAPTER THIRTY-FOUR

Parasol Labs
Ridgeland, South Carolina
August 12

Today was the day. Rohit's birthday provided the perfect distraction. The team gathered in the break room mid-morning, the standard time for their work celebrations. This area and the bathrooms were the two places in the lab without security cameras.

Rohit sat at the round lunch table as the team gathered around him. Very lit the candles on the cake at the counter while other researchers placed gift cards and small presents on the table. Malcomb Everett stood in the doorway wearing a forced smile and looking put out. Carson Kemp hurried in just as Very turned with the cake. As discordant voices began the song, Kemp set a small cookie tin on the table and said, "My wife's homemade peanut brittle." Then he joined in the cacophony.

When the cake had been eaten and the conversation completed, her coworkers returned to work amid well-wishes and pats on the back. Rohit carried the small passel of gifts to his desk while Very returned the cake to the fridge, then withdrew the special six-pack of her favorite microbrew. A bright pink bow topped one of the two center bottles. She carried it to the desk and set it with the rest of the haul.

Rohit looked up from his computer and poked his chin toward the beer. "Who's that from?"

"Me. You can pre-game for the concert tonight." Very grinned.

Rohit shook his head. "Awesome, thanks. Don't think I don't notice it's *your* favorite beer."

"And I'll be taking one for later," she said, slipping the bottle with the bow from the six-pack.

Pulling another bottle from the cardboard, Rohit toasted her. "Is it too early to start now?"

Very laughed, and Jeffrey delivered his signature flat look from the adjacent desk.

"Aww, come on, Jeffrey. You know you love me," Very goaded.

He licked the frosting from the plastic fork and stood. "If you need me, I'll be looking at mouse liver cross sections." After tossing the small plate and utensil, Jeffrey stalked to the lab at the back of the room.

Rohit started to speak, then sealed his lips. Very turned to see Dr. Kemp standing over her desk.

"Verity, a word."

"Sure thing," she replied as Kemp retreated. Very set the bottle beside her computer monitor and gave Rohit a wide-eyed look of mock terror. Her friend chuckled, and Very dutifully headed to her boss's office.

Very stood in the doorway and knocked on the jamb. "You wanted to see me?"

Her boss didn't look up from whatever he was reading on his computer. "Verity, yes, it's time for your annual psych eval."

"That's…sudden," Very said.

"No, no, it's all quite routine." Kemp fumbled through the files on his desk. "Just head on over to the wellness building."

"I have a mountain of work. Will it take long?" she asked.

"Hopefully, you'll be back to work this afternoon."

"Why, hopefully?"

"Hmm?" Kemp looked up from his screen.

"You said *hopefully* I'll be back to work," Very clarified.

Kemp took a sip of coffee, then stared into the mug as he spoke. "Just a figure of speech, dear."

"Okay." She started to leave, then turned back. "Oh, I had a breakthrough with that allergy drug. I sent you my findings and the reports from the testing center."

"We're onto human trials?" Kemp asked.

"Yes, first round. It's looking promising."

"All right. I'll take a look when I have a minute."

With a little salute, Very returned to her desk to fill out the forms, a strange cocktail of trepidation and excitement fizzing in her blood.

CHAPTER THIRTY-FIVE

Ridgeland, South Carolina
August 12

Alonso Mitchell leaned forward in his chair, looking closer at the security feed. Despite Krill's instructions to investigate the Vitruvian Society, Mitchell had returned to South Carolina. His instincts told him he needed to be close to the lab. He watched the monitor as Verity Valentine walked across the room and entered her boss's office. He toggled between cameras, noting the beer bottle blocking the button camera he had placed on her lamp.

He switched to the camera in Kemp's office. There was no audio, but he could read the body language as clearly as if there were subtitles. Kemp was uncomfortable, fumbling around on his desk. He knocked over a capped water bottle, righted it, then spoke to Verity.

Mitchell switched to a different camera angle and zoomed in on Kemp's monitor: a memo for a psych eval. Interesting. Mitchell put the pieces together immediately, despite not having been informed.

Krill wanted Verity off the board, at least until Mobilify was released, and he was using one of his old reliable methods to do it. Krill was going to send Verity to the place where her mother died, the Hale Center.

Krill wouldn't harm her; she was too valuable. A blood relative. Krill learned his lesson about eliminating his heirs when he had his own daughter murdered. No, sending Verity to Hale was the easy way to ensure Mobilify was released without a hitch. The last thing Krill needed was a rogue scientist shouting about side effects and price gouging.

Verity stood at Kemp's desk. She looked surprised but not shocked or panicked. Mitchell squinted at the black-and-white image of the young scientist. Could she have expected this move? Highly unlikely. And yet, Mitchell knew about Verity's mother–he knew every detail. If she was looking for proof...

Mitchell sat back, locked his fingers behind his head, and ran through various scenarios. He had the unshakable feeling that Krill had just been out-smarted. Krill was a brilliant tactician. Then again, he wasn't a surgeon; he was a butcher.

Krill was no fool, but neither was Ms. Valentine. Mitchell looked at the monitor and watched her thread her fingers in an obvious nervous gesture. However, the rest of her body language betrayed her true feelings. She was bouncing on the balls of her feet and leaning toward her boss; she looked... *eager.* Could she have anticipated Krill's move? Planned for it?

Holstering his sidearm, Mitchell scooped his keys from the table by the door. Krill may have thought he was handling the young woman, but Verity Valentine may have just outmaneuvered them all. The question was, had Krill stopped her in time? Had he prevented her from executing any additional espionage with Mobilify? Mitchell jumped into his car and headed to the lab.

CHAPTER THIRTY-SIX

Parasol Labs
Ridgeland, South Carolina
August 12

D r. Theodora Baker was reed-thin and pointy with the quality and appearance of a heron. Her dark hair was secured in a practical bun, and she wore round, tortoiseshell glasses that occasionally slid down her nose. Her smile was effortless and insincere as she gestured Very into the office.

Very entered the well-appointed room in a separate building on the Parasol campus. Through the window, she could see her lab across the compound. "Do you normally make house calls, well, work calls, I guess, to the satellite offices?"

Dr. Baker resettled her glasses on the bridge of her nose and sat in the armchair opposite the couch where Very had perched.

"Verity. That's an interesting name," Dr. Baker began as she scrolled through something on her tablet.

"It means truth," Very said.

"I'm aware," Dr. Baker replied without looking up.

"So, I guess I should tell you that my mental health is, um, healthy. Super healthy, in fact."

"I see you've been arrested twice." Dr. Baker looked up then.

"Well, yes. That's not new info. I disclosed it before I was hired. Stupid really. One was an animal rights protest—we were picketing a lab, not a Parasol lab," she chuckled. "I tried to bust in to free a bunch of bunnies."

"Yes, I see."

Then why am I explaining? Very wanted to snap, but she kept her cool. "The other time—I'm sure you have the details there. In college, at a local bar, a guy tried to slip something into my friend, Twitch's drink. I flattened him with a serving tray."

"You gave him a concussion."

"Damn right. Fucking rapist." Very shifted on the edge of the couch.

"You seem to carry a lot of rage." Dr. Baker returned her attention to the file.

"Not really. I'm basically a happy person. Just when someone tries to hurt the people I love."

Without acknowledging the explanation, Dr. Baker moved on. "Let's talk about self-harm, Verity."

Very shifted uncomfortably. "All good there."

"Where did you cut?" Dr. Baker asked.

"My thigh. I only did it a few times." Very lied, pleased Dr. Baker had discovered the tidbit Very had planted in her own personnel file.

"And yet you were hospitalized for the severity of a wound."

"I wasn't trying to kill myself or anything. I just went too deep," Very explained.

"And you were thirteen at the time?"

"Twelve. My dad got me a great therapist. She really turned things around for me."

"So you haven't felt the urge to harm yourself since?" Dr. Baker posed the question like a trap.

"Nope."

"You don't think putting yourself in dangerous situations," she tapped the screen of her tablet, "That bar fights and violent protests are a form of self-harm?"

"Well, no. I think there were extenuating circumstances for both of those incidents. I don't go out looking for bar fights."

"And yet police have been summoned on two other occasions related to incidents involving you."

Very shrugged. "Drunk guys can get aggressive."

Dr. Baker removed her glasses. "Verity, I'd like to invoke the seventy-two-hour observation you agreed to when you signed your employment contract."

"What are you talking about?"

Dr. Baker held out the tablet, and Very crossed the small space to take it. On the screen was a copy of a page of her work agreement. Her initials were next to a clause explaining that if the Parasol staff deemed it necessary, the employee must submit to a psychiatric hold at the Parasol-designated facility outside of Washington.

Verity knew of the prestigious Hale Center. "You want me to go to Virginia for three days?"

"Correct. It's routine. I'd like you to speak with the staff psychologist and ensure you're in good mental health."

"That's really not necessary. I feel great, mentally speaking."

"I'm afraid it's non-negotiable. We will leave at once."

"And if I refuse?"

"Your employment will be terminated."

Very sank down on the couch. "I guess I don't have a choice."

Dr. Baker leaned forward. "There's another reason I'd like you to accompany me. Mr. Krill feels you may be a candidate for work at my lab at The Center. You'll go through the standard, in-depth psychological testing, but you will also tour our lab and see if my work piques your interest."

"That sounds pretty cool."

Very's relief must have been palpable because Dr. Baker aimed for what Very was sure was a reassuring smile and said, "This isn't some scene in a bad horror movie, Verity. A burly orderly isn't waiting outside to inject you with a sedative. Parasol values their employees. We want to ensure you are at your best in a whole-health sense."

"Yes, of course. I just hate to miss work."

"I'll make sure Dr. Kemp is informed. This is all fairly standard."

"I'll need to pack a bag."

"That won't be necessary. The Hale Center is fully equipped. Everything you need for a short stay will be provided."

An orderly appeared at the door holding a small tray. Dr. Baker took the paper cup and crossed the room to stand over Very. "I noted your aerophobia." She extended her hand.

Very eyed the two yellow pills. "Oh, uh, no thanks."

Dr. Baker released a patronizing sigh. "Verity, I am a medical doctor. Illnesses of the mind are illnesses, and like any other ailment, there are medications that treat them. A person with diabetes would not refuse insulin, nor should a person who suffers from anxiety refuse a sedative."

Very accepted the offering.

"I'll be right back." Dr. Baker stood and left the room.

Very saw the act for what Dr. Baker intended, a show of trust. Very could take the medication or not.

However, the camera in the ceiling belied the doctor's good intentions.

Without hesitation, she lifted the paper cup to her lips and tipped it back. She thought about texting an update or an apology. Darwin had to know she had hoped for this little deviation in the plan. In the end, she decided making contact was too risky. Plus, she knew Steady was out there. It was almost as if his energy shifted the air around him, which was absurd scientifically. Nevertheless, for whatever reason, Very seemed attuned to his presence. Steady was watching. Hopefully close enough to see what was happening but far enough away not to interfere.

Dr. Baker exited the room and met her nurse in the hall. Without breaking stride, she passed off the iPad and proceeded to the small security room. She opened the door to find the guard, as instructed, had the monitor displaying the room she had just left. The man vacated his seat, but Dr. Baker remained standing. She watched as Verity took the pills and chased the sedative with the bottled water that had been placed on the table. Verity crumpled the empty cup and dropped it in the pocket of her lab coat.

Brushing past the nurse and the guard, Dr. Baker ordered, "Have the driver bring the car around. We'll leave immediately."

Steady sat in his jeep on the shoulder of the main road and looked through the high-powered binoculars. Beside him in the passenger seat, Tilly eyed a pair of frolicking squirrels in the adjacent field. Very had just walked into a building marked "Wellness."

Was she sick?

There were no internal cameras in that building, or if there were, Twitch couldn't access them, so Steady sat and waited.

Finally, he clocked movement at the door of the Wellness building. He grabbed the binoculars and watched as a man in green scrubs helped a wobbly Very into the back of a car. A moment later, a brisk woman in a suit followed. It had to be the same woman Steady's pals at the airfield had seen arrive via private jet.

Steady called Nathan with an update, then texted Herc and Chat for backup. He also sent a message to his buddy at the airfield. He started the jeep and floored it, leaving a curtain of dust and gravel in his wake.

Observe-and-report wasn't cutting it. Time to get creative.

CHAPTER THIRTY-SEVEN

Parasol Pharmaceuticals Jet
August 12

Theodora Baker looked past her patient's sleeping form to the landscape outside the plane as it circled the private airfield. This was her domain.

The Hale Center sat nestled in the rolling hills of Virginia horse country. Although built in 1977, the sprawling Colonial Estate looked as though it had punctuated the landscape for nearly as long as nearby Mount Vernon.

Founded by a team of doctors from elite Universities, the Center was designed to modernize mental health treatment. The Center's founder theorized that by offering other medical services, including cosmetic surgery and physical rehabilitation, the institute could destigmatize psychiatric treatment—as well as bankroll research and pro bono services.

To this day, The Center remains the bellwether for in-patient mental health treatment. Operating with an eight-figure endowment, accrued primarily through the donations of Parasol Pharmaceuticals, doctors at Hale treated patients with issues ranging from mild anxiety disorders to profound psychosis.

Despite the Hale Center's mission to minister to any and all that needed assistance, over the years, the facility had morphed into a mental health fiefdom with a distinct caste system. The main building, a three-story Georgian brick estate with a columned facade and dormered rooftop, boasted amenities exceeding any luxury hotel. Clients—doctors and staff never referred to them as patients—could dine at any of the restaurants on the grounds, order an in-room massage, and use the spa. Staff on hand included therapists (talk, behavioral, addiction, divorce, hug, pet, and food), sleep coaches, personal trainers, aestheticians, equestrian trainers, yoga instructors, meditation guides, psychiatrists, and nutritionists. The main building welcomed guests, including Oscar-winning actors, billionaire entrepreneurs, professional athletes, and two former First Ladies.

The rear patio and pool area were bordered by two cloistered walkways that extended for over one hundred yards and led to the stables, golf course, and walking trails.

Half a mile away and connected only by a service road at the perimeter of the property was another treatment area: the PDC building–treatment and long-term housing for Psychotic, Delusional, and Clinically Insane patients.

There were no pleasant euphemisms in this section of the Hale Center. Patients were patients, and their ailments were not "conditions" or "issues;" they were illnesses. The facility was not a "treatment center" or a "wellness retreat."

It was a prison.

This was the realm of Doctor Theodora Baker. It was the only private hospital of its kind in the country—an entirely self-funded facility dedicated to treating only the most extreme mental illness. The vast majority of funds went to this secure area that paying clients never knew existed.

The hospital's goal was to cure severe mental illness and rehabilitate those with diseases of the mind. Dr. Baker's noble intention, as outlined in the hospital's mission statement, was "through traditional and alternative methods of treatment, restore healthy cognitive function and create productive, moral members of society."

Theodora Baker was a beacon of promise in the psychiatric community. She dedicated nearly every waking hour to her cause. She worked tirelessly to expand mental health treatment for veterans and the homeless. Over holidays and on her vacation time, Dr. Baker flew to war-torn countries to treat soldiers with PTSD and victims of violence. An entire room in her residence housed her humanitarian and medical awards.

Her staff was her family. Her patients were her children. Dr. Baker's selfless dedication to her practice had earned her the nickname "Saint Theodora," a moniker that she patently refused to allow anyone to use in her presence.

As expected, the recovery rate at The PDC was low, and the death rate was high. Patients were lost to suicide and violence and occasionally brain tumors or illnesses. If the number of patients who died in a given period was out of the ordinary, no one in the government or the larger medical community batted an eye. Because when dealing with the kinds of cases Dr. Baker willingly took on, there was no "ordinary."

As a result, Dr. Theodora Baker had created her own unregulated testing facility with an unlimited supply of human guinea pigs.

There was no debating the fact that Dr. Baker had a god complex; she, however, would insist that she was a benevolent god, that the end justified the means. The breakthroughs in the coming years would place her squarely in contention for a Nobel Prize.

She had complete autonomy and conducted experiments with the aid of her most trusted and like-minded associates. There was only a small price to pay in exchange for this ideal work environment. She, on rare occasions, was forced to do the bidding of her benefactor, Armand Krill. There was only a small price to pay in exchange for this ideal work environment.

Krill had problems from time to time that she helped him eliminate. Only certain people were candidates for Dr. Baker's services. If Krill had other messes and other means of cleaning them up, that was none of Dr. Baker's concern.

She recalled the first time she had done the bidding of Armand Krill. Patricia Krill. After working with her father for three years at Parasol Pharmaceuticals, Patricia took it upon herself to put a stop to the long list of unethical practices taking place at the company. She had slowly and carefully accumulated damning evidence; she just hadn't done it carefully enough.

When her perfidy was discovered, Patricia Krill took her young daughter, Amelia, and ran. For a year, Patricia Krill remained hidden, working as a nurse in a small town. But eventually, her father's hounds tracked her down.

Twenty years ago, Krill brought his own daughter to the Hale Center, claiming she was violent, self-destructive, and delusional. After weeks of trying to bring Patricia Krill to heel, Dr. Baker called Armand to explain that the experimental medication they had given his daughter had triggered a stroke, and she was not expected to survive. Krill had acknowledged the information by hanging up the phone. Three days later, Patricia Krill died.

Theodora Baker neither knew nor cared what Armand Krill's long-term plans were for this young woman. For now, she had been instructed to keep Verity Valentine at the Hale Center. She would process the data when it became available.

Verity Valentine would either become a research assistant or research. Dr. Baker was equally pleased with either.

Leaving Verity to the orderlies, Dr. Baker stepped down the airstairs, where she was met by her admin, an efficient young woman named Rose. Dr. Baker neither liked nor disliked people; they simply performed a function in her life. However, she thought she would have affection for her quiet, capable assistant if she were capable of forming attachments.

Rose handed her a tablet. "I'm sorry, Dr. Baker."

"When did this happen?"

"Early this morning. The patient John-381 suffered a massive stroke forty-three minutes after administering the second dose. He died seventeen minutes later."

"I see." Dr. Baker returned the tablet to Rose and said, "Record the results in the file."

"Of course. And patient Jane-62 is ready for the next phase of testing."

Dr. Baker sat in the passenger seat of the golf cart while Rose climbed behind the wheel. "Excellent. We can begin after you get Ms. Valentine settled in her room."

Rose stepped on the gas. "Will she be a Jane patient?"

Dr. Baker glanced over her shoulder as the orderly carried a still-sleeping Verity off the jet. "Undetermined."

CHAPTER THIRTY-EIGHT

Parasol Labs
Ridgeland, South Carolina
August 12

Micah, the Head of Security at the Parasol Labs, sat behind the desk in his cramped office and monitored the surveillance cameras as employees filtered out of the building. He paid particular attention to the people leaving the second-floor lab where Verity Valentine worked. It was impossible to see if they were doing anything suspicious, especially because Micah didn't know what qualified. He also knew if he missed something, it would be his head. Micah certainly wouldn't tell Mr. Krill he had returned to Ms. Valentine's beach house in a second attempt to surveil her and been chased off again. He'd settle for making careful observations at work.

Dr. Kemp left first. Micah checked his watch. Four o'clock was early for Kemp, so Micah made a note. An hour later, Verity's deskmates, Rohit and Jeffrey, came out together and then parted ways. Micah checked off each lab worker as they left the building. Malcomb Everett was the last one out. He was checking his designer watch and hurrying to his Tesla. Micah watched the sleek car exit the lot. He'd love to have a ride like that someday. He scanned the remaining cars, imagining himself behind the wheel of the luxury models. That's when he spotted Mitchell.

Micah couldn't suppress the shiver that ran down his spine. He didn't know exactly what Mitchell did for Armand Krill, but he knew it was off the books and probably illegal. Micah continued to watch the security feed as Mitchell passed the receptionist on duty at the entrance, took the stairs to the second floor, and walked down the hall to the lab. Micah spun his chair to check another monitor as Mitchell swiped his access card and entered. Micah noticed Mitchell was watching himself on the security video through his phone, occasionally disappearing from view, wandering into blind spots, and changing the camera coverage.

Mitchell left the main room and went down to the storage facility. After checking the sample refrigerator, he charged back up the steps. For a long minute, Mitchell stood over Verity Valentine's desk with his back to the cameras, just staring. Then Mitchell looked directly into the lens, his expression so intense, Micah rolled his chair back a foot. Jesus, the guy freaked him out. It was Micah's job to watch the monitors; he was doing nothing wrong. Then again, maybe it was time for his break.

Mitchell climbed into his car and called Armand Krill.

"She's not working alone. I think a sample of the earlier version of Mobilify has been removed, and unless I miss my guess, it's being delivered to Ms. Valentine's contact at ProbeX labs."

"I see," Krill said.

"Do you want me to intervene?"

"That won't be necessary, Mitchell. Stand down."

"Sir..."

Krill's response was a whipcrack. "I'll handle it, Mitchell. Get back to New York. You need to focus on the other matter."

Mitchell squeezed his eyes closed. The Vitruvian Society. Krill was obsessed.

"Understood." Mitchell paused. "And the sample?"

"I don't like repeating myself, Mitchell." The call ended.

Alonso Mitchell tossed his phone onto the empty passenger seat and started the car. He assured himself that Armand Krill had something up his sleeve. He always did.

CHAPTER THIRTY-NINE

The Hale Center
August 12

Steady pulled the jet into the hangar at the Hale Center's private airfield and shut down the engines. After grabbing the uniform jacket and hat, he waved for Tilly, who was curled up in the copilot's seat. He straightened the pup's orange coat, clipped on her leash, and jogged down the airstairs where a mechanic was already beginning the post-flight check. A man with a clipboard met him halfway to the office.

"Who are you?" the man asked.

"Your regular pilot got the stomach flu. Crapped his pants on the tarmac." Steady often found a particularly graphic explanation prevented further inquiry.

Ignoring the dog, the man made a face and accepted the paperwork Steady handed him.

"Is there a place to get a burger around here?"

Making the log entry, the man didn't look up when he said, "Take a golf cart to the main building. There's a restaurant just off the lobby. Stay clear of the fenced facility." The man pointed with his pen.

With a cordial tip of his pilot's hat and a tug on the leash, Steady made his way over to the row of golf carts and zipped out of the hangar. He stopped on the path and glanced through field binoculars to the ominous fenced-off area where a slender orderly with a porn star mustache was wheeling a sleeping Very to a side entrance. While they waited for the automatic door to open, Steady watched as the man leaned down until his face was next to Very's.

And then he licked her cheek.

Steady had never in his life felt his blood boil, but as he stared through the binoculars, he wanted to blow the guy's head clean off his shoulders. Steady was confident he could make the shot from this distance, but he left the Sig in its holster. Guns blazing was not the way. Whatever was going on here was more complicated than a simple psychiatric evaluation. Beside him, Tilly growled. Steady patted her head, appreciative of the show of support.

The door buzzed open, and Very disappeared into the building. Steady continued to watch as another orderly came outside, hid behind a tree, and smoked half a cigarette. A few minutes later, two female nurses in white scrubs came out and ate at a picnic table in a small patio area. Returning the binoculars to his jacket pocket, Steady stepped on the gas and continued to the main building.

He could find what he needed in the less-secure facility.

In the early evening, wearing the scrubs he had borrowed from a supply closet, Steady hunched in the bushes outside the fenced facility and scanned the area by the side door as person after person came and went. He patted Tilly's head as she crouched beside him, also keeping watch. He was waiting for someone who bore the slightest resemblance to him and having shockingly bad luck. The door buzzed open, and a reed-thin black man and a curvy nurse wandered over to the patio.

"You've got to be kidding me," Steady muttered. Tilly put a paw over her nose, equally frustrated.

Finally, the smoker from yesterday slipped out and snuck over to the trees near where Steady waited. Dirty blond hair, just shy of six feet—close enough. Wasting no time, Steady shot him in the ass with the tranquilizer dart and watched as the man sank to the base of a large oak with the unlit cigarette dangling from his lips.

After snatching the photo ID access badge from the lanyard around his neck, Steady texted Chat and informed him of the package he had left sleeping at the base of the tree. Then, with Tilly by his side, he strolled into the building like he'd been working there for years.

CHAPTER FORTY

The Hale Center
August 12

Very opened her eyes, relieved she had been able to feign sleep for what had only been the second time in her life she had been on an airplane. Thankfully it had been a short, uneventful flight with an obviously skilled pilot. She had buried her face in the couch where they seated her and pretended to be passed out.

There was no clock in the room, but she guessed it was about seven based on the soft light in the summer sky. Very had never seen the inside of a psych ward before, which was odd considering how this institution had altered the course of her life. The room was pleasant, the walls a pale teal, the decor minimal. There was a folded patient gown on the end table, and, reasoning she had better change before someone did it for her, she snatched it up and slipped into the bathroom.

The lavatory was also as she had expected–no mirror, nothing breakable, no sharp edges. Leaving her underwear on, Very removed her blouse and work pants, folded them neatly, and set them on a small table next to a plastic bud vase with an artificial flower. She dipped her finger into the cleavage of her bra and fished out the two valium tablets she had palmed in Dr. Baker's office at the lab. Glancing around for a hiding place, Very spotted a paper cup dispenser beside the sink. She pulled out half the sleeve of cups, dropped the pills into the top one, and replaced the stack. After slipping on the green hospital gown, she stepped out into the main room, where the orderly who had licked her face was standing with a tray.

"Oh, you're awake." The disappointment in his voice made Very queasy. He had long sideburns and a narrow goatee. The neck of his scrubs revealed the edge of an elaborate tattoo. Very could see the piercing holes in his ears and nose; he must not be permitted to wear jewelry on shift.

"Yep." She strolled across the room and stood on the opposite side of the bed.

"Dinner." He set the tray holding a covered dish, a juice box, and a pudding cup on the bed. After snatching up the dessert, he tipped it her way and ran his eyes over her body. "I'll catch you later."

About an hour later, an older nurse with a kind smile appeared at the door, pushing a rolling cart filled with small paper cups. She came beside the bed, scanned Very's hospital bracelet, and handed her the pills.

"Am I allowed to ask what I'm taking?"

"Of course." The nurse retrieved a tablet from the cart and swiped the screen.

"A sedative and a multivitamin."

Nodding, Very accepted the cup and tipped it into her mouth. She had practiced this in her own bathroom many times.

"Open," the nurse instructed.

Very obeyed and showed the nurse the pills on her tongue. Then she accepted the water and drank it, opening her mouth again to prove she had swallowed them.

Satisfied, the nurse pushed the cart out the door and continued down the hall.

After settling back on the bed and holding the book to block the camera in the ceiling, she swiped her tongue along her upper gumline and pushed the pills onto her chin. She worked them onto the pillow, then adjusted herself to hide them beneath the sheet. A presence had her glancing over the book. Backlit, the silhouette of a man filled the doorway. He rested both forearms on opposite sides of the jamb.

"Better not let them catch you stashing those pills, Darlin'."

Very shot up in bed and whisper-shouted, "Steady? What the fuck? What are you doing here?"

"I believe someone requested a therapy dog. Third floor?"

It was then she noticed the leash dangling from his hand. He stepped fully into the room with Tilly in her orange assist jacket at his side. Very slid out of her bed and came to her knees beside the gorgeous pup, signing good girl with one hand and hugging her with the other. Tilly rested her head on Very's shoulder.

She looked up and, with none of the previous venom, repeated, "What are you doing here?"

Steady strolled across the room with his signature ease and sat on the bed. "Rescuing you."

She followed him and returned to her spot, mindful of the gown's open back. "I didn't ask you to help, Steady."

"I know, Darlin'."

Damn that, *Darlin'*. It got her every time. She continued to scold him, but the words had no heat. "Did I say fucking rutabaga?"

Tilly set her head on the mattress, and Very gave her a scratch.

"What? 'Steady asked.

"That night? In the bar? Our code word? Did I say your stupid, made-up vegetable?"

"It's not made up. Wait. We're doing that?"

"You have to leave. Now."

"Look, Very. I know what you're doing. I know you smuggled information out of Parasol Labs and gave it to a rival." He tipped his head from side to side in a gesture Very found annoyingly endearing. "I don't know why, but I know what. And I know they are onto you."

She moved her face a breath away from his. "That's the plan, you big dope."

"What?"

"You need to leave. I know what I'm doing," she said.

"Care to share?"

Very cast her eyes up to the ceiling. "Let's go for a walk. Tell the nurse the meds made me nauseous, and you're taking me for some fresh air."

"Copy that." He winked.

He slapped his thighs and started to stand, then stopped. "Oh, and one other thing."

"What?" she asked.

He leaned over and kissed her gently. "Hi."

His pillow-soft lips met hers for a split second, and everything melted away. He had followed her to Virginia because he thought she was in danger. Very had never wanted or needed to rely on anyone before, but she allowed the fleeting thought that if she needed Steady, he would be there.

"Hi," she whispered back when he pulled away.

"Ready for that walk with your therapy dog, Miss Valentine? You're lookin 'a little green around the gills."

Steady had somehow gotten ahold of an access pass and swiped them through the different rooms. No one questioned them as they made their way down to the main floor. They passed through a lounge and a game room and, after tapping the key card to the panel beside a set of french doors, walked out to the patio.

Very wrapped both hands around his strong arm and led him into the garden. They wandered down a winding path past azaleas and peonies. Tilly stayed at Steady's side as Very walked ahead, scouting out a quiet spot to talk.

"That hospital gown doesn't cover much. It's giving me ideas."

She made no effort to cover her backside as she spoke over her shoulder. "Me too."

They came to a clearing where an enormous statue of an angel with spread wings, blowing a trumpet to the dark sky, stood atop a marble plinth. The sculpture glowed in the fading sunlight.

Steady took her hand. "Talk to me, Darlin'."

Very traced the petals of a bloom and said, "I've been with Parasol for four years. Almost the entire time, I've been working on an arthritis drug called Mobilify that is going to market in a few days."

"Okay."

"In the first round of human testing, a couple of years ago, we tried two versions of the drug in double-blind studies against a placebo."

"No idea what you just said, but I get the gist."

"There were differences between the two versions of the drug–absorption rate, duration, stuff like that. There was also something else. One version of the drug produced a side effect that was significant but still within the acceptable levels for FDA approval."

"What side effect?" he asked.

"Blurred or double vision. The other version of the drug didn't produce that side effect and was equivalent in every other way. But Parasol proceeded with developing the version of Mobilfy that caused the vision issues."

"Why?"

"Because Parasol also happens to manufacture the most commonly pre-scribed drug to treat blurred vision."

"They're double dipping," Steady surmised.

"Exactly. It also happens to be one of Parasol's most profitable drugs."

"So, you came up with a plan to smuggle a sample of the earlier version of Mobilify to the string bean?"

"Who?" She made a face.

"The guy you met up with at the diner."

"Yes, the night you followed me."

"I wasn't the only one. One of Krill's goons was there watching you."

Steady held her face, rubbing a thumb along her cheek. It was a simple gesture, but Very took so much comfort in his touch.

She nodded. "I know. We wanted Krill to find out. It's part of our plan."

"*Our* plan?"

"I have a partner. He goes by Charles Darwin. We've been planning to bring down Krill for a long time."

"Charles Darwin, eh?"

"Yes, and I'm Marie Curie."

"Cute."

"Don't tease me. You guys all have nicknames. When I first moved here, I couldn't tell who was who."

"We have nicknames and call signs for a reason, Darlin'. On the SEALs, you never wanted to use real names over comms. The less the enemy knew, the better. So, you and Darwin have the right idea."

"He wants this as much as I do. We're going to get Armand Krill."

"So, how does this nuthouse figure in?"

Very waited a long moment before she spoke. Then, with a deep breath, she said, "The woman who runs this place, Doctor Theodora Baker? She killed my mom."

Steady eyes widened at her declaration. "Whoa."

"For years, decades really, Dr. Baker has been working on a drug to treat the most extreme mental illnesses. I've tried to look into it, but the significant research is locked down tight in the lab here."

"What kind of drug?" Steady asked.

"It's a form of neuroinhibitor intended to treat severe psychosis."

"What? Like a chemical lobotomy?"

"Well, sort of. They don't do lobotomies anymore. Even the more up-to-date surgery, a lobectomy, is extremely rare. There are drugs that exist, but they also disable normal brain function. The *benevolent* Dr. Baker is attempting to create a drug that not only inhibits psychosis but produces functional members of society."

Steady narrowed his gaze. "Do I detect a note of sarcasm in your voice?"

"Theodora Baker is the farthest thing from a humanitarian. Dr. Baker murdered my mother, and I think she did it with that drug. She calls it Comply."

"Oh, shit. Very."

"I know it's a lot. And I know it sounds crazy, but I swear, Steady, it's true."

"Very."

"Yeah?"

Steady put his hands on her shoulders. "I'm not goin 'anywhere."

Very held onto his wrists. "You're not?"

"Nope. Now tell me everything."

"Okay, but you'll have to give me a minute. I'm not used to people sticking around. I need to process."

"Well, since we're killing time." He kissed the daylights out of her. Very felt his hand slip into the open back of her gown and pull her closer.

"Now I want you." She ran a hand down his torso.

"How 'bout you get me when I get the rest of the story?" Steady said.

She leaned back an inch. "How do you know there's more?"

Steady thought about Chat's assessment of Very that night at the bar when he kissed her for the first time. *Sometimes people open their cover, so you don't read the pages.* "Because I took the time to read your pages."

She didn't look confused by his oblique comment. In fact, she seemed pleased. "That's… good to know."

Steady lifted Very by the waist and set her on the base of the angel statue. Resting his big hands on her thighs just below the hem of the flimsy gown, he waited.

"My birth name is Amelia Krill. My mother was Patricia Krill. Her father, my grandfather, is Armand Krill."

"Of Parasol Pharmaceuticals. Your target."

Very watched as Steady processed the information. After a moment, he nodded for her to continue.

"When I was little, my mom worked for Parasol. She was the oldest child, and Armand Krill was grooming her to take over the company. She noticed a disturbing pattern."

"Let me guess. Parasol was developing drugs with side effects that they also sold a pill for."

"Exactly. My mom collected evidence on a cholesterol medication that caused hair loss and a cancer drug with a side effect of a rash. In both cases, Parasol had a version of the drug that minimized the side effects but proceeded with the development of the flawed medication."

"What happened?"

"She confronted Armand Krill, her father." Very grabbed the end of her pink ponytail and held it. "Years ago, the Krill family was wealthy. Armand's great-grandfather made a fortune in the early nineteen hundreds pioneering and selling aspirin and over-the-counter painkillers. The family was part of the New York elite. Then they lost it. Krill's father was a society playboy with more money than sense, and he squandered millions on an extravagant lifestyle and bad business deals. Krill went from being a prince to a pauper. He became obsessed with rebuilding the family fortune and reputation. So when my mother threatened to ruin him," she choked on the words.

Steady finished for her. "He had his own daughter killed."

"When my mom figured out what he was planning, we ran. My mother took me, and we left in the middle of the night. We lived for a year in a small town in Delaware. One day, Krill's men found us."

"What happened?"

"My mom worked at a hospital. She was a trained nurse. She had a plan in place for if her father ever tracked her down. They came and took her while I was at the hospital daycare. She had a friend who knew the situation and got me before Krill's men could. We escaped, and I spent my childhood in Brooklyn."

"You were," Steady cleared his throat. "Safe?"

Very pressed her hand over Steady's heart. "Yes."

Steady nodded, relieved. "And your mom?"

"They brought her here. Armand claimed she was psychotic and delusional. With Krill's permission, Dr. Baker treated her with an experimental drug, and she died from a stroke. I know that experimental drug was an early version of Comply. Dr. Baker has been testing it on human patients for years. She's a modern-day Dr. Mengele. I want to find her research and prove that she's using people as human guinea pigs. This facility serves the homeless and the poor–people with no voice and no power to stop her. I'm going to stop her."

"That's risky business, Darlin'."

"You know that's my catnip," she said with a smile.

"Very, I'm serious. These people have killed for money; they've killed for power. Hell, they've killed for convenience. Let's get the fuck gone."

"I can't." Very searched his eyes. "I can't."

"I know," he sighed. "Worth a try."

Steady toyed with the hem of her gown, his fingers gently crossing the border of the fabric. She saw the desire in his eyes in the encroaching darkness.

"What about that story turned you on? The danger?" she asked as she spread her legs, allowing him access.

"You. Your honesty. Knowing the real you is the hottest thing I've ever experienced."

He caressed her thigh and smoothed the gown back into place. "Whoever's watching you has noticed your absence." He jerked his head to Tilly, standing alert and staring down the path they had followed. A moment later, timed outdoor lights illuminated the garden and patio.

"We better get back," she said.

Steady pulled her down from the statue and wrapped her in his arms. "Very, please be careful. What little I know about this place does not give me the warm fuzzies."

"Don't worry. I will."

He held her at arm's length and smiled as he said, "They better not fuck with your crazy."

"Aww, you like my lunacy?"

He fiddled with a lock of her hair. "It's growing on me."

Very scanned his face, then looked over his shoulder into the darkness. "What will you do?"

"Wait for you." He withdrew a yellow bandana from his pocket and fluttered the cloth. A moment later, Tilly appeared by his side.

"What do you mean?"

"I'm not leaving you here alone, Very. The orderly I borrowed the access pass from will be indisposed for the next few days, thanks to Chat and Herc. I'll be around."

She was afraid the threatening tears would fall if she spoke, so she nodded to the grass. After she composed herself, she said, "It's a seventy-two-hour hold."

"Then that's how long we stay. But listen, Darlin', if anything happens, if you need to get out—" He rested his hands on her shoulders. "I'm going to drop some essentials by your room later. If things get too hot, get out of there.

Head straight to the back of the property. There's an outbuilding on the other side of the service road that runs along the perimeter. I'll find you."

With a chaste kiss to her forehead and a whispered, "Be careful," Very let Steady lead her back to her room. He lingered by the door with Tilly while Very brushed her teeth and climbed into bed. She gave him a soft smile as she switched off the light.

In this most foreign and dangerous environment, Very felt safe.

CHAPTER FORTY-ONE

New York City
August 13

Brushing by well-dressed tourists and businesspeople heading out for the day, Alonso Mitchell walked through the marble-floored lobby of the Manhattan Four Seasons Hotel and rode the elevator to the sixth floor. After going through his customary routine of changing rooms–the hotel never questioned his requests when Armand Krill was footing the bill–he cleared the small living area and bedroom and took a seat at the desk.

It was ten a.m. when he booted up his laptop and accessed the security camera he had installed outside ProbeX Labs. Krill was distracted by his high-society aspirations, and Mitchell was determined to keep Krill's mind where it needed to be.

ProbeX bore no resemblance to Parasol Labs. It was nothing more than a converted warehouse in a decrepit section of Cleveland. The company had created a breakthrough asthma medication in the early 2000s but had stalled since. With venture capital money gone and generics cutting into their profits, ProbeX was barely staying afloat. There was no security to speak of, and the parking area was a rutted, unguarded lot. It had been nothing at all for his contact to install surveillance.

Resting his forearms on the desk's surface, he scrolled through the footage until the activity he was looking for caught his eye. An overnight delivery truck pulled up to the front entrance, and a uniformed man hopped out holding a small package. Before he reached the front door, the skinny guy Verity had met at the diner came out. He accepted the package from the deliveryman and disappeared back inside.

Mitchell emailed the footage to Krill–more evidence to spur his boss to action. After snagging a bottle of fancy tropical juice from the minibar, he crossed through the bedroom, heading for the shower. His thoughts strayed to Verity Valentine. What was she doing at the Hale Center? She was more of a wild card than Mitchell had expected. He'd need to keep an eye on her. He pulled out his phone and messaged Hale Center security.

Armand Krill's Manhattan home was lifeless as usual. It always saddened Mitchell that such a spectacular structure built for grand entertaining and hoards of family sat like a museum display, impeccable and haunted. In a grand castle, on a golden bed, Krill slept alone.

After making his way up the elegant staircase, Mitchell followed the hall to Krill's office, his expression grim. When Krill looked up with his signature impatient gaze, Mitchell spoke.

"The sample was delivered to ProbeX Labs this morning. I emailed you the footage. Your granddaughter has an accomplice. Someone took the sample after Ms. Valentine left for her psych eval. I think it was slipped into a thermal container disguised as a beer bottle."

Krill appeared uninterested as he shuffled through some paperwork on his desk.

Mitchell took a step forward. "Would you like me to retrieve the item?"

"No. That won't be necessary."

"Sir, with the original research and the sample of the alternate version of Mobilify, ProbeX Labs could have a competing drug on the market, a *superior* competing drug on the market, in a matter of months."

"I'm aware of the implications, Mitchell."

Mitchell waited; Krill was calm, confident. Mitchell remained stoic as he observed his employer.

"I don't waste my time following a rat through a maze," Krill said. "I destroy the maze."

Mitchell never expressed emotion of any sort in front of Krill. He did his job efficiently and professionally—never more than he was asked, never voicing his opinion.

Krill saw the bigger picture. He was always one step ahead. Mitchell was counting on it. He turned to leave when Krill called him back.

"Mitchell, don't return to my office until you have information regarding Vitruvian. That is your task. You do not prioritize your assignments, I do, and your primary objective is getting me everything I need to know about the Vitruvian Society. Correction: getting me everything there *is* to know about the Vitruvian Society. The ProbeX Labs situation is no longer your concern."

"I'll have something by the end of the day." Without further comment, Mitchell left.

CHAPTER FORTY-TWO

The Hale Center
August 13

Very's first full day at the Hale Center had been uneventful. She met with a staff psychologist and took a lengthy personality test. The whole thing felt like a charade. Reclining on the bed, she thumbed through a paperback she had found on the bookshelf, *The Princess Bride*. She flipped to a section of the book about Inigo Montoya's plan to avenge his father and reread it. She didn't know the time, but Very heard the minutes tick by in her head. It couldn't be much past five in the evening. She wasn't a *patient* patient, but Very needed to wait until the ward emptied before acting.

Setting the novel aside, Very wandered into the hall just as the evening shift change was happening. The jerk who had licked her face was parked in a rolling chair behind a nurse's station, laughing at something on his phone. Apparently, he was working a double.

Her stomach churned. This was the opportunity she had hoped for, and yet, now that the moment had arrived, she was afraid. She had prayed for this eventuality, prepared for it. Now she just needed to step up. Why was she hesitating? She had plotted for over a decade, since she was old enough to understand what Theodora Baker and Armand Krill had done to her mother. The time had nearly come.

Adopting a casual air, Very meandered through the ward, noting the posted shift times and fire exits. Rounding a corner, she came upon a patient in pajamas, sitting in a chair, cuddling and talking to a filthy stuffed lion.

"Hi," she said softly.

"Hugo likes you. Hugo thinks you're pretty," the man replied without lifting his head.

"Thank you."

He looked up then. "Hugo hopes you find what you're looking for."

Very backed away with a half-smile and shook off the haunting words. She *was* roaming the halls; the guy probably assumed she was lost. That must have been what he meant.

She had been so lost in her thoughts that she hadn't noticed another patient sidle up next to her until the woman grabbed a fistful of her hair.

"It's pink." The woman was about Very's size and looked to be in her mid-forties. She was obviously medicated.

"It is pink," Very confirmed as she pulled her hair free.

"I'd like pink hair," the woman said.

Very released an awkward chuckle. "Well, it's easy enough to get. It's just temporary color."

"I want your pink hair." She snatched another fistful.

For someone so out of it, she had a remarkably strong grip.

"There you are, Helen." A nurse gently brought her hand over Helen's fist, and the patient released Very's tresses. "The movie is about to start."

"Pink hair!" Helen shouted.

The nurse guided her patient around Very. "It's *Moana*, your favorite. Moana has pink flowers in her hair. Let's go see Moana's pink flowers."

"*Moana*."

With a wave of thanks to the nurse, Very hurried back to her room.

Very accepted the dinner tray. Before the disgusting orderly, whose name tag read "Jimbo," could get too familiar, she said, "I'd be so grateful if you could swipe some extra towels for me. I use a lot of towels after I shower."

With a lecherous smile, he disappeared out the door. Very hurried to the bathroom with her bag. The satchel had been searched when she arrived, but the nurse was looking for weapons and drugs, not what Very had hidden. She pulled back the frayed split in the shoulder strap, withdrew the small device, and tucked it into her bra. After retrieving the sedatives she had stashed in the cup holder, Very returned to bed, peeled back the lid of the dessert cup, and pushed the two pills from the bathroom and the two from under her pillow into the pudding. Jimbo returned with a stack of towels and set them on the back of the toilet tank. Then he came and sat on her bed.

With a finger tracing her shin through the blanket, he asked, "How did you plan on thanking me?"

Very picked up the pudding cup, dipped her finger in, and gave it a stir. She withdrew her finger and sucked off the chocolate. Handing Jimbo the pudding and the spoon, she said, "Wait and see."

He accepted her offering and leaned over the tray to whisper, "I'll be back after lights out."

"Lights out," she repeated.

"I'm here all night."

"Me too," she replied.

Jimbo took what Very was sure he thought was a provocative bite of pudding, turning the spoon upside down and cleaning it with his tongue. Her eyes widened with feigned interest. He stood and strolled out of the room.

An hour later, Very crept to the door. Jimbo was sleeping soundly in front of the security monitors. To her right, a guard was loitering at the nurses' station, texting or playing a game. The nurse on duty was out of sight, but Very could hear her arguing with someone on the phone in a break room.

Wearing the pale green pajamas set out on her bed, Very moved down the hall to the staircase. Dr. Baker's lab was on the second floor at the back of the building. She had memorized the floor plan months ago.

The stairwell hummed in the fluorescent light, and the steps were cold under her bare feet. The lurch of the air conditioning kicking on had Very jumping, and she hurried to the floor below. The push-arm of the fire door may as well have been a gong for all the noise it produced, but when she peeked out into the dim hall, it was empty. Dr. Baker didn't want prying eyes down here.

Very moved silently to the lab entrance. The access panel was the same system they had at Parasol. She could only hope the security protocols were similar as well. She slipped into a vending machine alcove and waited. Her thoughts drifted to Steady and their encounter in the garden. *I'm rescuing you.* She shook her head in a silent laugh even as her heart warmed.

Soft footsteps caught her ear, and Very scrambled back to the alcove's entrance. A guard came down the hall and passed her, heading for the lab entrance. There was one thing about the doors to the labs at Parasol, and Very hoped the same was true of the entries here; they closed slowly.

The guard swiped his access card, and the panel flashed green. He pushed open the door and entered. Very waited, one second, two—she had practiced this at Parasol. The door was falling closed. She rushed down the short hall, slipped through the narrow space, and dropped to the floor. The guard was walking through the dark lab, and Very crawled to the open kitchenette. Hiding in a corner, she waited for the guard to complete his cursory inspection. When the door clicked shut behind him, she returned to the main lab area.

Dr. Baker's office was in the far corner, a glass box that overlooked her domain; it was dark and locked. Along the opposite wall was a row of rooms. Two were marked as Procedure Rooms: A and B. Very stood before the one marked B and leaned closer to peer through the narrow, vertical window above the knob. It was a benign-looking exam room, a place where a child might wait for the pediatrician. The harmless sight weighted the air with dread. She stepped back and scanned the row. Flanking the procedure rooms were two offices, both with the doors open. One appeared unoccupied. The other, at the back corner, must belong to Dr. Baker's assistant. After the flight from Parasol, Very had overheard Dr. Baker speaking to the woman, Rose.

Something was off about the dimensions of this room. Very looked up at the ceiling and estimated she was about where her room would be located one floor above. But the third-floor hall continued on another fifty yards. A wall and an ominous steel door abbreviated the lab where she stood. Whatever was behind it was big.

Very placed one foot in front of the other until she was standing at the darkened doorway of Rose's office. It was an austere space but certainly not sinister. There was a simple desk with a computer, a lamp, and what looked like a few framed photos. The only other furniture in the room was a sturdy bookshelf with a cabinet at the base and medical texts above.

With cautious steps forward, she entered. The walls were sage, and the carpet, a dark pine, giving the room the green glow of virtual reality. The spines of the books stood like soldiers, and Very moved slowly by, the gold-lettered titles announcing the disturbing contents of each volume. She sat at the desk and woke the computer with a gentle shake of the mouse.

Although expected, the light from the monitor was startling, and Very nearly ducked to avoid the beam. She pulled the small device from the underwire seam in her bra and inserted it into the drive. A moment later, the password was overridden, and four files were displayed on the desktop, each titled with a code. She clicked on one. In the folder, Very found extensive research on a drug intended to combat auditory delusions—treating patients that heard voices. After the pages of chemical data came a section that had

Very shrinking back; she was torn between reading on and running from the room. There were two simple words at the top of the page: Test Subjects. She opened one link after the next and scanned the files; words jumped off the page, punching her in the gut: *violent, comatose, stroke, embolism.*

Very checked the dates on the research. This drug was years away from legitimate human trials, maybe decades. And yet, Dr. Baker had compiled this data.

She was experimenting on the patients here.

She looked at another file, a study on traumatic brain injury, another list of nameless patients. Another series of terminal side effects: *persistent vegetative state, grand mal seizure, aneurysm, myocardial infarction. Time of Death: 11:43, Time of Death: 1:18, Time of Death, Time of Death, Time of Death.*

Patient after patient, terminal result after terminal result. Through a sheen of tears, Very checked the next file and found what she was looking for: experimental drug HS-3408-93.

Dr. Baker called it Comply.

Reading through the data, Very reluctantly admitted that the science was fascinating. Twenty years ago, Dr. Baker attempted to treat violent, unmanageable patients chemically when doctors were still using barbaric surgical options. In reality, Dr. Baker was the barbarian. Wrapped in the cloak of humanitarianism, she had founded this safety-net mental hospital with the express purpose of having access to an unlimited supply of patients she could treat like lab rats.

Very scrolled through years of patient files. Down down down the list until she saw it. One of the earliest files had a final entry date of November 5, 2002. The day her mother died.

Her hand trembled on the mouse as she hovered the cursor over the file. Just as she mustered the courage to click, a clattering crash had her surging to her feet.

CHAPTER FORTY-THREE

The Hale Center
August 13

Steady moved silently down the dimly lit hall. The patient rooms were quiet, the nurse's station empty.

He told Very he'd be waiting for her at the back of the property, but he needed to take care of something first. Steady checked her room. As he suspected, it was empty. Although he had to look twice; she had done a decent job of arranging the pillows into a sleeping form. Steady quickly placed the brown paper bag on top of a stack of towels in the bathroom and slipped back out to the hall. Very's whereabouts weren't his concern at the moment. He had other business on this floor.

Jimbo awoke suddenly, his bellow of pain muffled by the hand over his mouth. He looked down in horror at his leg.

A voice in his ear whispered, "Oh hey, look at that. You have a knife in your thigh."

Sweat beaded on his brow, and Jimbo tried to struggle, but the hand remained firm.

"Careful there, buddy. See, the femoral artery is just a hair to the left. I assume you know what that means, being a medical professional and all."

Jimbo froze.

"One slip and you bleed out. Fast."

The orderly gave a jerky nod.

"You and I are going to have a little chat," the man murmured casually. "The girl in the room across the hall? Remember her?"

Jimbo squeezed his eyes shut against the pain and nodded again.

"You don't touch her. You don't look at her. We Clear?"

Jimbo bobbed his head emphatically.

"In fact," the man continued, "you don't touch any female patient in this facility outside of what's required for your job." He wiggled the knife handle, the slight movement sending another bolt of pain through his leg. Jimbo choked on a sob.

"I'm watching you, James Michael Carnes, 148 Riverbank Road, Apartment 4B. How's your granny, by the way? If I catch you doing things you shouldn't be doing, if I hear you've been doing things you shouldn't be doing, this knife will do some damage higher up."

Jimbo felt the room start to fade. The man shook him back to consciousness. "You payin 'attention, Jimbo? If anything happens to the woman across the hall, if she so much as stubs her toe, I'm holding you personally accountable. Do you understand?"

When Jimbo replied with a shaky yes, the man rotated the knife ninety degrees and pulled it out. The world went black.

When Jimbo regained consciousness, he was alone at his station, his scrubs soaked with blood. He staggered to his feet and limped to the locker room, grabbing a first aid kit from a shelf.

The sound of a steel door running up a track had Very's heart pounding out of her chest.

She stood from Rose's desk and moved closer to the picture window to her left. Silence.

The sun had fully set, but the parking lot was bright with stadium lamp posts. Several cars occupied spots. Her view of the back of the building was blocked by a wall bordering a loading dock. Very could just make out the back of a delivery truck with the garage-style door raised and a man pushing a dolly stacked with boxes.

When the worker passed under a light and Very saw the words on the delivery packages, her blood ran cold: *Enteral nutrition.* That was the liquid sustenance for patients with feeding tubes. The man disappeared out of her field of vision. He was moving up the ramp and heading for the unaccounted-for area at the back of Dr. Baker's lab.

Very tamped down her paranoia. That room was probably a storage space. *Why the security?* Those men were making a standard delivery. *At nine at night?* There's a logical explanation. *There's a horrible explanation.*

Another man came into her line of sight, leaving the building and returning to the truck. Very covered her mouth with her palm and bit the heel of her hand. As casually as the guy with the boxes had done, this man pushed a gurney holding a black body bag. He muscled it up the makeshift ramp into the truck. The other man joined him with the now empty hand cart, then reached up and grabbed the dangling rope with a meaty fist. As he yanked the door down, the man glanced up at the window where she stood. Very fell to her hands and knees. Her mouth flooded, and her breathing was shallow. She sat back against the wall and calmed herself. A moment later, she heard the truck growl to a start and pull away.

From her spot on the floor, she had a clear view of the main room and entrance to the lab. She stared straight ahead as she counted her breaths and managed her fear.

Gathering her wits, Very found her feet and walked into the central area. She glanced around the vast, dark space, her eyes coming to rest on the back wall. It was painted an unobtrusive gray; there were no pictures or adornments to draw attention—just a blank expanse punctuated dead-center by that menacing door.

The light changed; it was more a sensation than physical distinction, but it was enough to pull Very's eyes to the front of the lab and the sliver of light creeping under the threshold. Next came the sound: footsteps in the silence and the soft beeps of the keypad lock. Very shrank back into Rose's office, staying out of sight. As she stood in the shadows of the Spartan room, the glow behind her blanketed her like a shroud. The computer monitor might as well have been a neon sign announcing her presence. She squeezed her eyes shut, willing the screen to sleep. On top of that, the device she had used to override the password and download the files was still sticking out of the processor. She feared snatching it now would restart the timeout countdown, keeping the monitor illuminated. Very stepped to the front of the office, closed the door as far as she dared, and peered through the gap as the keypad by the main entrance flashed green.

The computer screen dimmed to half-light.

Very waited, standing frozen in the darkness.

CHAPTER FORTY-FOUR

New York City
August 13

Armand Krill looked up from the contract he was reading to see Alonso Mitchell had returned. Krill waved him in. The antique grandfather clock in the corner chimed nine.

"I trust the late hour means you have found something."

"The Vitruvian Society still exists," Mitchell said, standing in his usual spot between the two guest chairs.

"I knew it." Krill banged a fist on the table. He rarely asked about Mitchell's methods, but in this instance, he had to know. "How did you discover it?"

"I found the jeweler that makes the rings," Mitchell replied. "An old man in Amsterdam. He has fashioned thirty-four rings over the past fifty years. His father made your grandfather's ring in 1947."

Krill nodded his approval and urged Mitchell to continue. He wanted to know every nugget of information, every tidbit about Vitruvian.

"From what I can see, they operate as an investment club. I matched the members you knew or suspected with SEC filings, but because the group's members are international, many of their transactions are spread across the globe. They make charitable donations, purchase companies, and invest. A member of the group, Cornelius Davenport, manages the account. The current value is one hundred and eighteen billion."

Krill swallowed before he drooled.

Mitchell continued, "The jeweler hasn't been asked to create a signet ring in ten years."

"That would have been Johan DeVold's ring," Krill commented absently.

"Correct. DeVold lives part-time in Amsterdam and collected the ring personally," Mitchell confirmed.

Krill opened a desk drawer and withdrew a leather ring box. He cracked open the lid and stared at the coveted jewelry. This had been his grandfather's ring. As a child, Krill had stared at it while his grandfather had regaled him with tales of the mysterious group. Young Krill imagined the Vitruvian members were Knights of the Round Table. The golden ring glinted in the lamplight. His finger ached for the weight of it.

Mitchell went on, "The group is cagey. They conduct business offline whenever possible. There is no electronic record of membership, bylaws, contact information, or meeting minutes. There have been rumors over the years of some questionable dealings. I managed to track down an old Wall Street Journal reporter who tried to write an exposé on the group in 1987. He supposedly had proof of ties to rogue governments. Vitruvian ruined him."

Krill lifted his lips in a wan smile. Every word from Mitchell's mouth had his heart pounding.

"Is that all?"

"For now," Mitchell confirmed.

Krill dismissed him by returning to the contract he was reading.

Mitchell, in an uncharacteristic display of disobedience, cleared his throat.

"What," Krill clipped.

"Sir, you've seen proof that the sample of an earlier version of Mobilify was delivered to ProbeX Labs."

Krill waved away Mitchell's concern. "It's being handled."

"But sir–"

Krill lifted his hand, silencing him. "When I say I have the matter in hand, that is all you need to know."

Mitchell took a step back. "Understood."

"I never underestimate your abilities, Mitchell. Please show me the same courtesy."

"Yes, sir."

Krill dismissed Mitchell for the second time, pleased the man had regained some subservience. After giving the paperwork his legal department had rushed over a final perusal, Krill signed his name in heavy scrawl and initialed in the appropriate spots. Everything was proceeding as planned. Now he could focus on more important matters, namely the Vitruvian Society.

With due reverence, he took one last look at the ring, snapped the box closed, and returned it to the safety of his desk.

Soon.

CHAPTER FORTY-FIVE

The Hale Center
August 13

D r. Baker's assistant, Rose, tapped the access code and entered the quiet lab. With clipped strides, she marched through the main room toward the source of the problem the delivery men had witnessed. Rose's practical heels clicked in the silence as she headed straight to the steel door in the gray wall at the back of the lab. After entering another code, she rotated the heavy handle with both hands and hauled it open.

When the soundproof door separated from its seal, Rose heard the commotion that had prompted the men to message her. She hurried to the source of the disturbance.

After administering the sedative, she set the room to rights, picking up a toppled instrument tray and resecuring the oxygen feed. That handled, Rose surveyed the area. Noting another problem, she texted the incompetent fools who had ruined her evening. With calm restored and the only sounds, the gentle hiss of oxygen and the soft bleeps of the machines, Rose headed to her office to update the file for Dr. Baker.

She shoved open the steel door with more effort than necessary. Rose had been pulled away from dinner with the handsome administrator she had been flirting with for months. She had cut the evening short, but perhaps if she hurried, she could still catch her date for a walk in the garden or a private nightcap.

Sending a quick text to her companion, she crossed the central lab, listening for the distinctive hiss and snick of the door sealing behind her. She didn't hear it. Rose looked back just as the confirming sound came. Her forceful push must have delayed the door's closing. Appeased, she continued to her office.

At the entry, Rose paused. The door was ajar, closed farther than she usually left it. She pressed five pale-pink fingertips to the surface and pushed it open. Everything was as it should be–the desk chair tucked in, the computer dark, the bookshelf in order.

And yet…

Rose wasn't a woman prone to flights of fancy, but she couldn't shake the feeling of disturbance in the air. She took slow steps as she examined the space, double-checking for any anomaly that would have spawned this sensation. Shaking off her irrationality, Rose woke the computer and quickly typed the relevant information. She would receive no praise for her management of the situation, nor should she. This was part of her job. Had she been accepted to medical school all those years ago, she would have been called into work at all hours of the day or night. This was no different.

When the update was completed, Rose logged out and stood. Using the camera on her phone, she quickly checked her appearance, then returned the device to her evening bag. With a final check of her surroundings, her eyes lingered on the open office door. Perhaps that was what had produced her disquiet. Even now, the door seemed out of position–not flush with the wall as usual.

She took a slow step forward, then another. The wood grain seemed to stare back at her, to dare her. A foot away, she extended her palm. Before her hand touched the surface, her text alert chimed, and Rose jumped back with an embarrassing startle.

A different excitement flowed as Rose retrieved the phone and read the text from her date. Yes, he was still at the restaurant and would love to continue their evening. With renewed enthusiasm–and a burning desire to dismiss this paranoia–Rose shifted her attention from the door to the doorway and walked out.

Then, knowing her mind wouldn't settle until she resolved her unease, Rose stepped back into the room and thrust the open door against the wall. It hit with a loud but satisfying bang. With an absurd relief, she turned and left the lab.

Ten minutes earlier...

When the vault door hissed to a close behind Rose, Very stole out of the office and crept over to the high lab table closest to the back wall. Concealed in the shadows, she waited, crouched under the extended lip of the table. Very patted her bra and felt the outline of the drive she had used to access the computer files. An eternity passed as she stared at the burnished steel door.

Finally, the door was thrust open, and Rose took determined steps toward her office. With only seconds to move, Very crawled the remaining feet to the rapidly shrinking opening and disappeared into the secret room. She remained crouched by the entry until she was sure her actions had gone unnoticed. Then she turned and faced the room.

Very stood in the vast space and stared in disbelief at the sight before her.

Row after row of patients, sedated or on life support or maybe dead. Very stopped counting at thirty. She held her hand over her mouth to stifle a cry, then slapped the other on top of it. At the end of the first line of beds, a man was sedated and restrained. Some of the equipment surrounding him was askew, and a medical flashlight was on the floor. This must have been what brought Rose to the lab in the dark of night.

Very tiptoed down the central aisle. She checked each bed, looking for what? She didn't know, but the need to acknowledge these people as human compelled her to look at each face. When she came to the last person, the man who had apparently woken up and fought back, Very paused and rested her hand on his arm. Words formed in her mind but couldn't seem to travel to her lips.

Behind her, a keypad beeped.

She fell gracefully to the floor and rolled under the disruptive patient's bed. Her heart beat erratically as she stared up at the mattress. A different door opened, this one at the back, and two men entered–she assumed it was the men from the truck she had spied through the window. The only sound was their footsteps as they moved through the space. Very heard the sound of a long zipper and the grunt of exertion. She risked a peek and watched as the men carried out another body bag. After an interminable minute, Very scooted out of her hiding place. She saw it then–the small, stuffed lion against the wall.

She retrieved the tattered thing, holding it against her chest for a moment, then placed it on the bed under the sleeping man's hand—a small comfort in this hellscape. Propelled by outrage, fear, and adrenaline, Very left the back room and ran out.

Returning to her floor, Very raced through the quiet halls, certain she was being pursued. She glanced at the security desk, relieved to find perverted Jimbo gone. Then she slipped back into her room. She set the flash drive on the nightstand and made a beeline for the bathroom.

After closing the door, Very fell to her knees and vomited into the toilet. When her stomach was empty and the dry heaves had stopped, she stood at the sink and splashed cold water on her face. She blindly grabbed a towel from the stack Jimbo had brought when the sound of crinkling paper drew her eye. Very picked up the brown lunch bag and looked inside. Steady's kindness and intelligence had her crying again as she withdrew the first item and examined the box. Medium sunflower blonde. She smiled. He had correctly guessed her natural color.

She quickly applied the hair dye and showered, then stepped back into the pajamas and wrapped a towel turban-style around her head. Leaving the remaining items in the bag on the toilet tank, Very went back to the bedroom; the lights would need to be out for this next step.

Preoccupied with her plan, it took a moment to notice Jimbo, the creep, standing there, looking pale as a ghost. In front of him, Dr. Baker sat in a chair beside the bed, wearing a superior smile and watching Very's every move.

CHAPTER FORTY-SIX

Very stood stock still and silent.

Dr. Baker spoke to Jimbo without turning. "Go and fetch the item from the vaccine fridge. Oh, and disable the cameras in this room."

Jimbo's face was pinched as he hobbled out.

Dr. Baker reached over to the nightstand and toyed with the portable drive. "I have to say I'm disappointed. Not only did you not wait for me to give you a tour, but you didn't look at the most recent studies."

Very crossed her arms and said nothing.

"The human brain is the great unknown. My colleagues explore the Solar System, the universe, Dark Matter, looking for what? Answers to questions they don't have, understanding theories they haven't formulated. Meanwhile, the most fascinating puzzle in science sits right on top of our shoulders. The brain is still a mystery, despite every scientific and medical advancement of the past century."

She stood and turned to the trolley next to her and removed the cloth revealing a glass cover over a human brain.

Very reared back, and Dr. Baker gave an indulgent smile. "It's a teaching tool, Verity. For example," She withdrew a pen from the breast pocket of her white coat and touched the glass with the tip. "This section of the brain is responsible for impulse control. But," She paused for effect. "It is also the area that triggers seizures. Each part of the brain controls multiple functions, many of which remain unknown. So you can see why surgery and medications are a tricky business."

Despite her revulsion, Very couldn't help but be absorbed by the topic.

"The only truly effective way to achieve meaningful results in neuroscience is through human trials. So I have made it my mission to treat the untreatable. To attempt to repair a profoundly broken brain."

"You can't make an omelet without breaking some eggs." Very's sarcasm was evident.

Dr. Baker was not amused. "It may surprise you to know, even with my unconventional methods and experimental treatments, my recovery rate is better than any other facility in the world."

"And your death rate?" Very pressed.

She ignored the question. "Comply is a revolutionary treatment for severe mental illness, Verity. But, even more exciting are the uses in healthy patients. Criminals, terrorists, and violent men can all be brought to heel with one dose. You can't imagine the interest this has garnered among certain governments and, shall we say, political factions."

Very couldn't resist a swipe. "How humanitarian of you."

Dr. Baker was unaffected by the insult. "Doing good isn't cheap, my dear. That's the bitter pill I have been forced to swallow. Not to mention, mankind doesn't always know what's best."

"Careful doctor, your god complex is showing."

That got a reaction. Dr. Baker turned to Very with fire in her eyes. Then she smiled. "I'm glad to see that spark of rebellion. It's difficult to assess the effectiveness of Comply if there's no fire to extinguish."

Very bolted for the door. Two hulking orderlies each grabbed an arm and hauled her back to the bed, securing her arms and legs in restraints. Jimbo limped into the room, holding a tray. Dr. Baker observed the row of vials Jimbo held and snapped, "Just one, you idiot." She snatched what she wanted from the tray. "Return the other ampoules to the vaccine fridge immediately."

Dr. Baker wheeled the IV stand over to the bed and attached the tube to the cannula, one of the orderlies inserted on the back of Very's hand. Very thrashed against her bindings while Dr. Baker tapped the syringe and then inserted it into the IV bag dangling from the stand. "Please stop that tantrum. I need to work quickly. For optimal results, Comply must remain at a precise temperature before it is administered."

Very's struggles were pointless. The men held her down as Dr. Baker released the drug into the IV. Comply was black in color, and Very watched as the inky drug stained the saline in the bag and slowly began to travel down the tube.

After replacing the empty hypodermic on the tray, Dr. Baker turned to Very and gave her knee a gentle squeeze. "You'll feel the effects immediately, but Comply takes about three hours to optimize. I'll see you in a bit."

She left the room with the two brutes trailing in her wake.

The dark drug moved down the thin plastic, a third of the way, halfway. She clenched and unclenched her fist, trying to force the thin tube from her hand.

Comply continued to flow toward her vein. Six inches. Three inches.

Very squeezed her eyes shut and forced a welling tear out of the corner. What waking nightmare awaited? Would she even survive?

A painful tug on the back of her hand had her opening her eyes. Very looked over to see Jimbo, looking like he might pass out, detaching the IV from the port.

Next, he loosened her restraints.

"Why?" Very asked.

Jimbo glanced over his shoulder to the empty hall, then returned his attention to his task. "Because your boyfriend is crazier than any patient in here. Because I value my balls." He moved around to the other side of the bed. "I'm getting the fuck out of here, and I suggest you do the same."

Very sat up and helped him finish releasing her. "Thank you."

"Don't fucking thank me. Just tell that asshole that I helped you."

"I will."

Quick as a flash, Very leapt from the bed, ripped off the towel covering her dyed hair, and darted into the bathroom. She grabbed the bag Steady had left and slipped into the hall. It took a few minutes of poking her head into rooms until she found who she was looking for. Helen, the patient she had encountered earlier, tore her gaze away from *Wheel of Fortune* and stared at Very with suspicion.

Very ignored her misgivings and said, "I brought you a present." She opened the bag and gave the wary woman a peek inside. Immediately her eyes lit up, and she applauded with tiny claps of excitement.

When Helen reached for her gift, Very pulled the bag away. "Come to my room. I'll put on *Wheel of Fortune*, and you can have your present."

Without hesitation, the woman followed Very down the hall and, without being prompted, climbed into Very's bed. Then she frowned. "I won't be able to see myself."

"Look." Very pointed to the window where their reflection was clear against the backdrop of the dark night. She handed over the prize and helped the woman put it on. Then she clicked on the game show, but Very's new friend had no interest in the spinning wheel; she stared at her reflection with fascinated delight.

The final item in the bag was a security badge belonging to a blonde nutritionist named Renee. Very was startled by the burn of jealousy that hit her as she wondered how Steady had managed to acquire the I.D. Brushing those feelings aside, she moved to the hall. Her pajamas looked enough like scrubs to pass for staff. She was barefoot, but there was nothing to be done.

Very tiptoed past Jimbo's vacated seat and moved down the hall. Then she stopped. Turning back to the security desk, Very moved behind it into the back room. The vaccine fridge was clearly marked. She opened the door and spotted the row of Comply ampoules ready to be used on Dr. Baker's next human guinea pig. Very searched for something, anything. There was no time. Then her eyes settled on the appliance in the adjacent kitchenette. She quickly performed the task and fled.

The next station was also empty. Very could see two nurses in the back room debating a vending machine purchase. Despite the overwhelming desire to break into a run, she continued at a brisk but contained pace.

Bypassing the elevator, she walked to the end of the hall. The security badge slid easily through the pad. When the light flashed green, Very pushed into the stairwell. She kept her head down as she descended, knowing there were eyes everywhere. With both hands on the metal bar, Very waited at the door and listened. She heard laughter—two male voices joking about a car. *Hey, man, give me shit all you want. I don't pay for gas, and I can park that baby anywhere.*

When the voices faded, Very pushed open the door and peeked out. The hall was empty. Marshaling the last of her self-control, Very managed her pace the final ten steps to the exit.

Standing in the open doorway, she stared into the darkness. The beckoning patio was illuminated with ground lights–the garden beyond, dark and sleeping. She stepped out onto the walk with a soft whisper on her lips.

"Steady."

Very had been abandoned by the people in her life. Her mother had been taken. She didn't know her family. She was used to people disappointing her.

Yet, somehow she knew Steady would be there. He was true. And as carefree and unconcerned as he appeared, Very knew Jonah Lockhart was deeply invested in the safety of the people he held close.

She hurried across the patio and into the garden, struggling to see in the dark. Her eyes caught the low red and white lights at the back of the property. The airstrip. She ran through the high grass, finally crossing a service road. Rocks were cutting her feet, but Very ran like a bomb was set to blow.

When she came to the runway, Very sucked in a breath and glanced around the area. The hangar was closed up. A row of golf carts lined the entrance. A fuel truck sat idle in the open garage. And there, through the window of the small outbuilding, she saw him. Steady. He was sitting at a desk with his feet propped up, reading a magazine like a businessman at breakfast.

And yet.

He was hyper-aware, his casual pose belying his innate readiness. As if to prove her point, at that precise moment, Steady looked up. He turned his head and stared out the window into the darkness. Very was halfway to him when he jumped to his feet, and as he opened the door, she threw herself into her arms.

"You're here," she said.

Steady didn't crack a joke or cop a feel; he simply held her like she was his most precious possession and replied, "I'm here."

Reluctantly, it seemed, he pushed her back just enough to see her face. He rubbed a loose tendril of hair between his fingers and hooked it behind her ear. "I miss the pink."

Very held onto his shoulders. "I'll get it back." He was an anchor in the storm.

"Good." Steady gave her a satisfied nod. Then he kissed her slowly, innocently. It was a simple act, lips to lips. But there was a surety in it, a promise. *We are together.*

His mouth hovered over hers. "You ready to fly?"

"Fly?" she repeated.

Dr. Baker picked up her desk phone and called the security hub.

"Yes, Dr. Baker?"

"Check the patient in room 312."

There was a pause while the guard's fingers typed.

"Oh, yes," he said, "The girl with the pink hair. She's in bed."

"Good." She ended the call.

Dr. Baker left her office and strolled to the back of the lab to check on her Comply patients. After that, she took the elevator to the third floor. When she stepped into Verity Valentine's room, it took her a moment to process what she saw. There, on the bed, was an older woman wearing a bright pink wig and watching television. Unwilling to accept the situation, Dr. Baker stepped into the hall and double-checked the room number. Finally, realization set in. "Goddamnit!" She rushed to the security center with her phone to her ear.

CHAPTER FORTY-SEVEN

The Hale Center
August 13

"Fly?" Very repeated, her stomach flipping.

"Well, we're at an airfield." Steady shrugged like it was the most obvious thing in the world.

"So, we'll fly," Very said, trying to convince herself. "I can get on a plane with you."

"Don't worry, Darlin'. We're not getting on a plane." Steady cupped her jaw and ran a thumb along her cheek.

"Oh, thank God."

Steady took her hand and pulled her toward the hanger. Rather than open the big doors, he veered around to the back.

"I've got a real treat for you."

They walked around the building to a circular platform.

Very halted. "A helicopter?"

"Tilly's already on board. That dog loves to fly. And this is not just a helicopter. It's a Sikorsky Pave Hawk. Bishop Security's latest toy. John, our pilot, left her for me when he dropped off Herc and Chat."

"How thoughtful of him."

"He's got family in the area." Steady grinned.

Very dug in her heels. "What about Herc and Chat?"

Steady stepped toward the bird. "Already on board. Probably already asleep. Come on."

Very followed, or, more accurately, was pulled along. "Oh, shit."

Steady stopped at the open hatch and said, "Have I ever let you down?"

She bent her forehead to his sternum and felt the calm beat of his heart. "Never."

Suddenly a series of security lights on tall poles lit up around the main building.

"Time to go."

Steady boosted Very into the cockpit and guided her to the seat on the right. He buckled them both in, secured their headsets, and fired up the helo. In no time, the ground was disappearing beneath them, and they were shooting low across the wooded outskirts of the property with Very screaming into her hands.

The blaring ring of his cell phone had Alonso Mitchell shooting up in bed. "Yes," he answered calmly, no sleep in his voice.

"Sir, this is Hendricks at Hale. You requested updates on Verity Valentine. She left the premises without authorization about thirty minutes ago using a stolen access pass. Looks like she had help."

Mitchell sat up and ran a hand through his hair. "All right."

"We're in pursuit."

Mitchell had to stop himself from laughing out loud. Who did this guy think he was? SWAT? Mitchell had seen the file of every guard in that place.

They were closer to mall security than law enforcement. If they actually caught her, and the person helping her was who Mitchell suspected, the guards didn't stand a chance. "Let her go."

"Say again."

The ice in Mitchell's voice was unmistakable. "Let. Her. Go."

The guard, Hendricks, replied, "Yes, sir."

Mitchell disconnected the call and swung his legs over the side of the bed. He had no idea what had gone down at the Hale Center, but Mitchell had his suspicions. Theodora Baker worked without restraints and was rarely met with resistance.

He smiled, impressed with the young scientist. Krill had needed Verity Valentine out of the way while he countered her move. But the feisty young woman had anticipated this course of action. She wanted evidence that her mother was murdered, and Hale was the place to find it. The question was, had she found the proof?

Mitchell crossed the five steps to the kitchenette and started the coffee. Standing barefoot in his boxers and T-shirt, he watched the dark brew trickle down. He grabbed the mug before the coffee finished brewing, causing a hiss on the element.

Cup in hand, Mitchell crossed to the window and looked out. This complicated game had yet another moving part.

CHAPTER FORTY-EIGHT

Bishop Security Helicopter
August 13

The helicopter swooped low over the dark trees as Steady flew them south toward home. *Home.* It was a strange thought for Very. She'd lived in so many places, but on that peaceful beach with Steady close by, she finally felt settled. She finally felt her life begin.

Steady's voice through the headset brought her back to the here and now. "You doin 'okay, Darlin'?"

"Compared to that hospital, flying is a piece of cake," she said.

"Good to hear because I gotta tell you, I have a long list of places I'd like to fly you."

"Is that so?" She smiled.

"You better believe it." As if to prove his point, Steady dipped the helo, and they banked to the left. Very gripped the armrests, then forgot her anxiety when she took in the view. She could see the Atlantic Ocean in the moonlight. It looked endless, like the possibilities.

"It's so beautiful. I feel like we could chase the clouds," she said.

"I'm glad you're taking to it, Darlin'. I don't think I could love a girl who didn't like flying."

Love? He must have misspoken. Yet, when Very turned to look at him, Steady was watching the horizon without a hint of regret or panic. Very settled into the thought. Could he love her? Could she love him back? For so long, she had refused to accept the concept of love. The people who were supposed to love you didn't, or if they did, they left anyway. Love had been too painful, too risky, so she had written it off. And yet, when she looked at the man beside her, she couldn't help but think her heart had gone ahead and made the decision without her. She never in a million years would have guessed this scheme of hers would have led her to Jonah Lockhart.

"God, I'm so glad I needed to keep an eye on you." Very squeezed his leg.

"What do you mean?" he asked.

"You know exactly what I mean. You were snooping, so I used our little nightly rendezvous to make sure you weren't interfering," she said.

Very felt a quick lurch in her belly–the kind of burning pain she felt when she spoke without thinking, said something she shouldn't. She could practically see the wall go up around him before he spoke.

"So, all that time on the beach? It was a ruse?"

Very's chest ached. She wasn't explaining herself well, and when she felt frustrated, she got feisty. "What's the big deal, Steady? You were watching me too. The telescope?"

"I didn't manipulate you, Very. I didn't make you think–" He shook his head as if banishing a thought.

Very reached for him again. His thigh was granite under her palm. "Steady, it's not coming out right. Yes, I was trying to keep you from interfering, but our conversations on the beach were real. My feelings are real. I would never pretend to be something I'm not. Who would do that?"

Very squeezed her eyes shut. She knew exactly who would do that to Steady: his birth mother, his awful first stepmother. God, she wanted to bang her head against the window. She didn't know what to say to make it right. She scanned his rigid profile, saw the tick of his jaw.

"Steady, it's not what you think. Please, you have to believe me."

She knew she had lost him before he said another word. His frown morphed into that carefree crooked smile, and his eyes took on that infuriating, easygoing twinkle. His mask was back in place; the hurt she had caused stuffed somewhere deep down. She used to think that cocky grin was the arrogant smile of a privileged man without a care in the world. Now she knew better. His expression revealed more pain than any grimace or tear-stained face. His laissez-faire appearance used to infuriate her. Now, it broke her heart.

"It's all good. Let's get you back to Beaufort." He winked at her, and Very felt her heart crack. He was back to being that unconcerned frat boy she hated. Well, she didn't hate him, she loved him, but she loved the real him. She would have given anything to see sincerity in his eyes, but she knew it wouldn't happen in this cockpit. So she stared out the side window into the darkness, and the two of them flew home in silence.

CHAPTER FORTY-NINE

New York City
August 14

The Cavalry Club manager led Armand Krill down the grand hall toward the life-sized portrait of Ben Franklin. Neither man spoke. When they reached the end, the manager turned right and proceeded to the closed double doors. Standing before the looming suits of armor, he asked, "Can I bring you coffee or breakfast, Mr. Krill?"

"No, thank you."

The manager depressed both handles simultaneously, pushed them open with a flourish, and stepped back.

Krill spotted Johan DeVold sitting in an oxblood leather wingback chair by an unlit fireplace. The patch over his eye made him look mysterious and hostile. Krill took the other seat. He opened his mouth to speak, but DeVold halted him with a hand.

"I think I know why you're here. I saw your expression when you noticed my ring the other morning at breakfast. Most people assume it's a family crest or a college club, but you recognized the symbol."

"Vitruvian," Krill said. "I want to join."

DeVold scratched his temple, the signet ring glinting in the lamplight. "While my gratitude for your actions the other day is profound, that is a favor I cannot grant."

"Why not?"

"Vitruvian is a closed society. I am a member because my father is a member. The investors are all descendants of the original five founders. Outsiders are not permitted."

Krill anticipated the response and withdrew a sheaf of papers from his briefcase. "Perhaps this will sway you."

DeVold looked at the information, then cast a surprised glance at Krill. "Your grandfather?"

"Yes," Krill confirmed. "I have his ring." He leaned forward again and produced the small leather box.

DeVold opened the hinged ring box and examined the same signet ring he wore. He expelled a weary sigh. "Even if the members were willing to overlook the generational skip, you fail to meet the other prerequisite. The portfolio requirements are non-negotiable. Vitruvian accepts only legacies and only billionaires."

Krill lifted a finger. "My net worth will hit one billion in the next six months. Twice that over the next five years."

"This new drug?" DeVold questioned.

"Yes," Krill explained. "Mobilfy. It's a revolutionary arthritis medication. I expect a fifty percent market share in six months. My net worth will triple."

"That's optimistic."

Krill leaned forward conspiratorially. "There are aspects of this drug's formula that make it exceptionally profitable." Krill would never reveal that the version of the drug he was releasing produced a side effect treatable with another Parasol-produced medication and that sales would surpass forecasts within a month. The implication in his words was enough.

DeVold's face was inscrutable, but Krill thought he saw a glimmer of admiration in DeVold's one visible eye. The diamond heir leaned back and crossed one leg over the other. "Membership review lasts for over a year. That should give you ample time to accrue the minimum net worth."

Krill frowned. He never imagined being in a situation where a billion dollars was the minimum amount for anything.

"I'll have to speak to my father," DeVold continued. "I have been a member for ten years, and in that time, no new prospects have been introduced. Frankly, I'm not even sure of the protocol."

"That's all I ask." Krill stood and extended his hand. DeVold remained seated and shook it. "I look forward to hearing from you."

Krill left the meeting feeling slighted. Yes, DeVold was a powerful man with untold billions, but Krill was his senior by more than thirty years, and the younger man had Krill feeling like a job applicant. He bottled the insult and reminded himself that if DeVold could clear a path to Vitruvian, Krill would shine his shoes.

PART FOUR

The Convincer

CHAPTER FIFTY

New York City
August 15

Armand Krill was finishing a conference call when his assistant poked her head in the door. Krill shot her an annoyed glance.

"Sir, I'm sorry to interrupt, but Johan DeVold is here to see you."

Krill kept his demeanor even as he ended the call. "Show him in."

Johan DeVold entered the office alone, but Krill could see his assistant and security lurking in the outer office. Even with the eye patch, DeVold was a striking man. Unmarried, as far as Krill knew, the man undoubtedly would not lack for female attention; his bank account was handsome enough. DeVold wasted no time with small talk.

"Armand, I have news."

"Please, sit down."

DeVold sat in one of the two high-backed leather chairs and crossed his legs. He had the bearing of a royal, making Krill feel inferior despite his position of power behind the desk.

"I spoke to my father. He is currently the president of the organization. What you know as the Vitruvian Society is now called Vitruvian Investments.

Many aspects of the group are secretive, but we are a legitimate investment club."

"I see."

"What I saw as a problem—your family's financial setbacks and expulsion from Vitruvian—my father found rather remarkable. To rebuild a fortune in the face of such adversity, well, he thought it commendable."

Much to his dismay, Krill found himself leaning forward onto the desk, his anticipation getting the better of him.

DeVold laced his fingers on his knee. "Vitruvian will accept your membership request."

Krill wanted to jump from his seat. DeVold stayed him with his next word.

"However."

Krill tethered his enthusiasm and listened.

"As I mentioned, the provisional period is one year. During that time, our people will observe your business dealings and social interactions. You must conduct yourself with the utmost propriety."

After taking a slow breath and fighting the urge to throw a paperweight at DeVold's head, Krill nodded.

"A year from now, your net worth must exceed one billion dollars, or the offer of membership is revoked."

"Understood."

"At that time, our advisory committee will meet with you to discuss the unique aspects of our investment strategy with the primary goal of generational wealth in mind." DeVold leaned in to share a secret. "Rumors abound that the Metropolitan Museum of Art is considering selling naming rights. Several of our members are aflutter at the prospect."

"I imagine I'll be too late to be in the running for that," Krill mused.

"A day late and a dollar short, as they say. The rights will sell in the billions."

Armand swallowed his embarrassment, and DeVold chuckled. "Don't worry, Krill. There will be limitless opportunities when you join our ranks. Last year two of our members vied to donate the new engineering school to their alma mater. They settled the matter over a game of billiards. These men will be more than business partners. They will be social allies, trusted advisors, and friends. Even an alibi, should the occasion call for it."

Krill heard the mirth in the younger man's tone, but something told him DeVold wasn't joking.

"There is a nominal initiation fee of five million U.S. due at once. It's more of a gesture than anything else, a show of intent. Vitruvian will invest the money as they see fit, but after you have been granted full membership, that money will become part of your portfolio."

"I freed up funds in anticipation of good news." Krill woke his computer. "Do you have the wire transfer information?"

DeVold made a meal of withdrawing a crocodile billfold from his inner breast pocket and removing a card. "Here is the account."

Krill transferred the funds. "Done."

"Congratulations, Armand. One year from today, you will receive an invitation delivered by messenger to attend a dinner at the Cavalry Club. You will be the guest of honor, and the members will welcome you into our ranks. Also, I'm sure it's unnecessary, but I have been instructed to remind you never to mention Vitruvian. The conventional wisdom is that the society doesn't exist, and we want to keep it that way."

DeVold extended his hand, and Krill shook it more vigorously than he had intended. Johan DeVold walked to the door, turned, and said, "Oh, and Armand, during this probationary period, do not wear the ring." Then he walked out.

Armand couldn't be bothered with offense at the directive. He had done it. He was twelve months away from restoring the Krill name to the Pantheon

DEBBIE BALDWIN

of American aristocracy. In defiance of DeVold's command, Krill opened the box and slipped the ring on his finger. Splaying his hands on the desk, he stared down at the adornment. He felt like a goddamned king.

Now he needed to ensure that nothing, *nothing*, interfered with the release of Mobilify.

Krill had grown tired of this amateur chess match with his granddaughter. Over the years, he had learned that sometimes brute force was infinitely more effective than strategy. The simplest way to win a chess match was not to lure your opponent's king into checkmate; it was to steal the board.

He picked up the phone and placed a call.

255

CHAPTER FIFTY-ONE

South Island, South Carolina
September 15

Very entered her rented beach house, tossed her bag on the overstuffed chair in the open living area, and hiked the canvas grocery bag higher on her hip. She was distracted; her mind was on a gorgeous pilot with a calm nature and a heart-stopping smile. It had been two days since he brought her home, and they hadn't spoken. How had this happened? How had she screwed up so badly? It was easy to blame other people for her misfortunes–her grandfather for his callous greed, even her mother for her recklessness, but with Steady, she was the one who had done the damage, and she was the one who needed to fix it. She was so overcome with this unprecedented urgent need that she wasn't paying attention. So when she flipped on the kitchen light to find Dr. Theodora Baker sitting in the breakfast nook, the steam billowing from the cup of tea before her, and two hulking men flanking the alcove, she screamed.

"Stop that," Dr. Baker sniped.

Very's brain quickly caught up. Dr. Baker wasn't here for a casual visit. Very had tipped her hand when she escaped from the hospital. Darwin would be disappointed with her rashness. It was too late to convince Dr. Baker she was interested in joining her team.

Very had ensured that Krill knew the sample of the earlier, better version of Mobilify had been delivered to ProbeX Labs for development. She had provided the distraction by being sent to the psych ward. Well, if Very were honest, she would admit she had gone rogue. Very knew Krill's connection to the Hale Center, and she knew he often used Dr. Baker to handle specific problems. She had done nothing to encourage Krill's actions; any suggestion that she wanted to go to Hale would be suspect. She, however, had been fully prepared to investigate Dr. Baker if that course of action occurred. Very had every intention of enduring her stay at Hale and finding out everything she could about Dr. Baker's dirty deeds–until she got caught. Escaping hadn't been the plan, and now she was facing the blowback of her impulsiveness.

Very began unpacking the groceries she had purchased while she spoke calmly.

"What do you want?" She placed the milk and yogurt in the fridge, set the filters beside the coffee maker on the counter, and stored a box of Frosted Flakes. Subtly, she nudged a plastic storage canister partially onto the burner Dr. Baker had used to heat the water for her tea. Then she pulled out the item she had purchased for Steady and set it on the counter.

Dr. Baker sipped her tea. "I want to help you achieve your true potential, Amelia Krill."

Steady sat on his deck with a mug of coffee in his lap and his bare feet propped on the wicker ottoman. Tilly was on the beach fighting with a seagull over what looked like the remnants of a sack lunch. The yellow lab was paws-down, ass-up guarding half a sandwich while the bird squawked and dive-bombed.

Very wanted to talk. Steady didn't. She was just another woman who had shown she couldn't be trusted, who used him to advance her own selfish needs. He never should have let himself care about Very Valentine. She said from the start she didn't believe in love. He honestly couldn't fathom how far down that path he had wandered. And now he was lost.

He set the mug on the glass-topped end table with a thunk. Tilly had given up her battle with the gull and was now dodging waves.

Steady was pissed, and what was magnifying his anger was the reason why. He wasn't upset about the lying per se or the manipulation. He was mad that Very had made him believe there was someone out there in the world who was different, someone who filled that empty space inside. Her admission in the helicopter was the worst betrayal yet.

The sliding glass door opened with a gentle swoosh, and Steady heard his dad's voice behind him. "I need to check the attic for my old fishing hat." Louis Lockhart walked down to the lower deck and stood beside the couch where Steady stewed. "You know, I think your mother is boxing up the things she doesn't like and hiding them over here."

Steady looked down reflexively. He wasn't wearing a Hawaiian shirt today, just a gray UNC T-shirt, but he had no doubt his mother had hidden the box of his grandfather's floral monstrosities in the beach house attic.

His father continued, "That way, if I raise a stink, she can still retrieve whatever she's carted off."

Steady sighed, "Yeah."

His dad took a seat in the wide chair and drummed his hands on the varnished wicker arms. "What's got you in a mood?"

"Nothing, I'm good."

"Son, I may have been born at night; I was not, however, born *last night*."

Steady leaned forward and locked his fingers between his thighs. "It's a woman."

Louis Lockhart chuckled. "Would this woman, by any chance, have a pink ponytail?"

"How the hell would you know that?"

"She jogged by last time I was here. If gravity hadn't been holding you down, you would have floated off after her."

"Her name is Very."

"Interesting name," his father said.

"Interesting girl."

"Clearly, if she's got you this twisted up."

Steady laughed despite his angst. "Yeah, she's somethin'."

"And I take it there's a complication beyond your aversion to romantic entanglements?"

Steady pulled a bandana from his pocket, walked to the edge of the deck, and waved the yellow fabric overhead. Tilly caught the flash of movement and came running. When the dog had eaten the treat Steady provided, she settled next to him on the couch. Steady rested a hand on Tilly's broad head and told his father everything.

"So you see? She's just like… she's not who I thought she was."

His dad sat quietly for a long moment, a look of regret in his pale green eyes. He moved his hands together, massaging his palm with his thumb. "You know, Jonah, June was twenty-two when I married her. Twenty-three when she had you." He held up a hand. "That's no excuse, but I'm working toward a point here. She talked about wanting to be a singer all the time–took music lessons, performed whenever she could. I dismissed it–thought it was a hobby. It was her dream. She told me as much."

Louis stood and moved to the couch. He, too, rested a hand on Tilly's sleeping form. "And Marissa, I don't think I ever knew what she wanted. I guess the money, the lifestyle."

"Dad, I won't let you take the blame for any of that. Nothing June or Marissa did was your fault," Steady insisted.

"Maybe not, but that's not the moral of this story."

Steady felt his confusion drift across his face.

"The point is, when you love someone, really, truly love them, your dream becomes making their dreams come true. Back then, I was so caught up in my dream of making the hotels a success that I never gave June's dream a lick of thought. That's not love. It's attraction; it's ego or vanity, but not love."

"So what's different with Lara."

His father smiled then. "I could say it was maturity or experience or self-reflection, but the truth is, it was Lara. *She's* what was different. I still think about that first day when she walked into my office for an interview, and you were raising hell in the corner. She wore a yellow dress and these red shoes with little bows on the toe. It wasn't a sexy outfit; hell, it wasn't a particularly professional get-up either, but one look at her, and I felt like I had been looking at black and white photos my whole life, and, suddenly, someone handed me a color picture."

His dad sat back, crossed his legs, and extended his arm along the back of the couch. "From the minute we met, I wanted to know everything about her. What made her happy? What were her dreams? And, by God, I set about finding ways to make them come true. And," His father held up a finger to emphasize his point. "As much as I want to do that for Lara, she does the same for me." He gave Steady's shoulder a squeeze. "Son, if you love this girl, maybe you should stop thinking so much about what Very did and start thinking about why she did it. Ask yourself what she wants. What are her dreams?"

"So, stop being a selfish asshole?" Steady gave his dad a cockeyed grin.

"Well, that's the abridged version."

"Thanks, Dad."

Louis Lockhart stood and wandered to the edge of the deck. Peering over the rail to the side of the house, he said, "Glad to see your mother's flower beds survived the renovation."

Steady grinned. "I know better than to mess with her garden. I told the guys anyone who steps on a plant buys the beer for a week. Not a single flower harmed."

With a low chuckle, his dad crossed to the sliding doors, giving Steady's shoulder another pat as he passed. "I'll grab that fishing hat and be on my way. I love you, Jonah."

"Love you too, Dad."

When his father had reclaimed the old hat and driven away, Steady returned to his musings. He knew Very was up to something, and he knew it was big. She was trying to bring her mother's killer to justice. How big of an asshole was he to get bent out of shape over a minor manipulation. Especially when he was doing the same thing to her for much less noble reasons. Very had a dream; she'd told him her dream, taken him into her confidence, and he was sitting here pouting instead of helping her make it come true.

Tilly lifted her head, dislodging Steady's hand.

"I know, girl. I'm an idiot." Those were the words he spoke, but he signed *good girl* to the dog.

Tilly ignored him and sniffed the air. Then leapt down and darted out to the beach. They didn't have a dog on their SEAL squad, but Steady knew the dog's pose; every combat fighter did. She lifted her nose higher, catching the scent, then she sat. That was her signal. She detected an incendiary device. Tilly returned to his side, and Steady gave her a treat–standard procedure when Tilly worked.

His eyes shot to the beach house next door. He could just make out the edge of a car in the front drive. Steady jumped up so quickly that his coffee mug hit the deck. After grabbing his Sig and phone from the house, he took off across the sand at a slow jog, mindful of the potential danger. Every instinct warned him that Very was in trouble, but he kept his pace. Was this all another part of her fucked up plan? Would he bust in and destroy a set-up years in the making? Or was she manipulating him into doing her bidding yet again?

Steady stopped, Tilly vigilant by his side. He looked down at the dog, who met his gaze awaiting a command. Fuck it. If she didn't want him sticking his nose where it didn't belong, then Very shouldn't have toyed with his heart.

Tilly nudged his calf, and Steady led her away from the shore to the cover of shrubs and angel oak trees that grew between their houses.

Amelia Krill.

Very paled at the use of her birth name.

"Yes, dear. We've known all along who you are. It's time for you to realize it too."

"What does that mean?"

"It's time to bring you peace, Amelia. To silence those conflicting voices in your head and let you return to your rightful place in the Krill dynasty." Dr. Baker paused. "What is that smell?"

Very turned to the stove and moved the plastic container off the burner. "I must have knocked it when I was putting the groceries away," Very muttered as she turned on the exhaust fan in the hood.

"As I was saying," Dr. Baker continued. "You're the heir apparent at Parasol Pharmaceuticals, Amelia. I'm here to help."

"What if I don't want help?"

"Amelia, did you look at the research you stole from my lab?"

"I… no. Not in depth."

"We'll go over it together. One thing of note, however, is that in recent years, I have perfected the drug we call Comply. It quiets a disturbed mind more effectively than any surgical procedure. It's humane and efficient. More notable, however, is the effect the formula has on a healthy mind. It renders the patient docile and highly suggestible. Regular monthly injections can modify behavior indefinitely."

Dr. Baker picked up the hypodermic needle that had been resting behind her mug. Before Very could turn to run, both goons had grabbed her.

"Relax, my dear. This is a sedative to keep you under control until we get you to Armand's home. Sometimes, Amelia, a patient doesn't know what's best."

Dr. Baker passed the syringe to one of the men restraining Very, and he stabbed the needle into her upper arm. Very broke free of his hold, grabbed the emptied hypodermic still dangling from her arm, and threw it across the room. She scrambled behind the couch, then collapsed onto the floor.

Steady had just ensconced himself in bushes when he heard Very's front door slam open. He couldn't see the SUVs until they entered his field of vision, pulling out of the driveway and onto the main road. Moving low and fast, Steady ran to Very's deck stairs and peeked through the window. The house was quiet. A sick feeling brewed in his gut as he slid open the deck door, gun drawn, and silently moved inside.

Steady remained calm as he took in the scene—a mug of the tea she hated (but kept for Twitch) cooling on the table, the signs of a struggle, the syringe on the floor. He knew the house was empty before he called out her name. "Very?"

After taking a slow turn around the room, Steady's eyes settled on something that made his pulse spike and his brow bead with sweat. There was only one item on the kitchen counter.

A rutabaga.

With his phone to his ear, he sprinted out the door.

CHAPTER FIFTY-TWO

New York City
August 15

The smile spread across his face like a fisher cracking granite as Krill read the text from Dr. Baker. Krill had to hand it to Verity Valentine. She had devised a brilliant scheme to ruin him. Unfortunately, like every opponent he had ever encountered, she had underestimated him. Krill had the mind of a chess master; he played out every scenario and planned for every contingency.

And he never lost.

"Excuse me, Mr. Krill?" His secretary stood in the doorway.

"Yes?"

"Dr. Baker and Miss Krill have arrived."

"Excellent. Show them in."

Krill returned to his desk and took his seat as Dr. Baker walked in, followed by two men hauling a subdued Verity Valentine–soon to be rightfully known as Amelia Krill–between them.

"This is how she behaves?" Krill asked, unimpressed.

Krill watched Theodora Baker as a flash of irritation passed her face, then cleared. She replied without emotion. "No. She's simply sedated. I need a controlled environment to administer Comply."

"You can use one of the guest rooms upstairs."

"I thought you might want to speak to her before we use the medication. She won't process information as effectively after treatment."

"Ah, yes, of course. I want the young lady to know how badly she's been beaten."

Krill directed the men to seat Amelia in the chair opposite his desk. "You gave it a valiant effort, my dear. I think your mother would have been proud. Unfortunately, you have failed to learn the same lesson. I cannot be outsmarted. I've lived too long, seen too much, and understand with crystal clarity how the world works, how people work."

Verity met his gaze, defiant. Krill nearly laughed. She would soon understand. Eventually, they all did.

CHAPTER FIFTY-THREE

Bishop Security Headquarters
Somewhere outside Beaufort, South Carolina
August 15

Steady was pacing a hole in Nathan Bishop's office carpet.

"Her whole op has gone FUBAR, and I don't know what the fuck to do? Where is she, Nathan?"

"Steady," Nathan said calmly.

"What?" Steady snapped.

"Get a hold of yourself."

"You don't understand. She's in over her head. She thinks these people killed her mother. Now they have her, and they probably want to kill her too."

"I understand. Trust me, Jonah. Nobody understands better than I do. Emily was in the hands of a madman twice."

"How did you keep your shit?"

"I didn't. Inside I was losing my mind, but I did what we always do at times like this. Focus on the op. Concentrate all that worry and fear on real, concrete things we can do to get her back."

"Yes, good. Real, concrete shit." Steady plopped into a guest chair. "Like what?"

"Twitch hacked into the security feed at the Hale Center. Very's not there."

Twitch appeared at the doorway as if the mention of her name had summoned her. She rested an open laptop on her pregnant belly. "I think I found her."

Steady jumped to his feet as Twitch set the computer on the small conference table and sat. Chat entered the room and joined her.

Nathan moved to the large table, and Steady did the same.

"Okay," Twitch lifted satisfied eyes to the group. "A Parasol Pharmaceuticals jet took off from the Kiawah Island private airstrip earlier today with a logged flight plan to Teterboro Airport."

"They're in New York," Steady said.

Chat rubbed her back. "As always, you are a miracle worker, and it is appreciated."

Steady knew his intuitive friend must have sensed Twitch's need for affirmation, so he jumped on board. "Twitch, you're amazing."

Her eyes clouded, and Twitch flapped her hands to wave the tears away. "Thanks, guys. Argh, pregnancy hormones."

Finn stuck his head in the door. "Everything okay in here?"

"Suddenly, Chat isn't the only psychic in the group," Nathan muttered.

Steady tugged at his hair. "Yes, Finn, your girl couldn't be better. Now can we get back to Very?"

Finn rolled a chair between Steady and Twitch, pushing Steady over half a foot. With a big hand on Twitch's lower back, he whispered softly in her ear. Twitch nodded and smiled.

"Twitch!" Steady bellowed.

She cleared her throat. "Sorry, Steady. One second." Her hands flew across her keyboard. "Got it. The address of Armand Krill's Manhattan home. That's the logical place to start." She tapped another button and sent the information to Steady. "The jet is ready for you at the airfield. The flight plan has been logged. Tox is already in New York with Calliope. She has some doctor's appointment her mother set up. Finn and Cam are good to go."

Steady stared blankly at his capable colleague.

"What?" Twitch asked.

"You did all that while I was sitting here bitching?"

"Nothing to it." She closed her laptop. Finn kissed her cheek.

"Twitch, thank you." Steady bussed her other cheek as he passed her chair.

Nathan looked at Steady. "Hold on for a minute. I don't think kicking down his door is the right way to go about this."

Steady retook his seat. "What did you have in mind?"

"Parasol makes several over-the-counter medications. Your family owns dozens of hotels, each one with a lobby gift shop, correct? Armand Krill isn't a man to pass up an opportunity. Let's see if we can arrange a meeting."

Twitch and Finn turned to him with matching expectant expressions.

Steady stood. "Set it up. I'll dust off a suit and head to New York." He looked around the table. These people, his second family, would do anything for him. "Thanks."

Nathan gave an understanding nod, then said, "What are you waiting for?"

Without another word. Steady ran out the door. As he raced through the building, a thought struck him. He had felt this way once before–that day in the desert hobbling with a busted leg to that broken-down Huey. It was as if his heart wasn't simply pumping blood through his veins. No. It was beating for someone else and for a reason far more important than just him.

His heart was beating for Very. It was beating for love.

CHAPTER FIFTY-FOUR

Very stood between the two guards, horror and hope intermingling into a nauseating cocktail in her stomach.

Armand Krill picked up a paper file, moved around his desk, and sat on the burgundy sofa in the small sitting area. Dr. Baker's men moved Very into the highback chair opposite.

Krill crossed his legs and tapped on his knee—index finger, middle finger, ring finger, pinky. Over and over. It was hypnotic. He recaptured her attention when he spoke. "Your attempts to undermine me have failed, my dear granddaughter. Although, I admire your determination. Few people have had the nerve to dare try."

Very stared daggers into Armand Krill's beady eyes. This man, her grandfather, was a devil in a three-piece suit. He should have been—well, it was a waste of mental energy listing all the ways he should have behaved as the head of a family. He wasn't her family, no matter what the DNA indicated.

Very fought against the sedative clouding her brain and said, "ProbeX has the sample of Mobilify. They can produce the medication without side effects in under a year."

"I thought you'd like to witness this." Krill reached for the file at his side, opened it, and signed a document with a flourish. Then he passed it to her.

"What's this?" Very asked.

"Parasol Pharmaceuticals newest acquisition." He paused, relishing the moment. "ProbeX Labs."

Very opened the file, her adrenaline spiking. "You bought the lab?"

"It was hardly a chore, Amelia."

"My name is Verity," she corrected.

Krill ignored her. "ProbeX was on its last legs. The owner was ecstatic after receiving my generous offer. The board signed off in under an hour. My signature on that contract finalizes the deal."

"You bought the lab," she repeated.

"Now that the matter is settled, Dr. Baker will attend to you." He flicked a hand dismissively. "Perhaps I will finally get a family member of some use."

CHAPTER FIFTY-FIVE

New York City
August 16

The house manager stood dwarfed in an archway three times his height and cleared his throat. Armand Krill nodded his approval to speak.

"Sir, Miss Amelia." The man stepped to the side, and his granddaughter appeared wearing a high-necked blouse secured with a bow and a knee-length pleated skirt. Her inconspicuous dark blonde hair was held in a low clip, and her hazel eyes were flat as she assessed the room.

Armand nearly smiled. Decades of a settled scowl had cemented his facial muscles in place, and now, at the age of seventy-three, the most he could manage was a slight lifting of the corners of his lips and a partial baring of his teeth. It was an action that conveyed disgust rather than joy and gave the young woman pause before she proceeded into the cavernous space.

She stood with her hands clasped and her head slightly bowed and waited.

"Good evening, Amelia."

"Good evening, g-grandfather."

"Please." He indicated the place to his right, and a jacketed man stepped forward to seat her and lay the linen napkin across her lap. She fiddled with the silk ties of the bow that hung from the neck of the blouse, then stopped and let her hands go limp.

Armand indicated with a glance at his empty cup that he was ready for coffee. The young man poured, then retreated as another uniformed server placed a fruit assortment on each silver charger.

Fully aware of Amelia's diminished capacity for emotion and opinion, he kept his questions fact-based. "What did you do this morning?"

"I started a biography of Eleanor Roosevelt and went for a walk in the garden."

Armand took a bite of cantaloupe and nodded to Amelia to do the same. "The weather was tolerable in the garden?"

"It was quite warm even at the early hour, but the path is shaded."

"Very good, Amelia."

They finished their breakfast in silence. Armand was impressed with Dr. Baker's progress. Comply was a wonder drug.

At the entrance to the dining room, Krill's house manager reappeared. "Excuse me, sir. The gentleman from Lockhart Hotels is here. He said you have an appointment."

Krill glanced at his granddaughter, his eyes lit with twisted pleasure. "Show him in."

Steady strode into the room, wearing a custom suit and holding a leather briefcase. He may look civilized on the outside, but beneath the surface, he was marshaling every ounce of willpower to stop himself from pulling out his Sig and blowing Armand Krill's head off. He took a beat to quell his rage. There was something far more important in this room than the snake at the head of the table.

Very sat to Krill's right staring down at her half-eaten breakfast. Her hair was the same dark blonde she had dyed it to escape the Hale Center, and her outfit looked like something out of a cult documentary. He willed her to look at him; he needed to see what was wrong. What had these monsters done to her?

He shifted his attention to Krill and, with an arrogant nonchalance, said, "Jonah Lockhart. I'm the CFO of Lockhart Hotels. As my assistant communicated, we are interested in using Parasol as the exclusive provider for over-the-counter medications in our lobby shops."

"I appreciate a man who gets down to business. My people have a proposal prepared. Let's go to my office," Krill said.

Steady observed as Krill whispered something to Very. He decided to improvise. "My parents are hosting an event in Charlotte tonight. They insist I attend. They're always trying to find me a wife. But these southern girls with dollar signs in their eyes have a little too much pluck for my taste. I train horses on my ranch. I don't have time to break a woman."

It took Krill all of ten seconds to do the math. He led Steady out of the room, then turned to the man who had answered the door. "Ask Amelia to bring us coffee in my office." He turned back to Steady. "If you'll follow me."

Steady tried to control his racing heart. It was such a foreign feeling, he worried he might be developing a coronary issue.

Krill led Steady into the cavernous office, and the two men sat at the conference table. Steady mapped the house's floor plan, noting alarms, security cameras, and points of entry. Krill's assistant brought two copies of a proposal and placed them in front of her boss. Krill passed one to Steady, and he pretended to look at the numbers.

A moment later, the air prickled, and Steady looked up. Very stood in the doorway with flat eyes holding a silver tray with a coffee service. She looked like a china doll.

It broke Steady's heart.

"Amelia, come in and set the coffee on the table. Mr. Lockhart, this is my granddaughter, Amelia."

Steady stood as Very placed the tray within reach on the long table. He came around Krill and held out his hand. "Amelia, a pleasure. I'm Jonah."

She looked confused for a moment, then placed her hand in his. She faltered at the touch but composed herself and said, "Hello."

Steady felt Krill's eyes on his back, and he forced himself to release Very's hand. She seemed equally resistant to the separation.

"Amelia," Krill said as he prepared his coffee, "it's warm today. Why don't you remove your blouse."

Very stepped away from Steady and obeyed without hesitation.

Krill sipped his coffee.

Steady had a momentary image flash in his brain of turning to Krill and killing him with one punch. It was brief but vivid.

Very, in a white camisole, stood in the center of the room like a department store mannequin. "Can I get you anything else, grandfather?"

Krill lifted a provocative brow to Steady. He didn't want Very to disappear, so he said, "Is it too early for lunch? I jumped on the jet at the crack of dawn and missed breakfast."

"Amelia, bring Mr. Lockhart some lunch."

"Yes, sir." She turned a passive gaze to Steady. "What would you like?"

"What do you suggest?"

Krill interjected, "Oh, you'll find my granddaughter doesn't hold many opinions of her own. She's here to meet your needs. Whatever you'd like to eat, the cook will prepare."

"A sandwich or a salad, please," he said.

Very nodded. "Cook is preparing a salad for our lunch, grandfather. Mixed greens with beets and goat cheese. Shall I bring that?"

"For two, Amelia," Krill ordered.

Very turned to leave, but Steady called her back. "See if the chef can throw in some rutabaga. I suddenly have a craving for rutabaga."

"Rutabaga?" Very repeated, her brow furrowed.

Krill thumbed through the proposal pages as he muttered, "That's an odd ingredient."

Steady lassoed every emotion going berserk in his body and said, "It's delicious. See if the chef has it handy. If not, c'est la vie."

When Very left the room, Krill redirected Steady's attention to the paperwork. He flipped through it but made a point of staring at the doorway. Krill watched him.

"Your granddaughter is charming." Steady forced a leering smile.

"She finds the greatest joy in serving others," Krill said.

"How is she like that?" Steady asked.

Krill's answer was simple. "Breeding. Take your time reviewing the proposal, and one of my people will be in touch. It's a standard provider contract we have with several retailers. Of course, we'd be happy to consider any accommodations you require. I'm looking forward to doing business with you, Mr. Lockhart."

"Not half as much as I am." Steady turned and left the room.

Halfway down the hall to the stairs, Steady met Very carrying the lunch tray. He wanted to shake the docile right out of her, but he needed to get her home, and then they could figure out how to fix her. Standing opposite her, the tray between them, Steady ran his thumb along her cheek. "I'll see you later."

He walked around her and proceeded to the stairs when he heard her say, "Steady, your lunch."

He froze, his hand on a finial carved into a large acorn. He looked at her still form and said, "What did you say?"

She repeated, "Your lunch?"

Steady stared at Very's back. She was still wearing just the camisole. He wanted to rip that fucking clip out of her hair, grab the ponytail in his fist, and kiss her back to sanity. He shook his head to clear his wishful thinking. As he descended the stairs, he muttered, "Shove it down gramps's gullet."

He threw open the front door and emerged into the stifling New York heat. He suppressed the urge to pick up one of the stone lions that flanked the entry and toss it through the bay window. Instead, he called Cam.

"How'd it go?"

"I think I need blood pressure medication. I may be having a heart attack."

Cam's chuckle was rich and soothing. "Hermano, you need your woman."

"I found her. Cam, we're gonna need a doctor. They gave her some drug. She's like a fucking robot."

All the humor left Cam's voice, "Copy that. I'll make the arrangements. Get her home."

PART FIVE

The Slip

CHAPTER FIFTY-SIX

New York City
August 17

Krill greeted Alonso Mitchell with uncharacteristic warmth as he brushed past him and took a seat at his desk. "Good morning, Mitchell. Your work is completed. I'll transfer your payment as usual."

"Thank you, sir."

"Amelia is back with me, Mobilify is selling like hotcakes, and I'll soon be a member of the Vitruvian Society. All in all, not a bad week, I'd say. Hell, I may even marry Amelia to the hotel chain heir."

"What?" Alonso Mitchell took a step forward.

Krill backpedaled. Mitchell had not been privy to the events of last night. "I had a prospect to the house, the entitled son of a southern hotelier. It could be an extremely lucrative arrangement. And he was quite taken with Amelia."

"Hotel chain, you say?" Mitchell took another half a step forward.

"Lockhart Hotels out of North Carolina."

Krill's hired gun stood still as stone, a strange look on his face.

"What?" Krill demanded.

Mitchell's explanation was halted by Krill's assistant, who was timid as she leaned into the room.

"Yes?" Krill snapped.

"There are three gentlemen here from the SEC."

Krill was curious but unbothered when he said, "Show them in."

After the men entered the room, the shortest and oldest of the trio stepped forward with his identification in hand. "Mr. Krill, I'm Joe Stoppard with the Securities and Exchange Commission." He held out a hand to his right, then his left. "This is Special Agent Corman and Special Agent Ravelli with the FBI."

Corman was thin and bald. Ravelli either had a short beard or needed to shave. Krill crossed his arms over his chest, then, realizing he had made the unconscious protective gesture, uncrossed them and flattened his palms on the desk. "How can I help you?"

"It has come to our attention that Parasol Pharmaceuticals has acquired ProbeX Labs."

"That is correct. I don't see how that is a concern for the SEC. Parasol is hardly a monopoly."

Stoppard's expression turned patronizing. "No, Mr. Krill, not a monopoly. Your purchase of ProbeX significantly impacted the value of the stock."

"I have no doubt," Krill replied.

Stoppard seemed annoyed Krill wasn't connecting the dots, but there were no dots to connect. Krill's investments were squeaky clean.

"Mr. Krill, you made a substantial investment in ProbeX Labs just days before Parasol purchased the company."

"That is not correct," Krill replied dismissively.

"Sir, you transferred five million dollars to Vitruvian Investments, which purchased the ProbeX stock through a shell company, and a poorly disguised one at that." Agent Stoppard withdrew a stack of papers from his breast pocket and passed them to Krill.

Krill flipped through the pages. "This can't be right. There's been some sort of misunderstanding." The SEC officer said nothing as Krill let the document flutter to his desk. "You certainly cannot arrest me for a misunderstanding."

Stoppard had a look on his face that made Krill want to kill him. Krill made a mental note of his name; he may not end his life, but he would unhesitatingly ruin his career.

"I can't arrest you for anything, Mr. Krill. The SEC is not a law enforcement entity. That's why these men are here."

One of the FBI agents stepped forward. "Armand Krill, you are under arrest for insider trading, stock fraud, and wire fraud. You have the right to remain silent—"

"I know my rights," Krill interrupted. The agent gripped his arm like Krill was a common thief and moved him to the outer office.

The FBI agent who wasn't manhandling Krill held the warrant open in front of his face. "We will be confiscating your computer and any paperwork related to Parasol Pharmaceuticals."

Krill barked to his assistant. "Get my lawyer." Then he turned his attention to Mitchell, who was lurking in the corner. "Find Johan DeVold. He can clear this up. His card is in my wallet."

Mitchell reached into Krill's breast pocket, retrieved the wallet, and looked inside. "It's not in here."

"Yes, it is, you idiot. His assistant gave me his card last week. Look again."

Mitchell looked up with a narrowed gaze. "Armand, it's not here. I'll get his contact information from your phone."

"I didn't save it," he barked. "Check the call log."

Mitchell scrolled through the list and shook his head.

"DeVold was insistent there be no…" Krill's voice trailed off as he finished the thought. "…electronic record." The blood drained from his face. "Get to the Cavalry Club. Find DeVold."

Mitchell snapped into action and was gone before Krill could add, "Find out what the hell is going on."

CHAPTER FIFTY-SEVEN

New York City
August 17

When Tox texted his brother, Miles, to say he had returned to New York for the doctor's appointment Calliope's mother had arranged, he was surprised where Miles had asked to meet.

Now, Tox stood in the posh men's lavatory of the Cavalry Club and watched his fraternal twin peel a fake scar from his cheek and remove an eye patch. Next, he popped out the colored contact lens from his uncovered eye and flushed all the items down the toilet.

"How was Calliope's check-up?" Miles asked.

"As expected. Her mother insisted she see this fancy OB. He did the same stuff her doctor in Beaufort does, told us everything is fine and sent us on our way."

"That's good," Miles said.

"So this is what you've been up to all week?" Tox pointed to the props disappearing into the plumbing.

Miles checked his reflection in the mirror. "The big fun is just starting."

"So where's the real Johan DeVold?" Tox asked.

"Johannesburg. Running his business. He's a homebody. His travel schedule is fairly light," Miles said matter-of-factly as he removed the dental prosthetic.

"Ready?" Tox asked.

"Now remember, no matter what, just do what I told you. If something goes sideways, I'll handle it," Miles cautioned.

Tox grinned. "You know, I took a drama class in college. I'm sure I could deliver a stirring monologue."

"Just stand there, Miller," Miles repeated. "No talking, no emoting, no nothing."

"You're sure?"

"Quite sure." Miles deadpanned. "Let's put this thing to bed; then you'll get the Peter Luger's porterhouse I promised."

Tox clapped his brother on the back. "You know, I was just thinking I needed some quality time with my baby bro."

Miles shoved him off and washed his hands in the marble sink. "I'm seven minutes younger, fool."

The phone in Miles's duffle buzzed. "Grab that, will you."

Tox knelt to retrieve it with his eyes on the door. "You're going to answer it? Now?"

"Four people in addition to you have that number. So yes."

Tox read the ID as it flashed on the screen. "Text ID reads *Trouble*. Fifty bucks says it's a woman."

Miles pulled a cloth towel from the stack and dried his hands. "It's Clara. Let me see." Miles read the text. "Tap a thumbs up on that."

"Clara?" Tox feigned ignorance as he did what Miles requested.

"You know who she is."

Tox held up the phone with a grin. "Trouble."

"I asked her to help out with this job. I thought it was the perfect way to do what her father wanted and keep an eye on her. All she had to do was play the part of my assistant and drop a pill bottle at the right time." Miles straightened his tie and shot his cuffs. "You'd think I was asking her to perform Ophelia."

"Is her part finished?" Tox asked.

"Not yet. Clara still has one crucial role to play. Then I can be done with her." He added, "Until, of course, she asks me to return the favor."

His twin didn't seem too broken up about that. Tox grinned and started to speak when Miles stopped him. "Don't say a word."

Tox dropped the phone back in the bag, slung the strap over his shoulder, and pushed off the sink. "Ready?"

The two men turned just as the door opened, and a pompous man wearing a jacket with the Cavalry Club logo stepped into the men's room.
*****

Two blocks from the club, Mitchell patted the small of his back, comforted by the presence of the Glock. He looked straight ahead, mission-focused. Krill thought his methods were so strategic, so astute; the truth was, Krill was predictable. And Mitchell knew better than most that predictability made for easy targets. Krill was getting taken for a ride. Mitchell knew it.
*****

The manager spoke with a stiff accent. "Sir, a word."

Miles and Tox stood side-by-side, staring at the older man. Miles took a step forward and spoke. "You can drop the act, Finster. The fish is fried."

Finster's stiff shoulders slumped as he said, "Thank fuck. I get so in character, I've been talking like a chump twenty-four/seven. My girl told me I even screw like a stuffed shirt. And that's no compliment."

Miles took the duffle from his twin and withdrew an envelope. He passed it to the man. "Job well done, Finster. The boys outside?"

"By the side entrance. That's what I came in to tell you." The man slipped the envelope into his breast pocket without examining the contents.

"All right. Let's go pay the fellas. My brother needs food."

Tox elbowed Miles as they strode with matched steps down the grand hall. "How the hell did you take over this whole joint?"

Miles replied, "You know what word can clear a building faster than anything in Manhattan?"

"Fire? 'Tox guessed.

"Nope." Miles turned the corner, heading for the alley exit. "Bedbugs."

One block from the Cavalry Club, Mitchell slowed his pace. He prided himself on expecting the unexpected. Krill used to jibe him; *you're like a boy scout, always prepared.* He *was* a fucking boy scout, and Krill was about to see just how prepared Alonso Mitchell was.

Miles stood at the alley entrance to the Cavalry Club and handed each person in the line an envelope of cash. They were dressed as waiters and maids and squash players and businessmen. Each cast member in their elaborate production laughed and joked. A man in a suit complained about the Jets quarterback to his buddy, who was wearing a chef's jacket.

Miles had taken over the entire establishment and filled the Cavalry Club with con men from Bushwick to Hoboken. The Mark, Armand Krill, had generously financed the operation with his initiation fee–with plenty left over for The Sting. When the last man had his cash, Miles bent down, picked up the sign, and affixed it to the fire door.

THE CAVALRY CLUB WILL BE CLOSED
FOR BUILDING MAINTENANCE.
MEMBERS MAY EMAIL THE MANAGEMENT
OFFICE WITH PRESSING MATTERS

"Finster, did you put the other one on the front door?"

"Yep, right across that bitch-ass logo." Finster held out his hand. "Good to see you, man. We don't do enough of these anymore."

Miles shook it and squeezed Finster's shoulder. "The confidence game is a dying art, my friend."

"See ya around." Finster ambled to the sidewalk and looked up the street. Before he took off, he turned back to Miles and said, "Looks like we might be getting some rain."

Miles walked to the edge of the alley and peered around the corner with Tox bent over above him. The real Cavalry Club general manager was peering through the glass doors and fishing a set of keys from his pocket. Josiah Greentree was a small but stern-looking man with square-rimmed glasses and an ebony walking stick.

Tox looked at his brother. "Now what?"

*****

Mitchell skirted a man standing beside a construction barrier on the sidewalk and rounded the corner. Immediately, he shrank back. Peering around the edge of the building, Mitchell watched as the man Krill knew as Johan DeVold was speaking with an older gentleman wearing a Cavalry Club staff blazer. The eye patch was gone. The scar was gone. This man was not Johan DeVold.

*****

Miles murmured to Tox, "Hang back," and came around the corner to the front of the club.

"Ah, Mr. Greentree, you're early. I thought we were meeting at five."

"Mr. Oglethorpe." The man greeted Miles. "I was in the neighborhood and thought I'd chance it. I passed by the building last week. There was certainly a lot of activity."

"At EnviroClean, we understand how awkward this situation can be. As we discussed, our staff dressed appropriately, entering and exiting the building.

Your effort to inform the members of the club's closing was successful. No actual members turned up. Any passers-by wouldn't be the wiser with our staff coming and going."

"You think of everything, Oglethorpe. It's why you're the best-reviewed service in the city," Mr. Greentree said.

The fake website had worked like a charm. "And the most expensive," Miles added with a chuckle.

"So?" Greentree rocked back on his heels.

"We've just finished the final inspection. The infestation has been handled. Most of the furniture was saved."

"Thank God."

"The few things that were unsalvageable were destroyed," Miles said.

"You're sure?"

"Mr. Greentree, the building is pristine. If you ever see a bedbug in the Cavalry Club, I will resign my post."

"Wonderful, wonderful. Thank you." Greentree extended his hand, and Miles shook it.

"My pleasure. The bill is on your desk. We came in just under the estimate."

"Excellent. I'll send the check today. Oh, is it safe to go inside?"

"Perfectly safe. Our patented treatment formula leaves no trace. It will be as if we were never here," Miles said with a gentle smile.

Greentree nodded and pulled open the etched glass door. "Thank you again, Oglethorpe."

"My pleasure. It's always rewarding to keep establishments like the Cavalry Club free of vermin."

"Indeed," Greentree concurred, disappearing inside the building.

Mitchell pulled out his phone and placed the FaceTime call. Krill's pinched face appeared on the screen.

"Well? Did you find DeVold?" Krill demanded.

"You need to see this." Mitchell checked his watch, then switched the camera angle as he rounded the corner.

As he headed toward the DeVold imposter and his entourage, something across the street drew Mitchell's attention. Still recording, he watched as the passenger window of a black sedan lowered, and the suppressed muzzle of a gun poked out. Two muffled shots were fired, and Mitchell redirected the phone to his side of the street where the man Krill knew as Johan DeVold lay on the sidewalk in a spreading pool of blood.

Mitchell turned the phone to his own face. "I need to get out of here."

"No. Show me what's happening," Krill insisted.

Mitchell pointed the camera to the action and shielded himself in the Cavalry Club doorway as men gathered around the body. A moment later, an unmarked SUV screeched to the curb. Four men in black ops military attire emerged in unison, collected the body, and drove away. Some of the men on the sidewalk climbed into the other SUV and followed. The entire event transpired in under a minute.

"Holy shit," Mitchell muttered as he hurried away.

"Mitchell," Krill whisper-shouted, "what the hell is happening?"

"I don't know, but this is much bigger than we suspected. DeVold, the man you knew as DeVold, is dead. Those men that came and took the body? That was black ops. Maybe government, maybe mercenary. Either way, you've stumbled into some dangerous shit."

Krill leaned so close to the camera Mitchell only saw his mouth. "Mitchell, I need you. Someone has set me up. Find out what happened at the Cavalry Club. Find out who's behind this."

"Yes, sir."

Mitchell ended the call and walked away. He didn't need to investigate further. He knew exactly who was behind it.

"Mr. Krill, we're ready." The FBI agent–Krill had forgotten his name–dangled a pair of handcuffs from two fingers. "You can have your attorney meet us at Federal Plaza."

Armand Krill stood with as much dignity as he could muster and extended his hands. He just needed time to think. He wasn't beaten. If he had to spend half his fortune, he would get to the bottom of this. He would never concede. Never.

CHAPTER FIFTY-EIGHT

New York City
August 17

Steady waited outside the Krill mansion, loitering under the awning of a designer clothing store across the street. He was unobtrusive, dressed in gray trousers and a matching long-sleeved T-shirt. His plan was pretty basic: wait until dark, sneak in the staff entrance, disable the alarm, grab Very, and run like hell. That strategy went out the window as he watched the men escorting Krill down the front steps and placing him in the back of a government car.

Steady looked down at the small duffle that held tools and supplies. Then he glanced up at the open front door of the Krill mansion. *Fuck it.* He took off like a starter pistol had been fired, bounded up the stairs, and burst into the front hall. There was one person in the foyer, a maid, who screamed and ran away. In the dining room, Steady spotted the house manager reaching for his phone to alert security. Steady took the stairs two at a time, throwing open doors as he passed. At the end of the corridor, he spotted Very. She was standing on the back staircase descending from an upper floor.

Without thought or stealth, he swept Very into his arms, tore down the stairs, and out into the street. Steady dropped Very into the passenger seat of the sleek rented sports car. When he snapped the seatbelt, he tucked a strand of brown hair behind her ear. "Don't you worry, Darlin'. We'll get you back, pink hair and all. You'll be crazier than a bee in a flower shop in no time."

Very met his gaze with confusion.

He closed the passenger door and hurried around to the driver's seat. He spoke as he pulled into traffic, expertly maneuvering the car. "You see, I'm sure you're a nice person, but you're not my Very. I need her back."

"Why?"

Steady looked straight ahead as he spoke. "Well, that's a hell of a question. I could tell you all the details. I could tell you what a firecracker she is or how much she cares about the people in her life. But the simple truth is I love her. I love her, and I want her back. Body and soul."

He looked over then. Very's face was turned away, but she was wiping a tear from her cheek.

"You big dope."

Steady inadvertently jerked the wheel to the right, nearly sideswiping a delivery van. He righted the car and continued downtown.

"Very?"

She shrugged. "I was faking."

"Faking?"

Very framed her face with jazz hands. "Faking."

"It's really you?" He ran a hand over her cheek.

"In the flesh." She laughed.

"How?" He checked the rearview mirror. "Hold that thought."

Steady pulled to the curb at a bus stop, hopped out of the car, and jogged back to the sedan that had slammed to a halt behind them. Krill's man emerged from the vehicle with a gun aimed at Steady's chest. Without hesitation, Steady came at him.

"What the fuck do you–"

Steady threw a jab to the guy's throat and a punch to his temple, knocking him out cold mid-sentence. He pushed the guy back through the open car door and set his head on the steering wheel with a less-than-gentle thud. Then he grabbed the fallen gun and returned to the rental.

"Now, where were we?" Steady floored it with a wink in Very's direction.

Very checked over her shoulder at the scene disappearing behind them, then leaned across the console and kissed him. "Hmm?" she said.

He momentarily pondered the logistics of taking Very in the front seat of a moving car in the middle of Manhattan traffic but reluctantly dismissed the idea. "You were explaining how you faked being drugged."

Very returned to her side and refastened the seatbelt. "Right. Like many vaccines, Comply is temperature sensitive. Before I left the Hale Center, I microwaved her samples."

Steady maneuvered the car through traffic with a grin. "So, when she injected you?"

"Nothing. The chemical degraded when I warmed it, and the vaccine was no longer viable. Dr. Baker had behavioral videos of patients in her files. So I just mimicked–"

With one hand on the wheel, Steady adjusted his erection. Very noticed.

"What about that turned you on?"

"What about that *didn't* turn me on? The most beautiful woman I've ever seen is whooping bad guys with nothing but her wits. It's the sexiest fucking thing I've ever seen."

"Steady, I'm sorry I didn't say it as soon as we got in the car. I was just–"

The red light was heaven-sent. He covered her mouth with his own.

"Steady," she breathed his name.

"Let's get you home."

"Oh, God. Are we flying?"

Steady ran his hand over her hair and held the side of her neck. "No, Darlin'. I want you to *want* to fly with me. So the plane is staying here for the boys, and we are going to hit the open road."

"Thank you."

"Everything is gonna work out just fine."

When he pulled back, his face was wet with her tears. "What's wrong?"

Very swiped at her cheeks. "I screwed up. My…," She paused for a beat. "My partner, remember? I told you about Charles Darwin. He and I had this perfect plan. Bring down Krill and stop the flow of money to the Hale Center. But that wasn't enough for me. I wanted Dr. Baker to pay for what she did to my mom. I wanted proof, so I deliberately tried to get them to send me for a psych eval. I added some tidbits to my personnel file to make it easy for Krill to exercise that option. I didn't know if he would resort to sending me to the Hale Center–it wasn't part of our original plan for that reason. It was too unpredictable of a variable. Darwin thought there were already so many moving parts. But I prepared for it, wished for it. I knew Darwin would be furious. He had planned everything down to the smallest detail. I jeopardized the entire thing by going off script."

More tears fell. Steady's chest ached. This lone woman was taking on corrupt corporations and criminals who had unlimited assets and power.

"Then it happened. Krill actually sent me to the Hale Center. It was a win-win for Krill and Dr. Baker. Either I joined forces with them, or I became their next human guinea pig. It was my one chance to get the evidence to bring Theodora Baker to justice. And I failed. I risked the entire plan and betrayed my partner for nothing."

"It's not over yet, Darlin'."

"I know. The plan was always to bring down Krill. Krill is the mastermind. He's the head of the serpent. It's just…Dr. Baker," Very looked at her feet. "She took my mom from me."

Steady's eyes burned at her declaration. Very always talked about her life and her childhood with this light, upbeat attitude. *Everything worked out. I had a really happy childhood.* He thought this might be the first time she actually admitted to herself that her mother's murder, being left all alone, was devastating.

"It's not over, Very," he repeated. "We'll figure this out."

Steady watched as Very steeled herself and regained her composure. He knew the next words out of her mouth wouldn't be good ones.

"Steady, I can't." She stopped. Started again. "I'm grateful for everything you've done." She rested a hand on his thigh. "But I need to finish this on my own. Darwin and I have to see this through."

Steady swallowed the pain. He remembered his dad's words. If you truly love someone, their dream becomes your dream. He wasn't going to let his petty insecurities fuck up any chance they had at a future. This was about her dream. This was about righting a twenty-year-old wrong. Steady wanted this for Very more than he had ever wanted anything for himself.

So, for the next eleven hours, while Very slept or ran into gas station convenience stores for snacks, Steady was on his phone in a hushed voice, making plans.

CHAPTER FIFTY-NINE

New York City
August 17

The two black Suburbans circled the block and came to a stop around the corner from the Cavalry Club. Tox hopped out of the rear car and hustled to the lead. The two men in the back seat got out, nodded to Tox, and climbed into the car he had vacated as it pulled away.

Tox settled in the back seat, reached over, and placed a hand on his brother's shoulder. "Oh, Miles. Why?"

Behind him, Tox's twin opened his eyes. "It's a good thing you made it in security because you suck as an actor."

Miles sat up, and after the driver tossed him a towel and a clean shirt, he set about wiping up the stunt blood and changing. He looked out the back window at the quiet street and spoke into an invisible comm unit. "Open it up, boys."

His men positioned down the sidewalk dropped their props–newspapers and brooms–and cleared away the barriers. Miles had used the classic New York excuse of filming a movie to keep pedestrians and cars off the block while the violent scene played out.

One of their men had already swept up the debris from the shootout and was hosing off the sidewalk like any other maintenance man on any other morning. It was a brilliant New York day.

"We need to head downtown." The driver pulled away and headed east to the FDR. Miles stretched his legs across the cargo space. "Just one last phase." He grinned like a kid on Christmas morning. "The Slip."

Tox asked, "There's more? This Krill guy thinks you're dead. He's going to jail."

Miles replied, "Don't underestimate a rich man's lawyer. Krill will spend whatever it takes to stay out of jail. The final step in a con is to ensure that the mark never realizes he's been taken for a ride." Miles squeezed his brother's shoulder. "We have to make him want to go to jail."

Tox laughed. "How the hell do you pull that off?"

Miles waggled his phone. "*Trouble.*"

Tox nodded, "Ah, Clara. She's certainly being helpful."

Miles speared Tox with a glare. "Put a cork in it. The Feds who arrested Krill owe me a favor. Plus, they were extremely receptive to the prospect of Clara facilitating a plea from Krill."

The SUV slowed to a stop on the outskirts of Federal Plaza, and Miles once again spoke into his comm unit. "Okay, boys, wait for Clara's signal. Then we're in and out in six minutes, or the real police will show up."

CHAPTER SIXTY

New York City
August 17

K rill sat in the back of the sedan and wallowed in his fury. On the humiliating walk to the FBI agents' car, an ill-mannered dog and its leash had gotten tangled in Krill's legs. Now his custom vicuña suit pants were covered in dog hair, and, with his shackled hands, he had no way to brush it off. So he stared at the white strands as anger fermented in his veins. He rubbed one pant leg against the other, trying to rid himself of the disgusting fur to no avail.

The two agents in the front seat were chatting about the Yankees. Krill paid them no mind. Suddenly, the air in the car shifted, and the tone changed. The bald one, Corman, if Krill remembered correctly, was speaking in a stage whisper as he drove.

"Ray Garrett got shot. Looks like a hired hit at some rich men's club on the Upper East Side."

The other agent nodded. "He gonna make it?"

"They lost him."

The driver slapped his partner with the back of his hand and jerked his head toward where Krill sat in the backseat.

"Let's just get this asshole to processing; then we can go. Ray was a good man."

Krill felt the blood drain from his face. He was sure he looked whiter than the wretched dog hair marring his suit. Mitchell had caught the man posing as Johan DeVold. This had to be the undercover FBI agent his captors were discussing. Mitchell had been there. Worse, Krill had ordered Mitchell to find DeVold while these agents were in the room.

The sedan pulled up to the curb at Federal Plaza. Corman opened the back door with the keys to the cuffs in his hand. He uncuffed Krill as he spoke. "Figured I'd save you the humiliation." The agent pulled Krill from the car and escorted him into the Javitz Federal building. After a brief elevator ride, the doors parted, and Krill was led down a quiet hall. The three men rounded a corner and stopped. A striking blonde woman was coming out of the restroom, wiping her nose with a tissue. She was wearing a black pants suit with red stilettos, and she had an ID badge around her neck. When she looked up, Krill saw her eyes widen with a flash of panic before she did a quick one-eighty and disappeared back into the bathroom.

It was DeVold's personal assistant, the woman who had given Krill DeVold's contact information and sat with him at breakfast. He would recognize those blue eyes anywhere. What the hell was that woman doing in the FBI field office?

Neither of his escorts reacted or spoke; they simply continued down the hall and deposited Krill in an interrogation room. The bearded agent said, "Someone will be in after your lawyer gets here."

Unaccustomed to being ignored, Krill sat for fifteen minutes when the door opened, and the blonde beauty slipped into the room.

"You? What are you doing here?" Krill demanded.

"Meinjeer DeVold was killed." She spoke with a flawless South African accent.

"Cut the crap. I know that man was not Johan DeVold. I saw your badge. Now tell me what's going on," Krill said.

"I could lose my job," the woman bit out. "You can't mention that you saw me."

"And what do I get in return?"

The woman glanced back to the hall, then stepped further into the room. "I'm a federal agent. The man you knew as Johan DeVold was my partner. We're investigating suspected terrorist activity at the Cavalry Club."

"Terrorist activity?"

"Yes. There's a secretive group that operates out of the club; they funnel millions to terrorist groups around the world. Ray, that's my partner, posed as DeVold to investigate a suspected terrorist and see who expressed an interest in joining Vitruvian–that's the group."

Krill's mind raced back, cataloging the times he had seen the man who claimed to be Johan DeVold. DeVold met with the mysterious Russian that first day. Krill had also seen DeVold speaking to the Arab man in the thoub at breakfast.

The woman continued, "We already suspect the assassin is linked to a club member." She explained about the Vitruvian Society and terrorist activity the FBI was investigating. What had he gotten himself into?

Why hadn't Mitchell uncovered any of this?

Krill knew what happened to suspected terrorists. They vanished into some dark hole in Guantanamo Bay or worse.

"We don't know how Ray's cover was blown. There may be a mole in the Bureau. For the sake of national security, for *my* sake, please don't expose me. Anyone who had contact with Ray, the man you knew as Johan DeVold, is in danger. These people will stop at nothing to keep their organization secret."

Krill's concern for this woman didn't amount to a hill of beans. His self-preservation, however, was paramount, and at this moment, it appeared the two interests aligned. He needed to get as far away from the Vitruvian Society as possible.

Krill rested his forearms on the scarred table, some of his bravado returning. "I will say nothing. You will say nothing. You agree not to mention my interest in Vitruvian, and I will forget about our entire encounter earlier."

"I can't do that," she snapped.

"I'm not a terrorist, and you know it. Don't waste time and resources investigating an innocent man. No one knows about my interest in Vitruvian but you."

The woman tapped a blood-red shoe on the linoleum. "Then why are you here? Under arrest?"

Krill waved away the question. "Unrelated matter."

The woman arched a brow.

"It's a business matter," Krill said.

Her eyes lit with understanding. "Ah, Corman and Ravelli's case." She laughed. "The Vitruvian Society engineered that. They probably suspected you were an agent."

Krill bristled despite the truth of the statement. "My attorney is on his way. I'll be leaving shortly."

"Prison may be the safest place for you."

"I won't go to jail," Krill insisted.

"Well, there's a silver lining if you do. An FBI agent wouldn't go to prison. If you get convicted, Vitruvian would know you weren't trying to bring them down."

"I'll worry about my safety," Krill said.

In an awkward gesture, the woman lifted her leg and placed a cherry-red stiletto on the seat next to him. Then, she leaned closer. "As long as no one saw you. Did they bring you in the back, through the garage? You should be fine."

Krill muttered his thought aloud. "We came in the front. They uncuffed me."

The woman's eyes widened in fear. "Why? Why would they do that?"

"I don't know. Corman said the handcuffs weren't necessary."

"I need to talk to my supervisor. It's probably nothing. Corman's in CID. He has no knowledge of our operation."

Krill shot to his feet. "He knew! He knew your partner had been shot. He was talking about it in the car."

The woman urged him to sit. "I'm sure it's nothing sinister. I'll talk to the SAC."

"The who?"

"Special Agent in Charge. Don't worry. If there is a mole, I can protect you. I can ensure the people inside this building know you're not a threat. Settle your matter with Criminal. I won't say anything about our involvement. No one has to know."

She said the words, but Krill watched as her eyes wandered to the surveillance camera mounted high on the wall. Then, she turned and left.

The overpriced attorney sat with Krill while he refused to answer questions. Finally, he was released pending an indictment he was assured was coming. Krill's mind was racing. The DeVold imposter had funneled his five million dollar initiation fee into Vitruvian, a suspected terrorist group. Then the group invested his money in a lab they had to know he was purchasing. Why?

The answer was obvious. The Vitruvian members, *the terrorists*, knew someone was investigating them undercover. That FBI agent was Johan DeVold, but Vitruvian thought Krill was working with him. Krill had certainly made it easy to suspect that. He had all but followed DeVold like a puppy whenever he had the chance. Krill had watched with evident fascination as DeVold greeted men with signet rings.

DEBBIE BALDWIN

Krill and his lawyer emerged from the Federal Building as the sun sank behind the tallest of the surrounding highrises. The plaza was strangely devoid of pedestrians. Police were scattered about. A uniformed officer was dropping evidence markers at various spots on the sidewalk. A crime scene photographer was snapping pictures of tire marks on the street. Krill approached the nearest cop.

"What's happening?" Krill asked.

"A woman was struck by a car and killed. Hit and run," the cop spoke matter-of-factly and continued with his work.

"What woman?"

"I don't have any information. Move along." The cop held a clipboard and pointed with the end of a ballpoint pen.

Krill's attorney tugged his arm, and the two men walked to the waiting car.

As Krill gave a final scan of the area, he saw it.

A blood-red stiletto lying in the street.

Krill threw himself into the back seat, his attorney climbing in behind him.

"What's wrong, Armand? You look like you've seen a ghost."

"That shoe," Krill whispered.

"What?"

"That red shoe!" he repeated. "She was going to protect me. She was going to make sure they knew I wasn't involved."

"Armand, you sound like a madman. Now I want to discuss negating the sale of ProbeX Labs. That should go a long way toward keeping you out of prison."

Krill looked out the window as he murmured, "An undercover agent wouldn't go to prison."

"What's that?" The attorney set his briefcase on his lap and flipped through the files.

"That's what the female agent said. The one who was killed out here."

"Armand, you aren't making any sense. I can certainly keep you out of prison. My main concern is the fine."

301

Krill turned and grabbed his attorney's lapels. "They can't get to me in jail."

The attorney clasped Krill's forearms and extricated himself from his grasp. "I don't know what you're talking about, but a minimum security facility is hardly a safe haven."

"That's not the point!" Krill shouted, causing the driver to look back.

Crossing his arms over his chest, the lawyer spoke to Krill as if he were a child. "What is the point, Armand?"

"If I go to prison, Vitruvian will know I'm not a government agent. I'm just a greedy bastard out to make money." Krill's eyes brightened with a stroke of brilliance. "Cut a deal with the Feds that includes prison time. One year, no two. Two is probably best. Pay the fine."

"Armand, you're not making any sense. I don't understand."

Krill snapped at his companion. "You're not paid to understand. You're paid to do what I tell you. Make the deal."

Duly cowed, the attorney deferred to his client. "Whatever you say, Armand."

Miles and Tox watched in the back of the blacked-out SUV as Krill witnessed the arranged scene unfold. Tox was late to this party, but he couldn't help but revel in the success of his brother's plan. Miles laughed out loud as Krill flung his slender form into the back of his town car. Tox pointed out the lawyer's disbelieving expression. Once the car had sped around a corner, the back door of their SUV opened, and Clara Gautreau slipped inside.

The space was cramped, but Clara squeezed in beside Miles. Tox observed his twin, saw how he kept his hands on the seat and his body stiff. He also noticed the slow inhale Miles took through his nose. He would never tease his brother in front of the beautiful blonde, but once they were alone, all bets were off.

After brief but enthusiastic introductions, Miles said, "Let's get out of here."

Clara replied, "Not until somebody gets my red shoe."

CHAPTER SIXTY-ONE

South Island, South Carolina
August 18

Steady pulled the car into Very's driveway and parked. There was fear in her eyes as she looked out the windshield. He leaned across the passenger seat and rubbed a tendril of light brown hair. "You'll be back to your old self in no time."

"Can you come in? There's still a lot we need to talk about."

"Glad you asked." He hopped out of the car and came around to help Very. Together they walked up the steps and into her house.

There, in the middle of the room, stood Alonso Mitchell.

Without hesitation, Steady charged, pummelling the older man with the full force of his body. Mitchell landed on his back on the hardwood, winded, and Steady took the opportunity to pound a fist into Mitchell's face. He pulled back his hand to hit him again when a grip on his wrist stopped him.

Steady turned back to look at Very. Beneath him, Mitchell groaned.

"Steady, stop!"

"Do you know who this asshole is?" he asked.

"Yes." Very smiled. "Steady, this is Charles Darwin. My dad."

After Steady filled a Ziplock with ice and helped Mitchell to the couch, he stood awkwardly next to Very and said, "Sir, uh, sorry for punching you. I had some facts wrong."

Mitchell drilled Steady with a hazel-eyed stare. When his eyes drifted to Very, he softened. "It's okay, kid. If you thought I was the bad guy, the plan worked." Mitchell's eyes bounced from Very to Steady, and he added, "I think we all need to do a little sharing."

Very grabbed them each a beer from the fridge. She took a seat on the couch and pulled Steady to her side. Mitchell and Very explained their plan for destroying Armand Krill. Krill, the man who had murdered her mother and changed the course of both their lives.

Mitchell readjusted the ice on his chin. After a long moment, he said, "This is going back, what? Thirty-five years now. I enlisted when I was eighteen. Came back from my third tour, and I was kind of lost." He took a fortifying sip of beer and continued, "I got a job in security at Parasol. Worked at the Midtown Headquarters, took any shift they offered, did any job. Worked my way up. After about three years, Armand Krill called me into his office and asked me to dig up dirt on a competitor. Computers were a new thing back then, but I had a knack. Nothing much impressed Krill, but I could tell he was pleased with what I found. From there, it snowballed. I became his, I don't know, his henchman, I guess."

Steady reached out and found Very's hand.

"One day, Krill called me in and said his daughter, Patricia, had just graduated from college and was joining the company. He was sending her to do a site inspection of a business in Mexico Parasol was buying. He told me to go with her for security."

Very smiled softly. "You can guess what happened next."

Alonso mirrored her expression. "I met Patricia at the Krill house to take her to the airport. Never in my life had I felt something like that. I was expecting to hate her. She was this spoiled, rich girl with her future laid out, and I was this aimless security guard with no life." He chuckled at the memory. "We sat in complete silence for the entire flight. Never said a single word. When we finally started talking, the pieces just fell into place. For six days, I was by her side. By the time we returned from that trip, I knew I'd never love anyone the way I loved Trish."

Very sighed. "It's so romantic. I love hearing that story."

Alonso agreed. "For the brief time we had together, it was pretty magical. Krill had other plans, of course. He had Trish set up with every rich jerk from Central Park West to SoHo. I'd go along on the dates as her driver and stew in the car while she ate some fancy meal. After every date, she'd get back in the car and say the same thing. "Lonnie, let's go somewhere private.""

Very leaned into Steady, listening. It was apparent she knew the story. It was also obvious she never tired of it.

"Of course, that's how Trish ended up pregnant." Alonso tipped his beer bottle to Very with a smile. "We devised a plan that was painful but necessary. She started seeing one of the society guys her father pushed on her, then announced she was pregnant, and they got engaged. Trish called it off after six months, had Verity on her own, and as far as anyone knew, she was a single mother. Krill was furious and wasn't quiet about it. That was really the start of the rift. Trish knew her father was doing some shady shit, but it wasn't until Krill berated her about having the baby out of wedlock that she started looking into Krill's dealings."

Steady said, "Armand Krill has had a reputation for questionable business practices for decades."

"Questionable doesn't begin to describe it, as I'm sure you know by now. Even back then, Krill was using the Hale Center to murder his enemies. Trish spent years carefully gathering evidence. I helped, but we had to be careful. We devised an escape plan. When Krill discovered what his daughter was doing, Trish took Very–she was called Amelia back then– and ran. I did what I could to derail the search without giving myself away, but eventually, Krill's men tracked them down. Trish and I both knew what we had to do. She was going to go with the guards, and I was going to keep Very hidden. The plan was to rescue Trish from the Hale Center as soon as I got Very safe, but by the time I got there–"

Alonso couldn't speak the words, but he didn't have to. His stricken expression, even all these years later, said it all.

Steady looked at Very. "So Mitchell was 'the friend 'who raised you?" When she nodded, he continued, "And right under Krill's nose. It was the last place that bastard would look."

Very added, "We lived in a brownstone in Prospect Park in Brooklyn. It was a surprisingly normal childhood."

Alonso laughed at that. "Then I did my job because my life took a huge turn. I finally felt like I had a purpose."

Steady encouraged him. "You were a single dad with a mission."

Very said, "Take Krill down."

"Exactly. I didn't keep the truth from Very. Trish changed her name to Verity because she was sick of all the lies. Justice was in her DNA." Mitchell's words were filled with pride.

"So for the next few years, I ingratiated myself with Krill getting better and better at the sneaky stuff he wanted done. When Very was in college, Parasol began human trials for Mobilify, a breakthrough arthritis medication."

Steady added, "And you knew he would be up to his old tricks."

Very nodded. "Finding a version of the drug that met FDA approval but also had a side effect that another Parasol drug could treat. Dad knew this was the opportunity we'd been waiting for."

"So you pretended to be sneaking a sample of the older, better version of Mobilify to a rival, knowing Krill would buy the company?"

Mitchell resettled the icepack on his chin. "We chose the perfect target—a struggling drug company where Very knew someone. Krill had been buying up vulnerable businesses to expand his empire. We set up the pins; Krill just needed to roll the ball."

Very added, "And it was a win-win because if we somehow miscalculated Krill's response, ProbeX labs could proceed with manufacturing the comparable drug."

"The real trick was sneaking the sample out of Parasol. Very was supposed to do it, but she was waylaid by Krill and his psych eval. So, I had to go in. Knowing security was keeping a close watch, I pretended to investigate and stole the sample myself." Mitchell gave Very a disapproving glance, and she grinned.

"Wow," Steady said. "I can't believe you pulled it off."

Mitchell continued, "The other crucial component was getting Krill to invest in ProbeX without knowing he had done it. That was the crime. That's how we were going to bring him down. I've known Krill a long time. I knew his arrogance and greed would get the better of him."

Steady reran the events in his mind. He still had a million questions. "And that's where this club in New York comes in?"

Very picked up the ball. "Dad knew Armand Krill had a fascination with the Vitruvian Society. It was an old secret society his grandfather had belonged to. It's long since defunct, but dad suspected, and I agreed, that if Krill thought the Vitruvian Society still existed, he would do anything to join."

Mitchell said, "And we were right. Even as I worked on the assignment, I couldn't believe how obsessed Krill was. He nearly stopped thinking about Very's espionage. I constantly had to keep him on track."

"Sounds like you thought of everything."

"Not everything." Very stood and went to the kitchen to pour herself a glass of water.

Mitchell sighed. "Very wanted to bring Dr. Baker to justice. She's the woman who developed the drug that killed Trish. I thought it was too much."

Very's eyes were filled with affection when she said, "You were right. I almost blew the whole plan. With Krill's downfall, Dr. Baker will lose her funding. That's enough for now."

Steady rubbed the scruff on his jaw. He wanted to wait until he was sure everything went to plan before he told Very. She settled back beside him, and Steady lifted his arm automatically, cradling Very in the nook.

Steady loved the feeling of Very tucked in beside him, but as he watched Alonso Mitchell walk to the freezer and refill the bag of ice, he couldn't help but think that here was yet another item on the long list of things Very hadn't trusted him with knowing.

He shifted. His phone vibrated against his leg, and Steady checked the text. The plan had been accelerated; the Feds wanted to move before the news of Krill's arrest broke. Steady had an op to run.

"Well, it's been a long day. I'll let you two catch up."

Very narrowed her gaze as she assessed him. "Okay."

With an abrupt nod, Steady turned and left. As he pulled the rental car out onto the main road, it wasn't lost on Steady that he, too, was still keeping secrets.

CHAPTER SIXTY-TWO

The Hale Center
August 20

Theodora Baker stepped down the airstairs of the private jet, eager to return to her domain at the Hale Center. Armand Krill's petty demands had distracted her from real work. Dr. Baker knew better than to bite the hand that fed her, but she detested being at his beck and call. She had research here that required her attention.

She glanced around the airfield, prepared to rattle off a long list of instructions to her assistant, Rose, but when Dr. Baker saw no one, her irritation mounted. With a huff of frustration, she marched to the row of golf carts and climbed in the nearest one. After figuring out the basic operating method, she zoomed off toward her office.

When the parking lot came into view, she slammed on the brakes. Dozens of responder vehicles filled the parking lot with their lights flashing. Police were roping off the area, and fire trucks lined the periphery. Doctors in white coats poured into her containment area. A pair of EMTs wheeled a corpse in a body bag toward a coroner van. Dr. Baker wondered idly which subject had died.

Partially concealed behind the row of trees that lined the service road, Dr. Baker watched in horror as animals in law enforcement windbreakers hauled computers and boxes from the building. One of the men tripped and dropped the stack of laptops he was carrying. Theodora Baker wanted to scream. Corralling her outrage, she abandoned the golf cart and slipped into the parking lot undetected. The Hale Center had been compromised, but all was not lost. Aware of societal ignorance and archaic laws, Dr. Baker had prepared for such an event.

Her most sensitive research and formula for her most recent and successful version of Comply were stored in a vault in her home–along with a new passport, credit cards, and everything she would need to start fresh. The apartment in Geneva was luxurious, and a new facility awaited. Beneath the humiliation and the inconvenience, Dr. Baker couldn't help but feel a modicum of pleasure at being freed from Armand Krill's shackles.

With thoughts of a new life and limitless power and resources, Dr. Baker walked to her Mercedes EQS, parked in a spot by the private entrance like any other day, and drove away.

Finn spoke into the comm unit from his spot behind a hedge. "She's on the move."

Nathan's voice came next. "Stay frosty, people. The feds are letting us take the lead here as a courtesy, and we have been advised that if the target evades capture, our next jobs will include hair nets and name tags."

Cam replied, "Copy. Twitch, you have eyes on the car."

"The tracker is functioning. Looks like she's heading home," Twitch responded.

A chorus of "copy," followed her words.

Theodora Baker pulled into the side driveway of her modest but well-appointed colonial in an upscale neighborhood. She lived well while maintaining an image of selfless dedication to the less fortunate. She had used her time wisely on the ride home, booking flights and making arrangements.

After parking in the immaculate garage, Dr. Baker entered the home through the kitchen and went straight to her first-floor office. Miraculously, no one had seen the jet land, and the secluded area where she parked was unguarded. She wasn't a believer in luck; however, Dr. Baker had the utmost faith in the incompetence of law enforcement.

She was not prone to paranoia, but the events at the lab had her checking the street through the window. A Mexican worker was trimming the neighbor's boxwoods. A black man sat behind the wheel of a cable company van, killing time before his next assignment. A woman in workout clothes walked a dog. As suspected, Dr. Baker had escaped the obtuse investigation at the Hale Center.

Dr. Baker crossed the room with efficient strides and stood before the traditional wooden door to what had originally been a closet. She pulled it open, revealing the steel door behind it. After entering the code and placing her thumb on the scanner, the lock released, and Dr. Baker stepped inside. When she had installed the vault, it was a different era. She had anticipated needing room to store boxes of paper files. With her assistant Rose's help, the research and records had been digitized and took up a fraction of the space. She placed the portable hard drive into a specially designed protective briefcase and snapped it shut. Her first task completed, Dr. Baker returned to the office before heading upstairs to pack.

The man sitting behind her desk stopped her in her tracks. His filthy boots were propped up on her spotless desk. He was wearing a ridiculous tropical shirt, and a mop of sandy hair framed a placid face. If it weren't for the gun in his hand, he would have looked more at home in a tiki bar. She was about to demand he leave, but he spoke first.

"Gotcha," he said. "Had a feelin 'you were hiding the really incriminating stuff."

She gripped the handle of the case with white-knuckle force. "Surely we can come to some kind of understanding. You're clearly not a police officer."

"Sugar, you should be wishing the police were here. The people I work for don't take kindly to scientists running off with drugs that could threaten national security."

Theodora recoiled. This was far worse than a straightforward arrest for the goings on at Hale. A good attorney could get her out of that mess in a heartbeat. This was Homeland or the NSA or worse.

The yard man and cable guy from the truck outside appeared in the doorway, now dressed like they had just come from a combat mission in the Middle East. Through the window, Theodora saw the parade of black SUVs pull to the curb.

The black man from the van stepped forward and took the case containing the hard drive. She thought it best not to speak.

Two suited men and two similarly attired women appeared at the door, looking as ominous as they no doubt were. One of the women stepped forward and spoke without providing identification or even a name. "Dr. Baker, come with us."

She turned to the man at her desk, who wore a self-satisfied grin as he pulled a cigar from the breast pocket of that appalling shirt and perched it between his lips.

"This isn't over," she said. At least they wouldn't get their hands on the hard drive. Maybe the country bumpkin would even get killed trying to open the case. The thought pleased her.

"Oh, not by a country mile, sweetheart. It's just getting started."

Reaching for any remnant of dignity, she cast a glance at the briefcase, barely holding back a smirk. Then, Theodora Baker followed the agents out of the house and into the waiting car.

Steady set the case on the desk. "Now, let's see what the good doctor was taking with her." He rubbed his hands together like he was preparing to crack a safe. "There's no lock."

Calliope entered the room with Tilly on a leash.

Chat stopped him. "Wait. I don't like the way she looked at it."

"What do you mean?" Cam asked.

"Before she walked out the door. She looked at the case, and she almost smiled. Take a closer look."

Calliope unhooked the leash. "Why don't we let Tilly do her job."

Tilly went to work, quickly circling the room. When she got to Steady, she sniffed the briefcase, then sat.

"She's signaling explosives," Steady said. "It's boobytrapped."

Chat stepped closer. "Ah, there's a thumbprint scanner concealed on the side to verify her identity. The case is unlocked because she wants the contents destroyed if an unauthorized person gets ahold of it."

Steady dropped to his knees and wrapped Tilly in a hug. Freeing one hand, he signed *good girl*, over and over. She, in turn, placed her too-big paws on his shoulders and delivered a long lick right up the middle of Steady's face.

After giving Tilly her treat and a good scratch behind the ears, Steady stood and lifted the case more gingerly than before. "Let's get this back to the office. We'll have to disarm it." He turned to the group, "Saddle up."

Steady returned his attention to his dog, kneeling down and burying his face in her yellow fur. Tilly had saved the information that would not only condemn Dr. Baker but give Very the closure she sought. It was his gift to Very, and because it meant the world to her, it meant the world to him.

Steady glanced up to see only Calliope remained in Dr. Baker's office, eyeing him with an unreadable expression.

"What?" he asked.

"Nothing," she replied. "It's just nice to see Mr. Free-and-Easy getting attached."

Steady laughed, "Yeah, I'm pretty fucking in love with this beauty."

Calliope gave him a soft smile. "I wasn't talking about the dog."

Then she turned and hurried to catch up with the guys.

Three hours later, emergency crews were still managing the fallout from Dr. Baker's experiments. Doctors were treating patients. Techs were attempting to locate families, and Federal agents were confiscating every computer and scrap of paper in the lab.

Steady and Nathan stood on the grass at the periphery of the activity and watched.

Nathan turned to Steady, "Let's walk."

The airstrip was at the back of the property, about two kilometers from where they stood. Steady wondered if it was a long enough distance to cover everything.

They rounded the building and wandered across the back lawn with Tilly trotting along at Steady's side.

"So when did observe-and-report become meddle-and-rescue?"

"Almost immediately," Steady confessed.

Nathan replied, "As I suspected."

"Suspected or intended?" Steady asked.

Nathan chuckled. "We've known each other too long, my friend."

"Why not just tell me to get involved if you knew I would?"

They entered the garden, following the slate walk through the summer blooms. The statue of the angel stood at the convergence of several paths in a clearing punctuated by marble benches. Steady's blood heated at the memory of holding Very in his arms.

"Jonah." At the use of his given name, Steady turned to look at his boss. "The lives we have led, the things we have seen–you can spot a threat a mile away. You can fly a tin can through a missile attack in a sandstorm. But there's one thing you, all of us, can't seem to spot when it's right in front of us."

Nathan didn't need to elaborate. Steady stopped walking. "You're wrong there. I know I love her. I do. Love isn't the issue. It's trust. Very confided in me to some extent, but she certainly didn't lay her cards on the table."

"Have you?" Nathan asked.

Steady ran a hand over his stubbled jaw. "Well, shit."

"You're both guarded when it comes to giving your heart, and you both have good reason to be. You just need to figure out if the risk is worth the reward. For me, with Emily, it has been… extraordinary."

The airfield came into view, and Steady eyed the sleek Bishop Security Gulfstream waiting on the runway. For the first time in his life, he looked at an aircraft and wasn't filled with unfettered joy. Like Very, he had only shared parts of himself; he hadn't let her see the sadness that lived within him, the self-doubt—the fear. Nathan was right. If he loved her, he was going to have to put his heart on the line.

They climbed the airstairs, and Nathan turned to the cabin while Steady headed for the cockpit. He settled Tilly in the dog bed, then made his way to the pilot's seat to begin the checks. He needed to get home. He needed to see Very. The dawning awareness settled.

Home and Very were one and the same.

CHAPTER SIXTY-THREE

Bishop Security Headquarters
Somewhere outside Beaufort, South Carolina
August 23

Steady found Twitch working on something at the conference table in Nathan's office. He set the plate down, then took a seat next to her.

"One Twitch special, a BLT with pickles. A PBLT."

Twitch grabbed the sandwich and took a huge bite. "Nobody makes them like you, Steady."

"The secret is to put the pickle slices right on top of the mayo on the bottom slice."

Steady watched in silence until Twitch finally set the sandwich down and met his gaze.

"Okay, spill it," she said.

"What?"

"Johah Lockhart, I know you didn't hunt me down just to feed me. What's going on with Very?"

"I'm not sure."

"Have you told her about the op? About bringing down Theodora Baker?"

"Not yet."

"Why the heck not?" Twitch asked.

"I'm waiting for, I don't know, the right moment."

"Steady, you nailed the person responsible for her mother's death. Any moment is the right moment." She rested a hand on his arm. "What's going on?"

"I don't think she's ever going to let me in. I don't know if I'll ever be enough."

"What do you mean?"

"Well, I told her I loved her, and she didn't say it back."

Twitch pushed away the plate and wiped her mouth with the paper napkin. "Steady, I'm going to tell you something about Very that few people know."

He rested his forearms on the table and leaned into Twitch.

"Very says 'I love you 'a lot."

"Great."

"Let me finish." She smacked his hand. "The phrase doesn't have much meaning to her, so she throws it around. I think it stems from her childhood. A lot of people who claimed to love her didn't back those words up. Very had to run from her own grandfather. Her mother abandoned her–not by choice, but still. She had to go live in hiding with her father, who was basically a stranger. For whatever reason, when she truly loves someone, she doesn't use those words. She says something else."

"What does she say?"

"I think you know."

Steady's mind traveled back to the first time they talked on the beach. Very looking in his eyes. *You big dope.* The night in the garden when she confessed her plan, *you big dope.* He thought of the car ride when he rescued her from Armand Krill's clutches. *You big dope.*

Steady shot to his feet. "She calls you a big dope? *That's* how she tells you she loves you?"

Twitch resumed eating. "It's kind of cute, actually. I don't think she's ever called a man a big dope."

Finn appeared at the entrance to the room, spotted Twitch, and crossed to where she sat. Twitch beamed at him around her sandwich.

"Just me?" Steady asked.

"Just you," Twitch confirmed.

"I'm not *a* big dope. I'm *the* big dope."

"Exactly," Twitch agreed.

Steady looked at Finn with a shit-eating grin. "I'm a big dope."

"I know," Finn said, taking a seat beside his love.

"I'm a big dope," Steady repeated, retook his seat, and swiped a cookie from Twitch's plate.

Twitch stood a little off balance, and Finn took her arm. "Uh oh." Twitch stared at the floor.

Finn came in front of her, concerned. "What's wrong?"

"I think my water just broke."

Finn smiled and tucked a strand of copper-colored hair behind her ear. "That's okay, angel. What do we need to do?"

Twitch looked at him with a puzzled expression, but Finn had turned to Steady.

"Why are you looking at me?" Steady asked.

"Finn." Twitch tapped him on the shoulder, but Finn was now directing his inquiry to Nathan, who had just come in.

"You need to go to the hospital," Nathan said.

"Right, right," Finn nodded. "They need to plug it up. She can't walk around leaking."

"Finn." Twitch tried again, but Nathan spoke at the same time.

"There's no plugging up, Finn. You need to take her to the hospital because she's having a baby."

"She's having a baby," Finn repeated.

Nathan nodded along, waiting for Finn's brain to catch up with his mouth.

Finn's eyes doubled in size. "She's having a baby!"

Bingo.

Twitch stepped around her partner, grabbed the placket of his shirt, and shook him. "*She's* standing right here. Go get my bag from the downstairs closet and meet me at the car."

Finn held Twitch close. "It's too soon. Isn't it too soon?"

"It's a little soon, Finn. I'm thirty-seven weeks, but yesterday at the appointment, the doctor said I was dilated. Didn't you pay attention?"

"I didn't know what that meant, and I was too embarrassed to ask. Every week something's effaced or dilated or contracting. It's like a fucking science test in that office."

Twitch scrunched her face up and held onto her middle. "Okay, I think we need to go."

Chat appeared at the door holding one of three go-bags Finn had packed.

Steady looked at Chat with wide eyes. "How the hell did you know she needed the bag? That's just freaky."

Chat replied, "Nathan texted me."

Finn took the duffle from Chat's outstretched hand. " Oh, shit, Auggie. Someone needs to get him from school."

Nathan gathered his things as he spoke. "I'll get Auggie. Steady, circle up with Cam and let Calliope and Tox know what's going on."

"Copy that." Steady kissed Twitch on the cheek. "Good luck."

Twitch held onto his forearm and whispered, "Very loves you, you know. You're her big dope."

Finn pulled her away and ushered Twitch out the door with the rest of the gang in their wake.

CHAPTER SIXTY-FOUR

Beaufort, South Carolina
August 24

Very poked her head in the door of Twitch's hospital room. Things had finally quieted after her Bishop Security family had descended en masse. A nurse had shooed everyone out, insisting the new mom needed sleep. Finn had run home to shower and change. As dawn broke, Twitch sat up in bed holding her son, Trevor Devlin-McIntyre.

"Do you want me to come back later?"

Twitch's face lit up as she whispered, "No, come in. Meet your godson."

Very made her way through flowers and stuffed animals and sat beside Twitch on the bed. The baby already looked like Finn, and Very ran the back of her finger down his soft cheek. "I may be biased, but I'm pretty sure he's the most beautiful baby that's ever been born."

"Don't make me laugh."

"How are you feeling?" Very smoothed back her friend's hair.

Twitch lifted her head from the bundle in her arms. "I need to tell you something."

"That sounds ominous."

"Not ominous. It's pretty awesome, actually."

There, in the early morning hours, Twitch sat with Very and explained what Steady had done: how he had worked with the Feds to set up a plan, ensuring that Dr. Baker's research was discovered and all of her evil acts were exposed. Very wanted to run to his house right then; her heart was so full she thought it might burst. But she needed to make sure Steady knew that she trusted him absolutely. She did. Very trusted Steady with her life. She trusted him with her heart.

"It's Saturday," Very grabbed Twitch's phone from the side table and handed it to her. "Can you text me Chat's number? I need to ask him for a quick favor."

Twitch complied, then asked, "What are you cooking up?"

"I think I know a way to show Steady how I feel." Very kissed the sleeping baby. "Wish me luck, mom."

Twitch laughed. "Good luck."

After promising to keep Twitch informed, Very left the room and raced out of the hospital to her car. And, with an unguarded heart, toward her future.

Steady pulled the jeep into his usual spot at the private airfield. He needed to talk to Very. He just didn't know what to say. Steady decided that to think this through, he needed to be in the one place that had always provided clarity. The sky.

Steady jogged across the tarmac, waving to the crew performing various duties. He greeted the mechanic doing the pre-flight checks on his Cessna with a slap on the back. Then he spotted Chat standing near the cockpit, hands in his pockets.

"Hey, what are you doing here?"

"Just helping out a friend," Chat replied.

Steady furrowed his brow and looked around. "Who?"

Chat walked in the direction of his truck like it was every day he showed up at the airfield and loitered around Steady's plane. "You," he answered. "Have a nice flight."

Perplexed, Steady opened the small door and climbed inside the plane. There, in the copilot seat, looking nervous but committed, was Very. Her pink hair was back, and her smile held a challenge.

"Very?"

"Take me flying," she said.

"You sure? 'he asked.

"I made it this far, you big dope. Don't scare me away."

You big dope. Steady's grin hit his ears as he slid into the seat next to her. "Darlin', I hope you know what you're getting yourself into."

"I know. I'm not doing this on a whim, Steady. I want to fly with you. Only with you."

"I'm not talkin 'about the plane." He leaned over and kissed her. He started to speak, but Very covered his mouth with her fingers. "I know, Steady. I know everything you did for me."

Steady rubbed his palms on his thighs. "Yeah, well, after our talk in the car on the drive home, I just couldn't leave things the way they were. Dr. Baker needed to pay. I wanted to give you that."

"That's not exactly go-with-the-flow."

He wrapped his hand around the back of Very's neck and pulled her close. "I take charge when it matters."

Steady felt her sharp intake of air.

"I see that."

"You matter, Very. You matter the most."

"Steady."

"You ready to fly with me?"

"I was falling for you even before you took Dr. Baker down, so yes, let's fly."

"I was a goner for you the first time you called me a pervert," he said with a laugh. "So, buckle up because, Very Valentine, your feet may never touch solid ground again."

"No more secrets. I trust you. With everything. I love you, Jonah Lockhart."

"You… love me?"

"I think I've been looking at it all wrong. Like love was a decision–the way I decided to bring down Krill and planned to avenge my mother. But falling in love… It's something else. Do you remember those double stars you showed me that night on the beach?"

"The binary stars, sure," he said.

"Nobody knows why they are bound together. They just are. I can't explain it, but sharing your orbit feels like where I was always meant to be. I just do. I love you."

Steady cradled her face in his hands. "I love you, too, Darlin'. Like I never thought I could."

CHAPTER SIXTY-FIVE

Beaufort, South Carolina
August 31

At the entry to Nathan and Emily's dining room, Steady took in the scene as he held tightly to Very's hand. The dinner table was packed. Finn was holding baby Trevor and adjusting his blue cap while Twitch looked on next to him. The baby flailed his little arms and took hold of his father's pinky as Finn looked at Twitch with delight at the gesture. Auggie, their eight-year-old son, was sitting on Finn's right and putting one of the baby's socks back on. Tox had his arm around Calliope and was laughing at something his twin brother Miles said. Cam's fiancée, Evan, was holding Nathan and Emily's daughter, Charlotte, while the parents wrangled the toddlers, Charlie and Jack, into their highchairs. When the twins were secured, Nathan kissed Emily on the temple, took her hand, and led her into the kitchen to grab the food. Chat's bright smile was broad as he listened to some crazy story Herc was telling him.

Steady remembered the feeling of watching his brothers as they found love. He recalled the certainty in Nathan's eyes when he discovered Emily's true identity and Tox's ferocity when Calliope was in danger. Cam had risked his life to save Evan and then flown across the country to stand on her doorstep and beg her for a chance. And Finn, if anyone at the table deserved a happy ending, it was Finn.

Steady also remembered that odd sensation he had of being incomplete, of imagining Very's hand reaching out for his but finding only empty air when he reciprocated. He hadn't realized at the time what his heart was telling him.

Now he understood.

Very squeezed his fingers just then, and Steady pulled their joined hands to his lips. What he loved the most about Very was her innate ability to know what he felt, what he needed. He hoped he did the same for her. Steady wanted to. Every day. For the rest of his life.

Tox noticed them first. "Well, if it isn't the happy couple."

Calliope elbowed him in the ribs, and he pulled her close. Nathan and Emily returned to the room, each carrying a huge lasagna. Evan passed baby Charlotte to Cam–who cuddled the ten-month-old to his chest with the expertise gained from holding many nieces and nephews–as she hopped up to help.

Steady and Very took two of the three remaining seats and joined the party. Tox was already expediting, scooping steaming portions of lasagna on plates and passing them out. Evan followed Emily from the kitchen. She held an enormous salad bowl, and Emily carried a basket brimming with garlic bread.

Steady was excited for the meal, but he was more excited about the guest of honor.

When the doorbell rang, he helped Very scoot out of her chair. She hurried to the front door and returned a moment later with Alonso Mitchell by her side. The table fell silent before Very held up her hand. "Everyone, this is Alonso Mitchell, my dad."

Steady jumped to his feet and came to the front of the room. It was his first time seeing Mitchell since Steady had punched him. On top of that, it was his only time meeting the parent of a girlfriend, and he was uncharacteristi-

cally nervous. Something that wasn't lost on his brothers, who seemed to be enjoying his discomfort.

"Sir," Steady held out a hand. "It's great to see you, sir. Again, sorry, sir, about the, you know." Steady mimicked a punch.

Mitchell's face revealed nothing as he shook Steady's hand. "I was a boxing champion in the Rangers. We may have to step into the ring. Give me a chance to even the score."

Steady paled, and Mitchell barked a laugh. "Relax, kid, I'm joking. Very loves you. That's all that matters to me." Still gripping Steady's hand, he wrapped his other arm around his daughter. "Now quit calling me "sir" and let's eat."

Emily crossed to the threesome. "Welcome, Alonso. I'm Emily Bishop. Come sit. We're so happy you're here."

"Thank you." Mitchell tipped his head, and the group moved into the room. Miles stood and embraced his old friend. Steady heard Tox's twin murmur, "We did it, Lonnie."

When Mitchell was seated, he said to the table, "I imagine you have some questions."

Calliope and Emily had both been reporters, so the women were peppering Alonso with questions before Steady could think of where to begin.

When Alonso finished explaining how he and Very had brought down Krill, Tox looked at his brother. "And Miles? How do you fit into the picture?"

Miles took a slow sip of wine. "I've known Lonnie for years. Never knew he had a daughter." He tipped his glass to Very. "Nice to meet you, by the way." He took over the story. "A while ago, a congressman had been caught taking a bribe from Parasol. I was hired to make it go away. Lonnie was my contact at the company." Miles set down his glass and stared at the flowers in the centerpiece. "Something about him. I don't know. Maybe like attracts like."

Alonso said, "After we met a couple of times to handle the bribery situation, Miles looked at me and said, 'Lonnie, 'He's the only person besides

Trish who has ever called me that. 'Lonnie, let's grab a beer. 'We went out, talked about nothing. I don't know what he could have possibly figured out from that one encounter, but as I got up to leave, he said, and I'll never forget this, 'Lonnie, if you ever need any help with anything, just give me a call."

Miles opened his jacket and pulled out two Cubans. Passing one to Alonso, he said, "Taking over the Cavalry Club was my idea."

Alonso accepted the cigar. "I told him about Krill's obsession with prestige, about the Cavalry Club and the Vitruvian Society. This evil grin spread across his face, and he said, 'Lonnie, we're going to run a con. 'The plan was always to get Krill to hand over the money he thought was an initiation fee to join Vitruvian and then funnel that money into ProbeX Labs stock."

Miles lifted his wine glass. "All while providing a poorly concealed path the SEC could trace back to Krill."

Evan asked, "So everything at the Ridgeland lab: downloading the research, smuggling out the sample was all done intentionally to get Krill to buy out the rival lab?"

Alonso answered, "It's Krill's M.O. I knew if I dropped the right bread-crumbs: a struggling company that could be had for a song, a threat to what would be his most profitable drug, Krill would do what he always does, crush the little guy."

Nathan said, "And meanwhile, Krill was unwittingly and illegally investing in ProbeX, the company he was about to acquire."

Cam refilled Alonso's wine glass. "That was a work of art."

Alonso toasted Cam. "Miles deserves all the credit. I'm more of a guns-blazing kind of guy. Miles has finesse."

Chat pushed his plate back and leaned forward. "So, what's next for Alonso Mitchell?"

Alonso smiled. "We thought relocation was a good first step."

Steady put his arm around Very. "Mr. Mitchell is going to move to Beaufort."

Alonso shook his head. "Thinking about it anyway. I'm fifty-two years old. I think it's high time for a career change."

When dessert was served, Steady slipped away from the table and wandered out to the back porch. Miles and Alonso were down on the patio smoking their cigars. Laughter surrounded him as Nathan appeared at his side.

"Dishes are done. Children are asleep. All is right with the world."

"Our definition of that has certainly changed over the years."

"Or maybe we just never knew what it meant," Nathan said.

Steady snapped his fingers. "Yes, I think that's it."

Side-by-side, the two men stared out into the night.

"Thank you, Nathan."

"For what?"

"You know."

Nathan clapped him on the back. "Sometimes, we all need a nudge. That's why we're here, Steady. We're a family. A patchwork family but a family nonetheless."

"Shall we find Very and Emily?"

"Always." Nathan turned and walked back into the house.

Steady looked up at the starry night and smiled. Yes, all was right with the world.

EPILOGUE

Very and Steady took a walk on the beach. The sun was low in the rosy western sky, and the breeze at their backs propelled them forward. Tilly ran ahead, frolicking in the surf.

Steady looked casual. At least, he thought he did. He was wearing a long-sleeved gray thermal and jeans. Funny thing: when Very moved in with him, his collection of his grandfather's Hawaiian shirts mysteriously disappeared.

He and Very had been living together for three months. Every day had been better than the one before it. Armand Krill was in prison, and his company faced even more scrutiny. Dr. Theodora Baker had not been seen since the day she disappeared with those ominous government officials. Very had left Parasol and started her own business. She opened a private evidence lab helping law enforcement and fighting for justice every day. She was beautiful and brainy and exuberant and perfect. And somehow, she had chosen him. His grandmother would say they were like apple pie and cheddar cheese; they shouldn't go together, but somehow they did. They still pushed each other's buttons, but now it was this heated foreplay that invariably ended in bed. Or on the kitchen table or the deck couch or the stairs or, one time, in the cockpit of his Cessna.

For all their unconventional quirks, it had been a revelation to discover that Very was surprisingly traditional. She wanted to be married and have a family. Of course, she was quick to mitigate her comments with add-ons like *there's no rush*, but the way Steady saw it, Very was it for him. The quicker he made an honest woman out of her, the better.

He had bought the ring a month into their cohabitation. And then, he waited. He wasn't stalling or unsure. He was Steady. He was looking for the perfect moment to present itself. But as days turned into weeks, and weeks turned into months, Steady realized that if Very Valentine had taught him anything (and she had taught him *everything*), it was that sometimes you had to take matters into your own hands.

So he came up with a plan. It wasn't creative like Cam's proposal or a grand gesture like Tox's, but it was something he hoped would show Very how much he truly loved her.

He pulled the yellow bandana from his pocket and flagged down Tilly, who returned to his side.

"Remember that first time we hooked up?" he asked.

Very took his hand. "How could I forget? I didn't realize you could be so *intense*."

Steady couldn't help but puff up, but that wasn't what he meant. "I'm talkin 'about after."

Very laughed. "I seriously thought you might swim into the ocean to escape."

"Don't think I didn't think about it."

"All that talk of living with you and getting a dog." She stopped walking. "Oh, my God. Steady."

"And taking walks on the beach, and my parents coming to visit. We're livin 'it."

Very turned and faced him. "Never in my wildest dreams did I ever think this is where we'd end up."

"Darlin', this isn't where we end up. This is where we begin."

He dropped to one knee.

"Steady?"

He gave her a beat to catch up, then said, "Verity Valentine, I'm not great with words, but you are my one and only. You showed me what love is, and I want to spend the rest of my life by your side. I want to fight with you, laugh with you, cry with you, and love you. All of it, everywhere, forever. Will you marry me?"

He pulled the ring box from his pocket and tipped up the lid revealing the three-carat oval pink diamond his sister, Laney, had helped him pick out. Very wasn't looking at the ring, though; her hazel eyes were pinned to his.

Steady felt like Christmas had come and gone by the time Very finally sank to her knees and threw her arms around his neck. She spoke into his shoulder. "You were pretty good with those words."

"Are you going to answer the question, Darlin'?"

She leaned back and placed her hands flat on his chest. "Jonah Lockhart, I'd marry you tomorrow. Yes."

"Hot damn." Steady plucked the ring out and tossed the box over his shoulder. Then he took Very's left hand and slid it on her finger.

"Oh, my God, Steady."

"My girl's gotta have a pink diamond."

"I love it."

"Are you happy?"

"I don't think I knew what happy was before I met you. I love you, Steady."

He frowned a little, and Very laughed. "You big dope."

Steady took his fiancée in his arms and kissed her with everything he had while Tilly danced around them.

When darkness had settled, they made their way home. Very tucked into her nook, and Steady's arm circled her shoulders.

"Are we going to wait to tell our friends until after we tell our parents?" she asked.

"I think you know the answer to that." Steady kissed her hair.

"They're back at the house waiting for us, aren't they?"

Steady pointed, and Very saw the deck lit up with candles and Tiki torches. Tilly smelled the steaks on the grill before the scent reached their noses and took off, running toward the group. Just before they hit the circle of light, Very stopped him.

"You made me a believer, you know. I love you, Jonah Lockhart."

"I love you, too, Very. Forever and always."

With Very's hand in his, they walked up to the deck. Amid a chorus of cheers and well wishes, Steady led Very into a future filled with friends and family and surprising, incredible, extraordinary love.

THE END

ACKNOWLEDGMENTS

Thank you to my proofreaders, Angela Howard and Kara Horton, and my editor, Peter Gelfan, for your invaluable assistance. As always, thanks to my technical consultants, Henry Arneson and Billy Fash. My heartfelt appreciation goes to Kristyn Fortner, author manager, social media goddess, part-time therapist, and friend. Without your input, Chemical Capture would not be what it is. Thank you to my family and friends for your belief and encouragement.

And, most of all, to the readers, thank you for your continued support. Another book in the Bishop Security series is coming soon!

FALL IN LOVE WITH NATHAN AND EMILY IN THE FIRST BOOK IN THE BISHOP SECURITY SERIES, FALSE FRONT!

False Front (Bishop Security #1)
By Debbie Baldwin

PROLOGUE

Two Years Ago ...

Emma Porter looked bored. No surprise there. It was her standard expres-sion—her failsafe. She, with some effort, avoided the imposing lighted mirror in front of her and kept her gaze on the screen of her phone. Her violet eyes, masked by colored contacts that turned them an unremarkable blue, glazed. It didn't help that the stylist was working his way around her head in a hypnotic rhythm, pulling long strands of honey-colored hair through his enormous round brush. He would have put her to sleep but for the incessant chatter. Sister, do you model? How has no one approached you before? Oh, they'd approached her. She gave her standard reply.

"Nope, just in school."

She checked her phone again. A text.

We're good for Jane Hotel. I talked to my buddy. Bouncer's name is Fer-nand. See you at 9!

The exclamation point annoyed her. You're a guy, she thought. Guys shouldn't use exclamation points when they text. She'd probably end up dump-ing him over it. She'd done it for less.

"Big night tonight? It's a crazy Thursday. Are you going to that thing at Tau?"

"No. Just meeting a friend for a drink."

A friend? She guessed he was a friend. She'd met him twice—no, three times; he'd kissed her on 58th Street before she got into a cab three nights ago: hence the big date.

"A friend, huh? Sounds like a date."

"Yeah," Emma sighed, "it's kind of a date."

"So, no one special? No BF?"

"Nope. No boyfriend. Just a date."

"Well, I imagine the boys are climbing through your window, gorgeous girl."

She wanted to say the last time a boy tried to climb in my window, security guards tackled him on the front lawn as a leashed German shepherd bared his teeth at his neck while Teddy Prescott cried that he was in my seventh-grade ceramics class, and he just wanted to ask me to a school dance. Instead, she buttoned her lip and checked her phone. Again.

"No, not so much."

"Well, my work here is done. What do you think?"

He ran his fingers up her scalp from her nape and pushed the mass of hair forward over her shoulders, admiring his handiwork. She managed as much enthusiasm as she could muster.

"Looks great. Thanks."

She grabbed her bag, left the cash and a generous tip—partly for the blowout, mostly for enduring her mood—and headed out.

The walk home was a short-ish hike. While Broadway up ahead was always jam-packed, the little Tribeca side street was surprisingly desolate. Scaffolds stood sentry, and crumpled newspapers blew across the road like urban tumbleweeds. Emma's footsteps clacked on the pavement, and her shopping bags swished against her legs. In the waning daylight, the long shadows reached out. Emma moved with purpose but not haste, running through the plan for the evening in her head. Across the street, a pair of lurking teens stopped talking to watch her. The jarring slam of a Dumpster lid and the beep, beep, beep of a reversing trash truck echoed across the pavement. Near the end of the block, a homeless man in a recessed doorway muttered about a coming plague and God setting the world to rights. Emma forced herself to keep her pace even but couldn't stifle her sigh of relief as she rounded the corner and joined the hordes. A businessman let out a noise of irritation as Emma forced him to slow his pace when she merged into the foot traffic. Yes, this was better. She hurried up Broadway and headed for home.

Spring Street was insane. The stores ran the gamut from A-list designer shops to dive bars and bodegas. Beneath the display window of Alexander Woo, a ratty hipster strummed a guitar. In front of Balthazar, there was a hotdog vendor. The street was dotted with musicians and addicts and homeless and shoppers and tourists and construction crews and commuters and students. There was a French crêpe stand next to Emma's favorite Thai place that was next to an organic vegan café. It was like somebody took everything that made New York New York—the art, the diversity, the music, the food, the bustle, the noise—and jammed it all onto one street. The street Emma called home.

Outside her building, a group of guys from her Abnormal Psychology class was coming out of the corner bodega.

"Hey IQ, what's up tonight? Heading downtown?"

"Maybe."

"Martin's parents' brownstone is on Waverly. Party's on!"

"Okay, I'll try to stop by."

"Cool."

The guys in her class had started calling her "IQ" freshman year. She was flattered at first, thinking it bore some reference to her intellect. A few months in, she discovered it was short for "Ice Queen." That was fine with her too. Whatever.

Her elegant but inconspicuous building sat just down from Mother's Ruin, her favorite pub, and next to a heavily graffitied retail space for rent. She waved to her doorman, who rushed to help her with her bags. "Hey, Ms. Porter. Shopping, I see."

"Hey, Jimmy. Yeah, just a few odds and ends."

He glanced at the orange Hermes shopping bag and raised an eyebrow but didn't comment.

"You want me to take these up?"

"Yes, please, Jimmy." She handed over the bags and pushed through the heavy door to the stairs, while Jimmy summoned the elevator.

As she climbed the seven flights, Emma felt pretty calm. It was just a date. People had them all the time. Normal people had them all the time. She was normal. Well, she was getting there, and this outing tonight was proof of that. She had met a cute guy. She liked him well enough, and he was taking her out. She was excited about it; well, the progress more than the date. Another box to check on the list. She could crow about it to her therapist next week. The guy, Tom, seemed excited too, based on the aforementioned errant exclamation point. That, and the fact that she had actually heard him high-five a guy over the phone when she'd said yes.

Her bags were waiting by the door when she emerged from the seventh-floor landing. She fumbled with her key and pushed the door open with her butt as she scooped her purchases from the hallway floor. As she walked into the small but tasteful apartment—well, huge and elegant by college standards but certainly low key for Emma—she was greeted by a squeal and then the vaguely familiar strains of Rod Stewart's classic, "Tonight's the Night," so off-key it was barely recognizable.

"Jeez, Caroline, could you take it down a notch?"

"Nope. Can't. Sorry."

Caroline Fitzhugh had been Emma's best friend since before they were born. That wasn't an exaggeration. Their mothers had grown up together, had married men who were themselves best friends, and were neighbors in Georgetown as newlyweds. The women were inseparable until Emma's mother crossed the line separating "life of the party" from "addict." Their pregnancies were well-timed. It gave the two women a chance to rekindle their friendship, and it gave Emma's mother a fleeting chance at sobriety. Their moms spent their pregnancies together, nearly every day for the nine months leading up to the girls' arrival.

Well, seven months and three weeks—Caroline was always in a rush to get places. After that, Emma's family moved to Connecticut, Caroline's to Georgia, and the girls saw each other on holidays and trips. Caroline knew Emma before. Before what one of her shrinks had euphemistically referred to as "the event." Before she was Emma Porter. Before she was from a small town near Atlanta. Before. Caroline was one of a handful of people with that knowledge. She knew Emma, and she protected her with a ferocity that rivaled Emma's father. Tonight, however, was a different story. Tonight, Caroline was pushing her out of the nest. It's time, she had said.

Caroline popped a bottle of Veuve Clicquot way too expensive for pre-gaming, declaring a dispensation on Emma's father's strict alcohol ban, and poured them each a glass.

"One glass, Em, to loosen up."

Emma answered her with a sip.

"Go get dressed. The LBD awaits."

The "little black dress" to which she referred was the Versace black crepe safety pin dress. It was the sexiest thing either of them had ever seen. The sleeveless dress hit Emma mid-thigh and was accented with mismatched gold safety pins at the waist and hip. Caroline had bought it for Emma on her credit card to avoid any questions from her father. He was generous to a fault, but anything remotely provocative was frowned upon. Emma garnered enough attention as it was, and a sexy dress only upped the ante. Now the dress was laying on her bed next to a pair of strappy sky-high heels and a small box holding a pair of diamond hoops. The outfit for the virgin sacrifice. She laughed to herself, then stopped abruptly, surprised by the term her thoughts had conjured: virgin. It was a word she never used because it had no meaning for her. She hated the word because the status of one's virginity was inextricably linked to one's past, and she couldn't dwell on what she didn't know. Therapists encouraged her to embrace a term that expressed her "emotional virginity," but Emma never could think of one. Her shrink was not amused when she suggested "vaginal beginner" and "hymenal newbie," so they let it slide. She could be an actual virgin after all. The point was that it shouldn't matter, and if everything went according to plan, after tonight it wouldn't. She could pop her emotional and/or physical cherry and move on. At this point, she just wanted to get the damn thing over with.

They had hours before she had to meet Tom. JT, her driver and body-guard, usually accompanied her out in the evening, but Caroline told him they were heading to a study group at a friend's in the same building, so he had the night off. She was on her own, and she was thrilled. Caroline pulled up the zipper on the dress and bounced around to Katy Perry, while Emma sipped tentatively on the same glass of bubbly. "Oh Jeez, Em, just drink it. One glass won't have you cross-eyed. It'll calm your nerves."

She was right. Emma was nervous. For obvious reasons.

Emma left Caroline at Mother's, their local bar, with some friends and ordered an Uber to head to the Jane Hotel. As Tom had said, the bouncer, Fernand, was expecting her. Not that she would have had any trouble getting in anyway—she never did—but that dress was like a VIP pass. The group of people waiting gave a resigned sigh almost collectively as Emma deftly moved past them and entered the elegant bar.

Tom had a table he was guarding with his life, and she made a beeline for him. When a guy at the bar grabbed her arm as she passed, not hard, just enough to stop her, Emma paused, stared at the hand on her bicep, and then slowly looked up at him with a perfected impassive glare. Ice Queen indeed. He released her without a word, and she dropped into the seat across from Tom.

"Hey, Gorgeous. You look amazing."

"Thanks."

"I didn't know what you like, so I ordered you a white wine."

She rarely drank. Well, that wasn't entirely true. She drank in one of her self-defense classes. Jay, her instructor, had insisted that she know how to do some of the moves "impaired," as he put it, so he'd fed her three beers and then had her train on the mat. She'd thrown up all over him. The wine did relax her, and they chatted effortlessly. It took Emma nearly an hour to polish off the drink, and when she returned from the ladies' room with a fresh coat of lip gloss, a second glass sat waiting.

What the hell. It was a big night.

It took her exactly four sips and ten minutes to realize what was happening.

Emma wasn't normal. Her father, in an extreme effort to get control of their world, made sure of that, and at this moment, she was thankful for it. Most girls would think the subtle blur of vision and the slight wave of nausea were due to nerves or too many drinks. But she knew exactly what was happening. She reached into her purse and texted her panic word, "lighthouse," to JT, but he was off duty. It could take him hours. She took a calming breath, keeping her heart rate as low as she could in her panic.

"I'll be right back. I think I left my lip gloss in the bathroom."

"I'll go with you. You look pale."

"No, no, I'm fine. Just dizzy from the wine, I guess. I'm a lightweight."

She forced a giggle. That appeased him. He didn't know she knew.

"Okay, I'll be waiting."

"Be right back," she repeated.

Emma took deliberate steps. When she glanced over her shoulder, she saw Tom throw some cash on the table and pull a key card from his breast pocket. She needed to focus on making her way down the hall. She couldn't get help in the bar; a stumbling, slurring girl in a bar would only bolster Tom's ruse. There was an elevator at the end, but as she made her way toward it, she stumbled and realized that it was exactly where Tom wanted her. She needed help or a hiding place, and she needed it fast. Whatever he had slipped in her drink was strong.

The symptoms were hitting her fast. She moved down to a janitor's closet. Locked. She started moving frantically hand over hand, keeping her balance on the wall, avoiding looking at the nauseating pattern of the wallpaper as it started to blur. Tom's footsteps were heavy behind her as he closed in. She got to another door, pushed it open, and stumbled into the room. A group of surprised suits looked up as she blinked at them with terrified eyes. The man at the head of the table stood.

"Jesus, are you all right?"

"No. Help."

She heard the man closest to her mutter, "she's wasted." The man at the head of the table moved like a flash. He was coming toward her, and she was losing her ability to discern whether she had put herself in more danger by stumbling into this room. He seemed to float toward her, and Emma started to shake.

"Not drunk. Drunk," she slurred. "Drugged," she amended. "Help."

"Jesus." He put his hands on her shoulders, and she instantly calmed. Emma tried to shake the fog out of her head, but it only got worse. When she looked up, she saw three of him. So, she looked straight ahead at his tie. A cornflower blue tie that hung between the open sides of his dark suit jacket. She grabbed it with both hands, crunching it in her fists. She tried to remember her training, but all that came out was a plea.

"Please."

He put his arm around her protectively and calmly spoke.

"It's okay. I've got you."

And with that soothing notion, she passed out in his arms, still clutching his cornflower blue tie.

Emma woke up nineteen hours later in a hospital room that looked like a suite at the Ritz. JT was standing at the side of the bed like a royal guard, a pissed-off royal guard. He felt responsible for her indiscretion; she could feel his anger and guilt. Her father dozed, ashen, in an upholstered leather armchair. The night was a bit of a blur, and she ran through a timeline in her head to catch up. She had as much of it recalled as she probably ever would. Other than the mother of all headaches, she was otherwise uninjured. When she lifted her arm, the one without the IV, to move an itchy strand of hair from her face, the final few moments before she blacked out came flooding back. There, in her hand, was the cornflower blue tie, still knotted, with the length of it dangling down her forearm. It was wrapped around her palm and knuckles. JT informed her with a perplexed smirk that the nurses gave up trying to pry it from her, and the man, who had not given anyone his name, had ended up pulling it over his head and wrapping it around her hand as they wheeled her away on a gurney. Completely unconscious, she had refused to let the thing go.

READ TOX AND CALLIOPE'S THRILLING LOVE STORY IN ILLICIT INTENT.

Illicit Intent (Bishop Security #2)

By Debbie Baldwin

CHAPTER THREE

New York City
April 16

Come on, come on, come on. Calliope Garland willed the indicator bar on the monitor displaying the percentage of download completion to move faster. *Fourteen percent, twenty-seven percent.* Then it seemed to stop at thirty-two percent as if it were deciding whether to continue. She rubbed the side of the CPU, encouraging the beast to comply. She checked the time on her phone: 10:17 p.m. The slick, suited brokers and analysts had abandoned their laptops and balance sheets for dirty martinis—and other pastimes with "dirty" as the descriptor—at a chic nearby nightspot *Stock* around the corner. The offices of Gentrify Capital Partners that occupied the top two floors of the Financial District tower were all but abandoned. The low hum of a vacuum cleaner down the hall and the faint voice of a newbie client-retention specialist trying to earn his stripes were all that remained. No one should interrupt her.

Her little undercover assignment was proceeding seamlessly. Farrell Whitaker, her boss at the news site where she worked, *The Harlem Sentry*, smelled a rat at this prosperous asset management firm, so he sent her in to investigate. She arranged to be hired as a part-time receptionist through a temp agency and had worked at the front desk for two weeks when she caught her target's eye. Calliope's editor had then arranged for the target's personal assistant to get wind of a massive federal investigation in the offing, and the woman had quit without notice. Badda bing, badda boom, Calliope was in.

Gentrify Capital Partners was housed in a soaring monolith at the bottom of Manhattan. The office was a shrine to eighties' financial corruption. From the sky-lighted two-story reception area to the interchangeable supermodel receptionists to the boys club of Ivy League analysts, the place was a throwback. It was as if the man who created it, Philip "Phipps" Van Gent, had developed his fantasy business model during the era of Ivan Boesky and Michael Miliken, and had duplicated that world without update.

Calliope had worked at *The Sentry* for nearly two years, longer than any of the other dilettante jobs she'd had over the past six years. She actually liked it, but it would soon be time to move on. Where would she go next? Maybe a nanny in London or an aid worker in Khartoum. She shook herself out of her revelry. First, she needed to make sure she didn't end her career as an investigative reporter with a literal bang.

At the moment, she was sitting at Phipps Van Gent's desk—nothing out of the ordinary. He often called her from the road to retrieve some piece of information or update a spreadsheet. Other than the late hour, there was nothing suspicious about her presence. Furthermore, the minions seldom popped in to see the boisterous CEO, on the rare occasion he was in the office. Despite the fact that half of this floor was a private apartment, and his office alone was bigger than most Manhattan studios, the eccentric man spent most of his time at his estate in Greenwich or on his yacht, currently anchored in Palm Beach. No subtle, hidden-gem locations for Phipps Van Gent; he chose the most obvious ways to display his wealth.

Fifty-eight percent. Calliope glanced around Van Gent's inner sanctum. Other than the desktop computer she was currently breaking into and his rarely-used personal laptop sitting open on the desk—a pin-dot of light at the top of the screen—one would hardly suspect this was a place of business. She wouldn't describe the office as gaudy, more like an elite hodgepodge. It was as if the decorator, or more likely Van Gent himself, had selected the most expensive item in any given category and put it in the room. Calliope guessed his tactic: if a potential client knew art, he or she would be impressed by the Rothko over the fireplace or the Hopper behind his desk. If they knew antiques, the imposing Goddard and Townsend desk would elicit a response. It was the same with the Persian rug, Tiffany lamps, and the ego wall filled with photos of Phipps with Oscar winners, heads of state, professional athletes, and so on and so on. It was the very definition of conspicuous consumption.

Ninety-one percent. She rolled her eyes. She could afford any or all of these items in her own right but preferred the sparse interior of her Brooklyn brownstone, decorated with thrift store furniture, quirky accents, and street art. The photos she displayed were of people and places that *mattered* to her: Calliope with her mother playing in the sand on a beach in Corsica, her dog, Coco, looking at the camera lens as if it were edible, her mother and stepfather looking at each other as if no one else existed.

She had conducted dozens of these surreptitious fact-finding missions. Most were as simple as watching who came and went or copying shipping records or a calendar. Computer piracy was a little out of her league, but Farrell had a bee in his bonnet about this particular story. Based on the proudly displayed photos of her publisher *Occupying Wall Street* years ago she could guess why. Nevertheless, her role had always been observer, not filcher. She should simply be telling Farrell that the files existed, not duplicating them. She shuddered at the implications of this little theft. Some people in some very high places were going to be livid.

Download complete. Just as she sighed her relief and reached to snatch the little flash drive from the port, she noticed another document on Van

Gent's desktop. It was titled "Golf Scores," but the "S" in "Scores" was a dollar sign: "Golf $cores." She clicked on it, and a password prompt appeared. She checked under the keyboard—where Phipps had told her his login information was kept—and sure enough, there, on another Post-It, was a second password. She entered it and viola. The document consisted of a single-page spreadsheet listing a series of numbered codes Calliope couldn't interpret.

Her computer genius friend immediately came to mind. *Twitch will know what this is.* Then, as if Calliope had conjured her, the disposable cell phone in her pocket buzzed.

"How did you get this number?"

"Please." Calliope could hear the mischief in her friend's voice. "How goes the wet work?"

"Nerve-racking."

"Oh, take a picture of his desk photos. Be interesting to see who's in Van Gent's inner circle. It'll take the Feds forever to get a warrant for that office."

Calliope turned back to the monitor and extended her hand to snap a picture of the cluster of framed photos on Van Gent's desk when a device mounted on the side of the screen started beeping.

"Shit. I'm setting off the cell phone detector on the monitor. I gotta go."

Calliope cut Twitch off mid-protest, pushed back in the chair to stay out of range of the device, and snapped the picture. Then she tossed the disposable phone into her purse and returned to the mysterious "Golf $cores" document.

When she tried to drag the document to her flash drive folder an ugly noise sounded and an additional password prompt appeared. She re-entered the second password, and the evil wonk sounded again. Double-checking the letters and numbers, she retried it and was denied a second time. In a final attempt, she entered the original login password. At the third failed attempt, a box appeared in the center of the monitor: *initiating security protocol.*

Now she was sweating. A countdown clock in the corner of the monitor was ticking down from five. Four...Three... At zero the screen went momentarily blank. *Was that the distant bing of the elevator's arrival?* No way was this going unnoticed. She imagined a tiny room with an IT tech sitting at a desk filled with monitors and drinking coffee from a Styrofoam cup while alarms clanged and red lights flashed, signaling the breach. Who knew? Phipps was a strange guy. At this very moment, his wall safe sat open above the credenza. She could see stacks of cash and documents. Honestly, if she took several thousand dollars and left a note on the safe door, she didn't think Phipps would care. It wasn't that money didn't matter to him, it was more like money wasn't real.

Calliope shook away the thought and returned to her task. Something bad was happening, something very, *very* bad. A progress bar appeared in the middle of the screen. Below it, commands flashed: *removing files, wiping backup server, clearing logs.* With each notification, a new progress bar would start and run up to 100%. Calliope didn't know much about computers, and she certainly didn't know if touching something would improve or exacerbate the situation, so she sat there and watched until the screen went dark and an ominous message appeared in the center of the monitor: *security protocol complete.* All the more reason to skedaddle. Just as she was reaching down to extract the flash drive, the imposing double doors to Phipps's office flew open with such force the knobs put a dent in the drywall.

Boof. Ten blocks north of Gentrify Capital, Miller "Tox" Buchanan was in the basement security room of a Chinatown office building. He was being held by two men and beaten by a third. The punch was nothing, but Tox needed to make this look good. A series of jabs and he stifled a yawn. Qi was maybe five-five, a full foot shorter than Tox, but he was well-built. Nevertheless, the blows were about the same force his buddies nailed him with when he told a bad joke. He just needed to keep these guys busy until his partner, Steady, got the cameras and bugs planted.

Their client's son had been abducted two days earlier by her estranged husband. She came directly to Bishop Security for help. The security company was an offshoot of defense contractor Knightsgrove-Bishop. Heir apparent, Nathan Bishop, had eschewed the CEO position in favor of running this humble branch. Bishop Security took a variety of national and international jobs—bodyguard to black ops—but the team's pride was The Perseus Project. Born of ghosts haunting Nathan Bishop after his childhood friend, now wife, Emily Webster Bishop, had been abducted, The Perseus Project worked to rescue victims of kidnapping. They rarely charged money, and they never received recognition.

This was exactly the type of case for which Perseus was created. The missing boy's father was a powerful man with connections to organized crime and enough money to buy silence. The good guys needed to break into his Manhattan offices, plant the cameras and bugs, put a trace on his technology, and have a quick look around; some damning evidence would be a useful deterrent to repeat attempts to abduct the child in the future.

Tox had the easy job: distract the security guys with a little poker—and a little cheating—until exactly 11 pm. To be fair, Tox didn't have to get caught cheating, but this beating was far less painful than listening to these jackasses' incessant chatter.

"You think this is funny, you fucking giant?" Qi's face was red with exertion.

Tox shrugged. He must not have been as good an actor as he thought. Qi shouted something over his shoulder in clipped Mandarin. A moment later Tox thought he felt the floor rumble. He was pretty sure he was imagining the *Jaws* theme. Then a man appeared in the doorway. The mammoth was nearly as wide as he was tall. This beating was about to take a bad turn.

"Hey, Qi, do you have the time?" Tox asked.

"Ten-forty-three. Why? You in a hurry?" The men holding Tox chuckled.

Shit. He had to kill seventeen minutes. Well, he knew he couldn't survive seventeen minutes of being beaten by this rhino. He could, however, survive seventeen minutes of being *chased* by him. In a vintage *Three Stooges* move, Tox engaged his massive biceps and pulled together the two guys holding his arms, then pushed them into Shamu. Qi pulled a Glock, but Tox quickly nailed him with a combat-booted foot to the chest, sending Qi flying back into the surveillance equipment, disrupting the feed. At least his partner could finish up undetected. *You're welcome, Steady.* A gunshot rent the air. Apparently, Gigantor realized he wouldn't be able to catch Tox if he ran. At six-five and two-thirty, Tox was by no means nimble, but his opponent had to weigh in at over four bills. The Ruger semi-automatic acted as an ersatz starter's pistol, and Tox bolted for the street.

The shout was even louder than the bang of the door, and the last vestiges of Calliope's composure dissolved. She flew to her feet, a flimsy excuse on her lips.

"Who's the luckiest bastard on the fucking planet?!!!"

Calliope didn't think Phipps Van Gent was expecting a response, and when she didn't reply, he continued.

"I am, Cathy." He hadn't bothered to learn her name. Cathy was the name of his former assistant. "I just won two hundred thousand dollars on one hand of poker." When her eyes widened, Phipps smiled with glib satisfaction. "Wanna know how?"

Calliope glanced briefly at the flash drive still sticking out of the computer and nodded.

Phipps stumbled and expelled an alcohol-tinged huff of air. He righted himself and, with the deliberate care of a drunk, tried to make the hand he used for support on the desk look casual rather than essential. "Because everyone fucking bluffs." He seemed to contemplate propping one hip on the desk, then reconsidered and flopped down on the taupe suede couch. He continued with his head on the butter-soft arm and his Gucci loafers propped up.

"I'm in a penthouse at the Wynn courting this whale. He's supposedly some totally infamous mobster, but he's worth a quarter of a billion, and he's looking for an asset manager. Money's money. It's all dirty, so what the fuck?"

He was talking to the ceiling now, and Calliope wondered if he realized she was still in the room. "I chased him around for two straight days. I finally landed him and got an invite to this high-limit poker game in his suite. The guy provided everything: coke, whores, cards, booze. Everything but sleep," he chuckled. "So the last hand, every asshole in the room wants to show how big his dick is, but I know I've got it. Not the dick stuff cause mine's nothing to write home about, but my hand of cards is something for the record books."

Calliope thought that her editor really might be onto something when he voiced his suspicion that Phipps Van Gent was a con artist running a Ponzi scheme. Phipps sounded more like a street thug than American ex-pat and the product of Cambridge and the London School of Economics that he claimed to be.

"It's hold 'em. I get dealt two fours down. The flop is a four, a four, and a nine. Right off the fucking bat, I've got four of a kind. *Four of a kind*, Cathy. Do you even get how rare that is? The odds of it…well, it's insanely rare, like Powerball rare."

He seemed satisfied he had made his point and continued the story. "The turn is a jack. I don't even remember the river because who the fuck cares? So I'm guessing someone at the table has a full boat, maybe a flush. Or they're all fucking bluffing. Doesn't matter. Lil' ol' me is sitting back and watching with four of a kind. Oh, it gets better. This other fucker, high as a kite, is out of cash, claims his credit card has some kind of travel block so he can't transfer funds, so he sends a guy to his room and comes back with this little tube and tosses it onto the table."

Phipps felt around in his carry-on bag to retrieve it, but it slipped from his grip and rolled across the rug out of reach. Calliope watched it roll. It was white and capped and only about twice as large, in both diameter and length, as the center tube in a roll of paper towels. Phipps extended his hand in a grabbing motion like a toddler asking for an out-of-reach toy, then abandoned his effort and continued. "Says what's in the tube will cover the bet."

He half-gestured toward the bar. "Pour me a scotch, Cath." Apparently, now they were on a wrong *nickname* basis rather than a wrong *first-name* basis. Calliope pushed back to stand and quickly snatched the flash drive, dropping it into her messenger bag that sat open on the floor. She fetched his drink, so nervous she didn't realize Phipps was still talking…"So I flip my hand and the guy, he shoots up from the table like a bull ready to charge. Then he drops dead.

"One of the hired goons starts doing CPR, and that's it for me. Anyway, glad I got cash from the other saps because the painting in that tube isn't worth shit."

With great effort, he sat upright, retrieved the tube with his foot, and popped off the cap. He upended it, and a small rolled canvas slid out. He unrolled it on the coffee table and weighted the edges with magazines. "It's a reproduction of a Titian called *The Thief's Redemption*. It's the schmuck on the cross next to Jesus. The original is in Barcelona. I Googled it. This isn't even the right size."

He reclined again, yawned, and closed his eyes. "Certainly a fitting title, because I got robbed." He chortled. "*The Thief's Redemption*." The scotch, perched precariously on the ridge of his gut, splashed in the glass. "Have my gal look at it on Monday. Could be it's something else, but I doubt it. Maybe I'll frame it and hang it at home. A memento of the one time Phipps Van Gent got taken."

He tossed the plastic tube that held the painting in the direction of the small trash can and yawned. "I don't mind losing money, but I do mind losing," he grumbled. She started to ask if he even wanted her to have the painting examined, but he was already snoring softly.

Calliope plucked the tube off the floor. With the intention of putting it in the recycling bin, she shoved it into her bag and headed for the door. She glanced over her shoulder at Phipps passed out on the couch—one hand in his pants, one still holding his scotch—and bolted for the elevator. She almost laughed at the fact that she hadn't uttered one word the entire time Phipps was there.

The ding of the elevator's arrival before she had summoned it surprised her. She thought about ducking around the corner into a vacant conference room but decided against it. She had every reason to be here and nothing to hide—well, stolen files aside. When the doors parted, Calliope studied the occupant. A late-night client meeting was par for the course at Gentrify; Phipps would meet a prospective client any time, anywhere—as evidenced by his recent junket.

The elevator doors slid open. The man in the car was handsome if nondescript. He reminded her of one of those spit-polished stars from the fifties movies her mom loved to watch. Although with his dark eyes, black hair graying at the temples, trimmed beard, and smartly tailored suit, this guy would be the villain. He brushed by her without so much as a glance, his Aquatalia boots silent on the terrazzo. As she entered the elevator and hit the button for the lobby, she noticed him pause, like an animal catching a scent, and while the doors closed she briefly glimpsed him resume his pace. *That will be a short client meeting.* She rolled her eyes and imagined that pristine man trying to rouse a passed-out Phipps.

Just as the car began its swift descent, a deafening blast met her ears, then a second, quieter with the distance the elevator car had gained. *Were those gunshots?* Surely not. There was no one on her floor except for a comatose Phipps and the suited man she had just seen standing in the middle of the expansive office floor. Unless he was shooting computer terminals with some hidden cannon, he couldn't have been the source. She was in that weird, paranoid panic mode, and the reminder of the late-night client and Phipps kept her blood racing. Once at the lobby, Calliope sprinted toward the security door. The guard watched her swipe her security pass to release the lock, then returned his gaze to the Islanders game playing on one of the monitors. She sprinted out into the New York night. And ran smack into a brick wall.

Tox looked over his shoulder and chuckled at the lug huffing and puffing behind him. He rounded a corner and barely broke stride when a black-haired butterfly of a girl smacked into him and landed on her bum on the sidewalk, the contents of her messenger bag scattering everywhere. Tox was about to sidestep her to fend for herself—man with a gun in pursuit and all—when he saw her sky-blue eyes and startled face. Her stunning, startled face.

"Calliope?"

"Tox?"

"No time. Let's go."

In her irrational panic, Calliope grabbed her bag from the bottom, upending it further. Her work phone smacked the pavement and shattered. She scrambled for the flash drive, the cylinder, the ruined phone, and the various odds and ends littering the sidewalk while Tox grabbed her around the waist and heaved her toward the open rear door of the black SUV that had screeched to a stop at the curb next to them.

"Need a lift?" Steady smiled from the passenger seat.

Tox grinned. "We could probably walk. That fucker's big as a glacier and twice as slow."

"Not his bullets, dipshit. Let's move."

As if to prove Steady's point, a bullet pinged off the armored tailgate. Calliope glanced over her shoulder to see an absolute elephant of a man with a gun. The man put his hands on his knees and heaved for air as their car rounded a corner and sped to safety.

Calliope had met Miller "Tox" Buchanan twice. The first time was on a street corner in SoHo when he gave her her dog. He had been bigger then. She remembered wondering if he was an NFL player or a bodyguard. It wasn't his size that struck her, though; it was his energy. He was this odd combination of arrogant asshole and teddy bear. Despite his obvious disinterest when he looked at her, she felt inexplicably drawn to him—like she could slip into the space under his arm and they could continue on down the sidewalk. She was hit with this overwhelming desire to peel the onion to discover what made Tox Buchanan tick. She'd also realized she had an overwhelming desire to peel the layers of his clothes off, so she quickly diverted her attention to the dog at his side before she started acting on any of those urges. She had scratched behind the pup's ears and rubbed her back, all the while repeating to herself, *don't gawk at the beautiful man, do not gawk at the beautiful man.*

And so, in an effort to ignore the gorgeous animal at one end of the leash, she had adopted the gorgeous animal on the other, Coco. Well, when Tox was fostering her, the dog's name had been Fraidy, short for Fraidy Cat. The rottweiler had been "fired" from her job guarding a warehouse because she was too friendly; she had actually been painted with graffiti by vandals as they defaced the building. When Calliope took the beautiful dog off his hands, her first order of business had been to change her name to something less demeaning: Coco Chanel.

Coco rarely left Calliope's side. She came to work with her at *The Harlem Sentry*, accompanied her on errands, and followed her around her cavernous Brooklyn Heights brownstone like she couldn't bear to have Calliope out of her sight. Her unwavering loyalty and undemanding presence were a balm in her chaotic life.

The second time Calliope had seen Tox was at the beachfront wedding of her coworker and friend, Emily Bishop. Calliope had brought her other work friend, Terrence, as her date. She needed the emotional support, and he wanted to ogle the mouthwatering military man meat—his words—who worked with Emily's new husband, Nathan Bishop. When the guys had invited Terrence to join them to "sugar cookie" a buddy, he hadn't asked questions, he had simply spun Calliope into the arms of Tox and scrambled off the dance floor after the men. Turned out, much to Terrence's dismay, that "sugar cookie-ing" someone simply meant throwing them in the ocean then rolling them around on the beach, coating them with sand. SEALs or not, boys will be boys.

Calliope was tall, nearly six feet in her four-inch heels, but when Terrence had twirled her into Tox, her forehead bumped his chin. She had struggled to find her footing as Tox steadied her. When she finally met his gaze, she saw something intriguing. He was smirking at first, like the cocksure jackass she assumed him to be, but then, as he held her gaze, the smirk had morphed into a sweet, almost vulnerable, crooked half-smile bracketed by dimples that melted her heart. His eyes reminded her of a dog's eyes, brown and glassy and longing. The attraction she felt wasn't sudden or jolting, like a spark or a zing; it was something indistinct and yet profound, like the force of the tide easing a ship into port. They'd stood still on the dance floor for a solid minute. Then, they both went stiff as boards and danced with the formality of middle-schoolers at a mandatory lesson. The phantom pain of the severed connection lingered, the sudden awareness of an ever-present absence, but Calliope refused to dwell on it.

Tox had revealed nothing about himself that day, and the reporter in her had been brimming with frustration, paradoxically adding to both his allure and his repulsion.

"Why do they call you Tox?"

"Long story."

"So, you were in the Navy with Nathan?"

"I work for him."

"Where are you from?"

"West of here." (They were on Nantucket. *Everywhere* in the U.S. was *west of here.*)

"Do you have family in the area?"

"So, Emily said you were from Greece or something?"

She had corrected him and then, for the rest of their dance, talked about herself in the same vague terms. When he thanked her and turned to reconvene with his friends at the bar, she stood on the dance floor with balled fists, feeling quite certain she had been, not manipulated per se, but maneuvered. When he glanced over his shoulder to meet her gaze, he winked, confirming her suspicions. She had refused to talk to him again the entire evening. And while her mouth was in full agreement, her eyes made no such promise. Calliope had to repeatedly scold herself for tracking his movements throughout the tent; she allowed herself a little leeway by rationalizing that he was so big, statistically, the chances that he would be in her line of sight were high. Right. Nevertheless, she had done what she could to ignore him.

Tonight she felt no such compunction.

Tox sat behind the driver, eyes forward. He was this remarkable combination of relaxed and focused, his body calm yet coiled. He had lost some muscle mass in the past year; he'd gone from "linebacker" to "running back," still strong and massive, but less…beefy. He also had been bald when she had danced with him that first time, but his dark hair was now a very short buzz cut; it was exactly the same length as the heavy stubble that covered his jaw. Everything about him flipped her switch. He wasn't the kind of handsome that starred in movies or appeared in cologne ads; he had the kind of face an artist might sketch, *Primal Man* or *Man Restrained*; the portrait would definitely have "man" in the title.

His sable gaze met hers and startled her from her uncharacteristic musings. He didn't smile, didn't cock a brow. He simply looked at her, placid. A scar on his forehead bisected his right eyebrow, giving his kind face an edge. Maybe she should give him a month.

Calliope had never had a relationship that lasted longer than a month. It wasn't a hard and fast rule; it was just that she never seemed to stick around long enough to entertain the notion of permanence. *Tox though...* As quickly as she conjured the thought, she dismissed it. If the parts of his body she couldn't see were as compelling as the parts she could, she would have a problem—not necessarily leaving him, but finding the next guy to fill his battered boots. He'd be a hard act to follow. And if she understood on some level that she was rejecting the idea of involvement with him because he might be the guy to make her rethink things, she didn't acknowledge it.

"So, how's your day?" Tox asked the question with genuine interest as if he had just picked her up from a nine-to-five.

"Um, good?" Calliope had a million questions, but her reporter instincts had fled.

"Good. Mine too."

"What...I mean why...I mean, what was that all about?"

"Just a little dust-up over a poker game. All good."

"A little dust-up?" Calliope thought about the poker game from which Phipps had just come; probably not the same stakes.

The driver, a striking African American man they called Chat, stifled a chuckle. The guy in the passenger seat—she couldn't recall his name—checked

GPS coordinates as they flew across the Brooklyn Bridge. A phone rang, echoing through the Bluetooth. Chat answered.

"Go Twitch. You're on speaker. Steady and Tox are here, and we picked up a passenger."

Steady. His name was Steady. Twitch was going to have a field day with this. For someone who saw the world in ones and zeros, she was shockingly romantic. Calliope could practically picture her sighing with her hands clasped under her chin. Having girlfriends was something of a foreign concept to Calliope. She was never in one place long enough to bond. Twitch and Emily Bishop had somehow wormed their way into Calliope's heart. At the moment, she was regretting the friendship.

"Hey, Twitch. It's Calliope. Tox bumped into me on the street, and the guys are giving me a ride."

Tox quirked a brow, pointing to himself and then her while mouthing, *I bumped into you?* Calliope ignored him.

The incessant click-clacking on Twitch's keyboard paused. "Interesting."

"Not interesting. The opposite of interesting. Mundane, in fact." *Stop talking.*

"Okay." Twitch resumed her typing with the trademark twinkle in her voice.

Twitch already knew most of it, but Calliope explained for the benefit of the men in the car.

"Farrell Whitaker, my crazy editor, has me pulling the threads on another of his conspiracy theories. He thinks Phipps Van Gent, the hedge fund billionaire, is up to something."

"Crazy like a fox," Twitch responded. "The Feds are on him like chrome on a bumper. Lots of chatter. I'd like to take a peek at what you discovered tonight."

Steady saved her from having to explain the computer nightmare.

"First things first, Twitch," he admonished.

"Right. Sorry. Got distracted. This one was almost too easy. No fun at all. The client's ex-husband has a nanny cam routed to his phone and laptop. The little boy is at the father's country house. Already got the location. Nathan's in town for a board meeting, so he's handling the extraction with Ren."

Calliope fingered the flash drive in the bottom of her now nearly empty messenger bag. Most of her makeup and sundries were scattered on Broad Street. A wave of dread washed over her. She felt her keys, but not her wallet. The conversation in the car faded as her ears started to buzz.

"What's wrong?" Tox laid a hand on her shoulder, sensing her distress.

"My wallet. It fell out of my bag when I dropped it."

Steady chimed in. "Forget it. It's gone by now. Do you have your bank's app? You can block your cards right now."

"Yeah, I'll do it when I get home. This work phone had a fight with the sidewalk and lost." She held up the shattered phone with two fingers.

Tox squeezed the shoulder he was still touching. His hand was so big his fingers touched her spine. "It's just a thing, Cal. Things can be replaced." He spoke like a man who had lost something that could not.

Calliope loved her name. She always corrected people when they shortened it or mispronounced it, but the endearment coming from this fierce giant warmed her as much as that big paw on her back. God, that hand felt good. She sighed.

"I know. It's just another inconvenience in a very inconvenient night."

Tox retrieved the cylinder that had once again rolled out of her bag and flipped it over one-handed. "Let me guess. A map to the secret vault where Phipps Van Gent has hidden billions in gold and the nuclear launch codes."

"No motherfucker named *Phipps* has nuclear launch codes," Steady grumbled. Chat chuckled. He was proving the irony of his nickname tonight. Other than answering Twitch's call, he had not uttered a word so far.

"Nothing even remotely that exciting," Calliope clarified as she took the tube. "Phipps got scammed in a poker game. He won what he thought was a valuable painting but turned out to be nothing." Calliope handed the cylinder back to Tox. "This is trash. I meant to put it in the recycling, but I got distracted."

Tox turned the tube over in his hand, then banged it on his thigh. "Mind if I take this? I have a leaky pipe in my kitchen and this might just do the trick."

"Sure thing. Glad to assist with your pipes."

Steady coughed into his closed fist. Tox gave her a look that nearly ignited her thong.

As they pulled up to her home, Chat spoke to her for the first time. "Calliope, do you have a security system?"

"Yes, of course."

"Make sure it's armed."

"Okay."

Tox gave her shoulder another comforting squeeze—although Calliope was beginning to think *comforting* wasn't quite the right word—and lifted his other hand in a motionless wave.

"Thanks for the ride guys." She addressed all of them but locked eyes with Tox.

Their black SUV idled at the curb until Calliope had climbed her exterior stairs, let herself inside, and waved through the glass sidelight.

Inside, Calliope turned to see her rottweiler, Coco, engaging in her wake up stretches: butt up, paws out, followed by back legs out behind her in a sploot. Coco produced a squeaky yawn and followed Calliope to the back of the house. Calliope lifted one foot in front of the other, suddenly overcome by profound fatigue. She aimed for the checkerboard porcelain tile floor of the kitchen. Depositing her cumbersome bag on the island she grabbed a bottle of water and headed for the stairs, the clittering of Coco's nails on the hardwood reassuring, the old stairs creaking as she mounted them.

Coco stopped on the landing and growled. Calliope noticed a strange, flickering light at the end of the upstairs hall. She stepped carefully, quietly, making her way toward the second-floor window overlooking the street. She finally breathed an inaudible sigh when she saw that a plastic grocery bag had hooked the neck of a streetlight, disrupting the beam each time the wind kicked up. She scratched Coco behind the ears as her trusty pet braced her front paws on the sill and gave a stern warning bark to the grocery bag.

"Come on, puppy. Let's get to bed."

Coco tossed another bark back at the offending bag and trotted into Calliope's bedroom. She was a docile, good-natured dog. She had once inadvertently caught a car thief when the perpetrator had misconstrued Coco's enthusiasm for a car ride as an attack. Coco's uninterrupted barking and pawing at the car door had delayed and distracted the man and caused such a ruckus, the car's owner came out to investigate. She napped in the sun, begged for belly rubs, and greeted visitors with a happy spin and a wet lick. But woe betide anyone who threatened Calliope while Coco was around. She may have been a sweet dog, but when it came to Calliope she could be a werewolf.

.